InvestiGATORS
Braver and Boulder

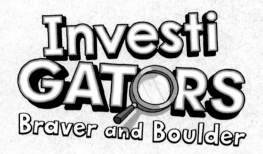

Investi GATORS
Braver and Boulder

written and illustrated by
John Patrick Green

with color by **Wes Dzioba**

:01

First Second
New York

To any buddy and every buddy

:01
First Second

© 2022 by John Patrick Green

Drawn on Strathmore Smooth Bristol paper with Staedtler Mars Lumograph H pencils, inked with Sakura Pigma Micron and Staedtler Pigment Liner pens, and digitally colored in Photoshop.

Published by First Second
First Second is an imprint of Roaring Brook Press,
a division of Holtzbrinck Publishing Holdings Limited Partnership
120 Broadway, New York, NY 10271
firstsecondbooks.com
mackids.com

Don't miss your next favorite book from First Second! For the latest updates go to firstsecondnewsletter.com and sign up for our enewsletter.

Library of Congress Cataloging-in-Publication Data is available

ISBN: 978-1-250-22006-6 (Hardcover)
ISBN: 978-1-250-84717-1 (Special Edition)
ISBN: 978-1-250-84942-7 (Special Edition)

Our books may be purchased in bulk for promotional, educational, or business use. Please contact your local bookseller or the Macmillan Corporate and Premium Sales Department at (800) 221-7945 ext. 5442 or by email at MacmillanSpecialSales@macmillan.com.

First edition, 2022
Edited by Calista Brill and Dave Roman
Cover design by John Patrick Green and Kirk Benshoff
Interior book design by John Patrick Green
Color by Wes Dzioba
Printed in China by Toppan Leefung Printing Ltd., Dongguan City, Guangdong Province

10 9 8 7 6 5 4 3 2 1

Chapter 1

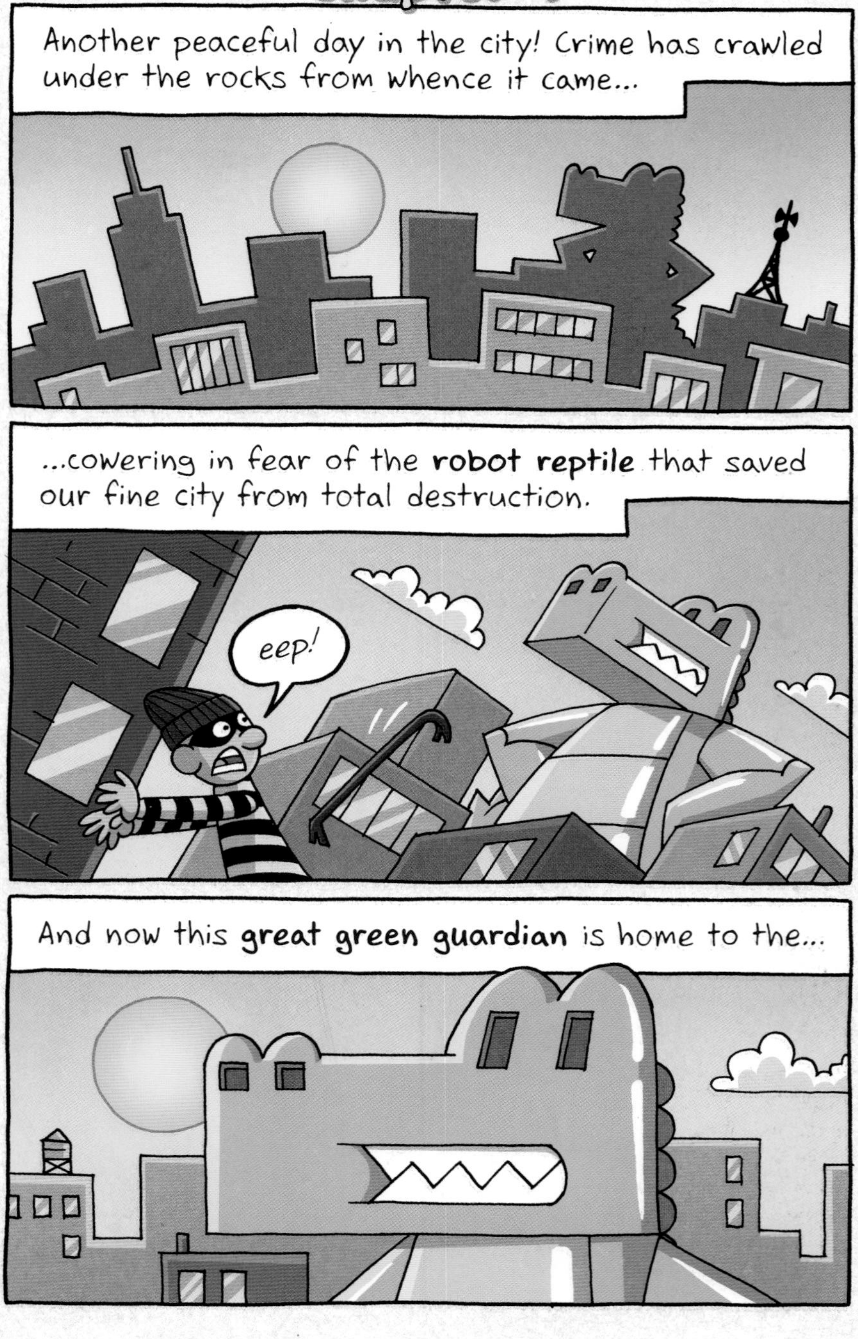
Another peaceful day in the city! Crime has crawled under the rocks from whence it came...
...cowering in fear of the **robot reptile** that saved our fine city from total destruction.
eep!
And now this **great green guardian** is home to the...

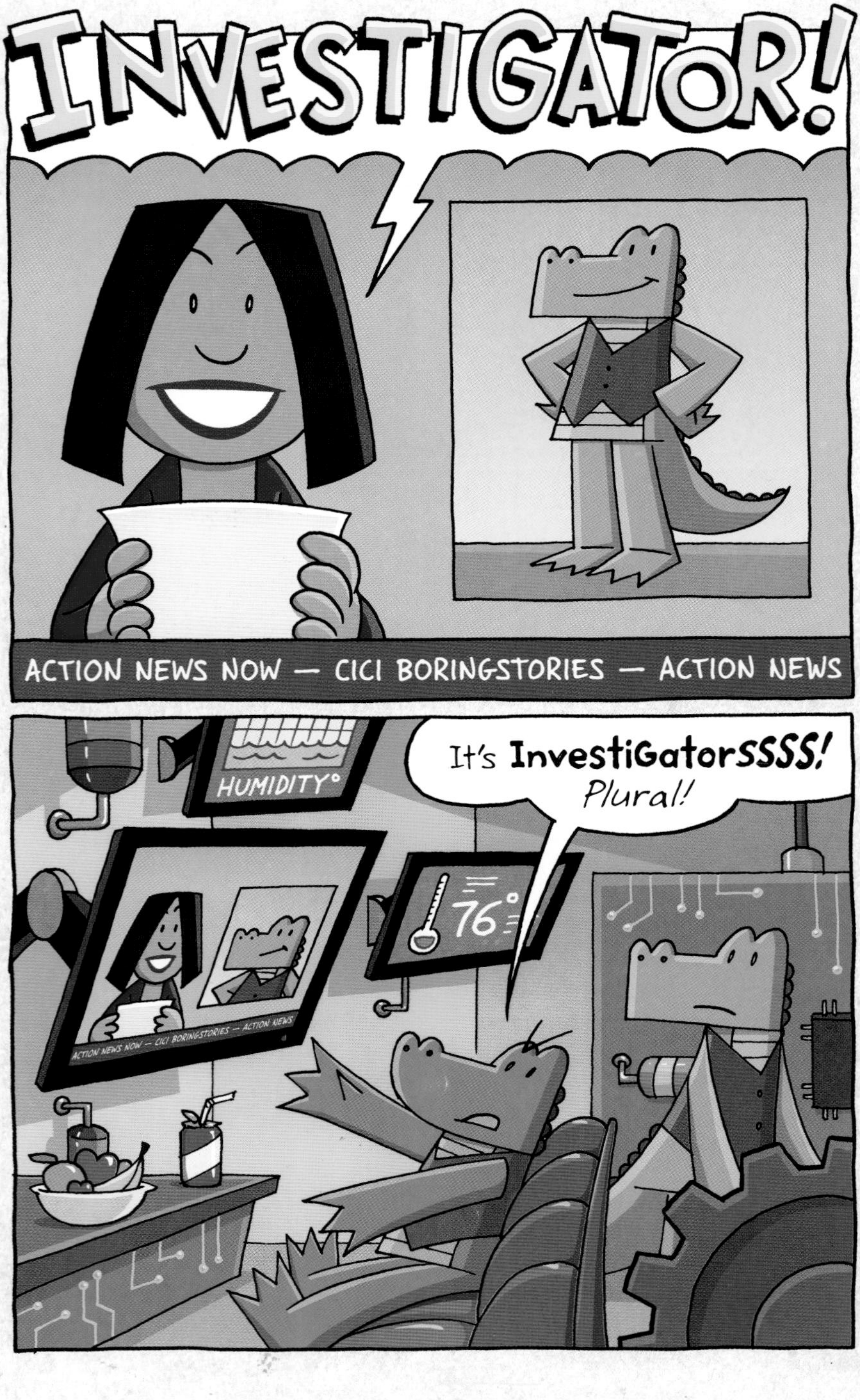
INVESTIGATOR!
ACTION NEWS NOW — CICI BORINGSTORIES — ACTION NEWS
HUMIDITY°
76°
It's InvestiGatorSSSS! Plural!

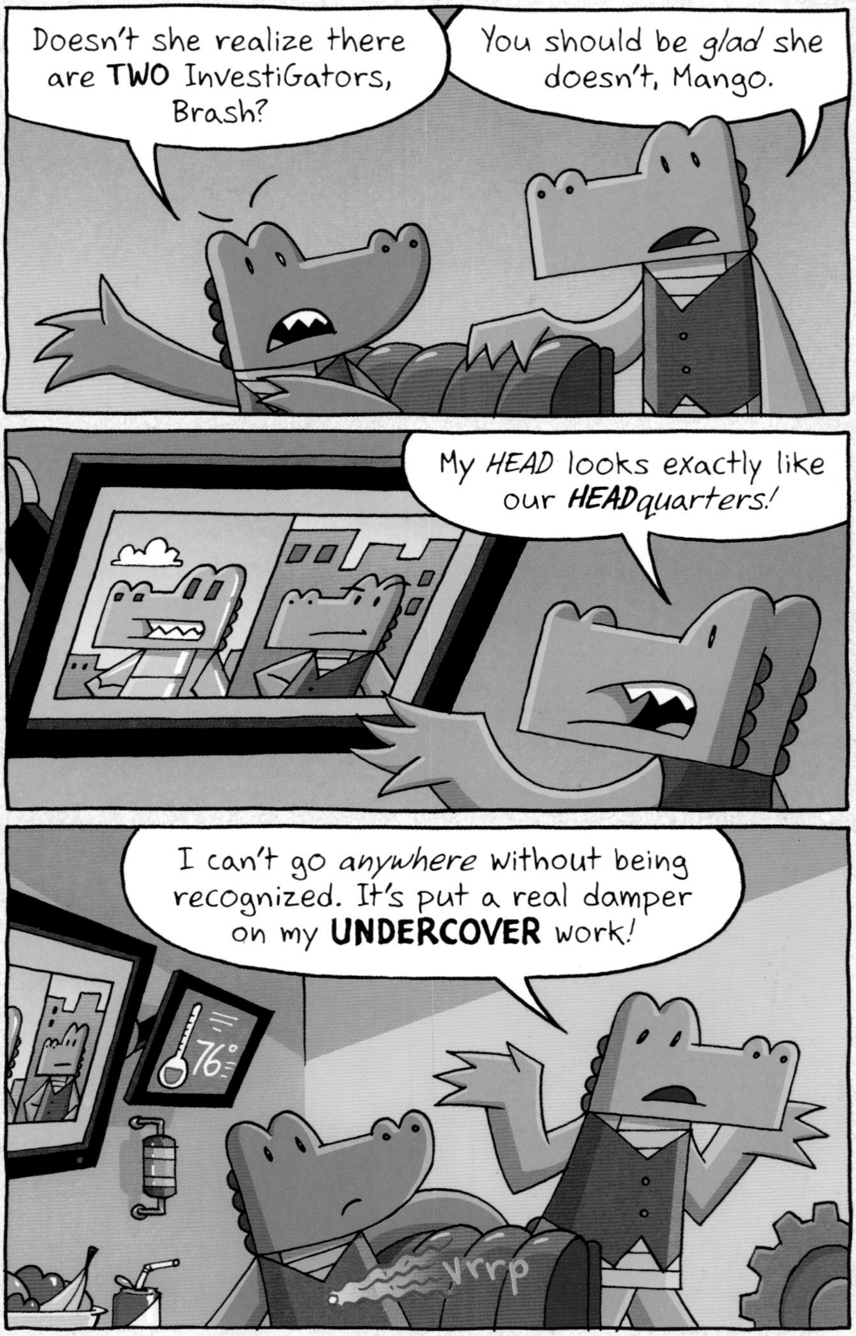
Doesn't she realize there are **TWO** InvestiGators, Brash?
You should be *glad* she doesn't, Mango.
My *HEAD* looks exactly like our ***HEAD**quarters!*
76°
I can't go *anywhere* without being recognized. It's put a real damper on my **UNDERCOVER** work!
vrrp

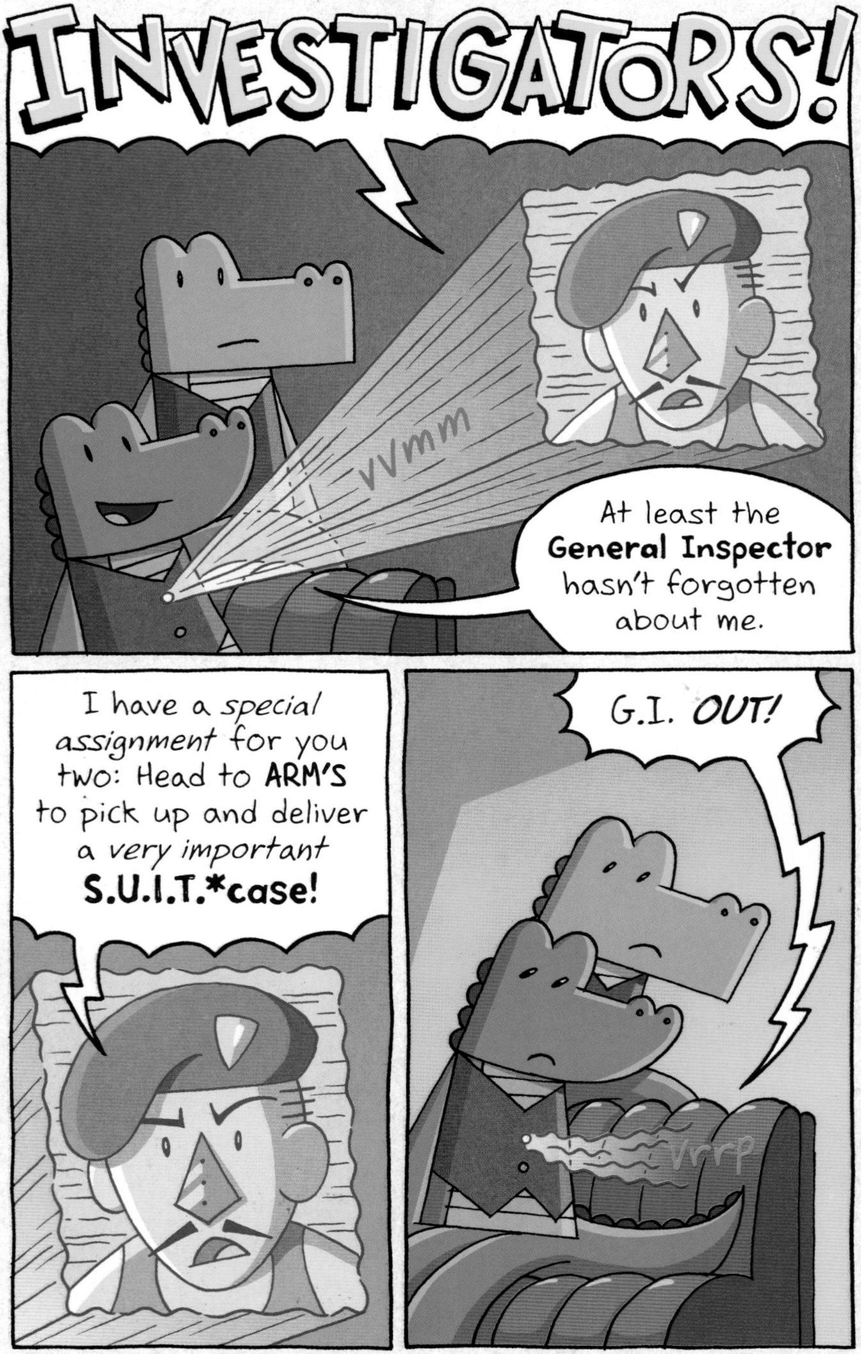
INVESTIGATORS!
VVmm
At least the **General Inspector** hasn't forgotten about me.
I have a *special assignment* for you two: Head to **ARM'S** to pick up and deliver a *very important* **S.U.I.T.*case!**
G.I. ***OUT!***
Vrrp

*Special Undercover Investigation Teams

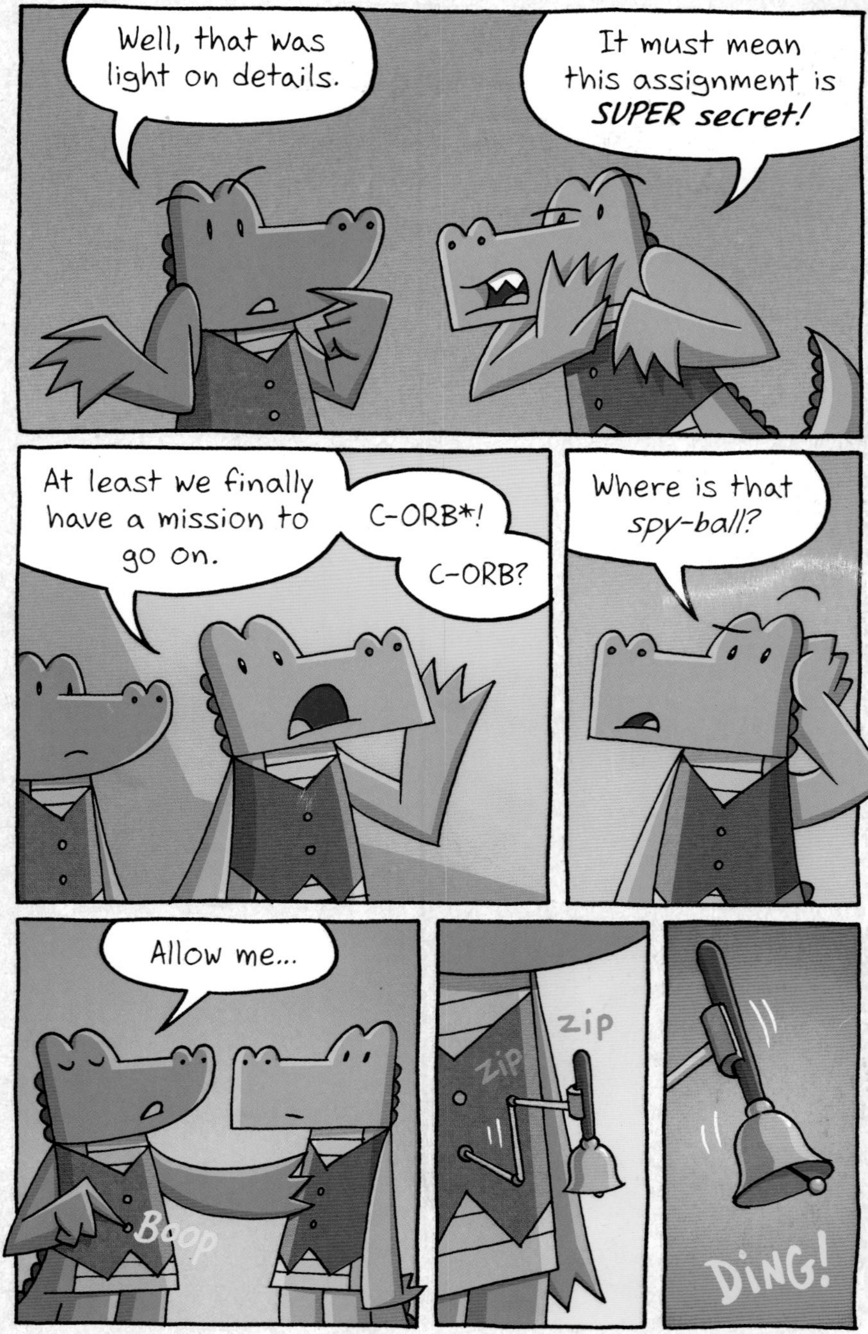
Well, that was light on details.
It must mean this assignment is SUPER secret!
At least we finally have a mission to go on.
C-ORB*!
C-ORB?
Where is that spy-ball?
Allow me...
Boop
zip
zip
DING!

*Computerized Ocular Remote Butler

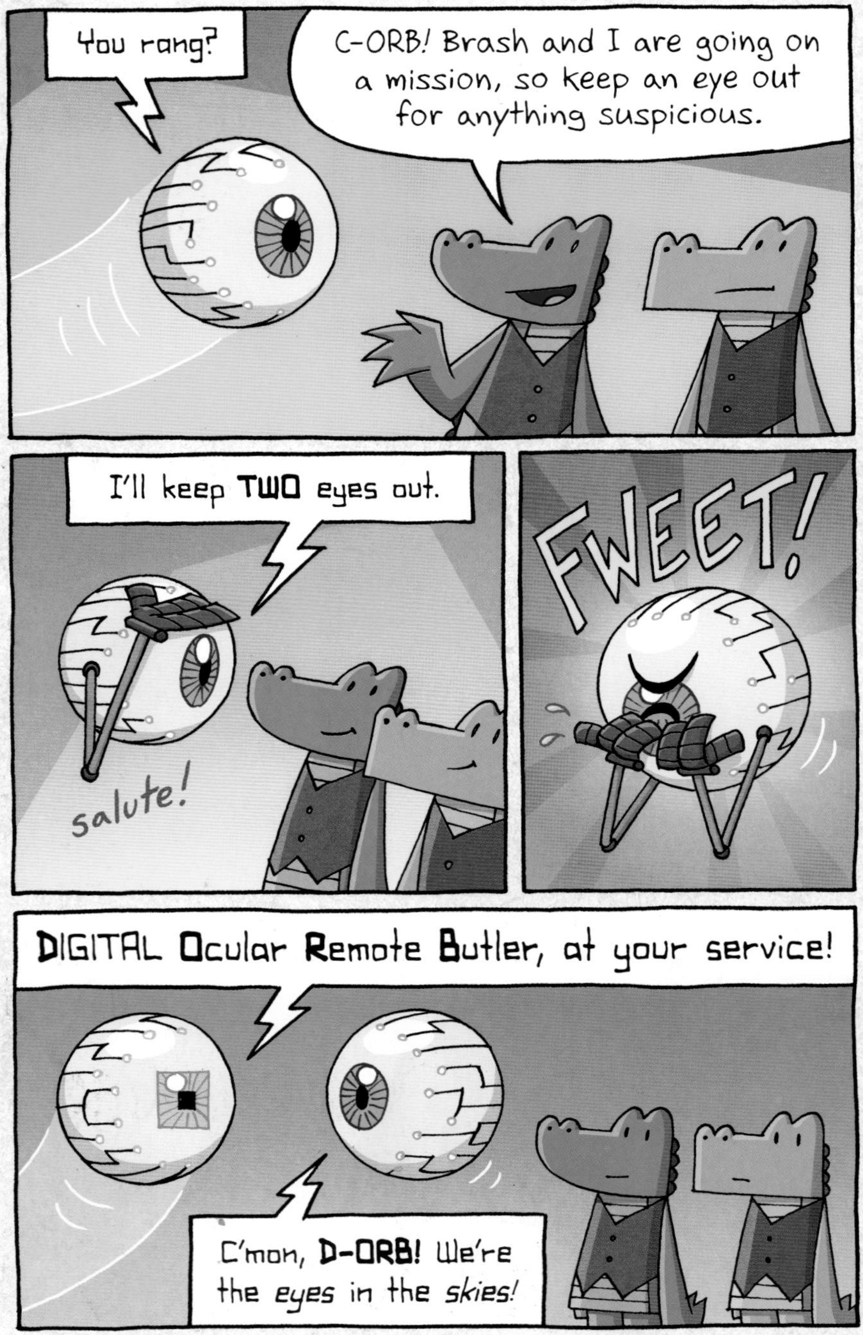
You rang?
C-ORB! Brash and I are going on a mission, so keep an eye out for anything suspicious.
I'll keep TWO eyes out.
salute!
FWEET!
DIGITAL Ocular Remote Butler, at your service!
C'mon, D-ORB! We're the eyes in the skies!

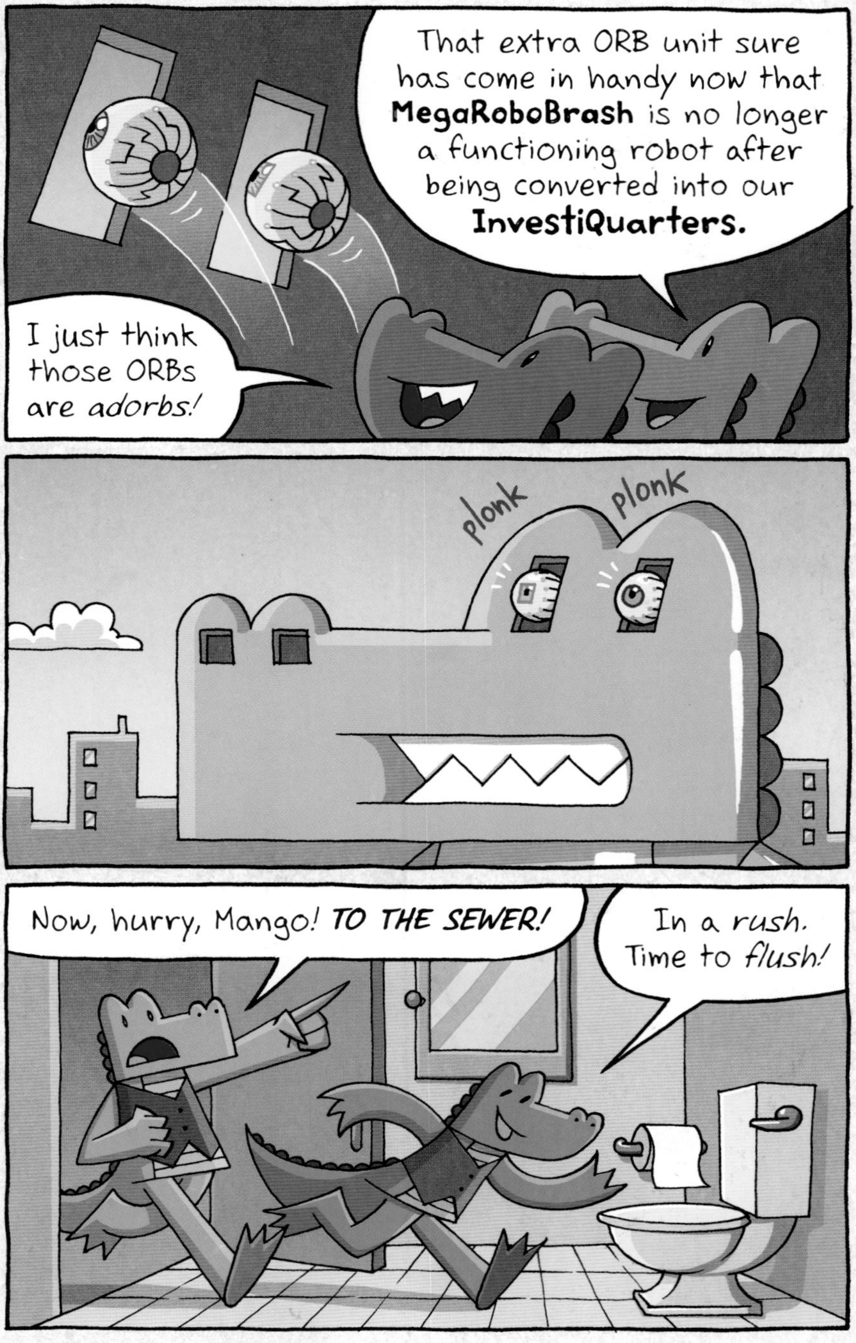
That extra ORB unit sure has come in handy now that **MegaRoboBrash** is no longer a functioning robot after being converted into our **InvestiQuarters.**
I just think those ORBs are *adorbs!*
plonk
plonk
Now, hurry, Mango! ***TO THE SEWER!***
In a *rush.* Time to *flush!*

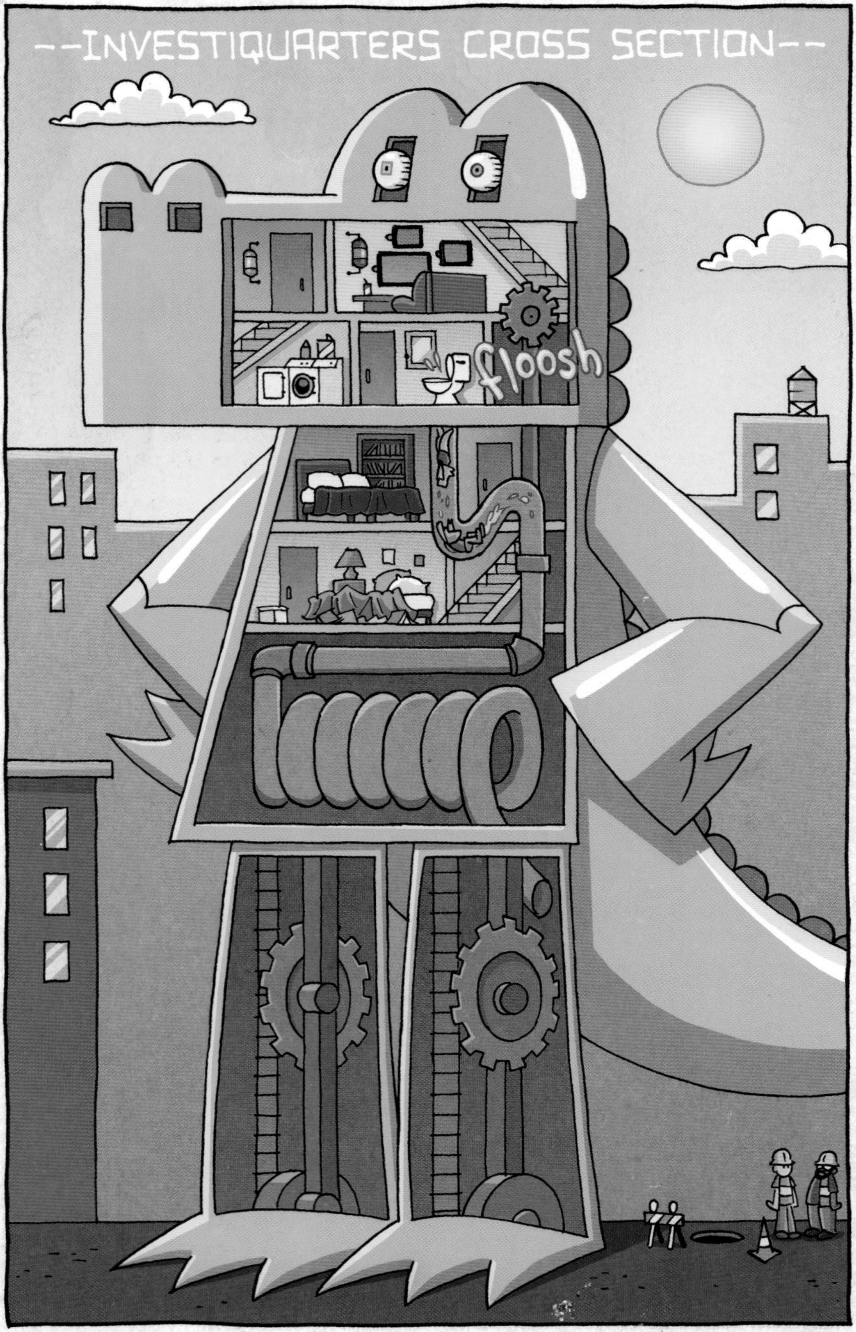
--INVESTIQUARTERS CROSS SECTION--
floosh

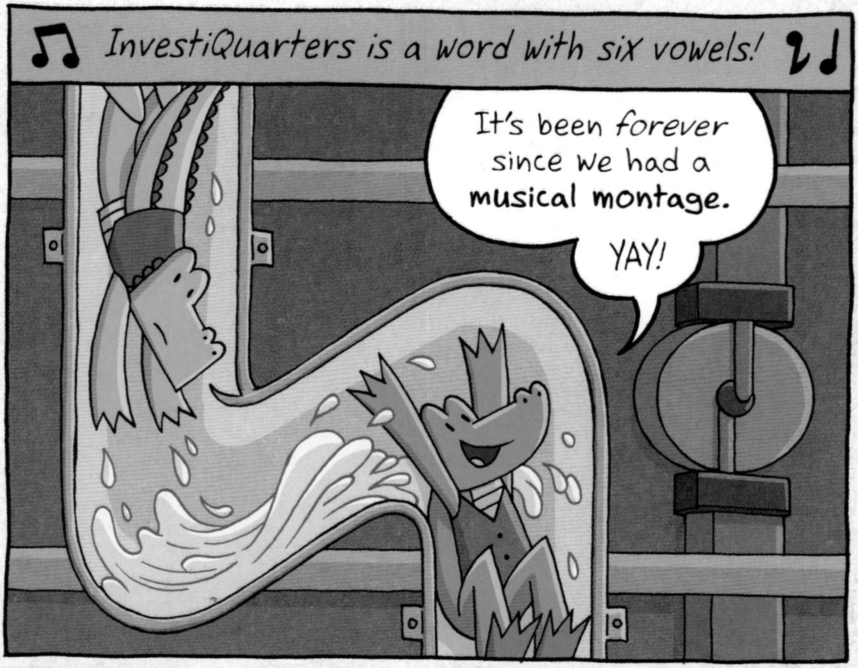
InvestiQuarters is a word with six vowels!
It's been forever since we had a **musical montage.**
YAY!

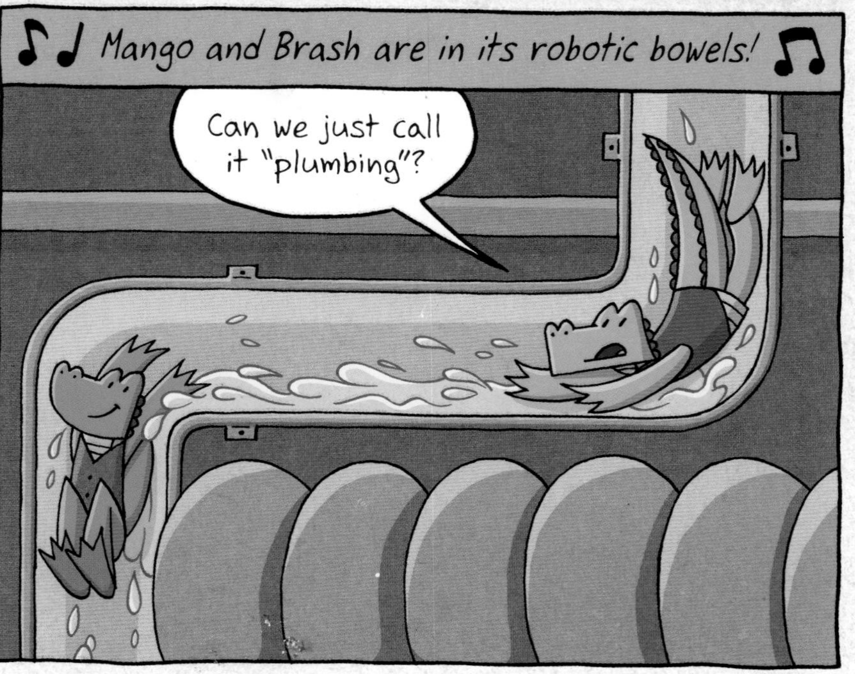
Mango and Brash are in its robotic bowels!
Can we just call it "plumbing"?

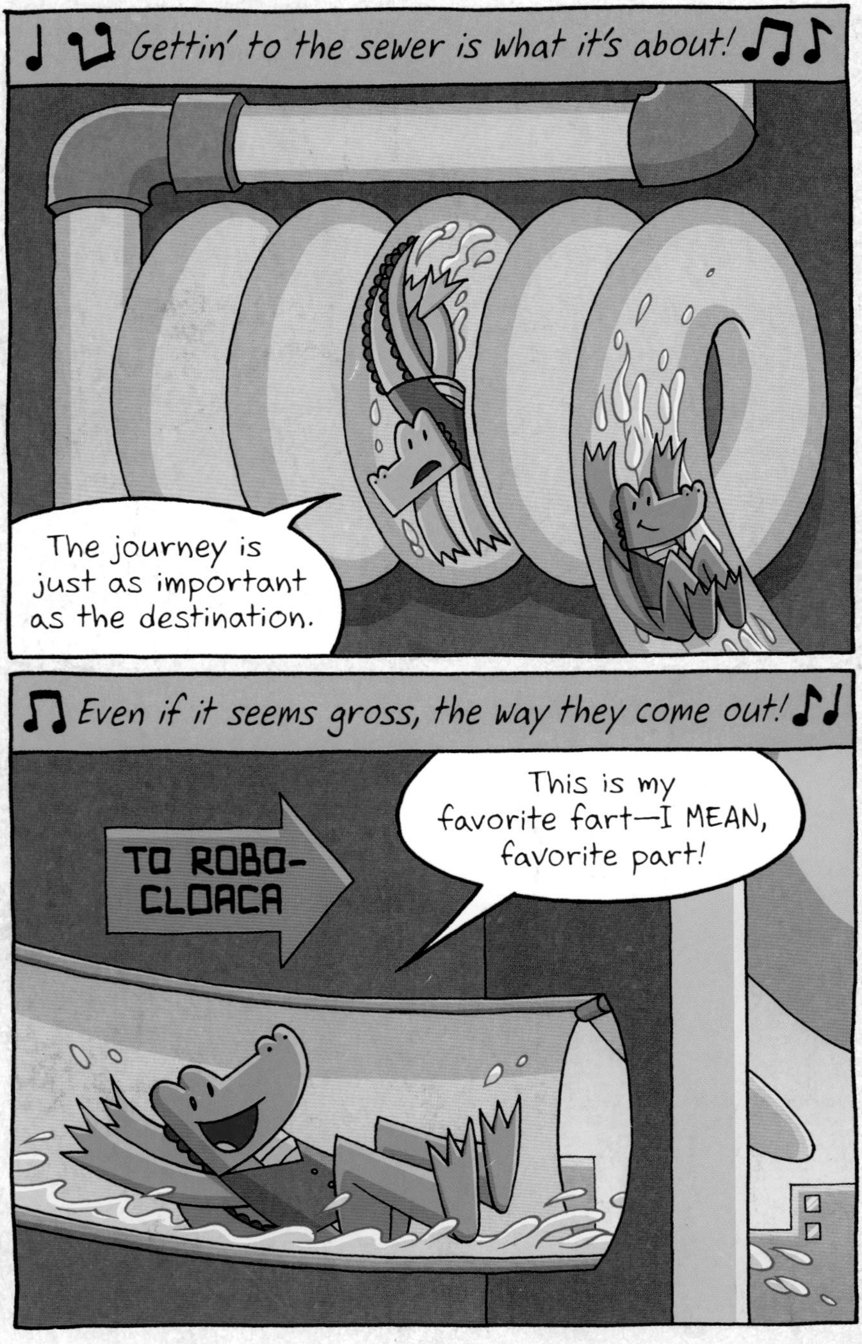
Gettin' to the sewer is what it's about!
The journey is just as important as the destination.
Even if it seems gross, the way they come out!
TO ROBO-CLOACA
This is my favorite fart—I MEAN, favorite part!

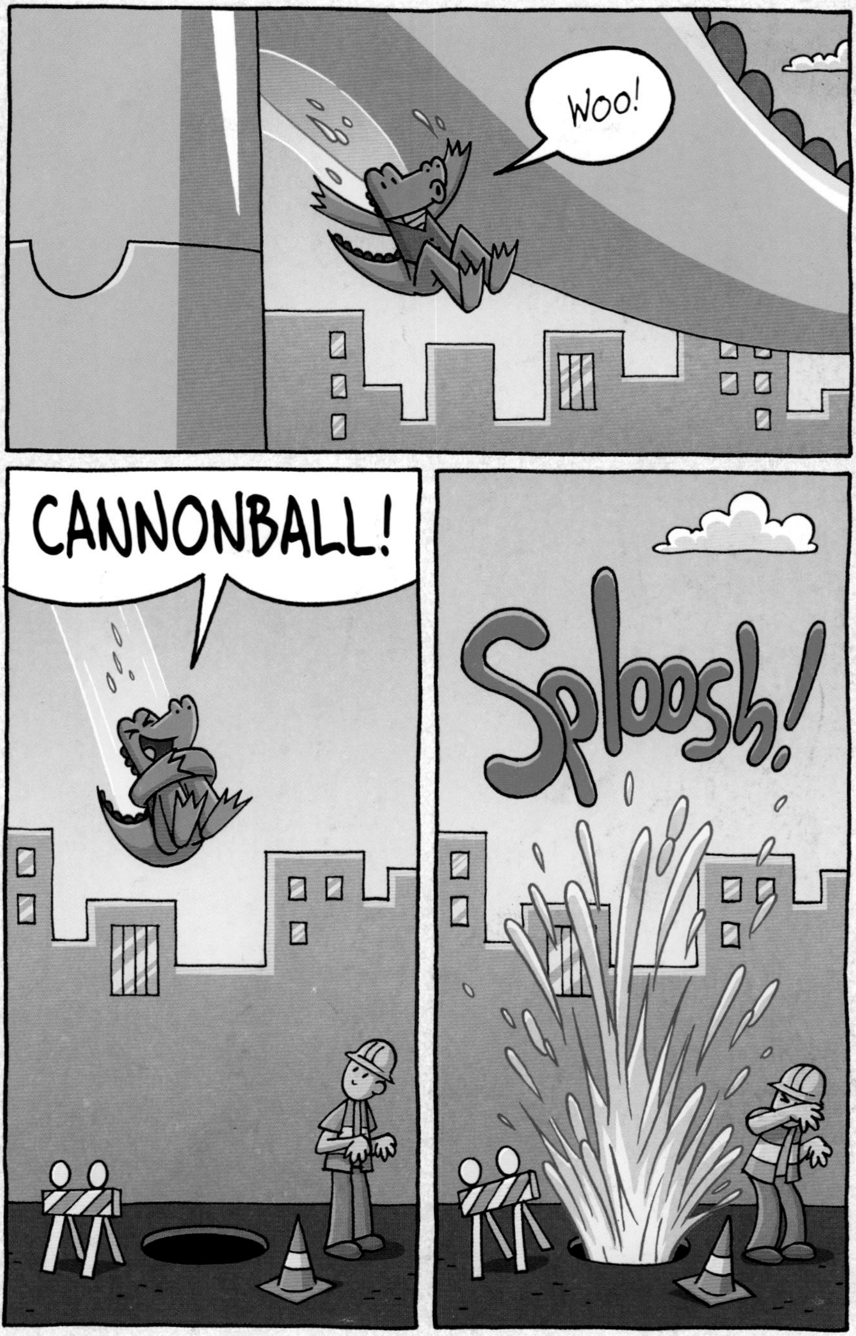
WOO!
CANNONBALL!
Sploosh!

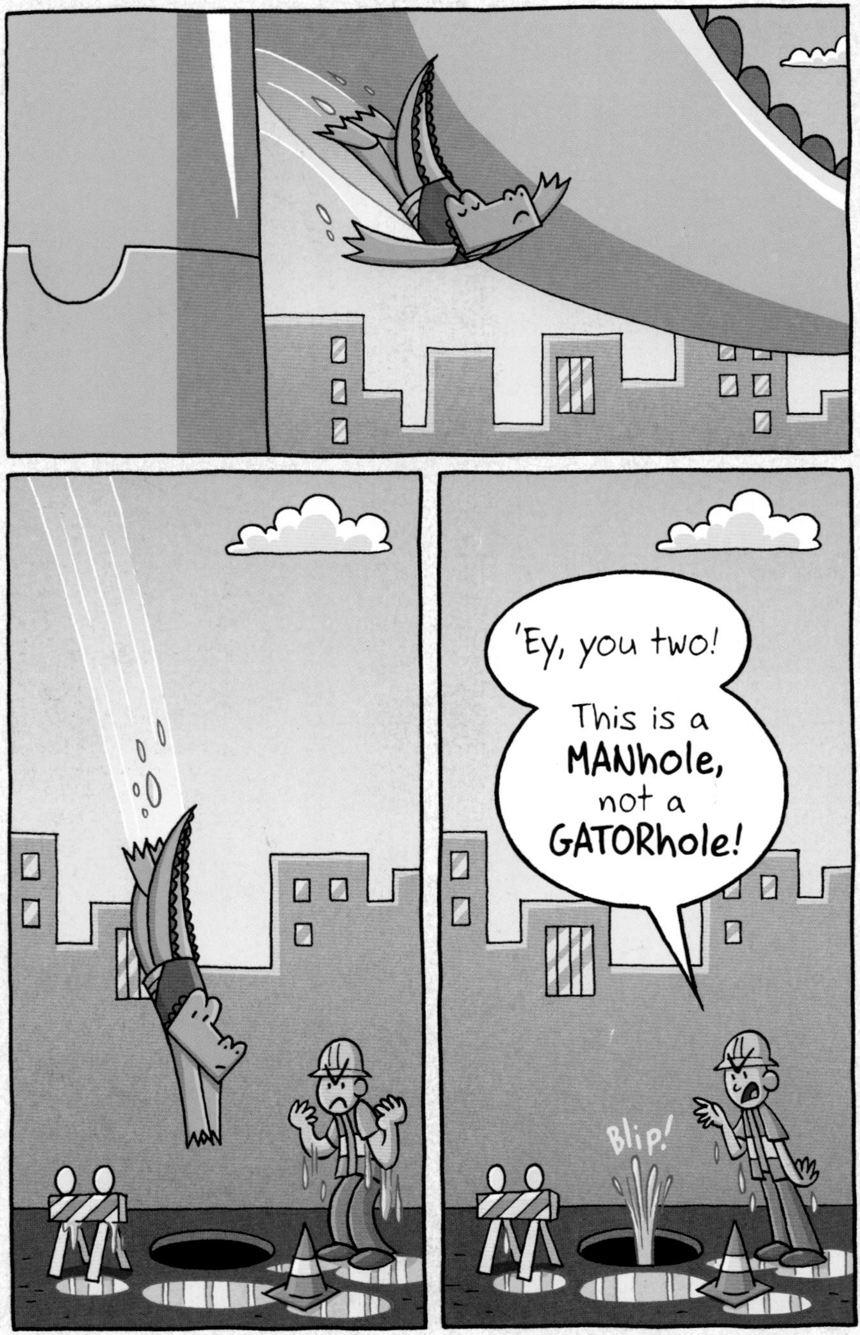
'Ey, you two!
This is a MANhole, not a GATORhole!
Blip!

Chapter 2

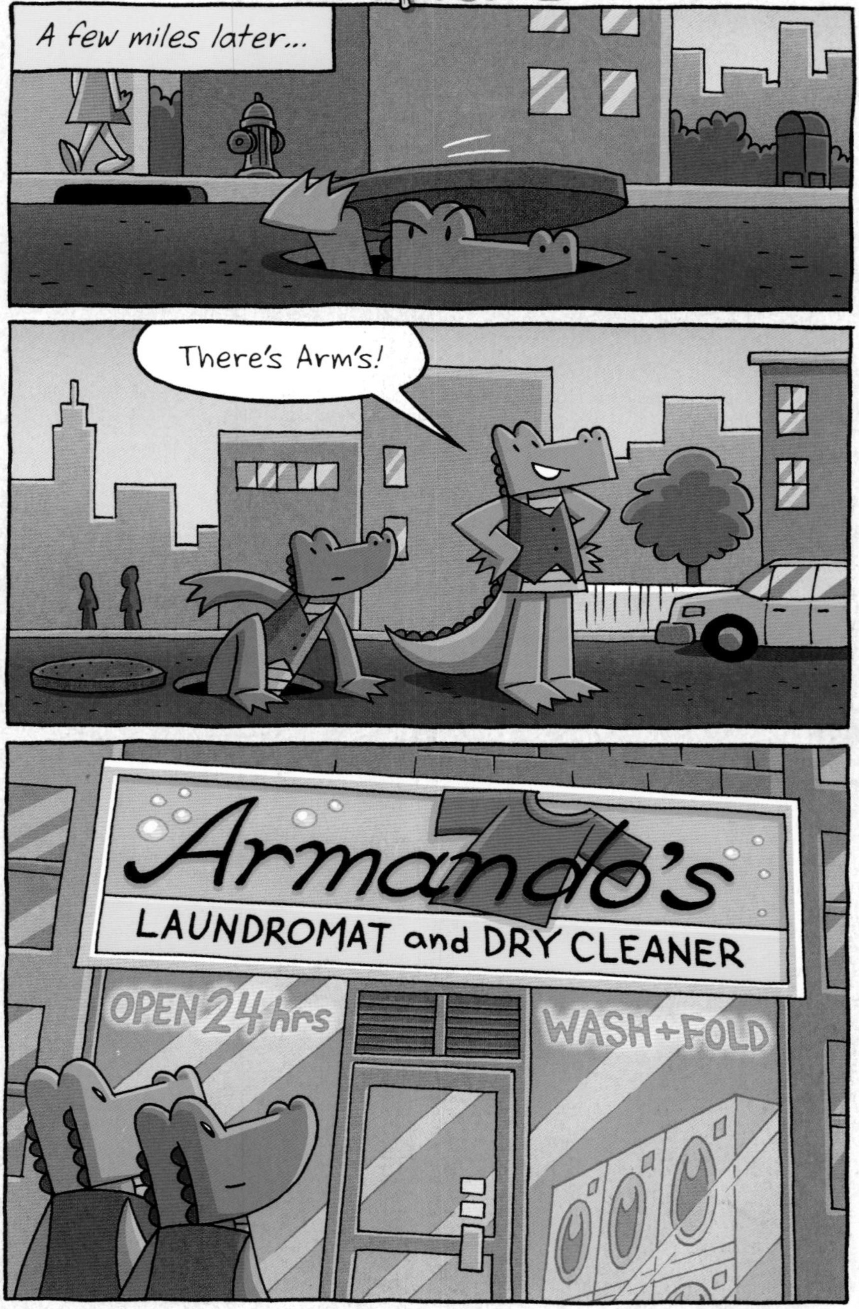
A few miles later...
There's Arm's!
Armando's
LAUNDROMAT and DRY CLEANER
OPEN 24 hrs
WASH + FOLD

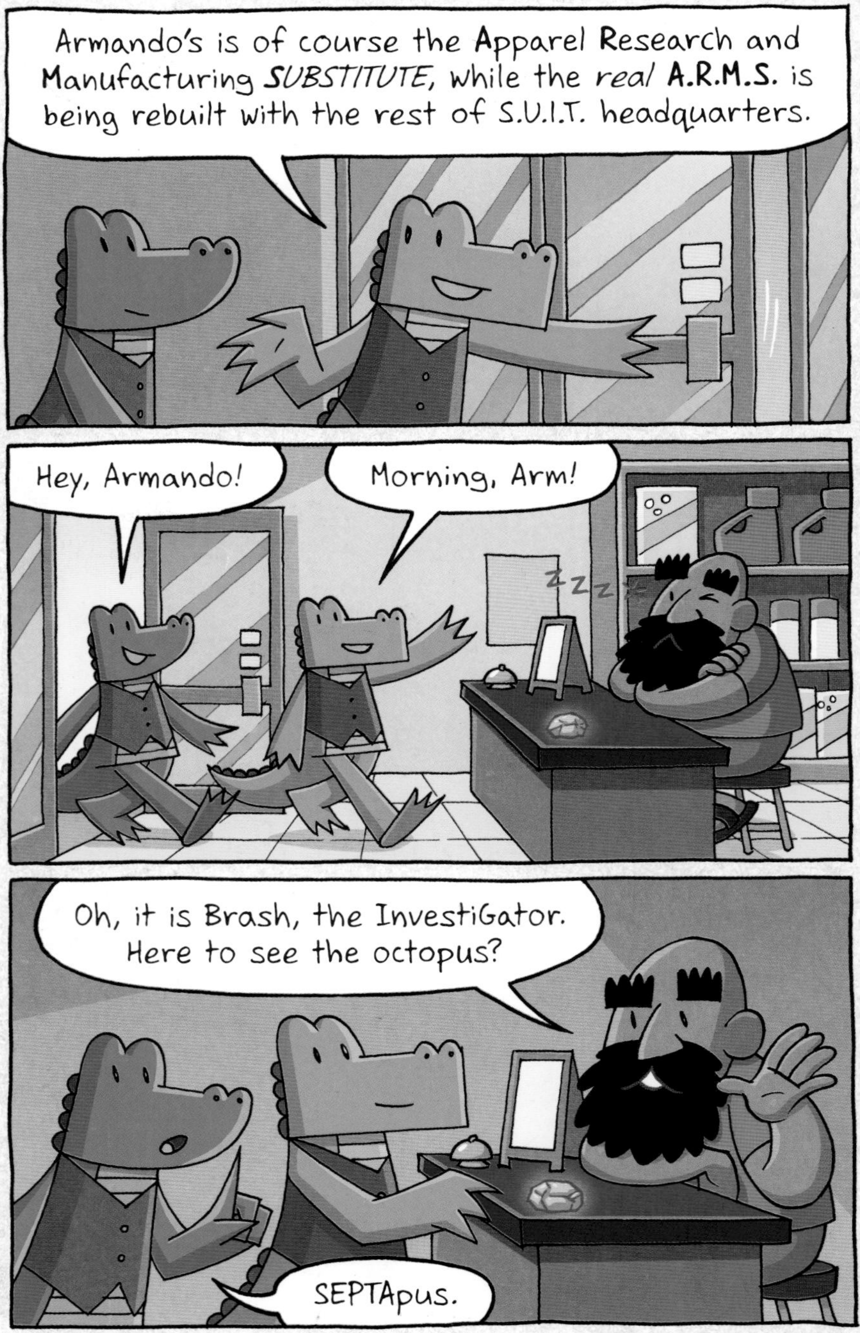
Armando's is of course the Apparel Research and Manufacturing *SUBSTITUTE*, while the *real* **A.R.M.S.** is being rebuilt with the rest of S.U.I.T. headquarters.
Hey, Armando!
Morning, Arm!
ZZZ
Oh, it is Brash, the InvestiGator. Here to see the octopus?
SEPTApus.

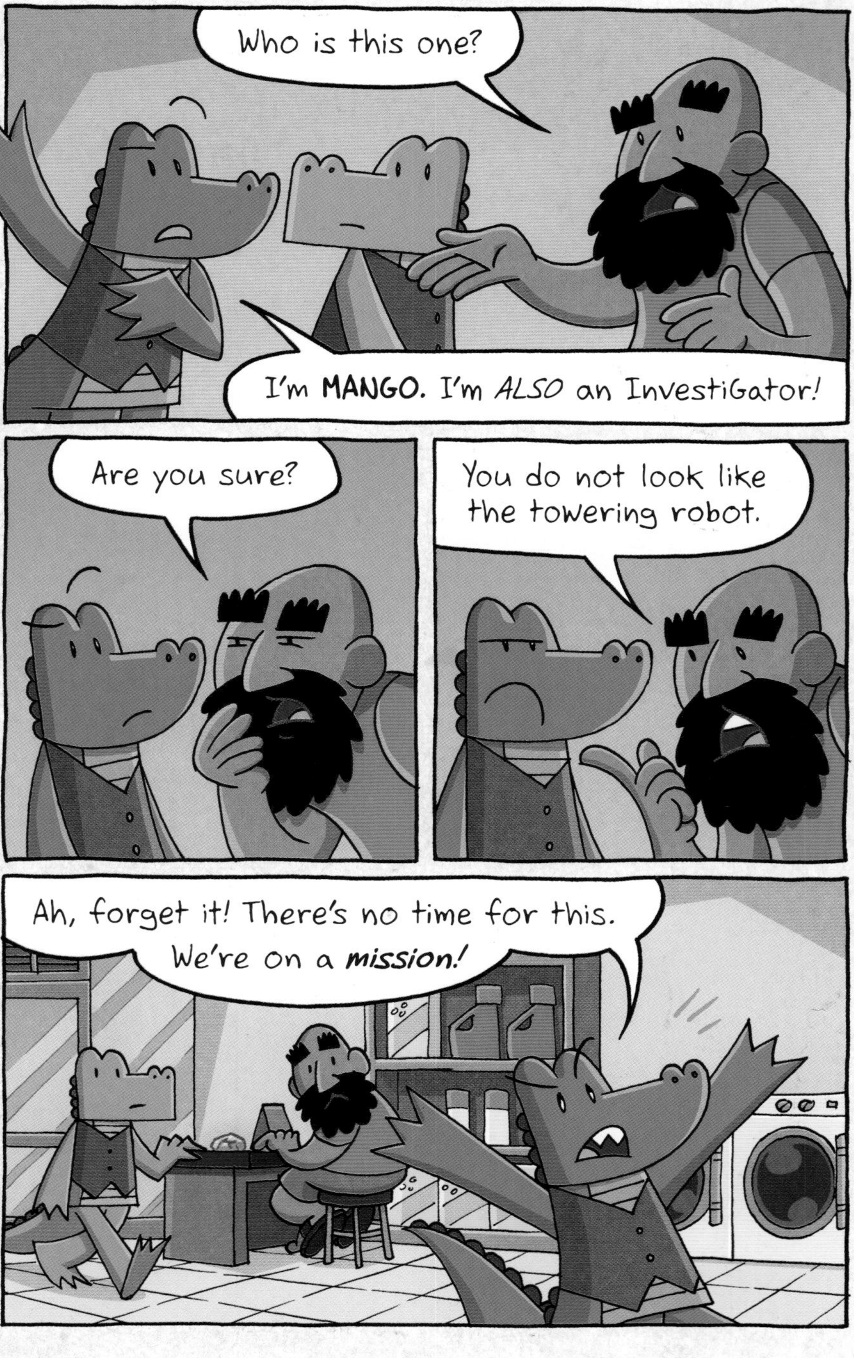
Who is this one?
I'm **MANGO.** I'm *ALSO* an InvestiGator!
Are you sure?
You do not look like the towering robot.
Ah, forget it! There's no time for this. We're on a ***mission!***

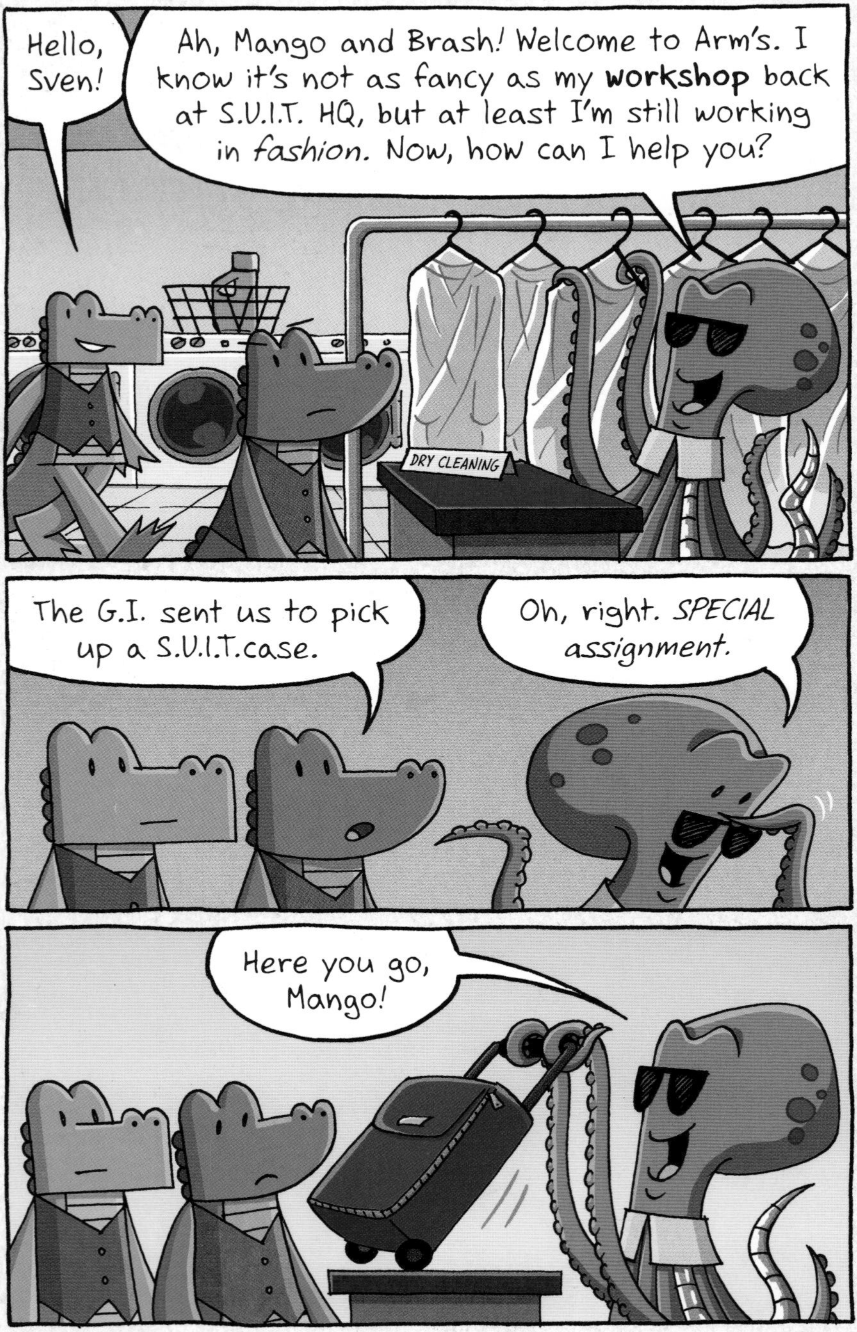
Hello, Sven!
Ah, Mango and Brash! Welcome to Arm's. I know it's not as fancy as my **workshop** back at S.U.I.T. HQ, but at least I'm still working in *fashion.* Now, how can I help you?
DRY CLEANING
The G.I. sent us to pick up a S.U.I.T.case.
Oh, right. *SPECIAL assignment.*
Here you go, Mango!

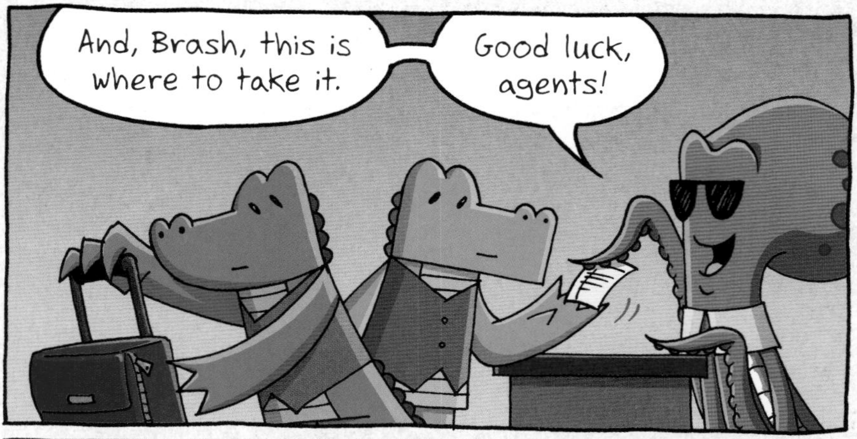
And, Brash, this is where to take it.
Good luck, agents!

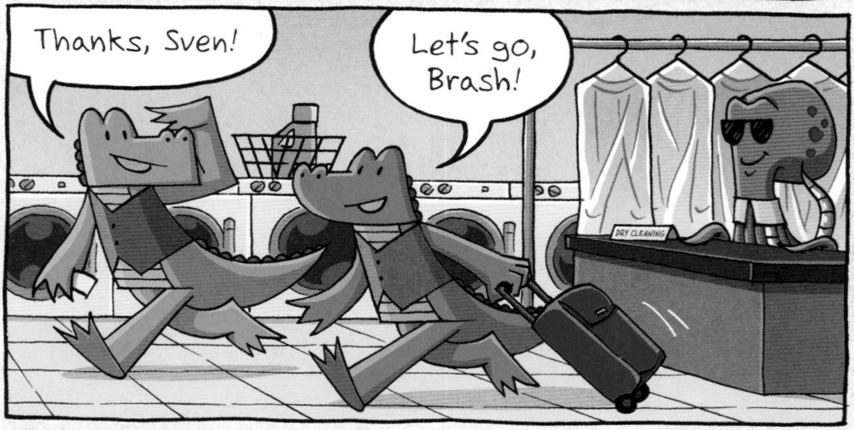
Thanks, Sven!
Let's go, Brash!
DRY CLEANING

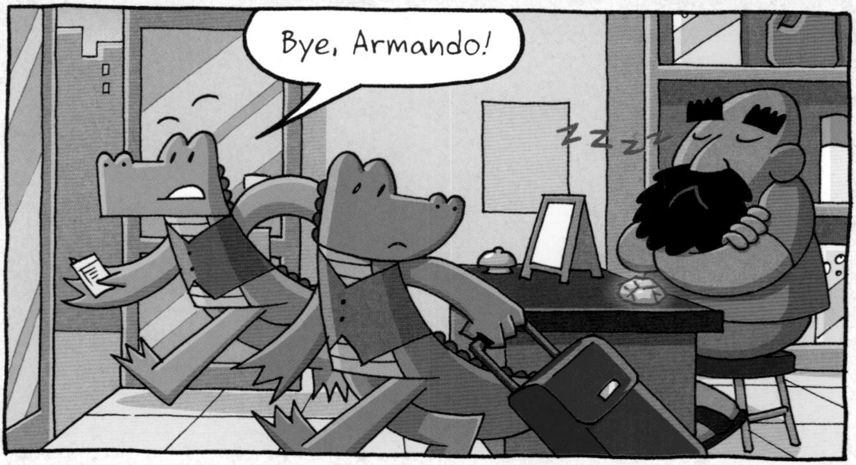
Bye, Armando!
ZZZZ

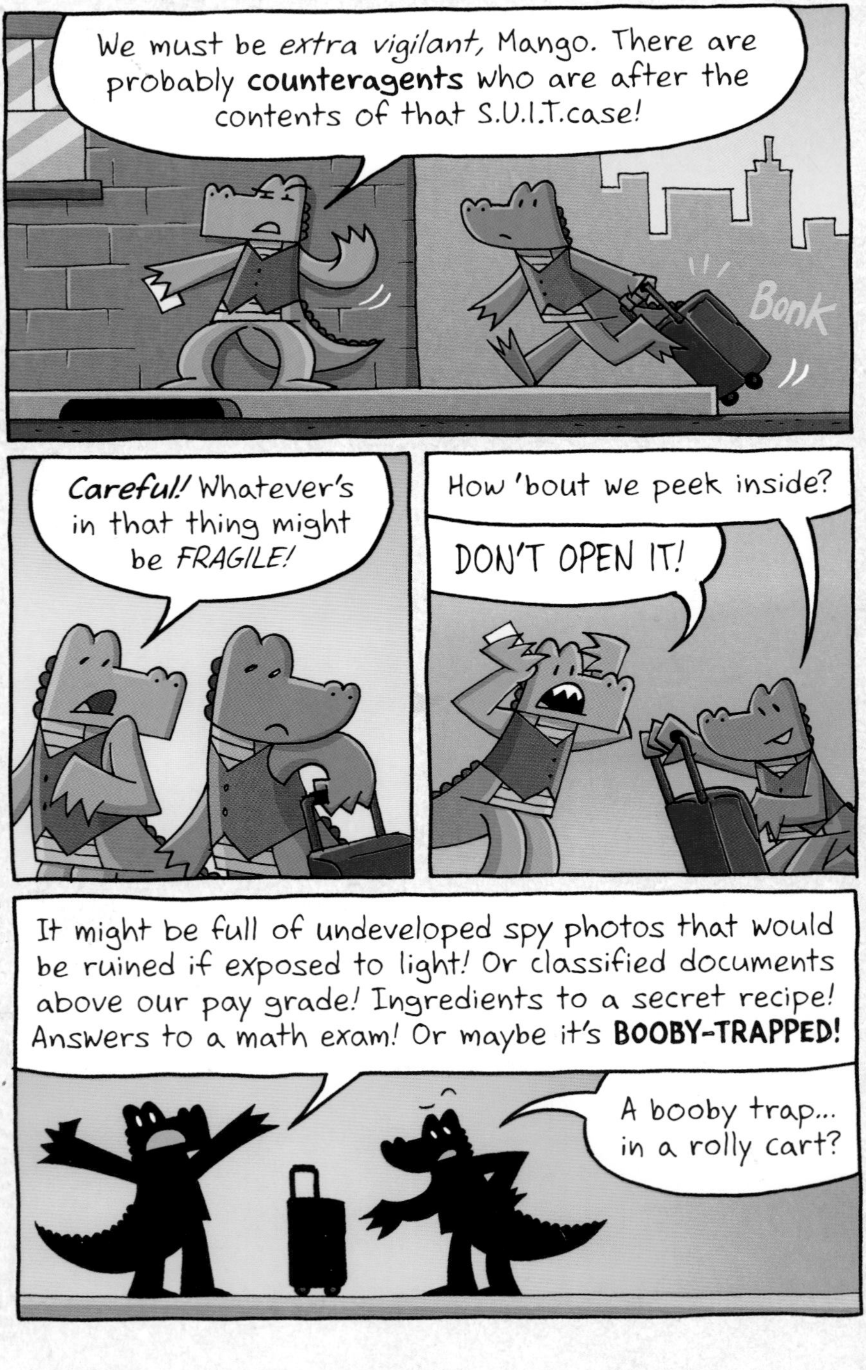
We must be *extra vigilant*, Mango. There are probably **counteragents** who are after the contents of that S.U.I.T.case!
BONK
Careful! Whatever's in that thing might be *FRAGILE!*
How 'bout we peek inside?
DON'T OPEN IT!
It might be full of undeveloped spy photos that would be ruined if exposed to light! Or classified documents above our pay grade! Ingredients to a secret recipe! Answers to a math exam! Or maybe it's **BOOBY-TRAPPED!**
A booby trap... in a rolly cart?

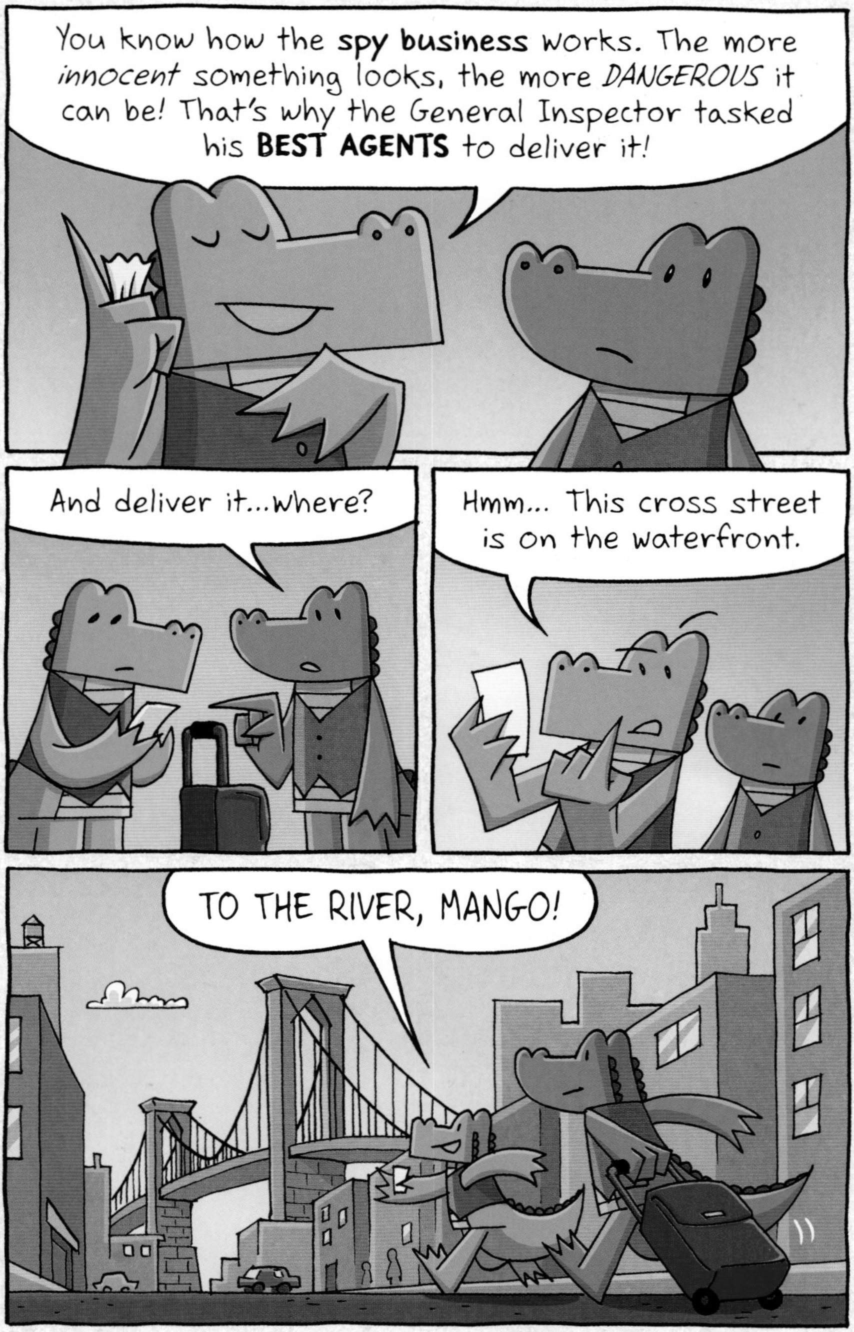
You know how the **spy business** works. The more *innocent* something looks, the more *DANGEROUS* it can be! That's why the General Inspector tasked his **BEST AGENTS** to deliver it!
And deliver it...where?
Hmm... This cross street is on the waterfront.
TO THE RIVER, MANGO!

Chapter 3

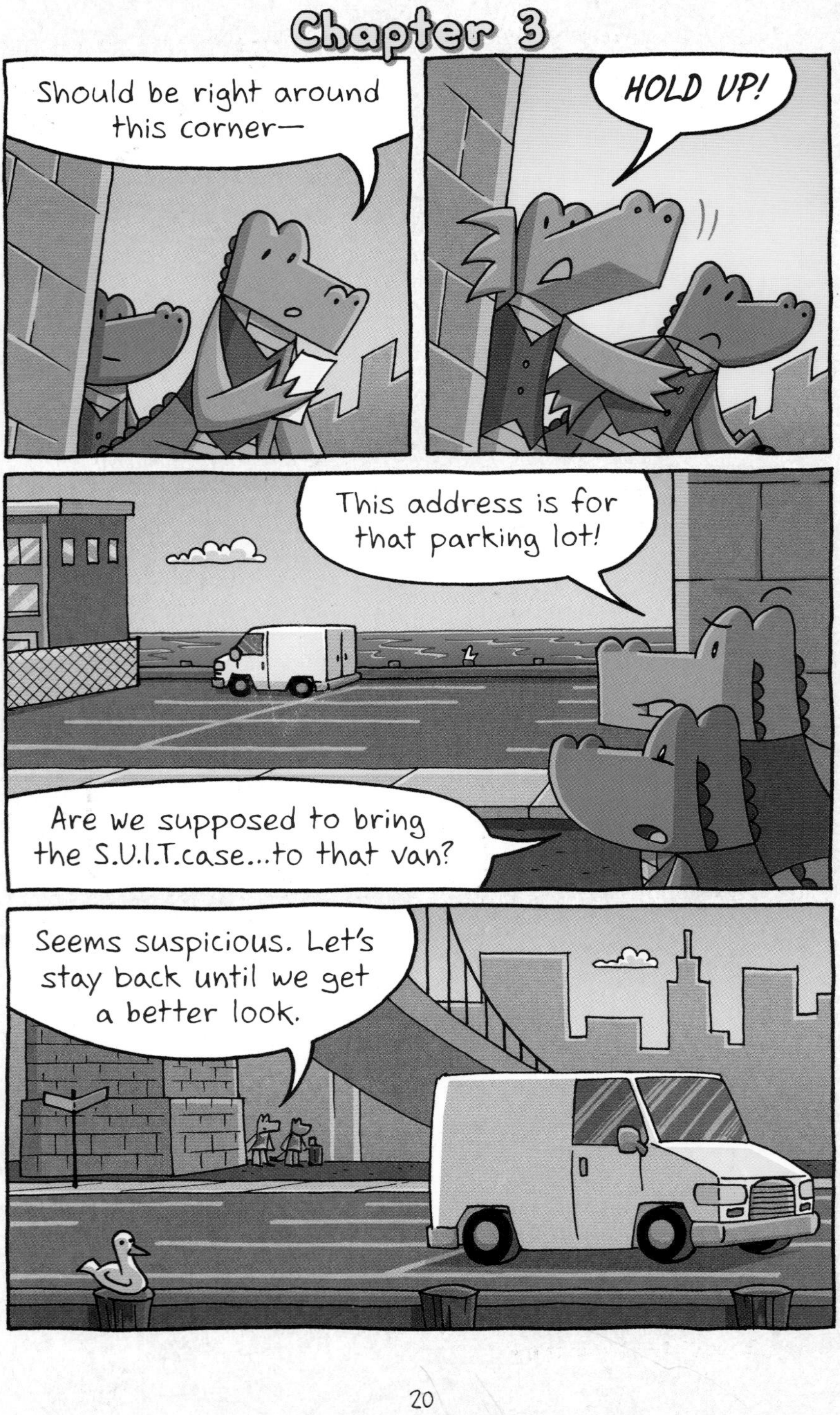
Should be right around this corner—
HOLD UP!
This address is for that parking lot!
Are we supposed to bring the S.U.I.T.case...to that van?
Seems suspicious. Let's stay back until we get a better look.

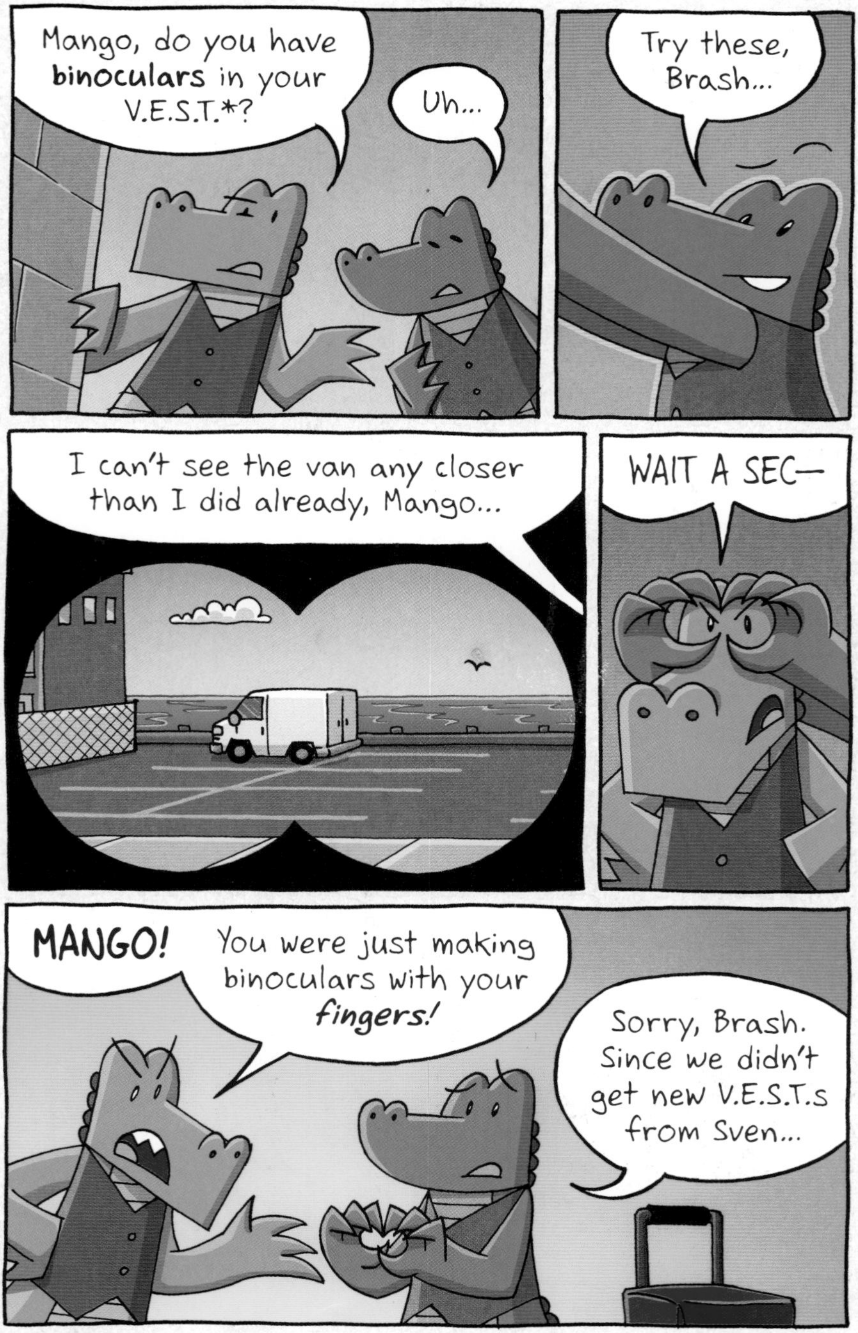
Mango, do you have **binoculars** in your V.E.S.T.*?
Uh...
Try these, Brash...
I can't see the van any closer than I did already, Mango...
WAIT A SEC—
MANGO!
You were just making binoculars with your ***fingers!***
Sorry, Brash. Since we didn't get new V.E.S.T.s from Sven...

*Very Exciting Spy Technology

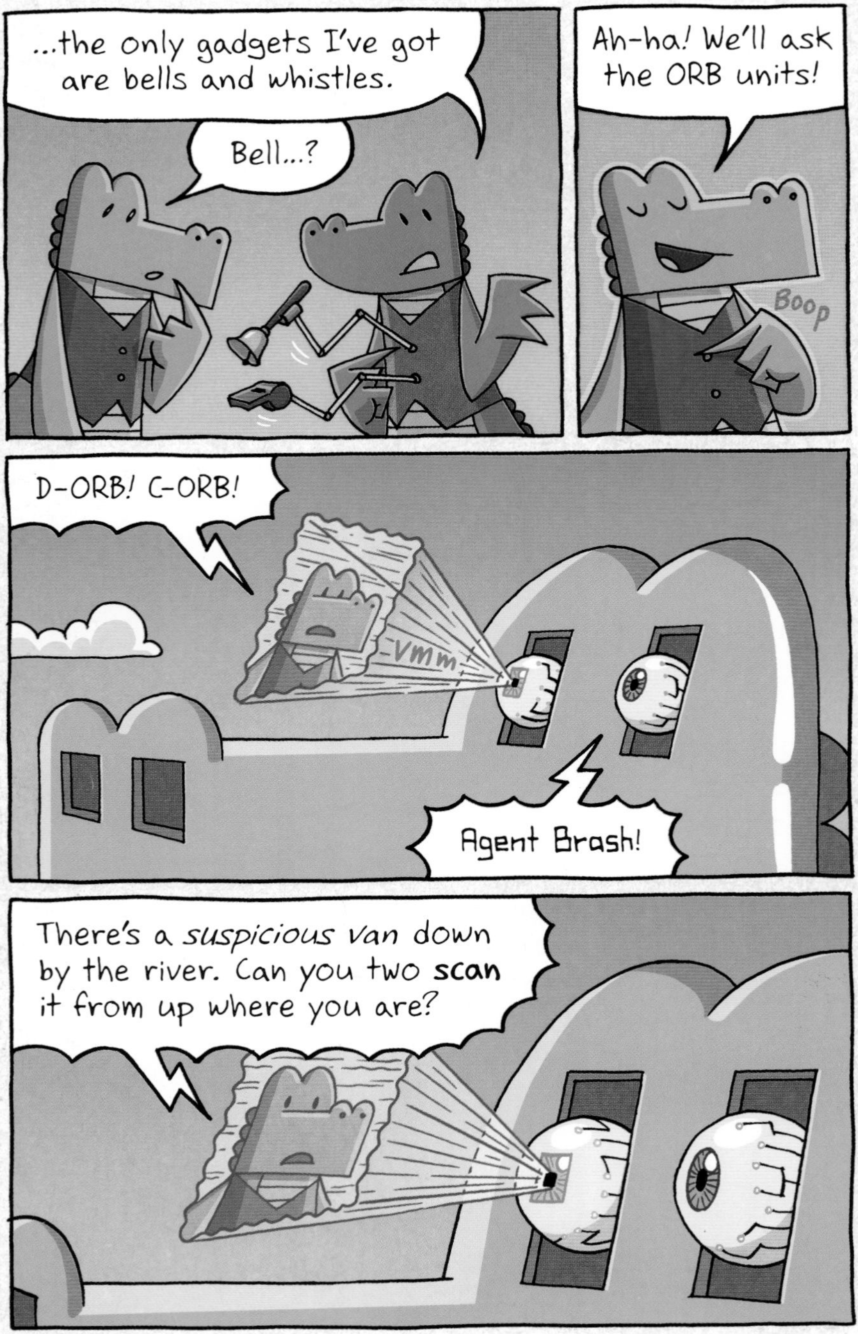
...the only gadgets I've got are bells and whistles.
Bell...?
Ah-ha! We'll ask the ORB units!
BOOP
D-ORB! C-ORB!
VMM
Agent Brash!
There's a *suspicious* van down by the river. Can you two **scan** it from up where you are?

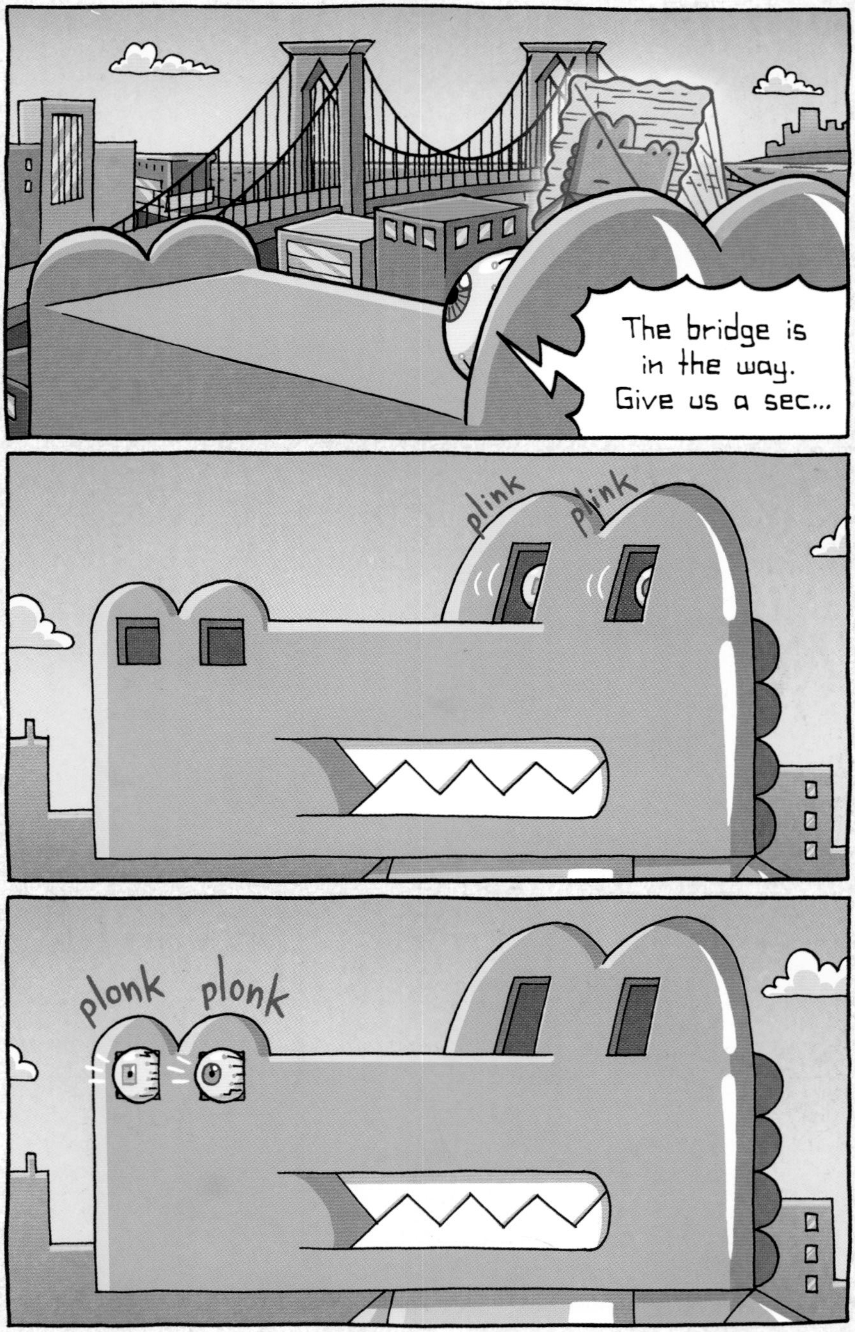
The bridge is in the way. Give us a sec...
plink
plink
plonk
plonk

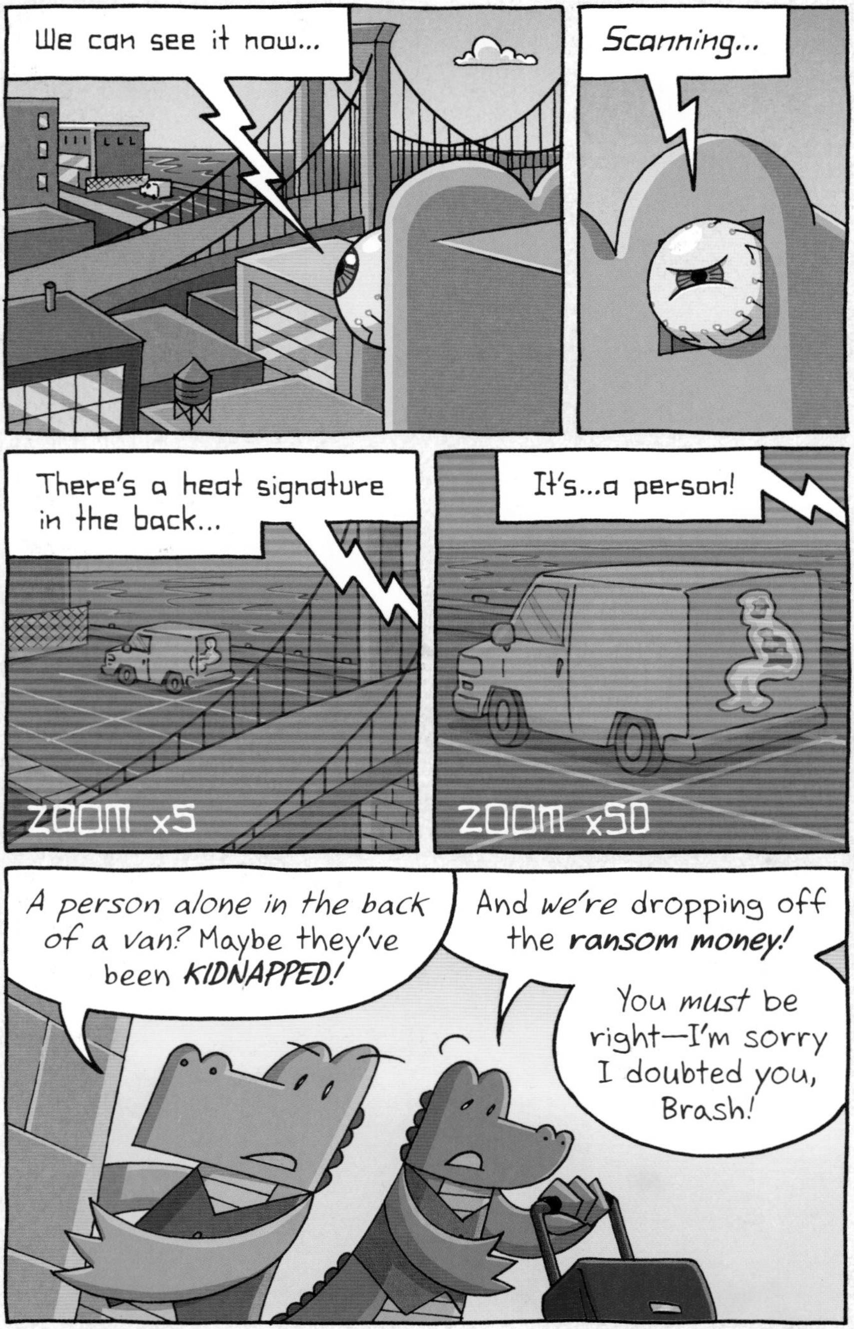
We can see it now...
Scanning...
There's a heat signature in the back...
ZOOM x5
It's...a person!
ZOOM x50
A person alone in the back of a van? Maybe they've been KIDNAPPED!
And we're dropping off the ransom money!
You must be right—I'm sorry I doubted you, Brash!

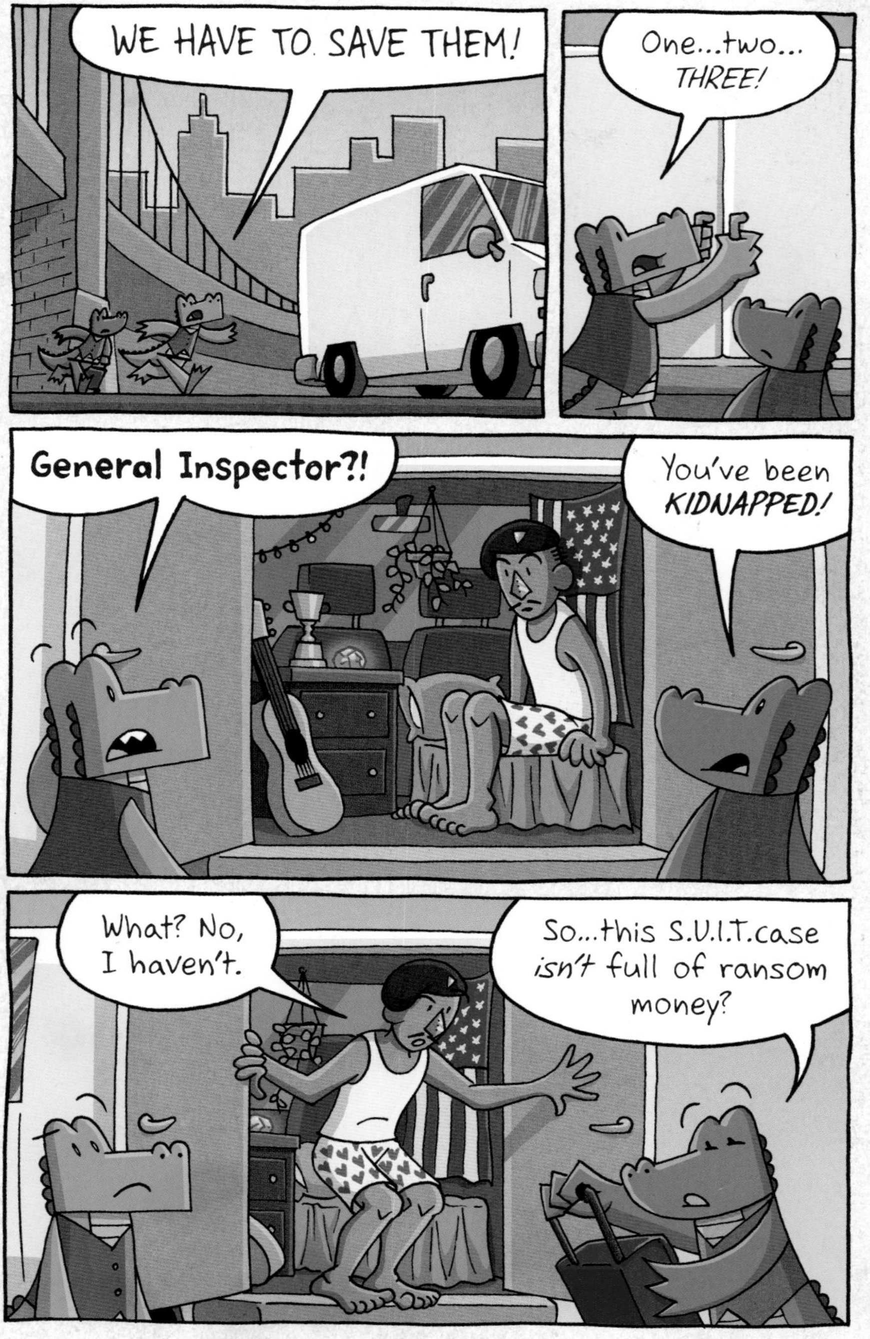
WE HAVE TO SAVE THEM!
One...two... THREE!
General Inspector?!
You've been KIDNAPPED!
What? No, I haven't.
So...this S.U.I.T.case isn't full of ransom money?

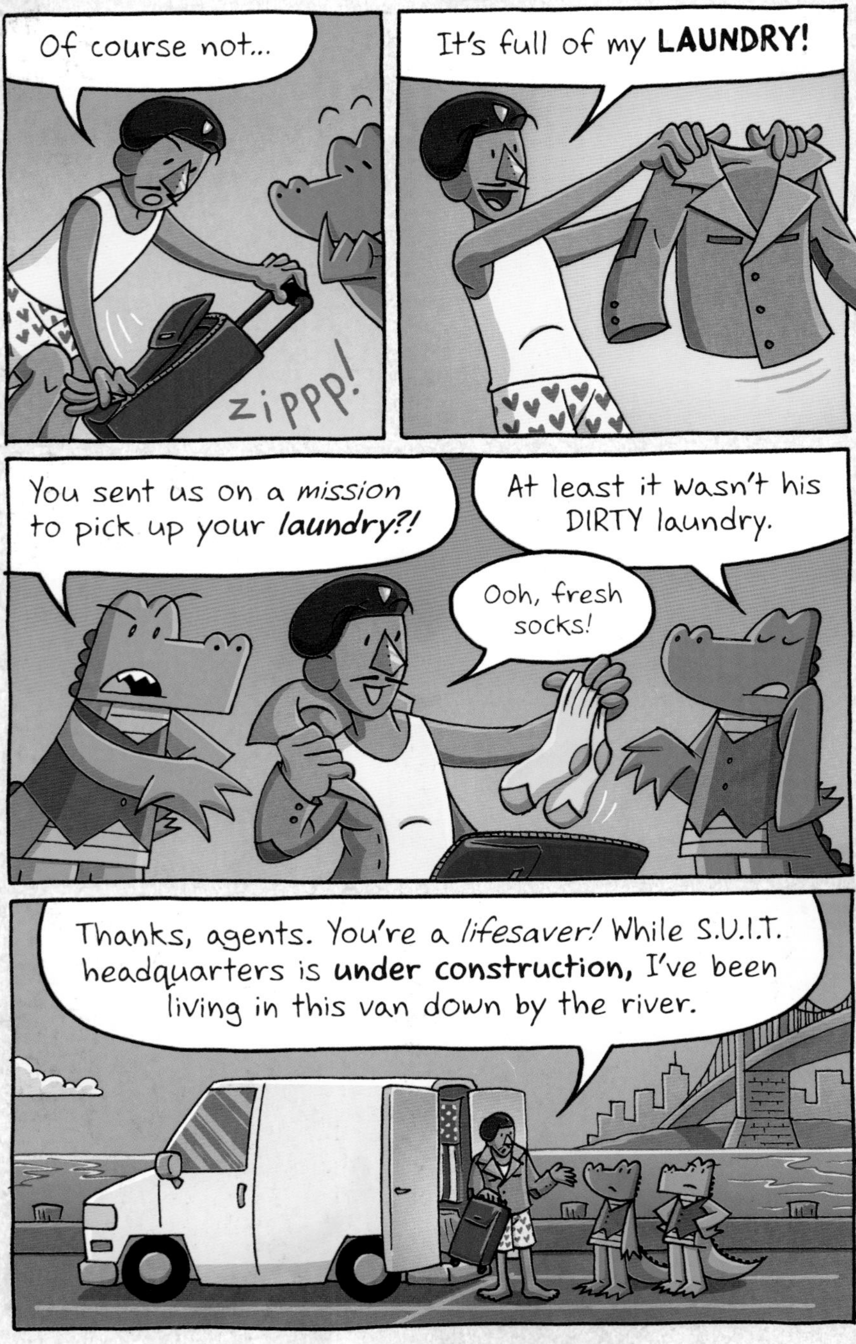
Of course not...
zippp!
It's full of my **LAUNDRY!**
You sent us on a *mission* to pick up your ***laundry?!***
At least it wasn't his DIRTY laundry.
Ooh, fresh socks!
Thanks, agents. You're a *lifesaver!* While S.U.I.T. headquarters is **under construction,** I've been living in this van down by the river.

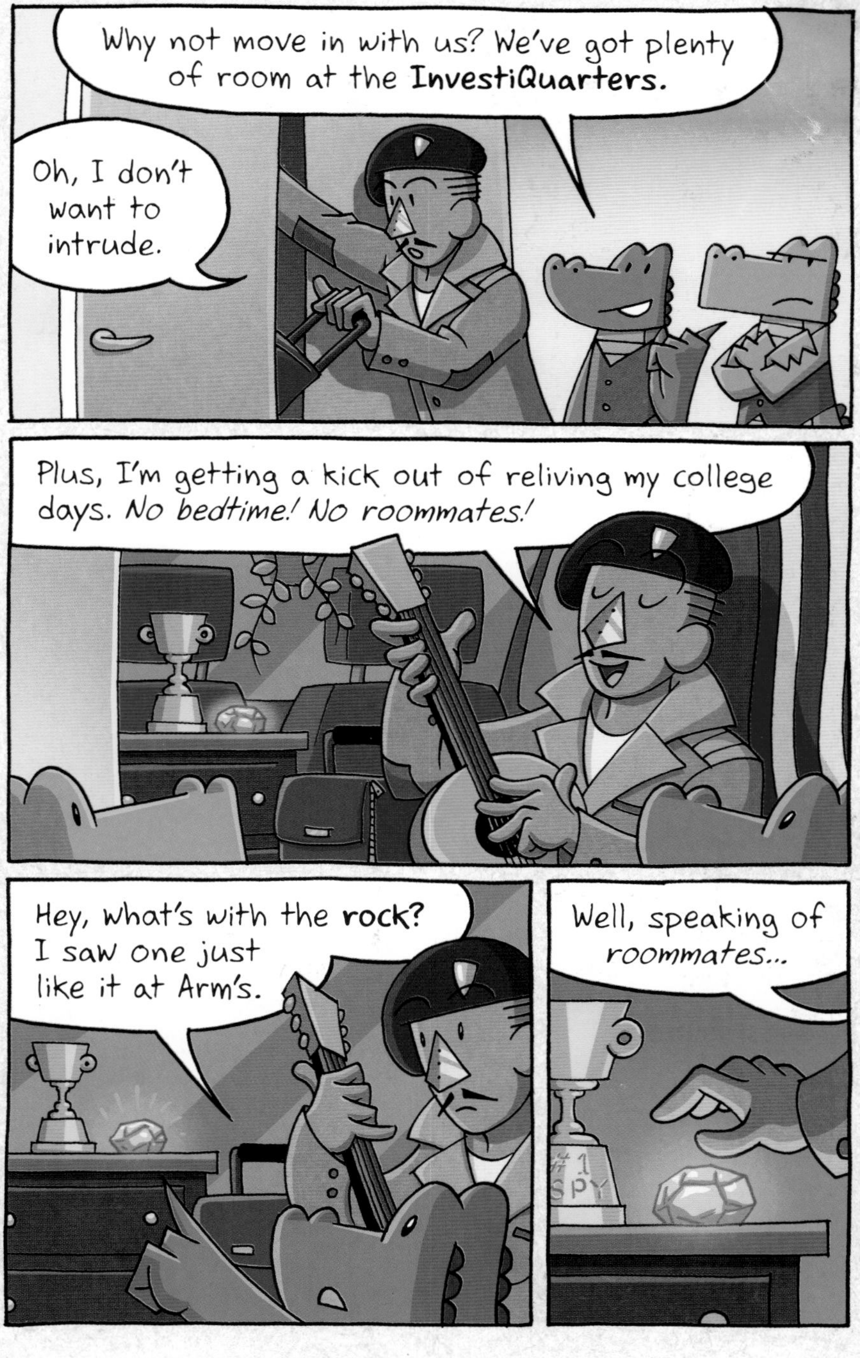
Why not move in with us? We've got plenty of room at the **InvestiQuarters.**
Oh, I don't want to intrude.
Plus, I'm getting a kick out of reliving my college days. *No bedtime! No roommates!*
Hey, what's with the **rock?** I saw one just like it at Arm's.
#1 SPY
Well, speaking of *roommates...*

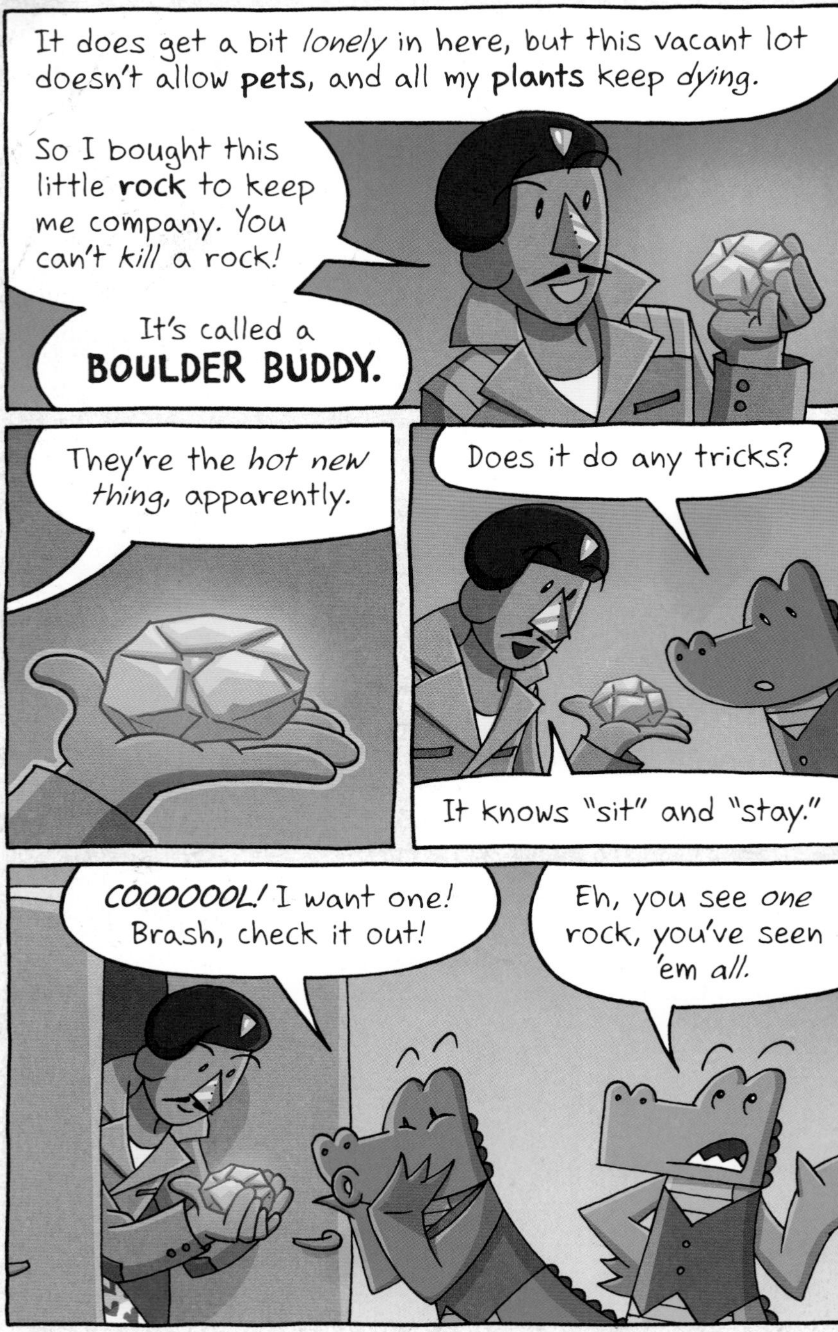
It does get a bit *lonely* in here, but this vacant lot doesn't allow **pets**, and all my **plants** keep *dying*.
So I bought this little **rock** to keep me company. You can't *kill* a rock!
It's called a **BOULDER BUDDY.**
They're the *hot new thing*, apparently.
Does it do any tricks?
It knows "sit" and "stay."
COOOOOOL! I want one! Brash, check it out!
Eh, you see *one* rock, you've seen 'em *all*.

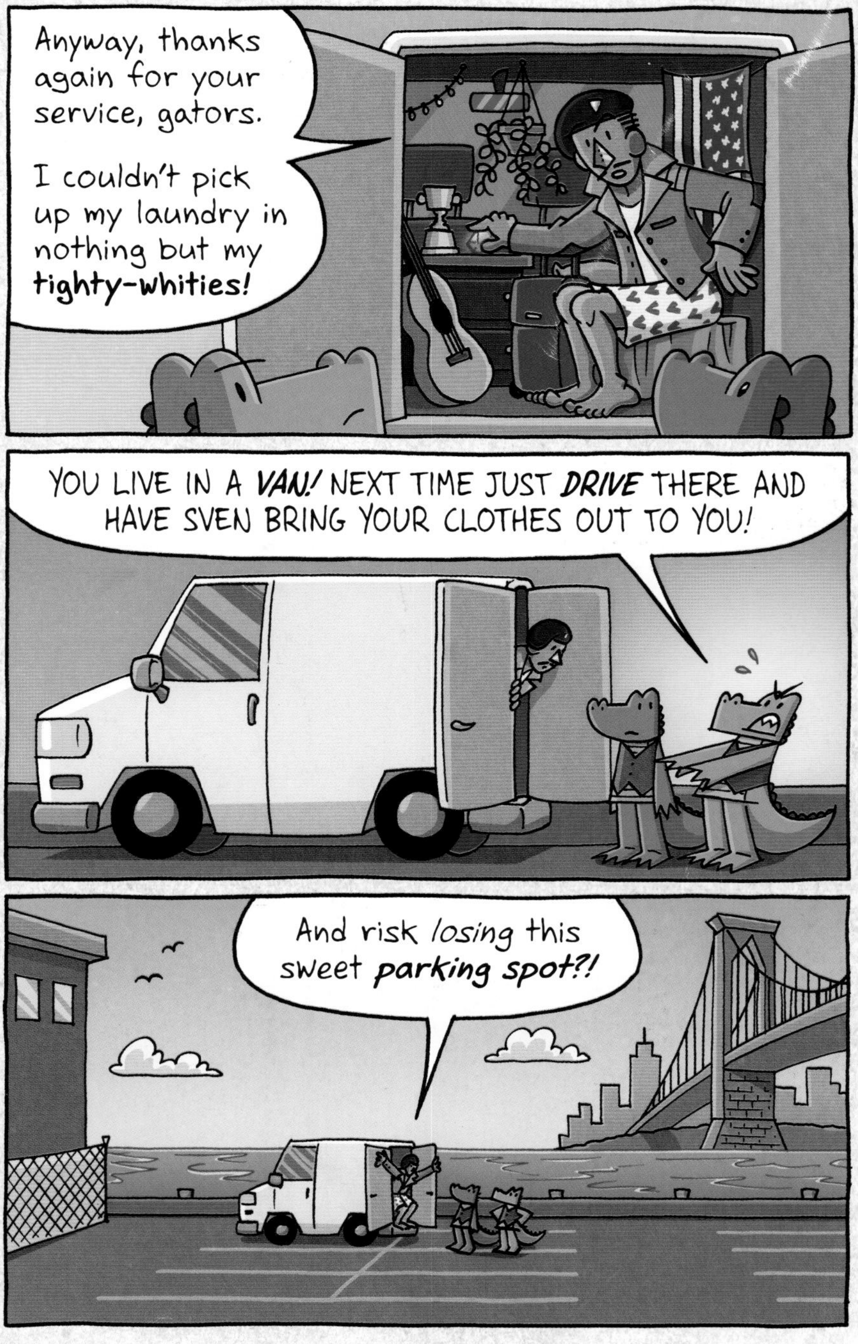
Anyway, thanks again for your service, gators.
I couldn't pick up my laundry in nothing but my **tighty-whities!**
YOU LIVE IN A ***VAN!*** NEXT TIME JUST ***DRIVE*** THERE AND HAVE SVEN BRING YOUR CLOTHES OUT TO YOU!
And risk *losing* this sweet ***parking spot?!***

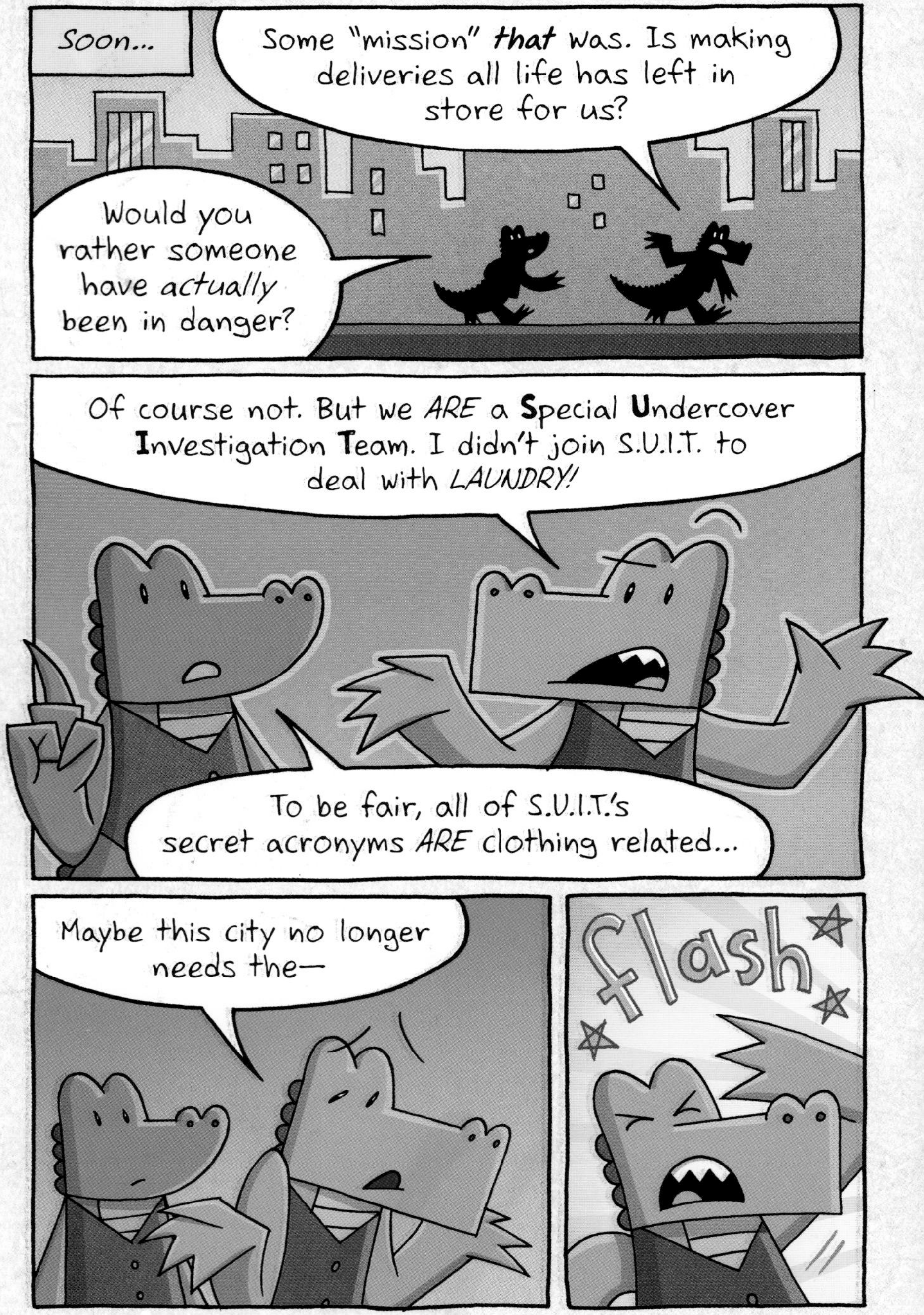
Soon...
Some "mission" ***that*** was. Is making deliveries all life has left in store for us?
Would you rather someone have *actually* been in danger?
Of course not. But we *ARE* a **S**pecial **U**ndercover **I**nvestigation **T**eam. I didn't join S.U.I.T. to deal with *LAUNDRY!*
To be fair, all of S.U.I.T.'s secret acronyms *ARE* clothing related...
Maybe this city no longer needs the—
flash

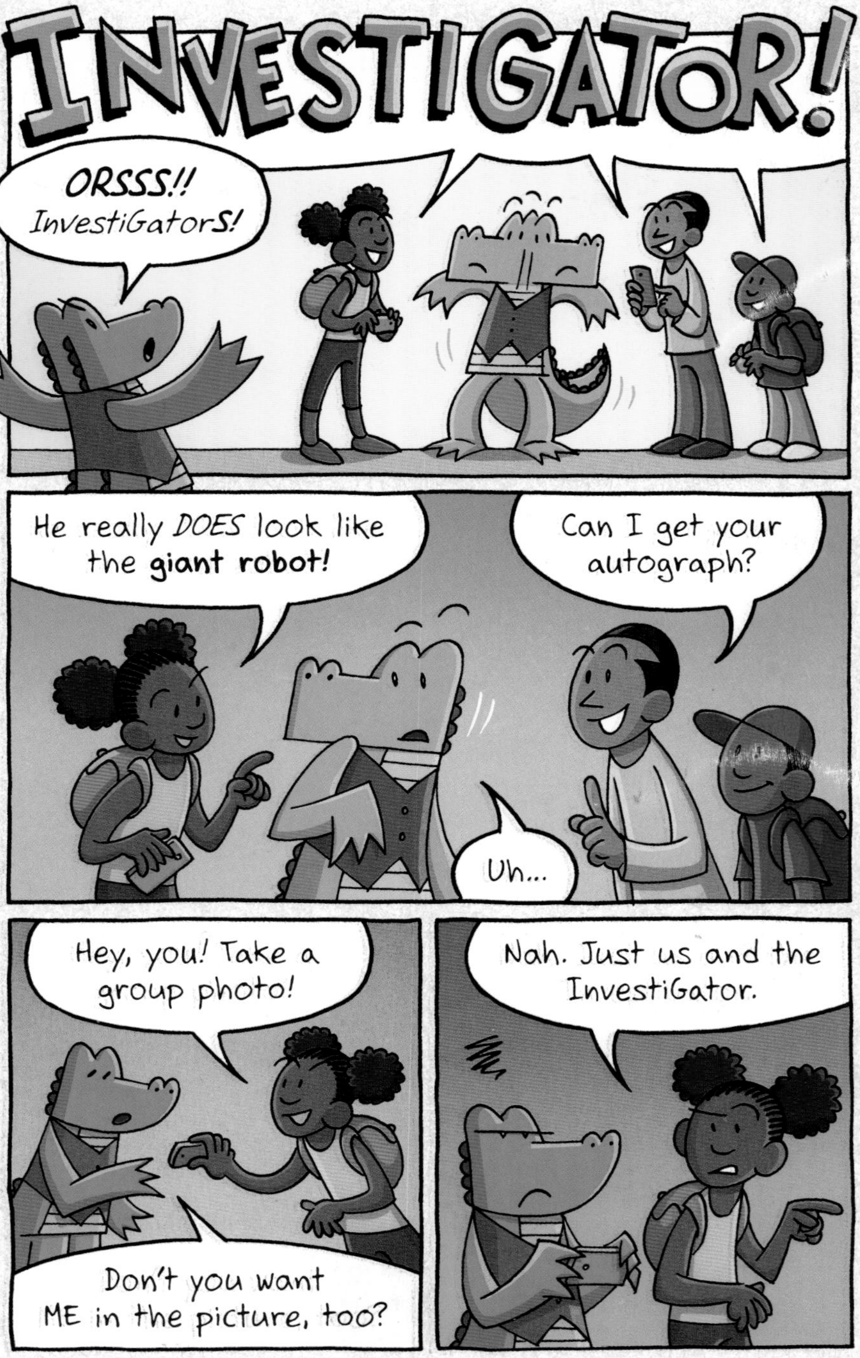
INVESTIGATOR!
ORSSS!! InvestiGatorS!
He really DOES look like the giant robot!
Can I get your autograph?
Uh...
Hey, you! Take a group photo!
Don't you want ME in the picture, too?
Nah. Just us and the InvestiGator.

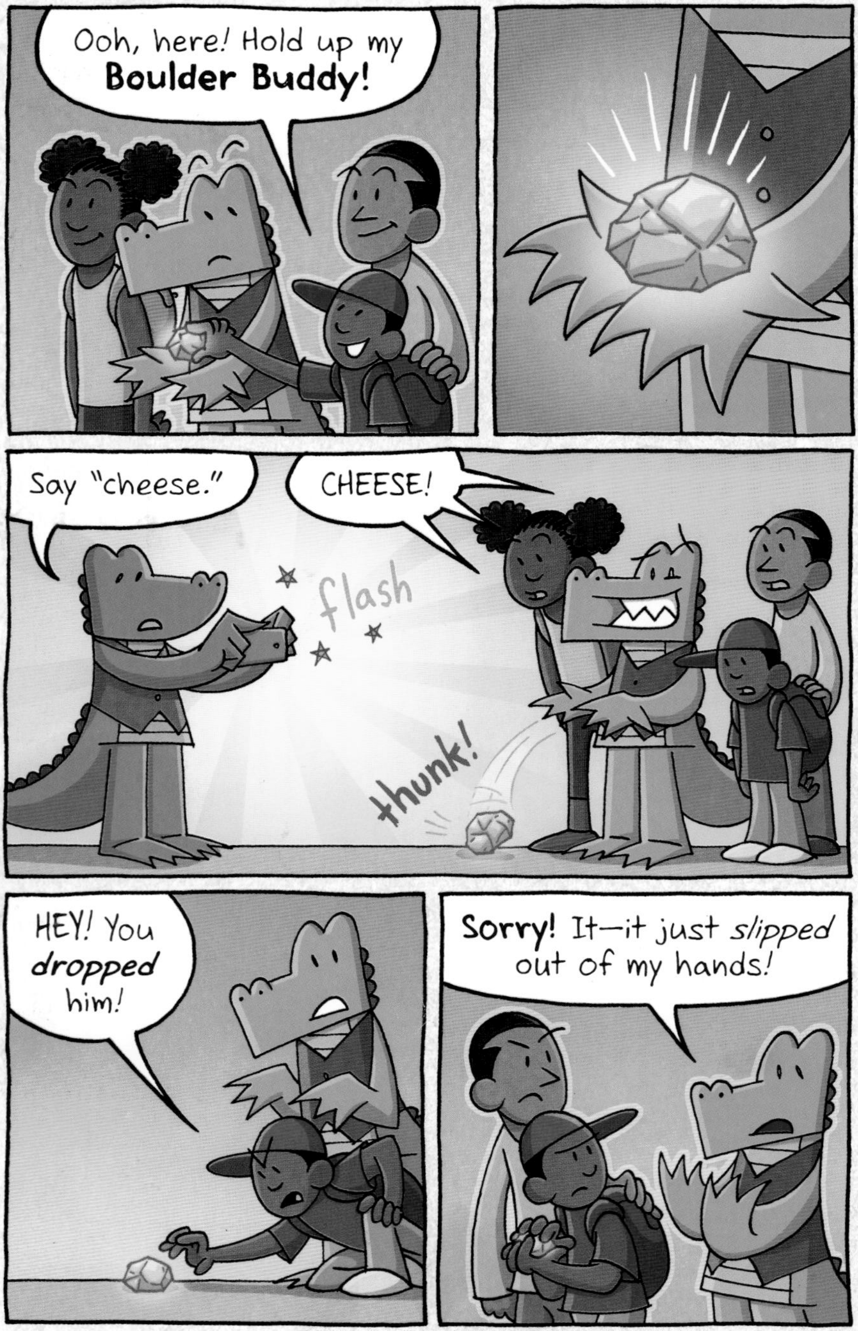
Ooh, here! Hold up my **Boulder Buddy!**
Say "cheese."
CHEESE!
flash
thunk!
HEY! You *dropped* him!
Sorry! It—it just *slipped* out of my hands!

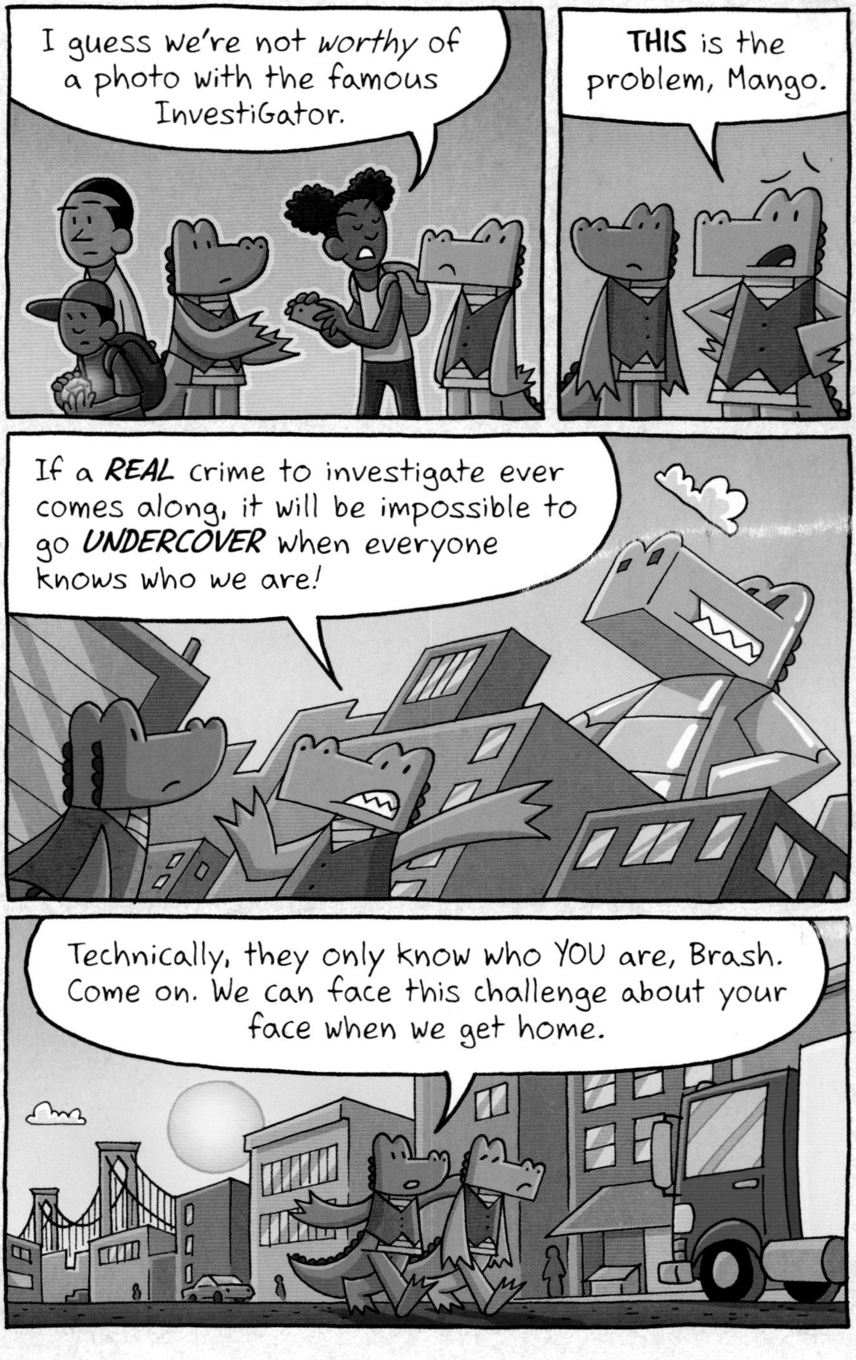
I guess we're not *worthy* of a photo with the famous InvestiGator.
THIS is the problem, Mango.
If a ***REAL*** crime to investigate ever comes along, it will be impossible to go ***UNDERCOVER*** when everyone knows who we are!
Technically, they only know who YOU are, Brash. Come on. We can face this challenge about your face when we get home.

Chapter 4

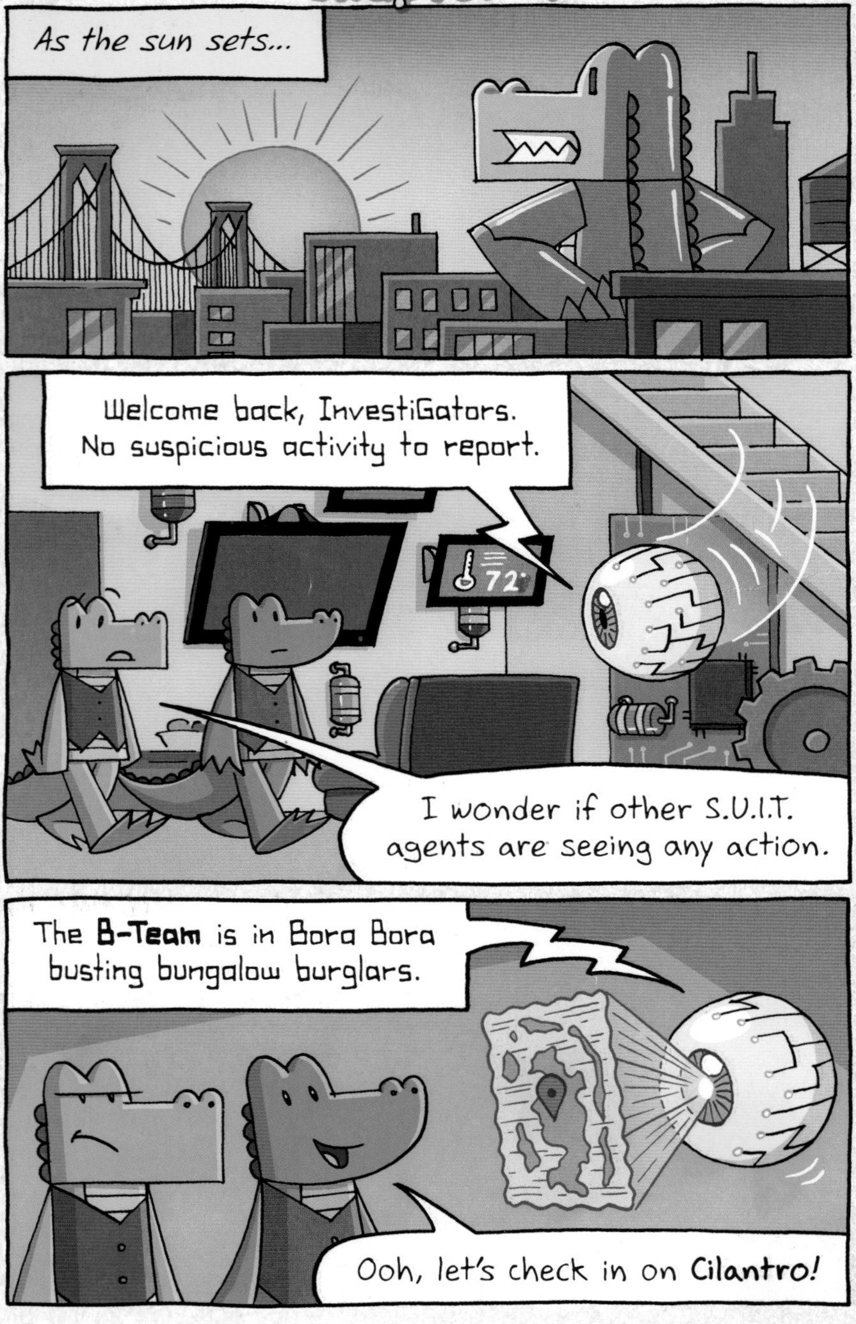
As the sun sets...
Welcome back, InvestiGators. No suspicious activity to report.
72°
I wonder if other S.U.I.T. agents are seeing any action.
The **B-Team** is in Bora Bora busting bungalow burglars.
Ooh, let's check in on **Cilantro**!

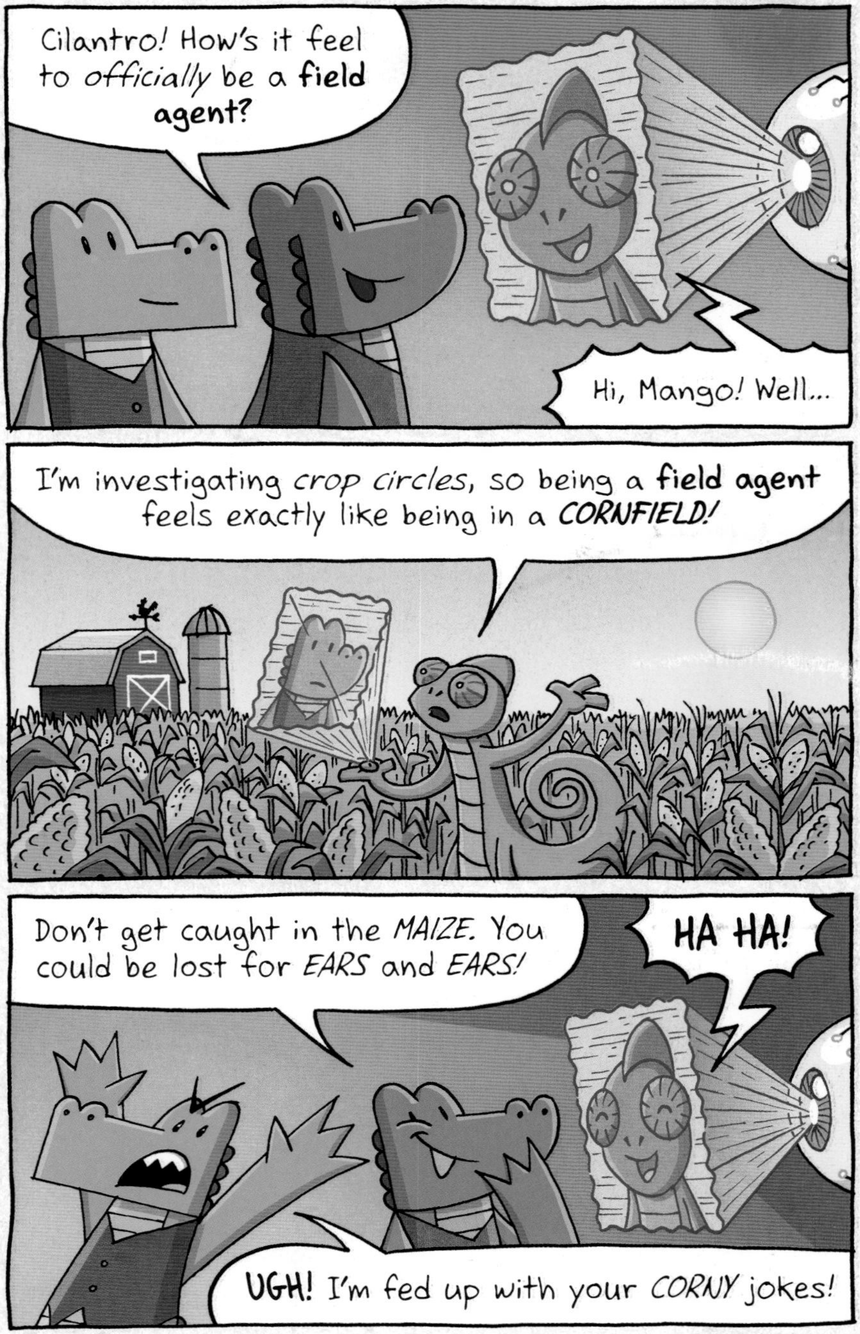
Cilantro! How's it feel to *officially* be a **field agent?**
Hi, Mango! Well...
I'm investigating *crop circles*, so being a **field agent** feels exactly like being in a *CORNFIELD!*
Don't get caught in the *MAIZE*. You could be lost for *EARS* and *EARS!*
HA HA!
UGH! I'm fed up with your *CORNY* jokes!

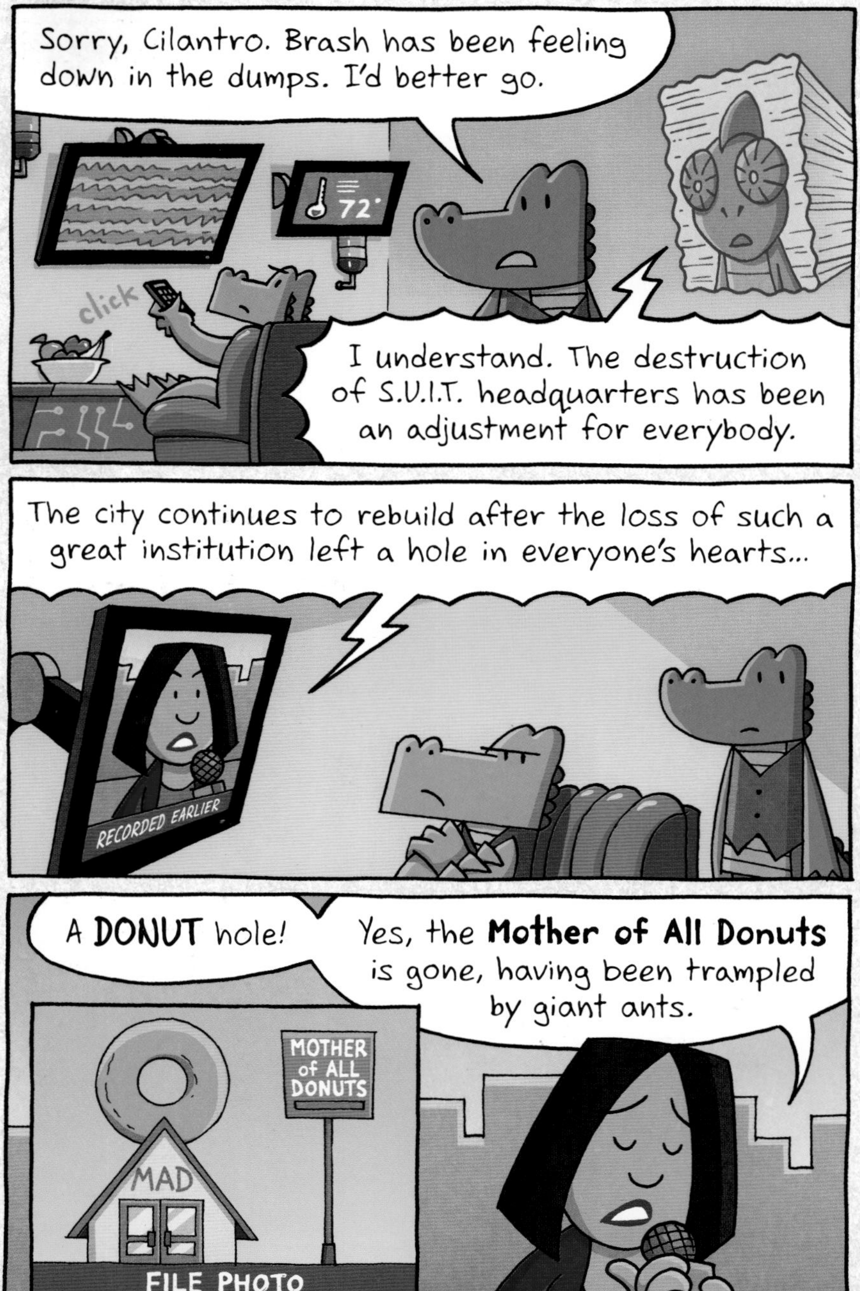
Sorry, Cilantro. Brash has been feeling down in the dumps. I'd better go.
72°
click
I understand. The destruction of S.U.I.T. headquarters has been an adjustment for everybody.
The city continues to rebuild after the loss of such a great institution left a hole in everyone's hearts...
RECORDED EARLIER
A **DONUT** hole!
Yes, the **Mother of All Donuts** is gone, having been trampled by giant ants.
MOTHER of ALL DONUTS
MAD
FILE PHOTO

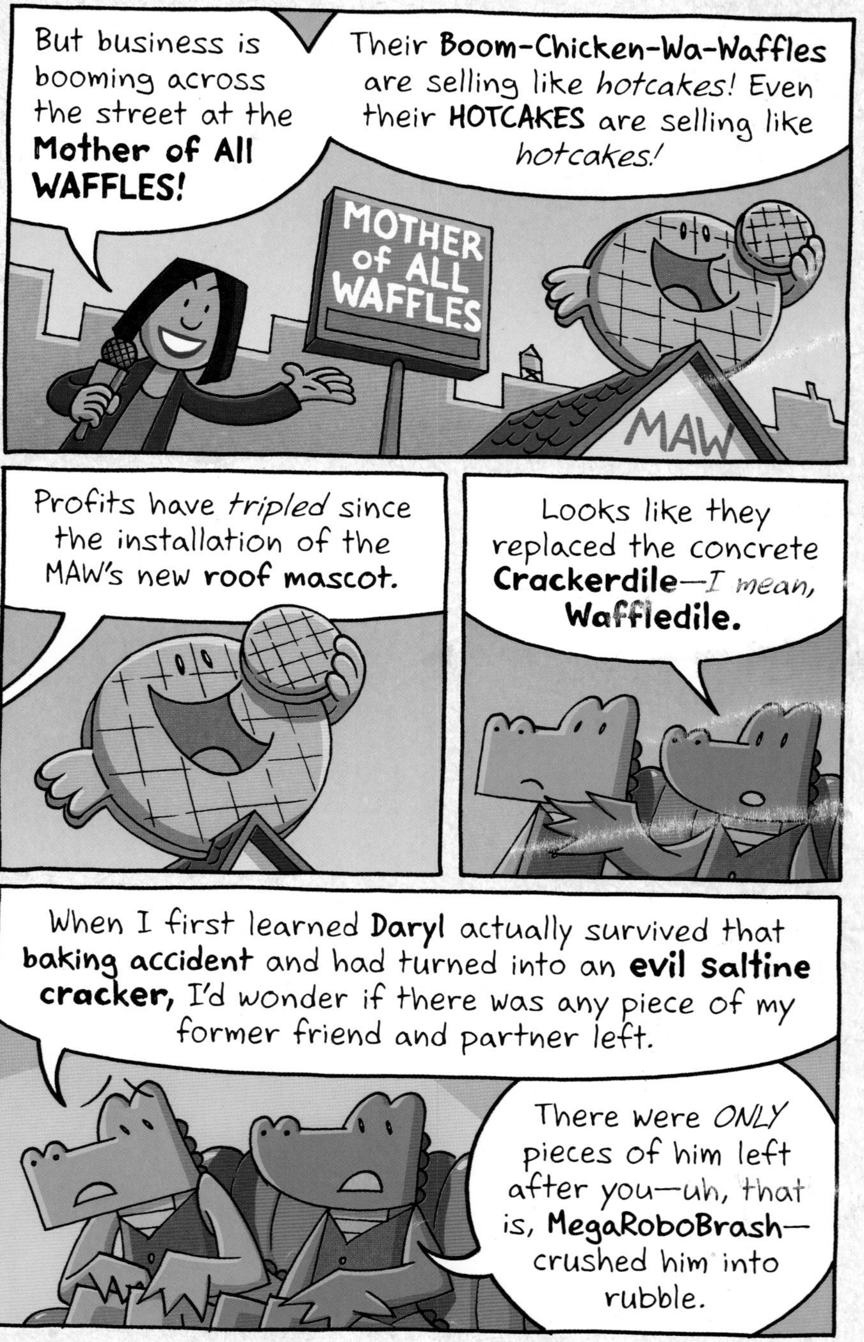

But business is booming across the street at the **Mother of All WAFFLES!**
Their **Boom-Chicken-Wa-Waffles** are selling like *hotcakes!* Even their **HOTCAKES** are selling like *hotcakes!*
MOTHER of ALL WAFFLES
MAW
Profits have *tripled* since the installation of the MAW's new **roof mascot.**
Looks like they replaced the concrete **Crackerdile**—*I mean,* **Waffledile.**
When I first learned **Daryl** actually survived that **baking accident** and had turned into an **evil saltine cracker,** I'd wonder if there was any piece of my former friend and partner left.
There were *ONLY* pieces of him left after you—uh, that is, **MegaRoboBrash**—crushed him into rubble.

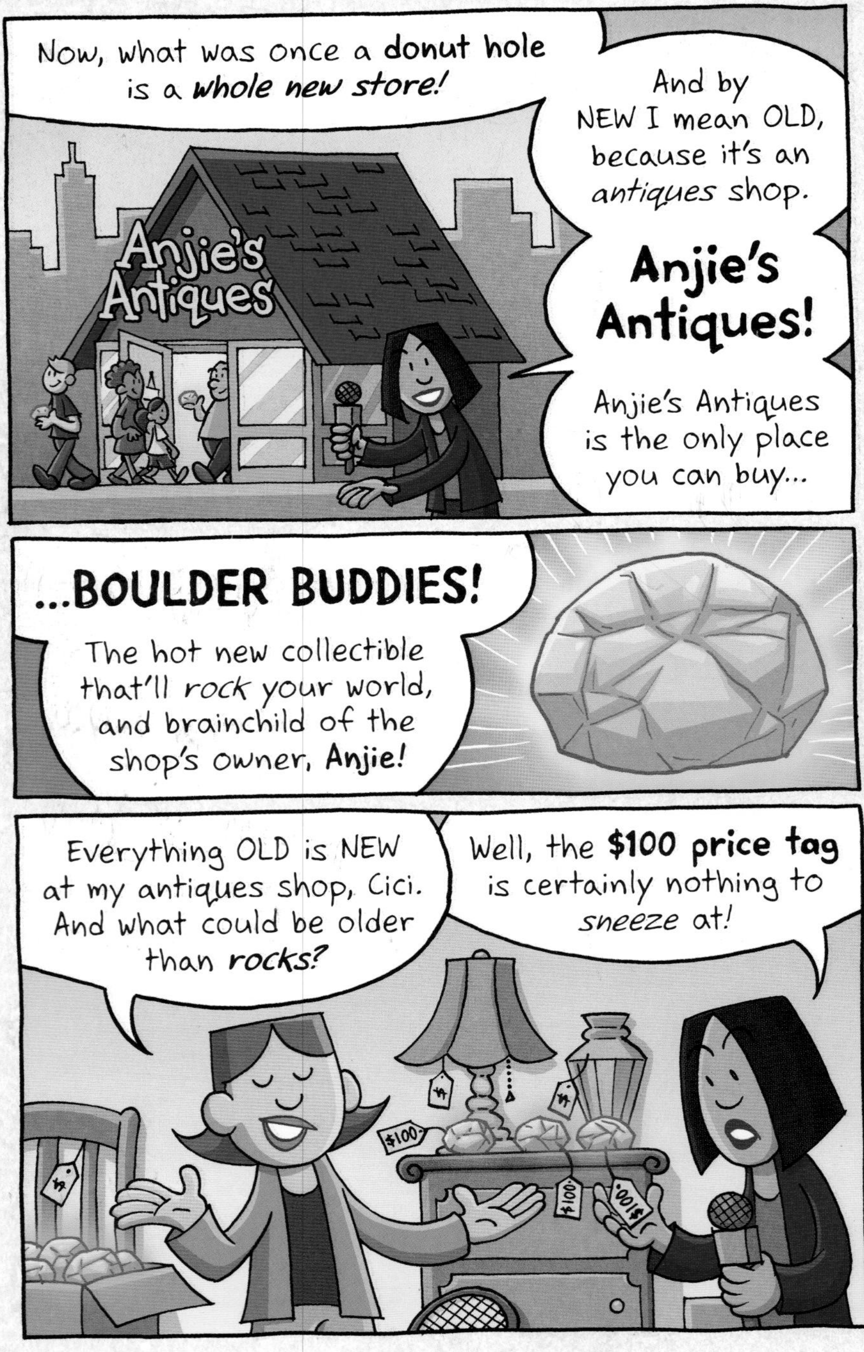
Now, what was once a **donut hole** is a ***whole new store!***
And by NEW I mean OLD, because it's an *antiques* shop.
Anjie's Antiques
Anjie's Antiques!
Anjie's Antiques is the only place you can buy...
...BOULDER BUDDIES!
The hot new collectible that'll *rock* your world, and brainchild of the shop's owner, **Anjie!**
Everything OLD is NEW at my antiques shop, Cici. And what could be older than ***rocks?***
Well, the **$100 price tag** is certainly nothing to *sneeze* at!
$100
$100
$100

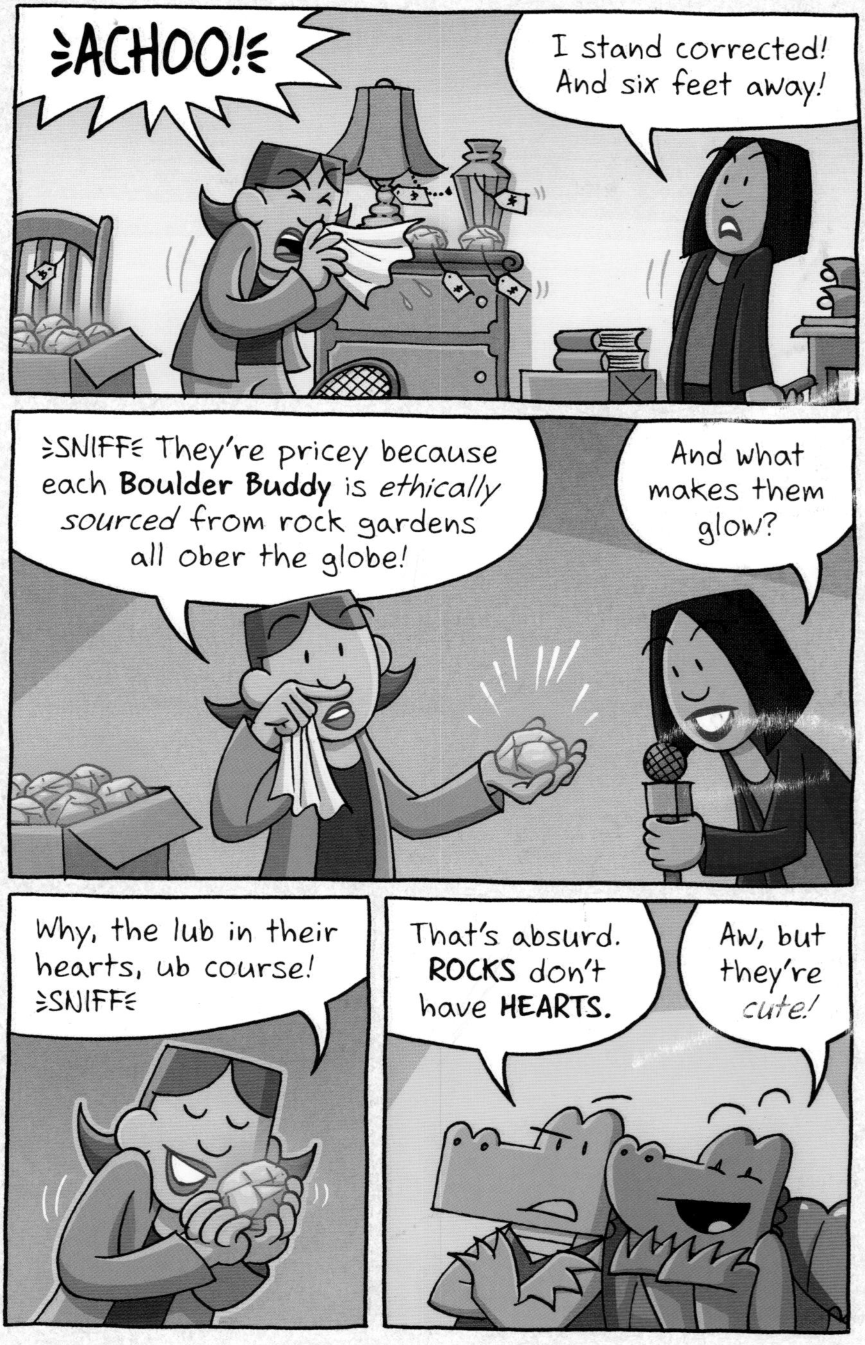

ACHOO!
I stand corrected! And six feet away!
SNIFF They're pricey because each Boulder Buddy is ethically sourced from rock gardens all ober the globe!
And what makes them glow?
Why, the lub in their hearts, ub course! SNIFF
That's absurd. ROCKS don't have HEARTS.
Aw, but they're cute!

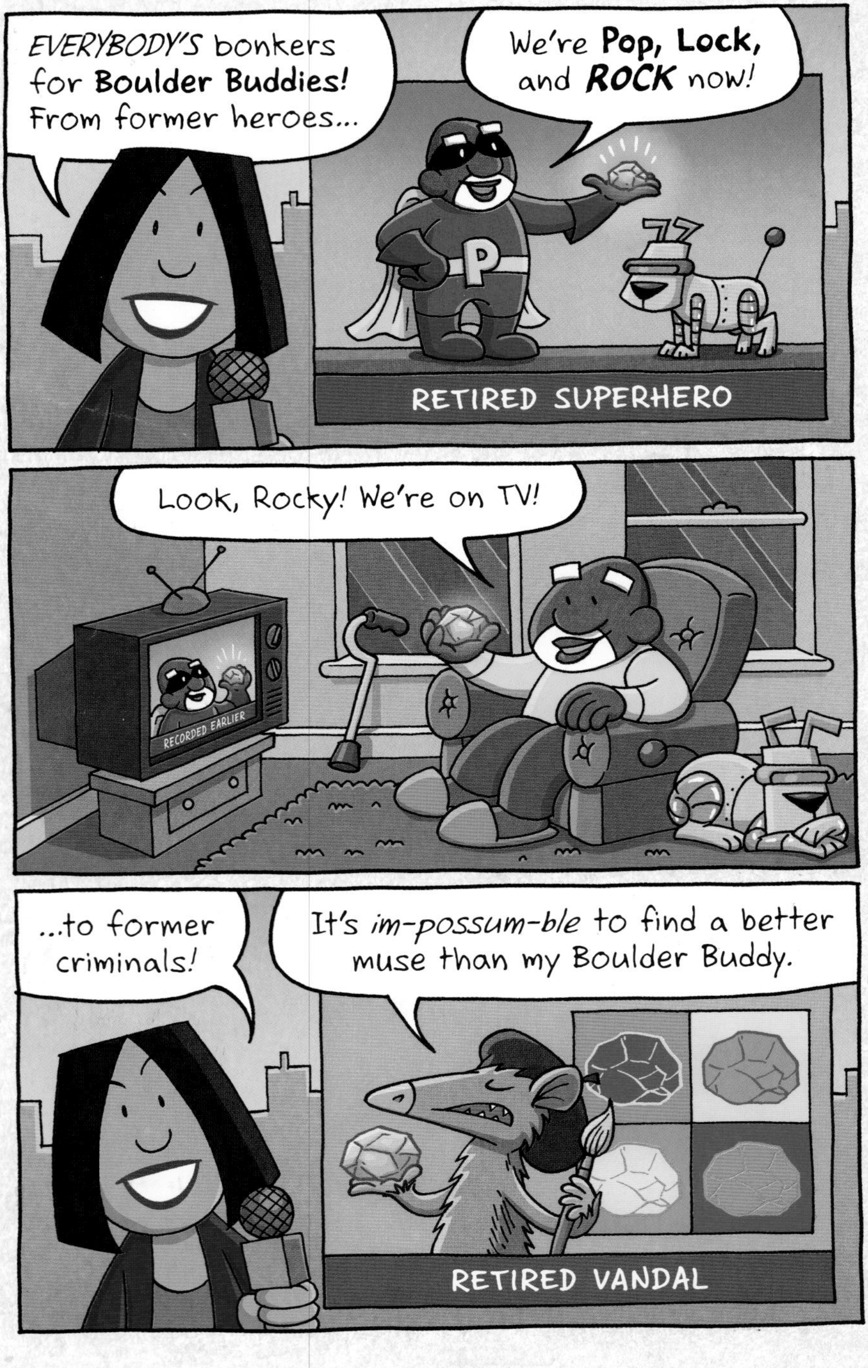
EVERYBODY'S bonkers for **Boulder Buddies!** From former heroes...
We're **Pop, Lock,** and ***ROCK*** now!
RETIRED SUPERHERO
Look, Rocky! We're on TV!
RECORDED EARLIER
...to former criminals!
It's *im-possum-ble* to find a better muse than my Boulder Buddy.
RETIRED VANDAL

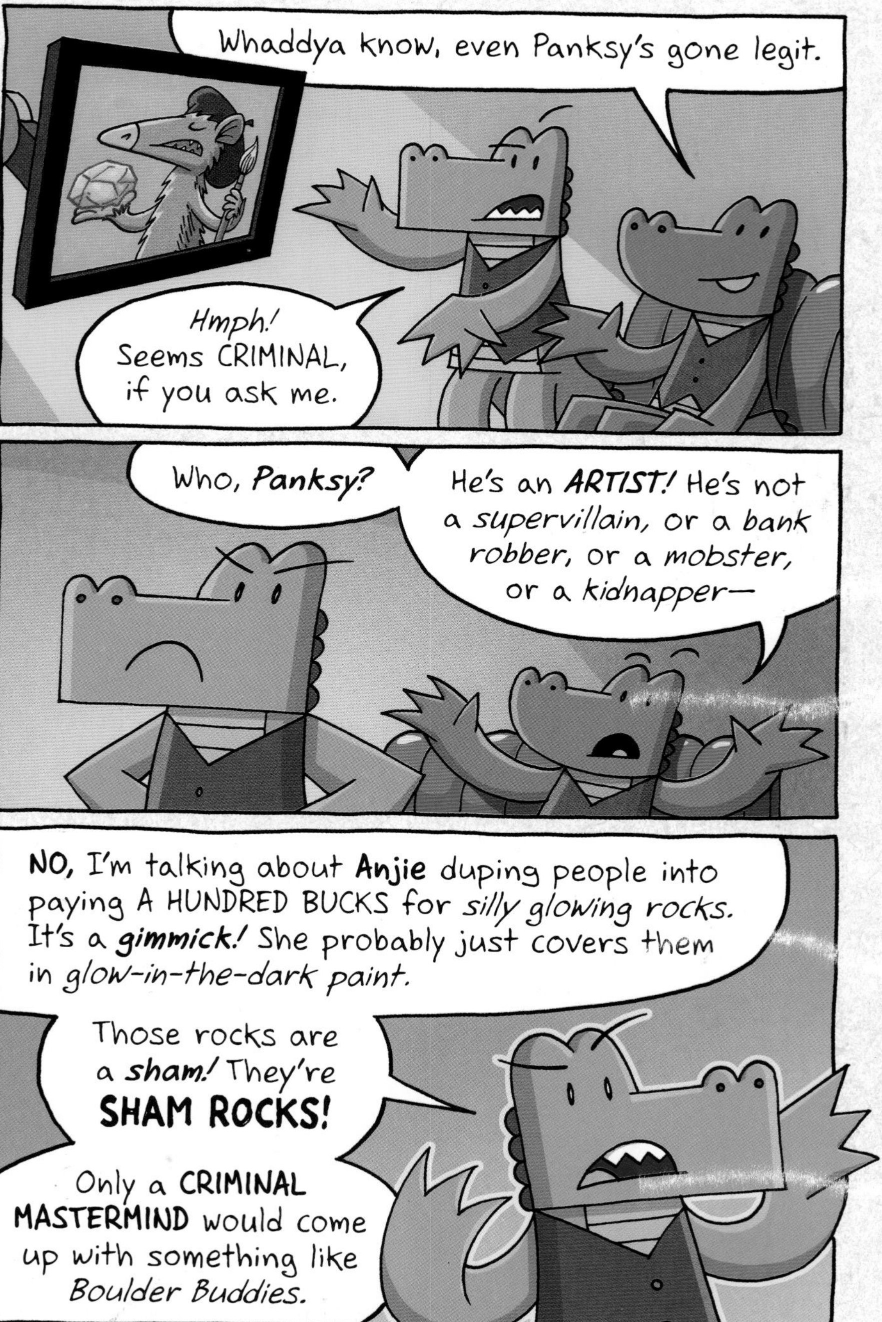
Whaddya know, even Panksy's gone legit.
Hmph! Seems CRIMINAL, if you ask me.
Who, ***Panksy?***
He's an **ARTIST!** He's not a *supervillain*, or a *bank robber*, or a *mobster*, or a *kidnapper*—
NO, I'm talking about **Anjie** duping people into paying A HUNDRED BUCKS for *silly glowing rocks*. It's a ***gimmick!*** She probably just covers them in *glow-in-the-dark paint*.
Those rocks are a ***sham!*** They're **SHAM ROCKS!**
Only a **CRIMINAL MASTERMIND** would come up with something like *Boulder Buddies*.

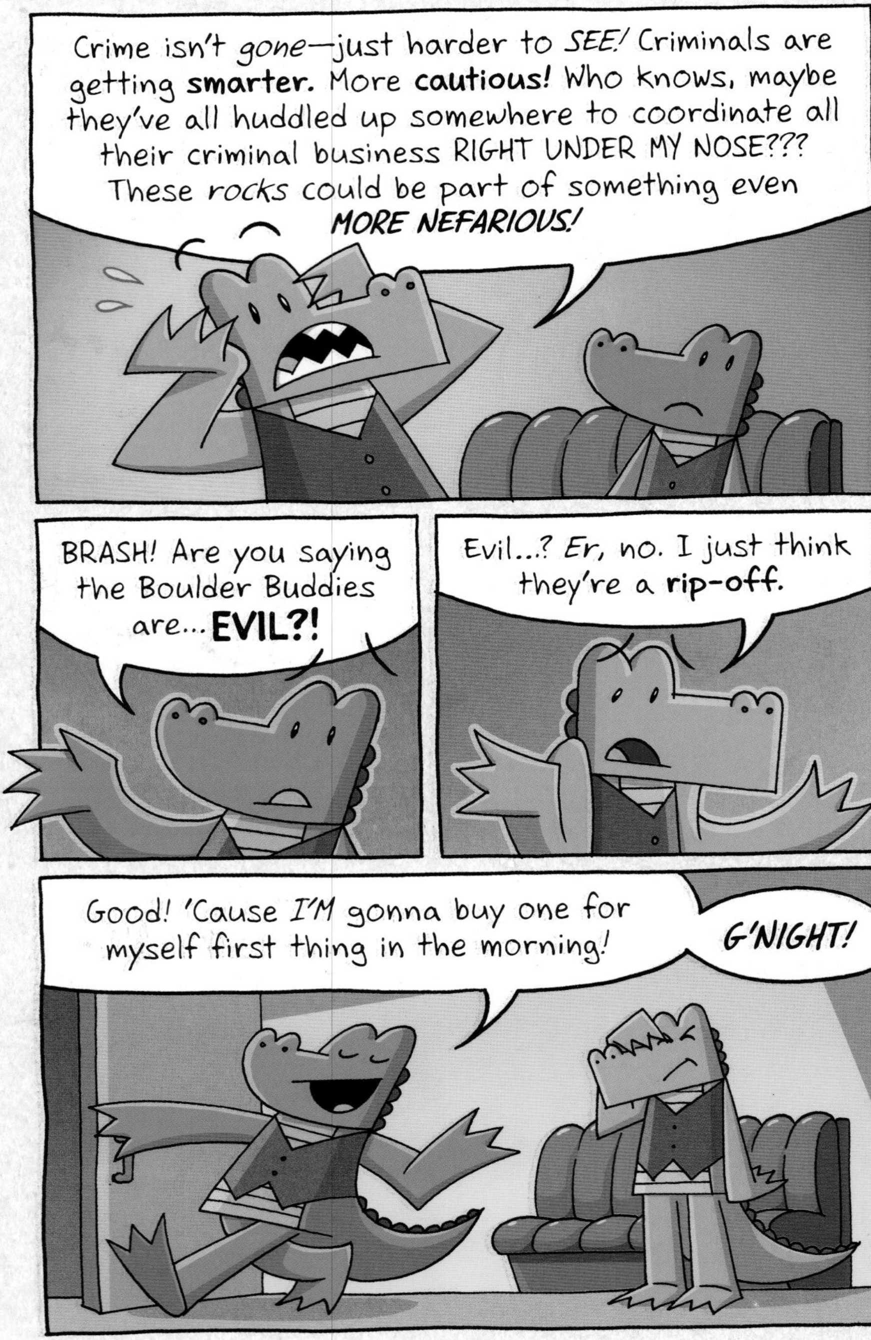
Crime isn't *gone*—just harder to *SEE!* Criminals are getting **smarter.** More **cautious!** Who knows, maybe they've all huddled up somewhere to coordinate all their criminal business RIGHT UNDER MY NOSE??? These *rocks* could be part of something even ***MORE NEFARIOUS!***
BRASH! Are you saying the Boulder Buddies are... **EVIL?!**
Evil...? *Er,* no. I just think they're a **rip-off.**
Good! 'Cause *I'M* gonna buy one for myself first thing in the morning!
G'NIGHT!

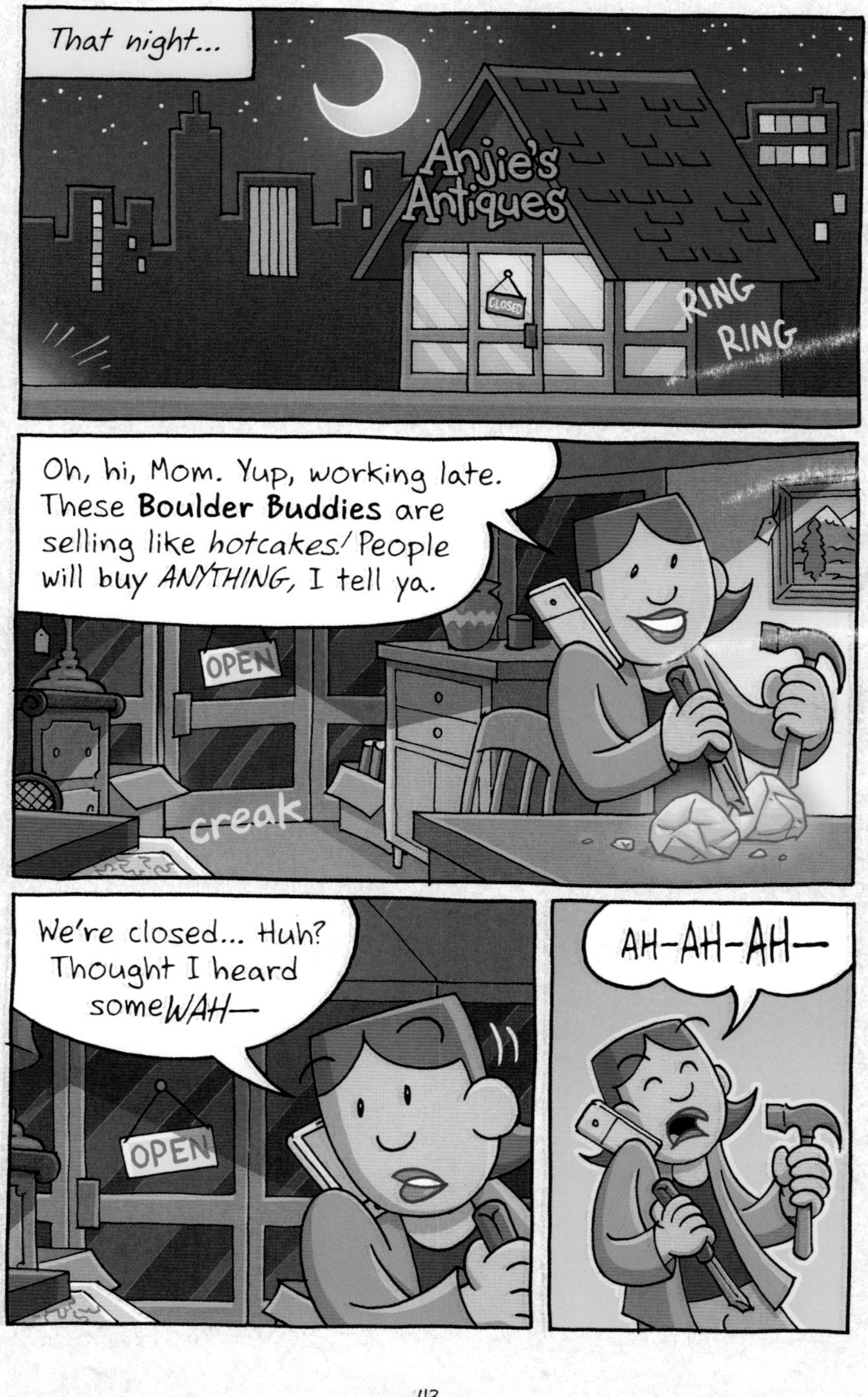
That night...
Anjie's Antiques
CLOSED
RING RING
Oh, hi, Mom. Yup, working late. These **Boulder Buddies** are selling like *hotcakes!* People will buy *ANYTHING*, I tell ya.
OPEN
creak
We're closed... Huh? Thought I heard some*WAH*—
OPEN
AH-AH-AH—

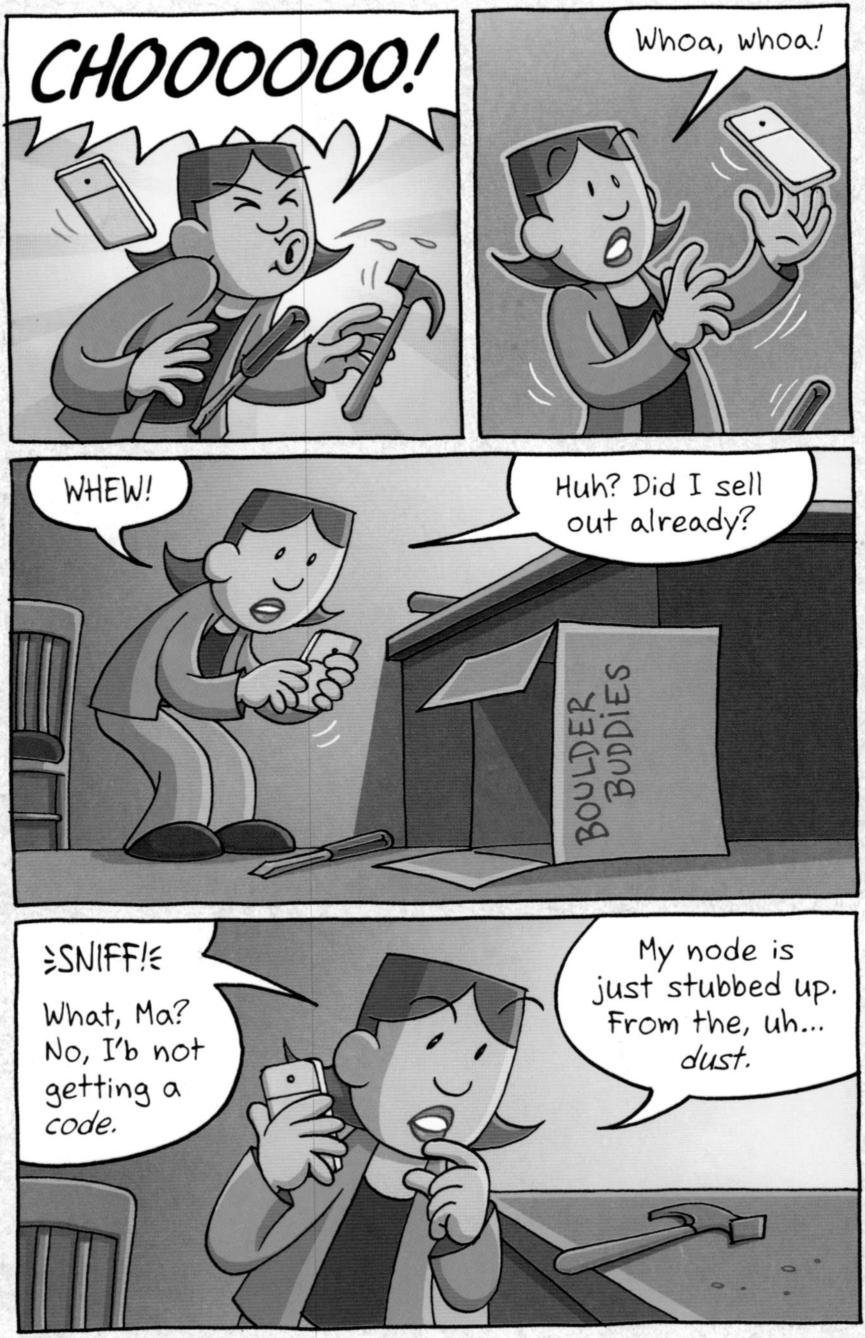
CHOOOOOO!
Whoa, whoa!
WHEW!
Huh? Did I sell out already?
BOULDER BUDDIES
SNIFF!
What, Ma? No, I'b not getting a *code.*
My node is just stubbed up. From the, uh... *dust.*

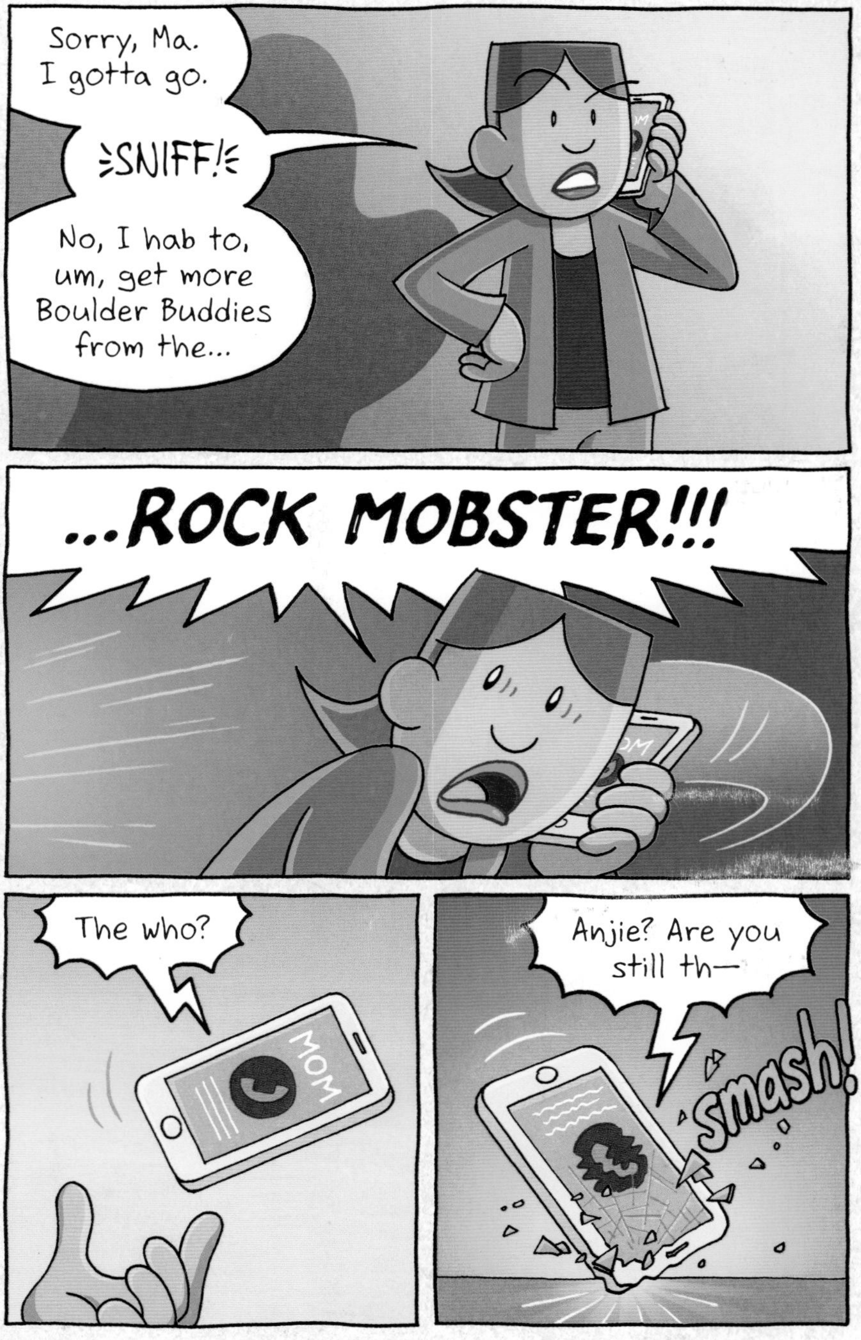
Sorry, Ma.
I gotta go.
SNIFF!
No, I hab to, um, get more Boulder Buddies from the...
...ROCK MOBSTER!!!
MOM
The who?
MOM
Anjie? Are you still th—
smash!

Chapter 5

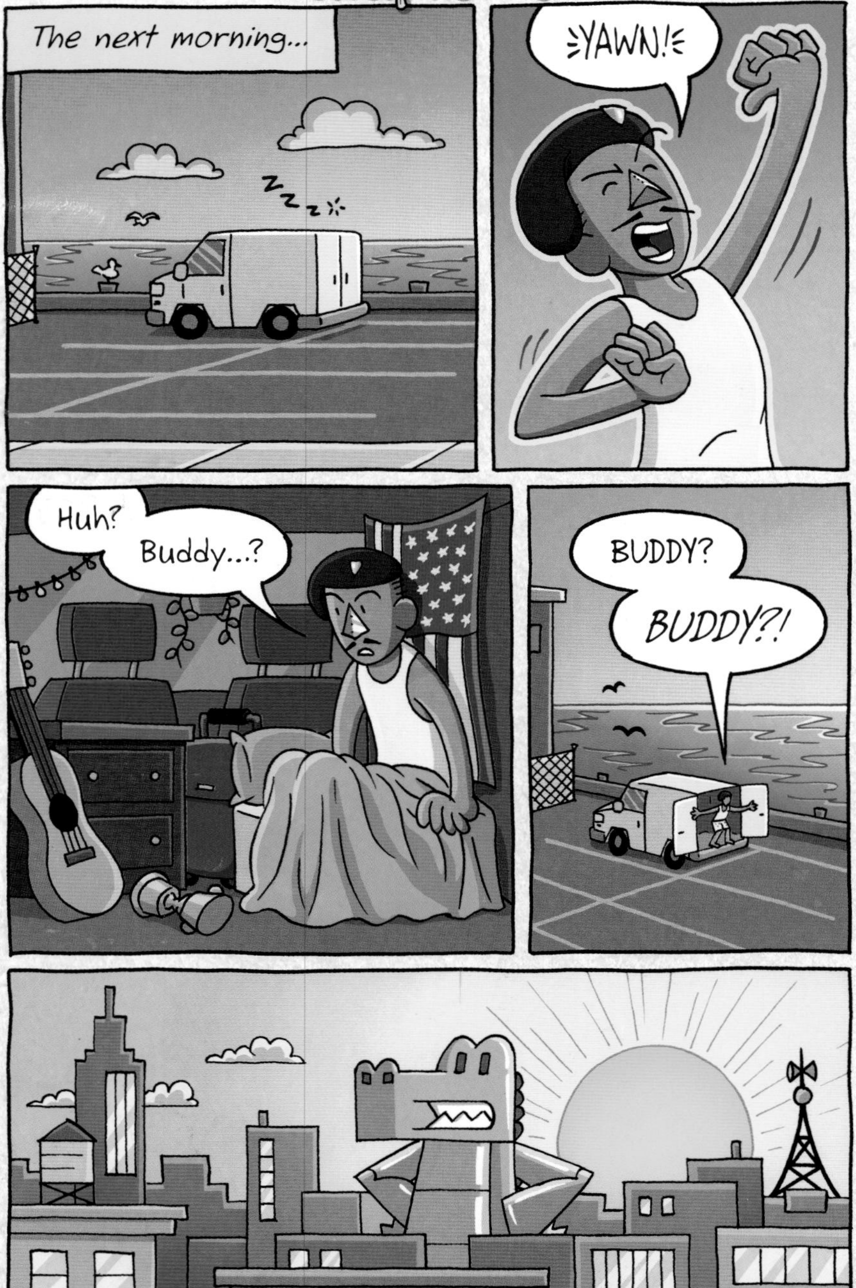

The next morning...
ZZZ
YAWN!
Huh?
Buddy...?
BUDDY?
BUDDY?!

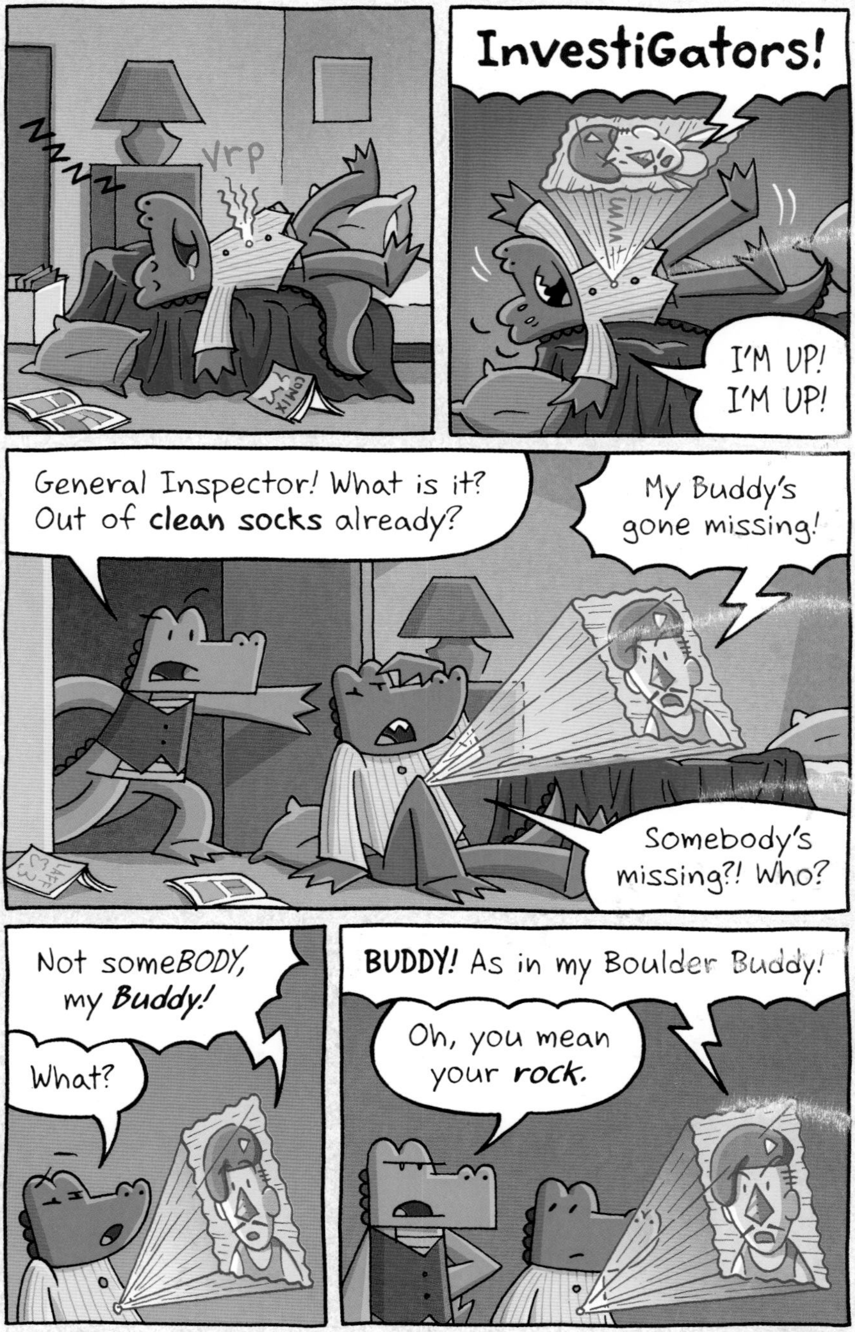
ZZZZZ
vrp
COMIX
InvestiGators!
I'M UP! I'M UP!
General Inspector! What is it? Out of **clean socks** already?
My Buddy's gone missing!
LAFF
Somebody's missing?! Who?
Not some*BODY*, my ***Buddy!***
What?
BUDDY! As in my Boulder Buddy!
Oh, you mean your **rock.**

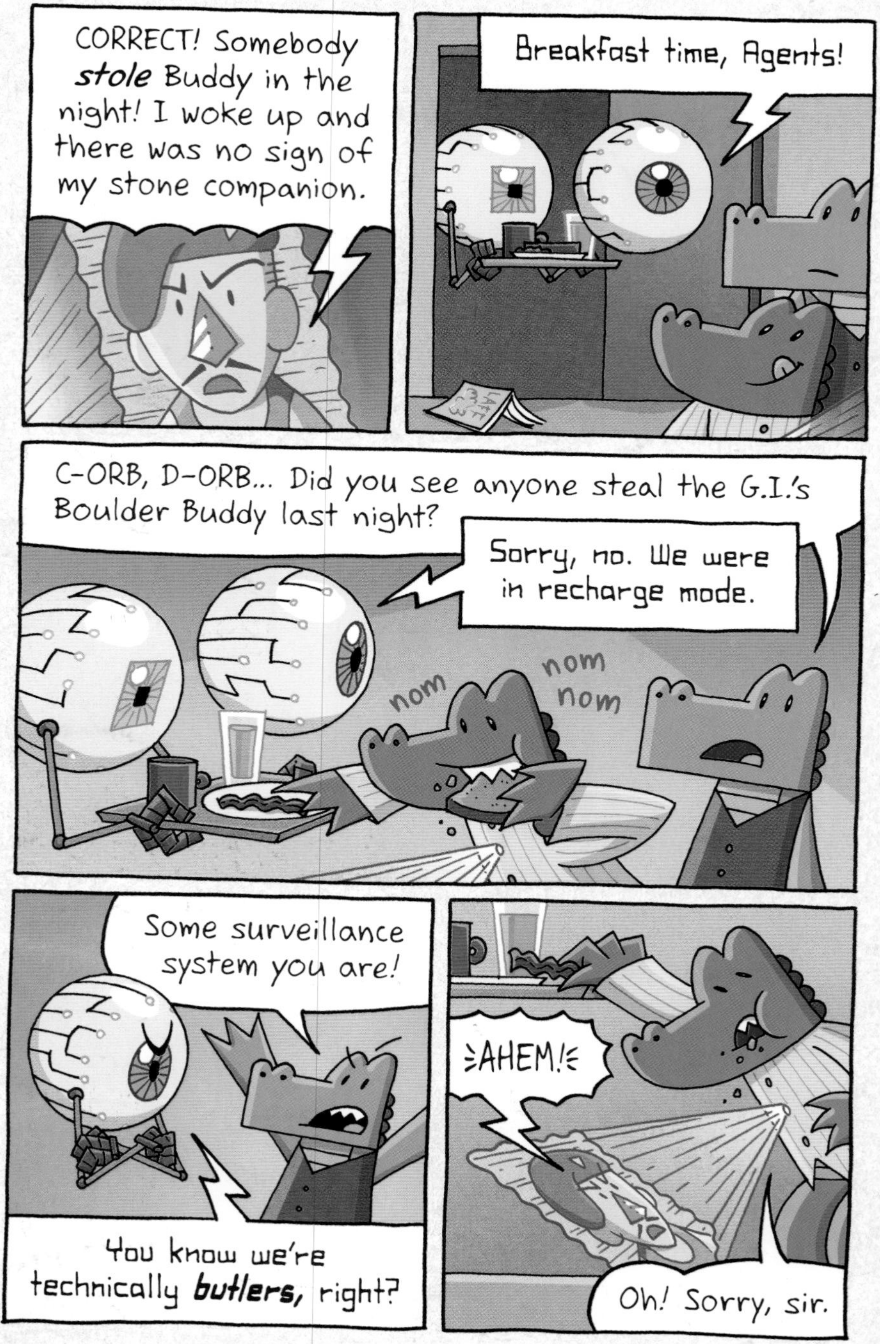
CORRECT! Somebody *stole* Buddy in the night! I woke up and there was no sign of my stone companion.
Breakfast time, Agents!
C-ORB, D-ORB... Did you see anyone steal the G.I.'s Boulder Buddy last night?
Sorry, no. We were in recharge mode.
nom
nom nom
Some surveillance system you are!
You know we're technically **butlers,** right?
AHEM!
Oh! Sorry, sir.

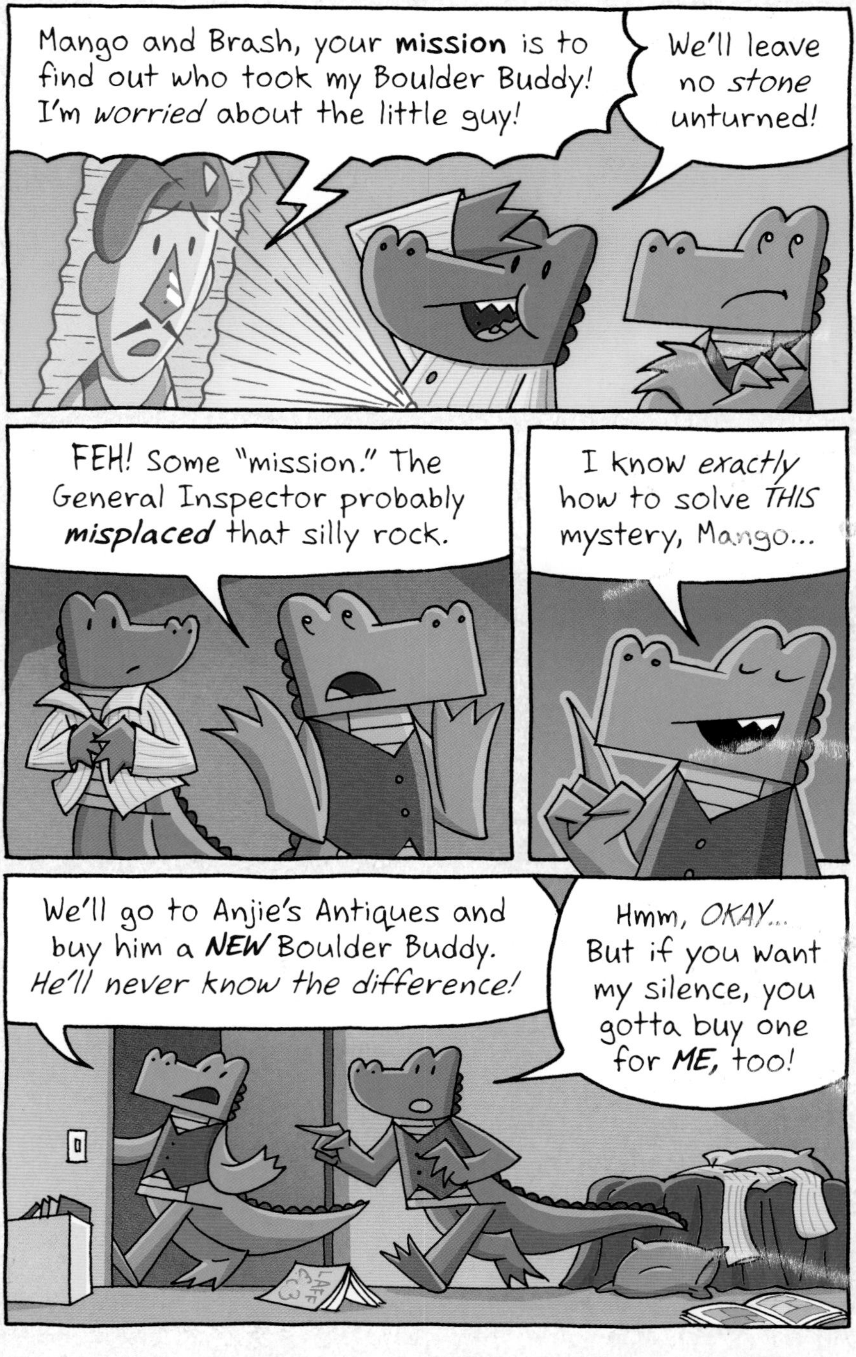
Mango and Brash, your mission is to find out who took my Boulder Buddy! I'm worried about the little guy!
We'll leave no stone unturned!
FEH! Some "mission." The General Inspector probably misplaced that silly rock.
I know exactly how to solve THIS mystery, Mango...
We'll go to Anjie's Antiques and buy him a NEW Boulder Buddy. He'll never know the difference!
Hmm, OKAY... But if you want my silence, you gotta buy one for ME, too!

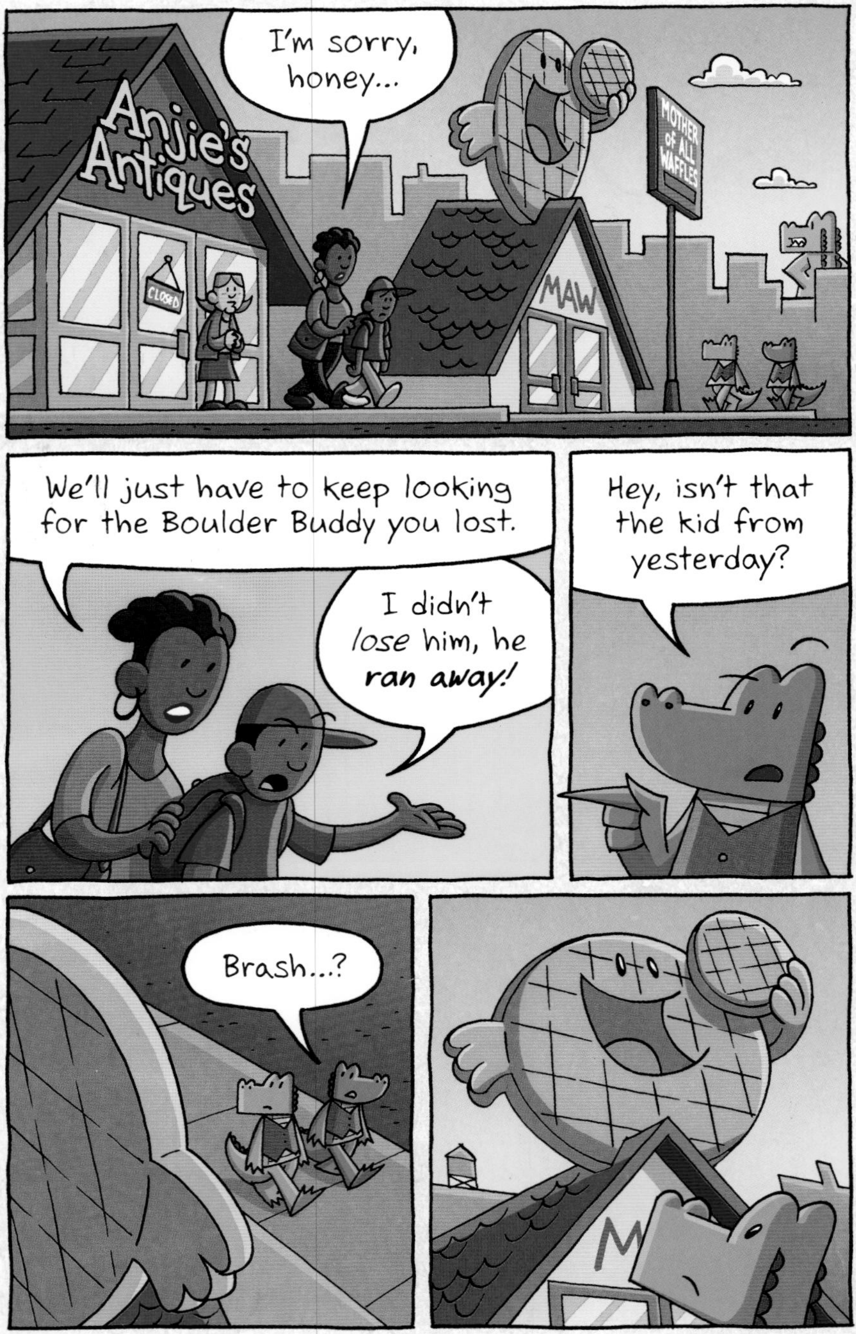
I'm sorry, honey...
Anjie's Antiques
CLOSED
MOTHER OF ALL WAFFLES
MAW
We'll just have to keep looking for the Boulder Buddy you lost.
I didn't *lose* him, he **ran away!**
Hey, isn't that the kid from yesterday?
Brash...?

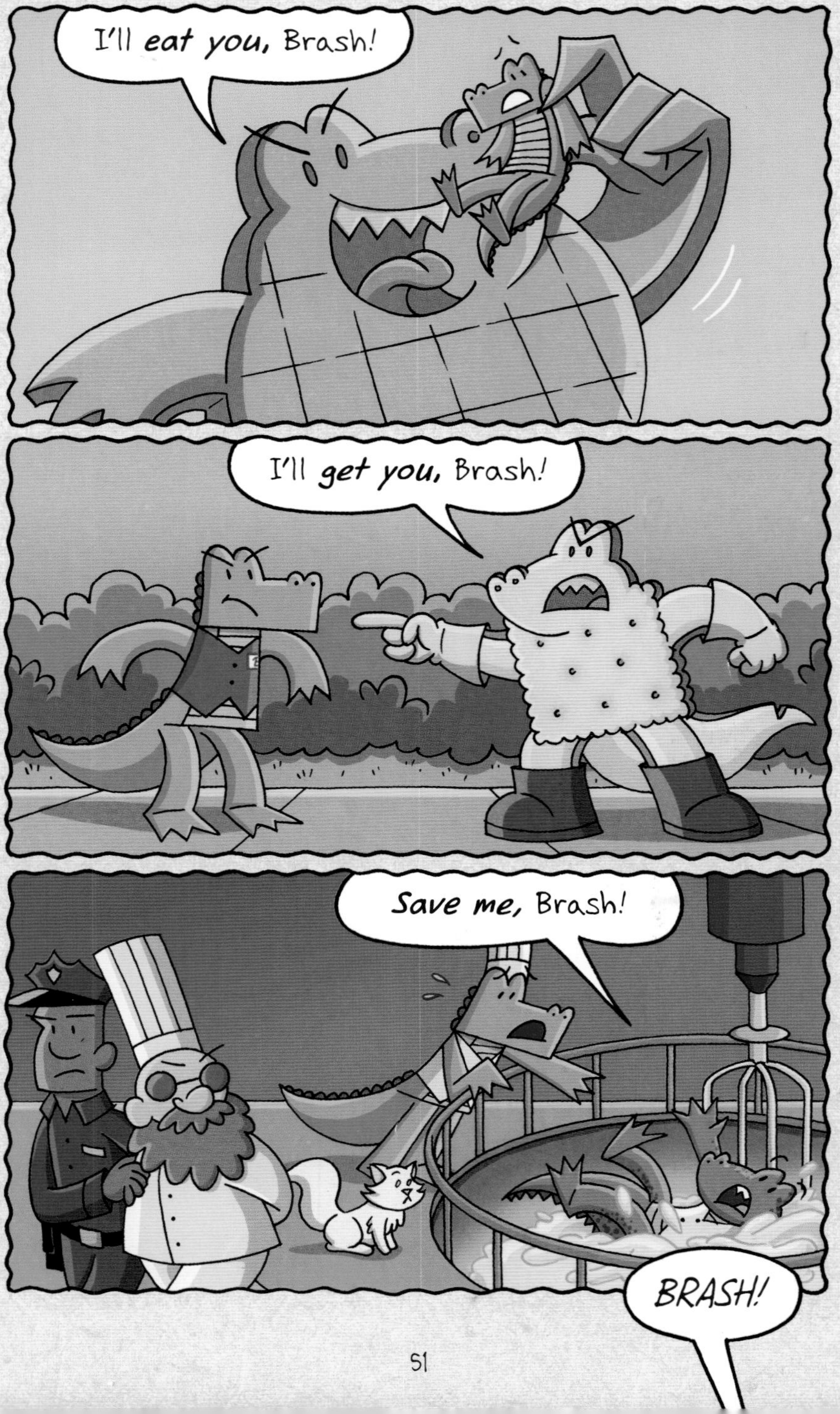
I'll eat you, Brash!
I'll get you, Brash!
Save me, Brash!
BRASH!

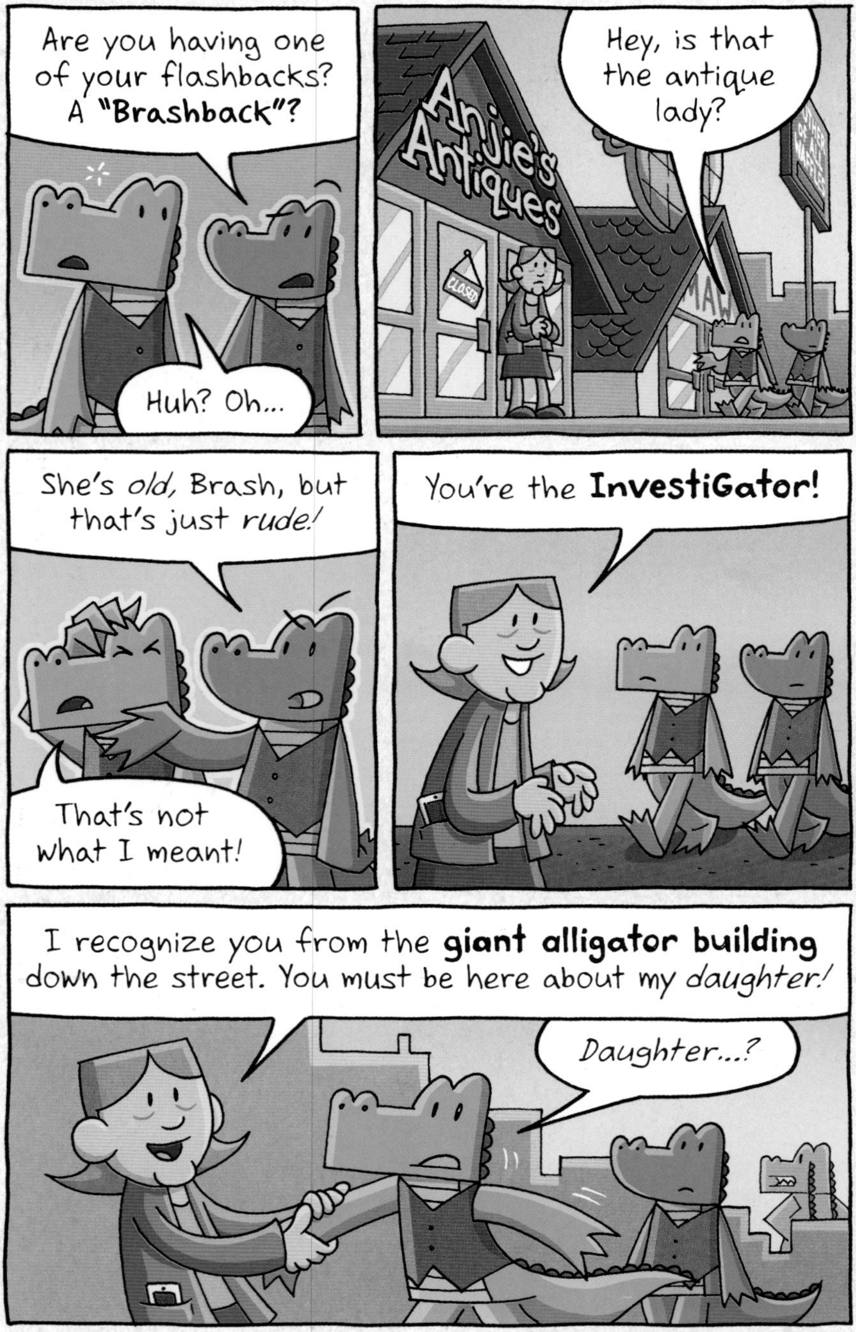

Are you having one of your flashbacks? A **"Brashback"**?
Huh? Oh...
Anjie's Antiques
CLOSED
Hey, is that the antique lady?
She's *old,* Brash, but that's just *rude!*
That's not what I meant!
You're the **InvestiGator!**
I recognize you from the **giant alligator building** down the street. You must be here about my *daughter!*
Daughter...?

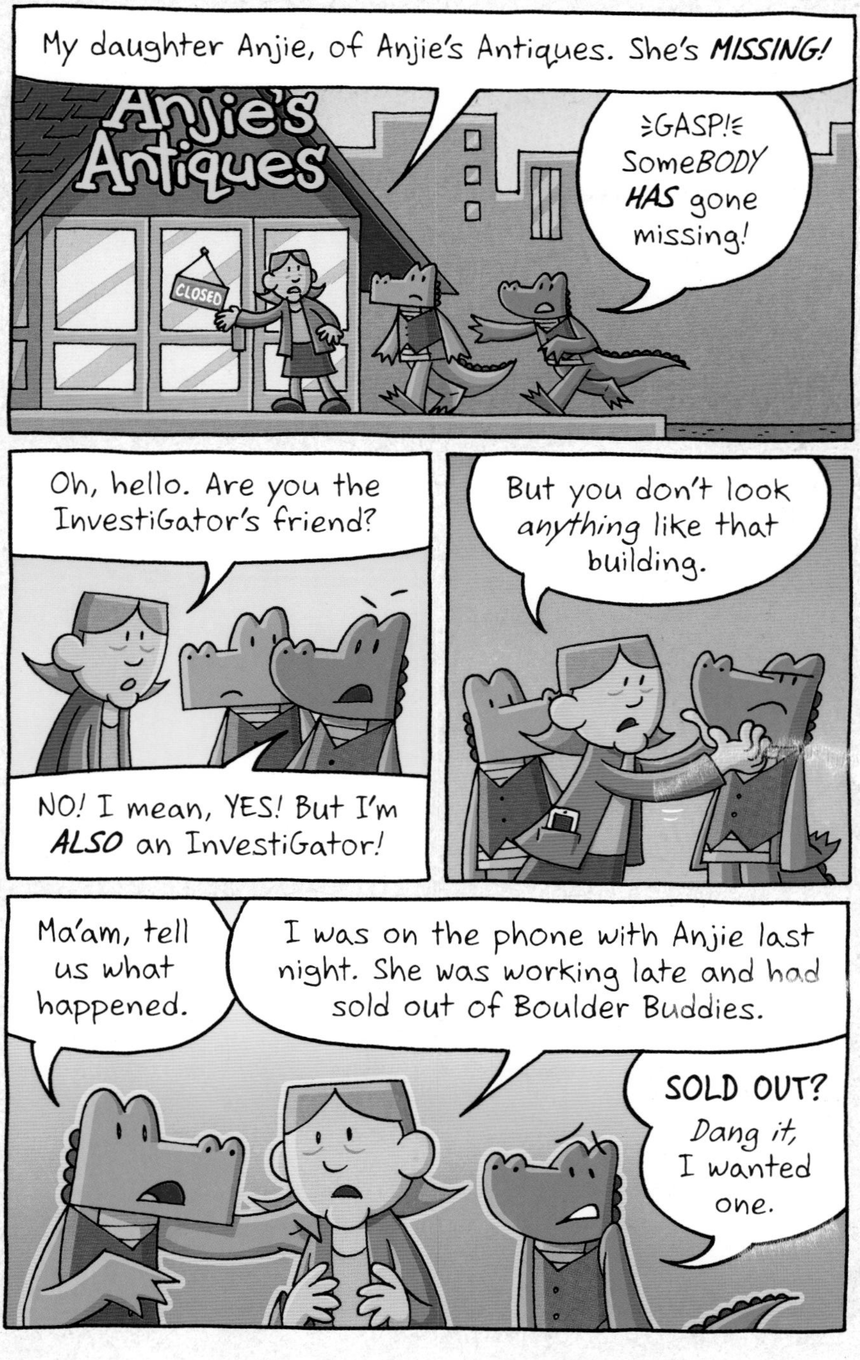
My daughter Anjie, of Anjie's Antiques. She's **MISSING!**
Anjie's Antiques
CLOSED
GASP! SomeBODY **HAS** gone missing!
Oh, hello. Are you the InvestiGator's friend?
NO! I mean, YES! But I'm **ALSO** an InvestiGator!
But you don't look *anything* like that building.
Ma'am, tell us what happened.
I was on the phone with Anjie last night. She was working late and had sold out of Boulder Buddies.
SOLD OUT? *Dang it,* I wanted one.

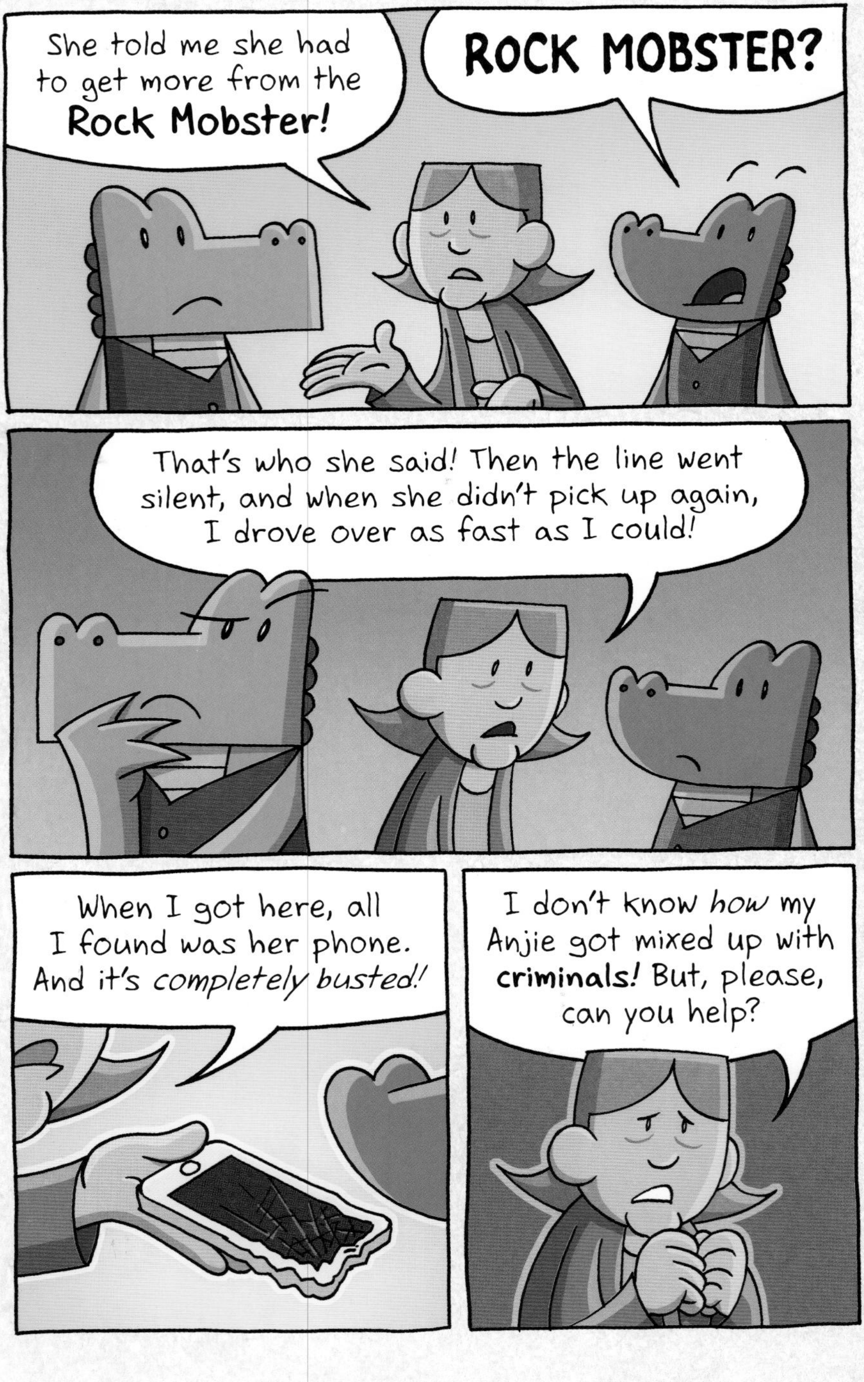
She told me she had to get more from the **Rock Mobster!**
ROCK MOBSTER?
That's who she said! Then the line went silent, and when she didn't pick up again, I drove over as fast as I could!
When I got here, all I found was her phone. And it's *completely busted!*
I don't know *how* my Anjie got mixed up with **criminals!** But, please, can you help?

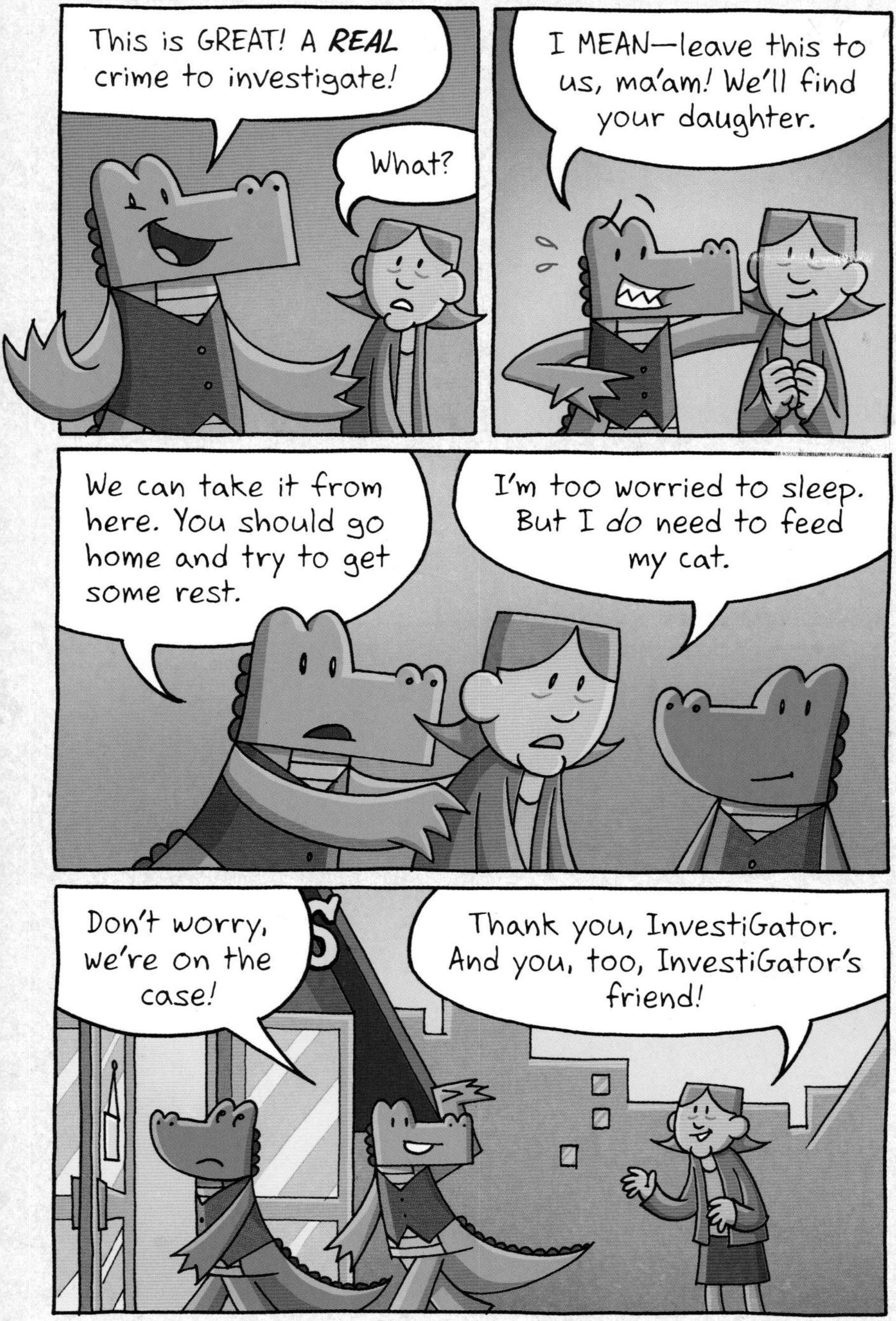
This is GREAT! A **REAL** crime to investigate!
What?
I MEAN—leave this to us, ma'am! We'll find your daughter.
We can take it from here. You should go home and try to get some rest.
I'm too worried to sleep. But I *do* need to feed my cat.
Don't worry, we're on the case!
Thank you, InvestiGator. And you, too, InvestiGator's friend!

Chapter 6

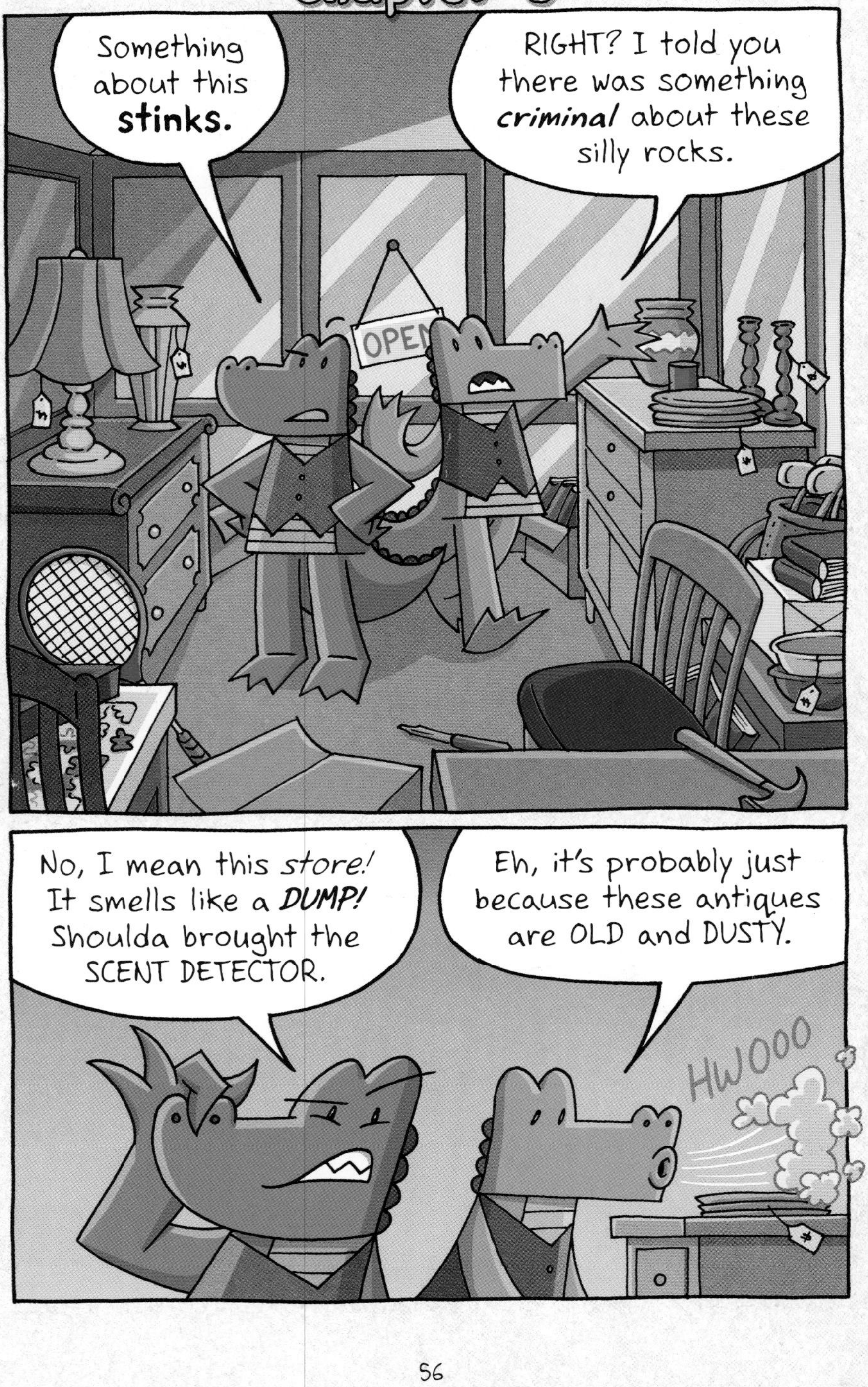
Something about this **stinks.**
RIGHT? I told you there was something ***criminal*** about these silly rocks.
OPEN
No, I mean this *store!* It smells like a ***DUMP!*** Shoulda brought the SCENT DETECTOR.
Eh, it's probably just because these antiques are OLD and DUSTY.
HWOOO

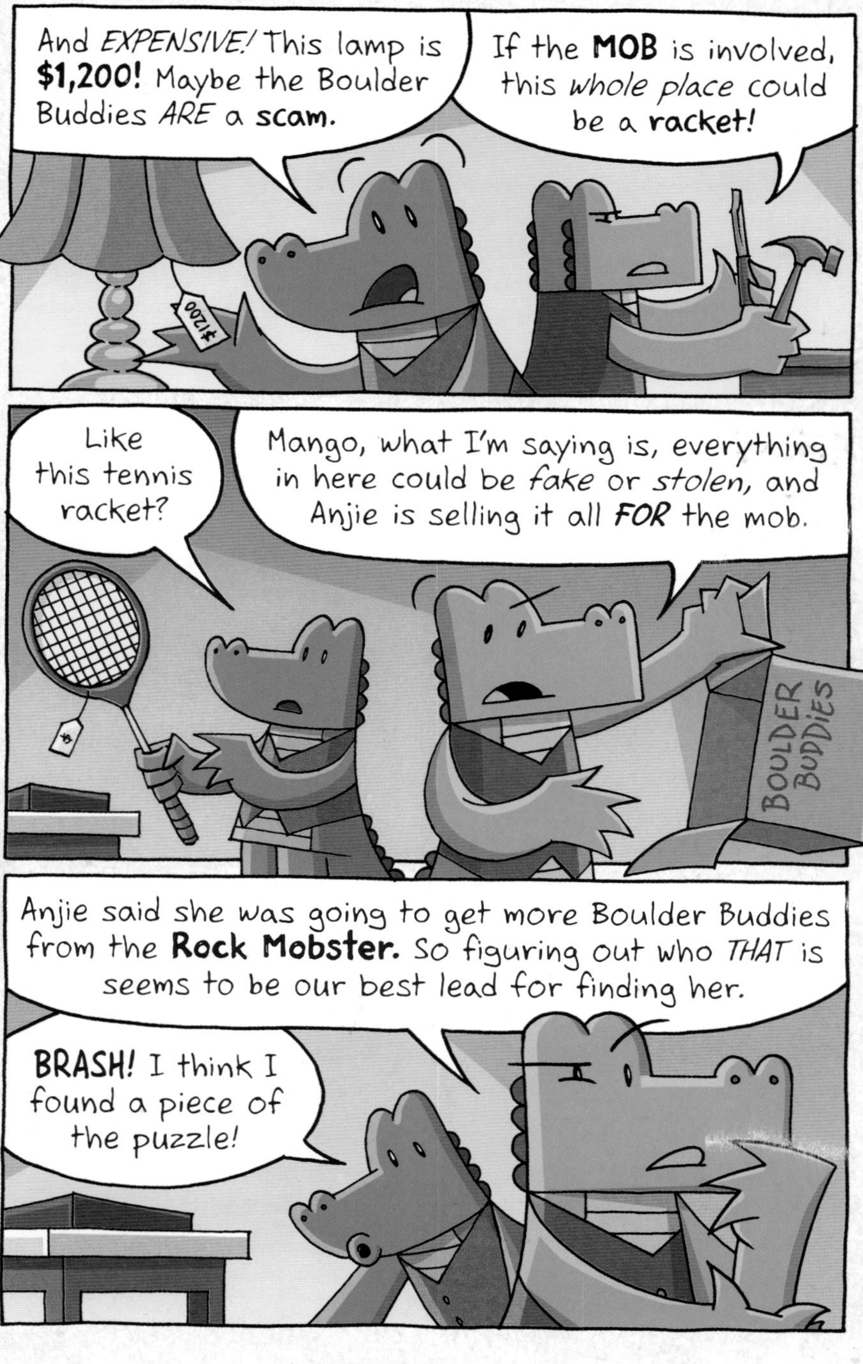
And EXPENSIVE! This lamp is $1,200! Maybe the Boulder Buddies ARE a scam.
If the MOB is involved, this whole place could be a racket!
$1200
Like this tennis racket?
Mango, what I'm saying is, everything in here could be fake or stolen, and Anjie is selling it all FOR the mob.
BOULDER BUDDIES
Anjie said she was going to get more Boulder Buddies from the Rock Mobster. So figuring out who THAT is seems to be our best lead for finding her.
BRASH! I think I found a piece of the puzzle!

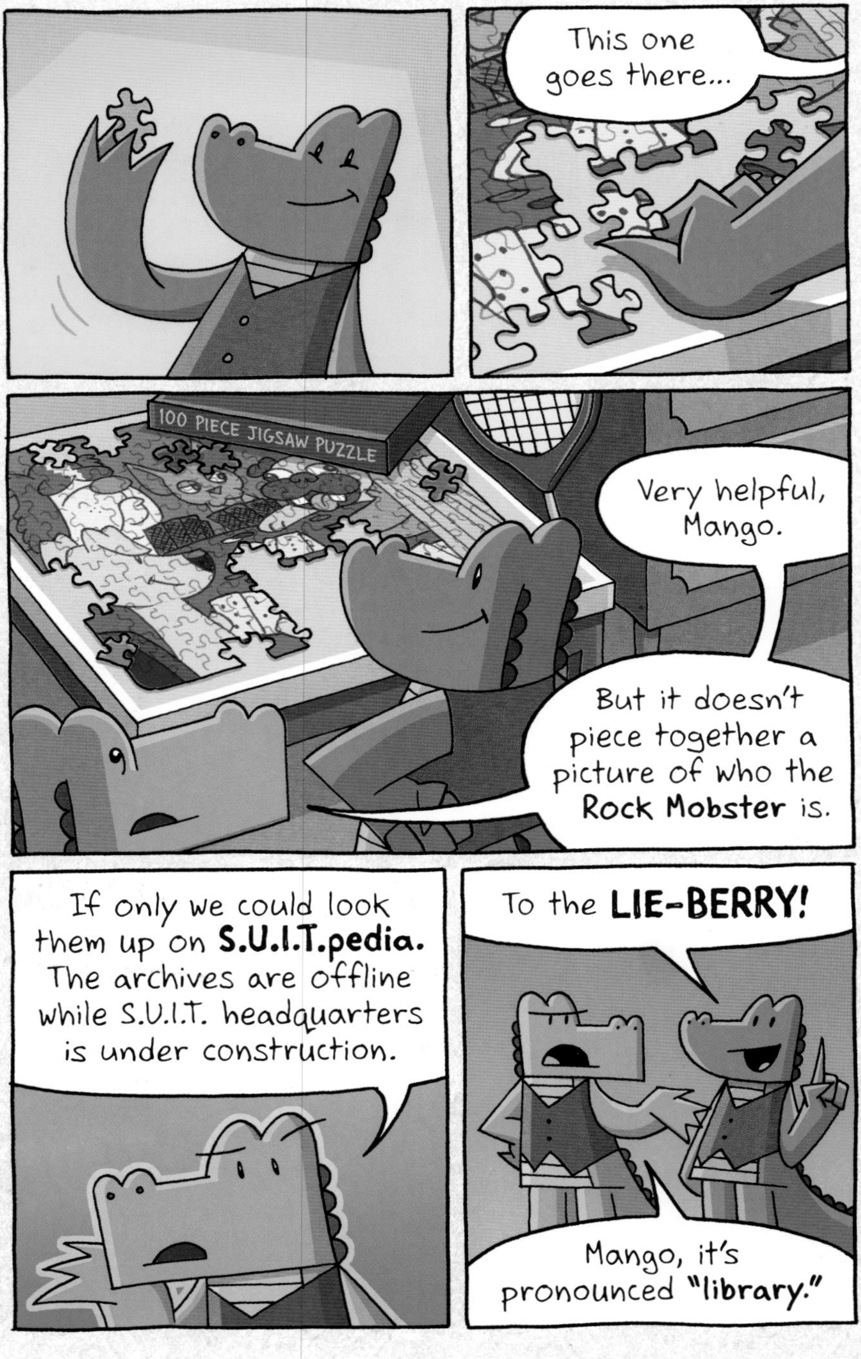
This one goes there...
100 PIECE JIGSAW PUZZLE
Very helpful, Mango.
But it doesn't piece together a picture of who the **Rock Mobster** is.
If only we could look them up on **S.U.I.T.pedia.** The archives are offline while S.U.I.T. headquarters is under construction.
To the **LIE-BERRY!**
Mango, it's pronounced **"library."**

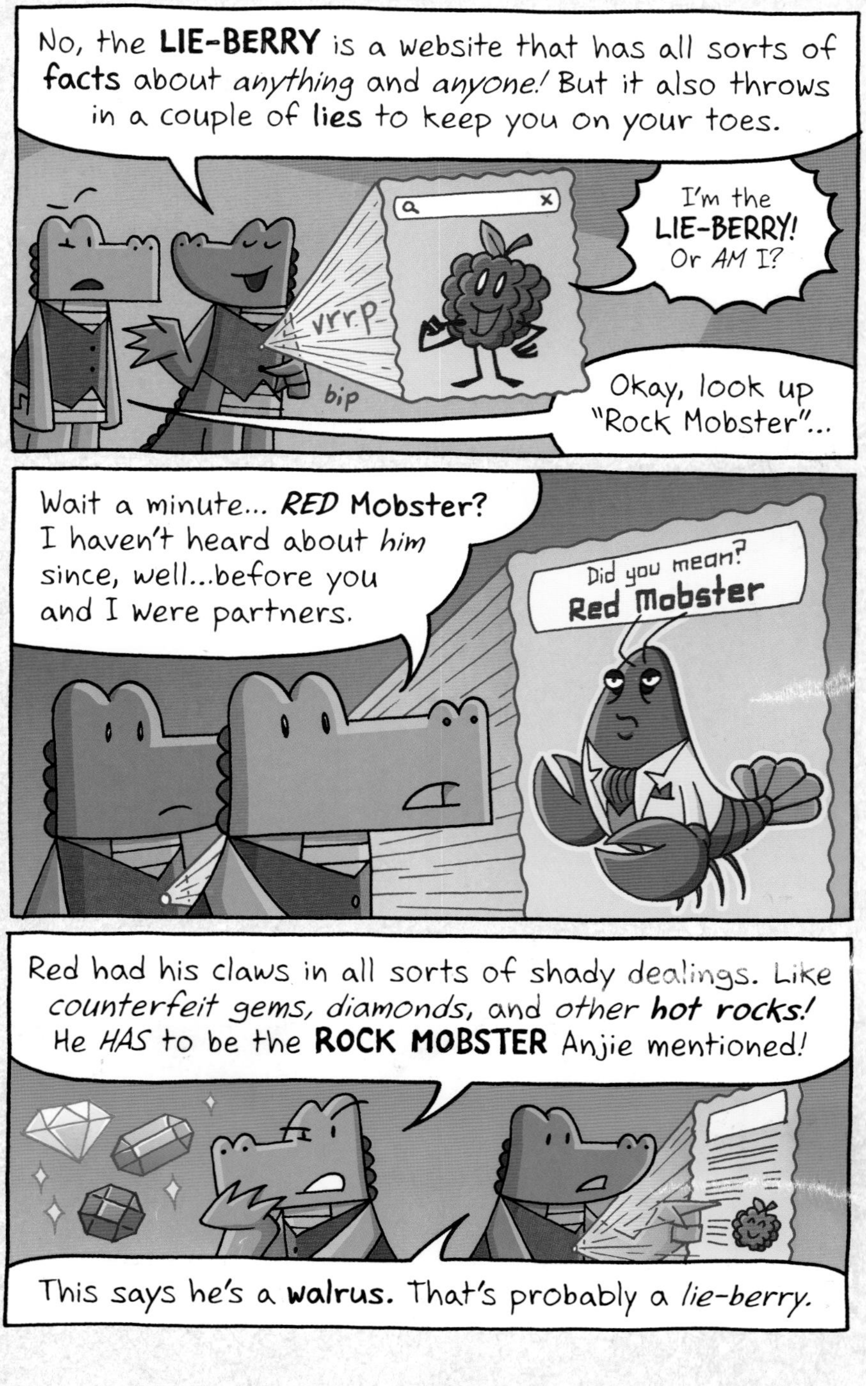

No, the LIE-BERRY is a website that has all sorts of facts about anything and anyone! But it also throws in a couple of lies to keep you on your toes.
I'm the LIE-BERRY! Or AM I?
vrrp
bip
Okay, look up "Rock Mobster"...
Wait a minute... RED Mobster? I haven't heard about him since, well...before you and I were partners.
Did you mean?
Red Mobster
Red had his claws in all sorts of shady dealings. Like counterfeit gems, diamonds, and other hot rocks! He HAS to be the ROCK MOBSTER Anjie mentioned!
This says he's a walrus. That's probably a lie-berry.

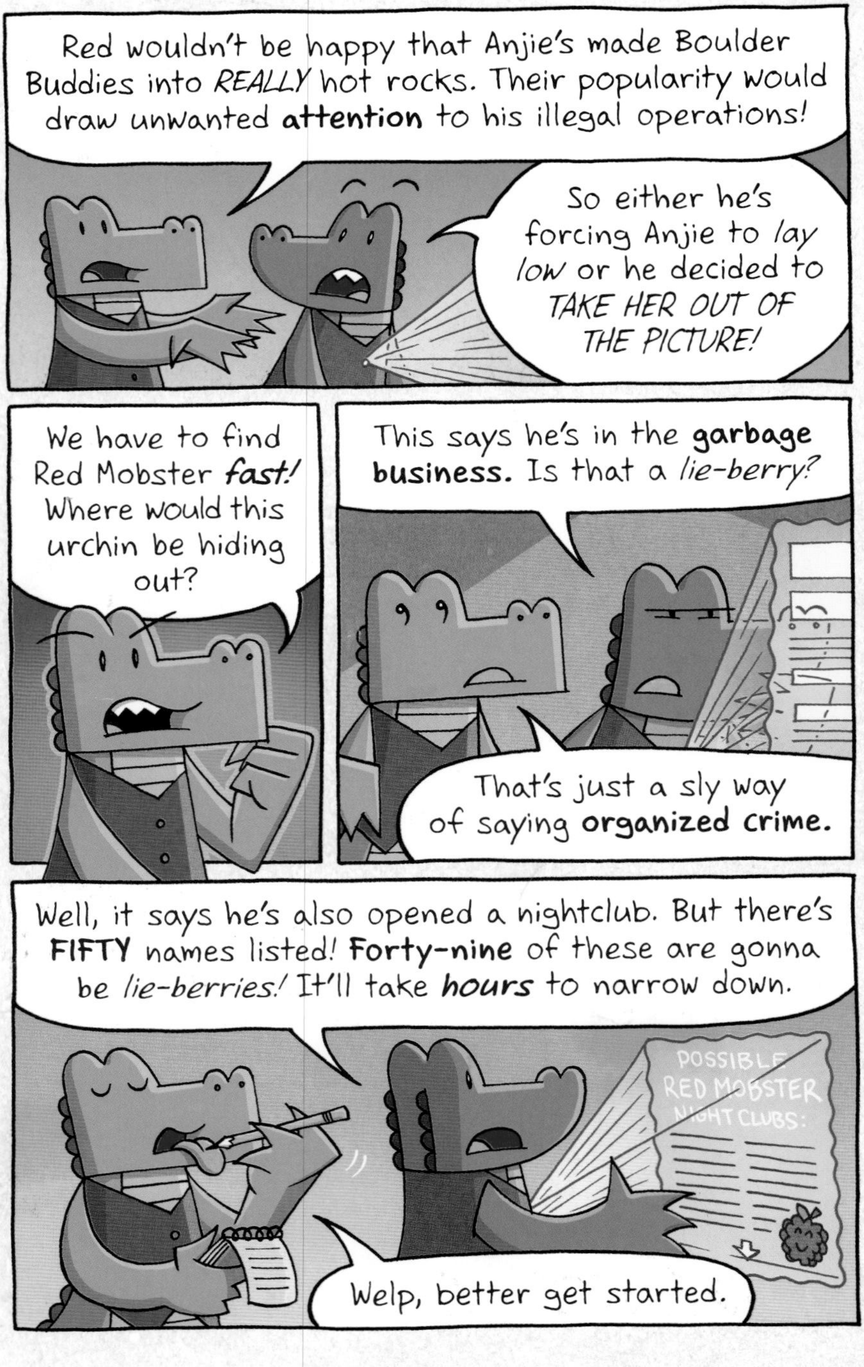

Red wouldn't be happy that Anjie's made Boulder Buddies into *REALLY* hot rocks. Their popularity would draw unwanted **attention** to his illegal operations!
So either he's forcing Anjie to *lay low* or he decided to *TAKE HER OUT OF THE PICTURE!*
We have to find Red Mobster *fast!* Where would this urchin be hiding out?
This says he's in the **garbage business.** Is that a *lie-berry?*
That's just a sly way of saying **organized crime.**
Well, it says he's also opened a nightclub. But there's **FIFTY** names listed! **Forty-nine** of these are gonna be *lie-berries!* It'll take **hours** to narrow down.
POSSIBLE RED MOBSTER NIGHT CLUBS:
Welp, better get started.

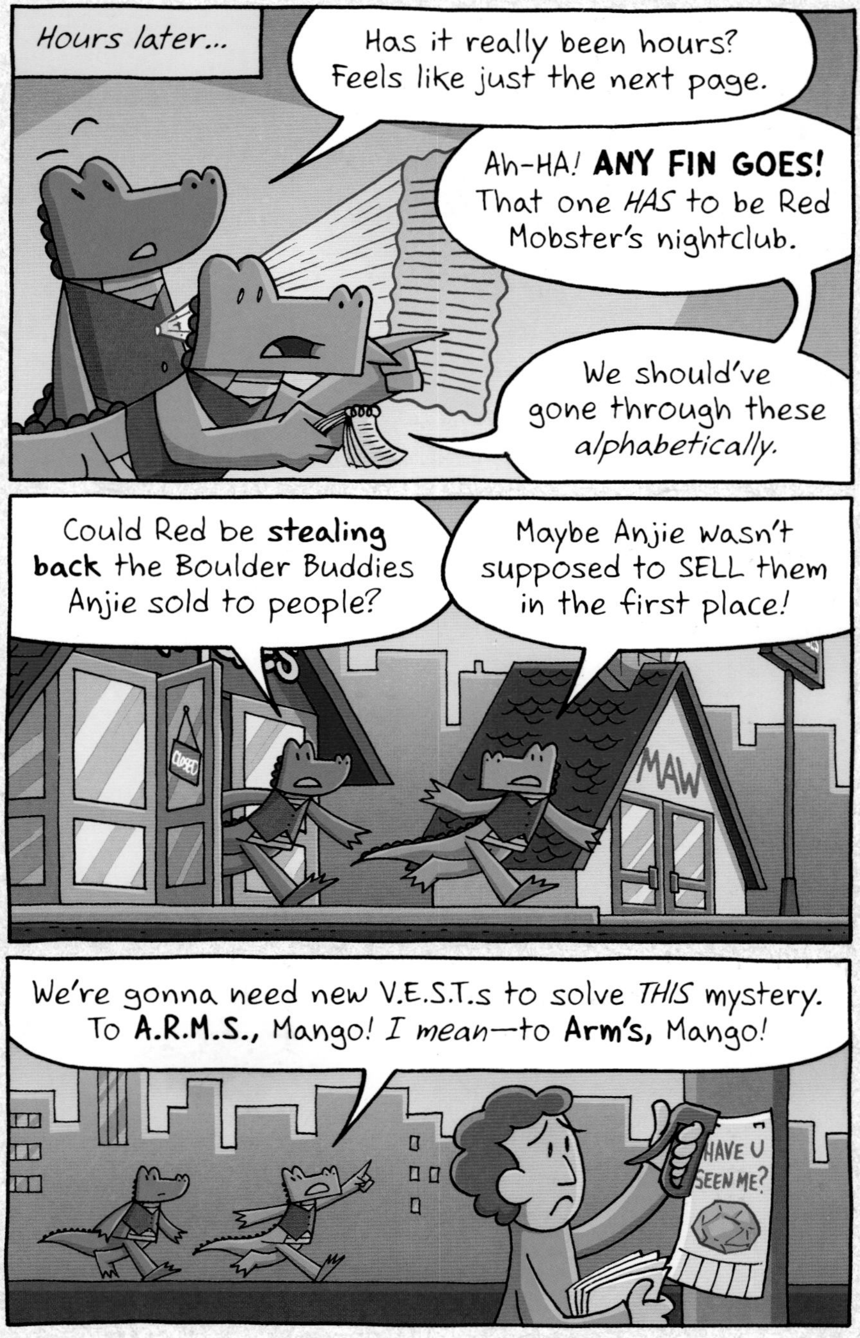

Hours later...
Has it really been hours? Feels like just the next page.
Ah-HA! **ANY FIN GOES!** That one *HAS* to be Red Mobster's nightclub.
We should've gone through these *alphabetically.*
Could Red be **stealing back** the Boulder Buddies Anjie sold to people?
Maybe Anjie wasn't supposed to SELL them in the first place!
CLOSED
MAW
We're gonna need new V.E.S.T.s to solve *THIS* mystery. To **A.R.M.S.,** Mango! *I mean*—to **Arm's,** Mango!
HAVE U SEEN ME?

Chapter 7

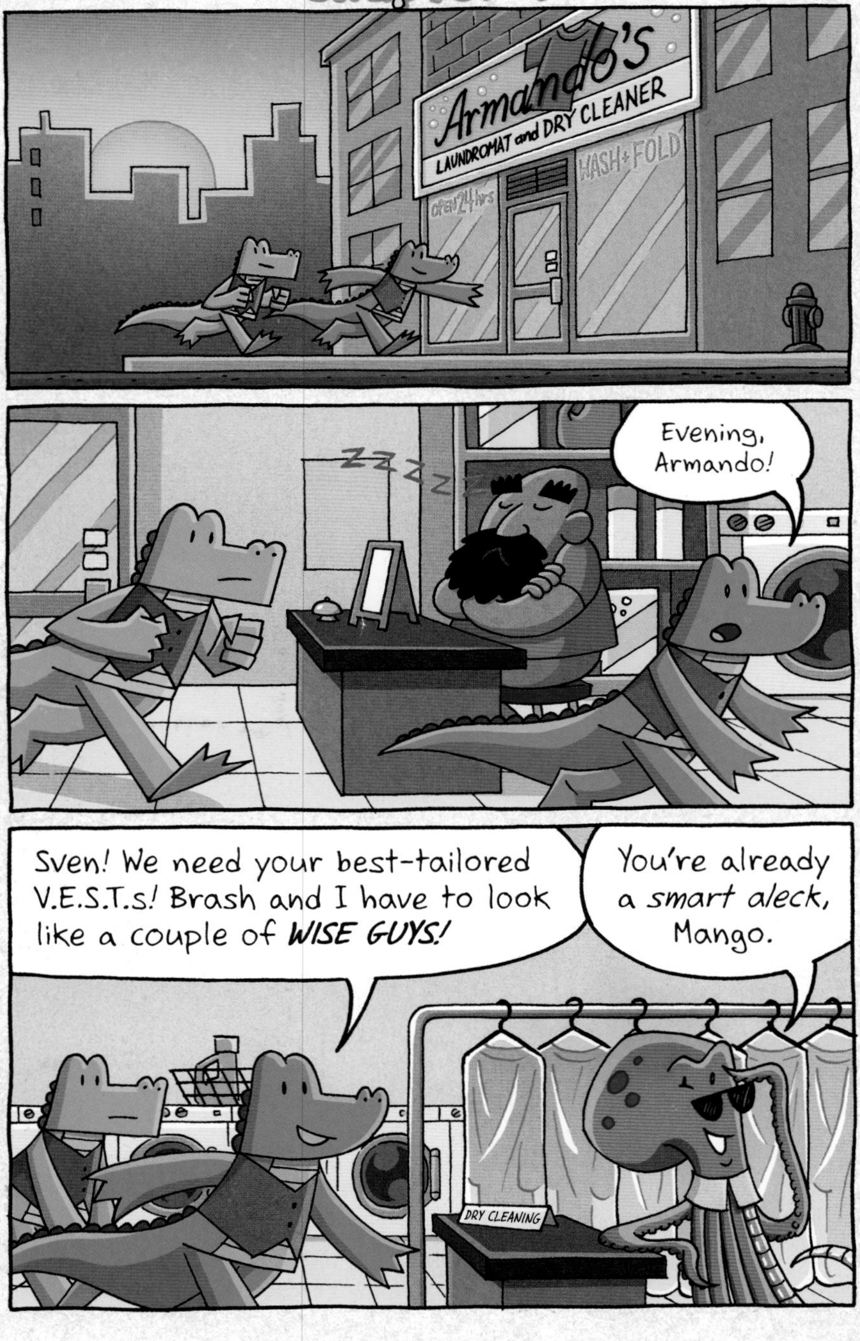
Armando's
LAUNDROMAT and DRY CLEANER
WASH + FOLD
OPEN 24 hrs
ZZZZZ
Evening, Armando!
Sven! We need your best-tailored V.E.S.T.s! Brash and I have to look like a couple of ***WISE GUYS!***
You're already a *smart aleck*, Mango.
DRY CLEANING

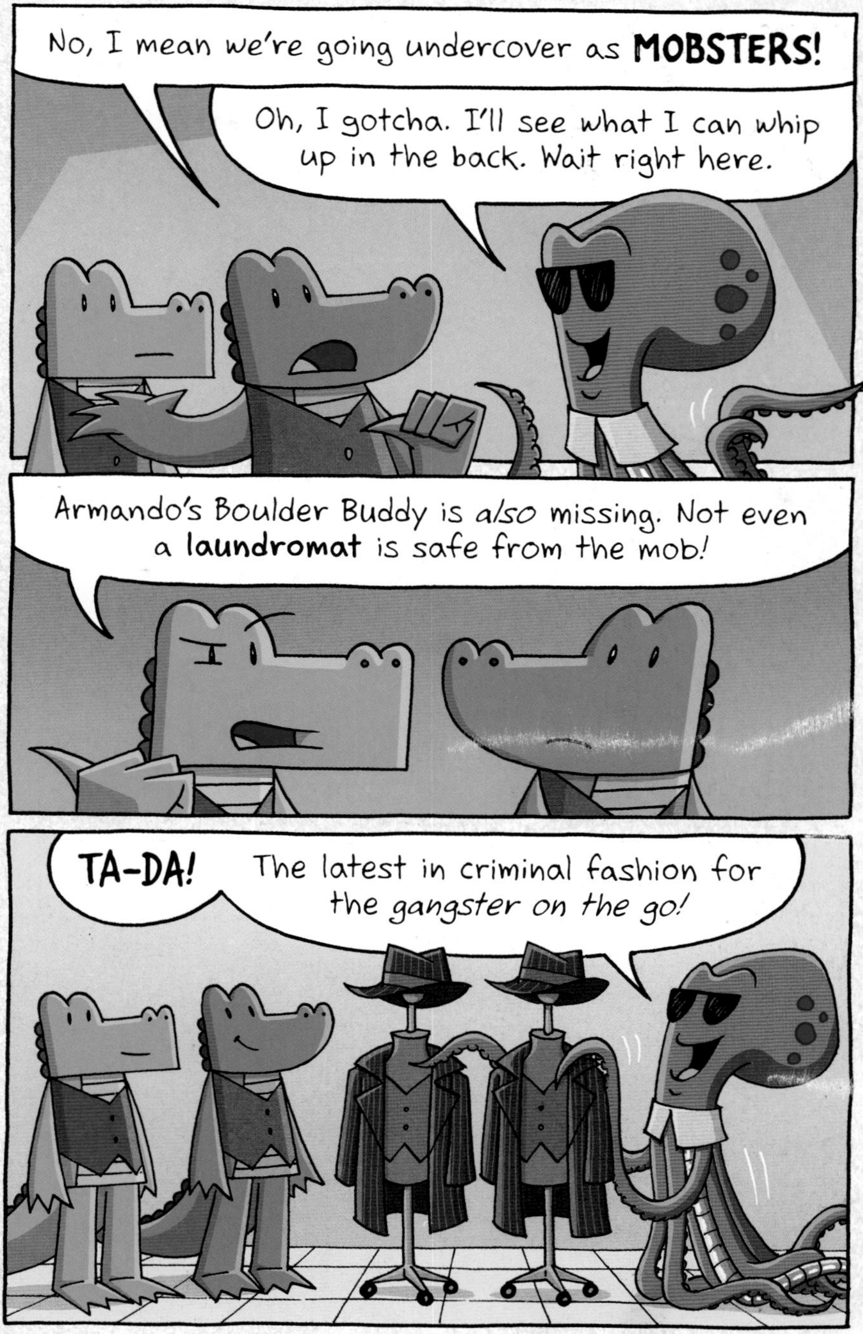
No, I mean we're going undercover as **MOBSTERS!**
Oh, I gotcha. I'll see what I can whip up in the back. Wait right here.
Armando's Boulder Buddy is *also* missing. Not even a **laundromat** is safe from the mob!
TA-DA!
The latest in criminal fashion for the *gangster on the go!*

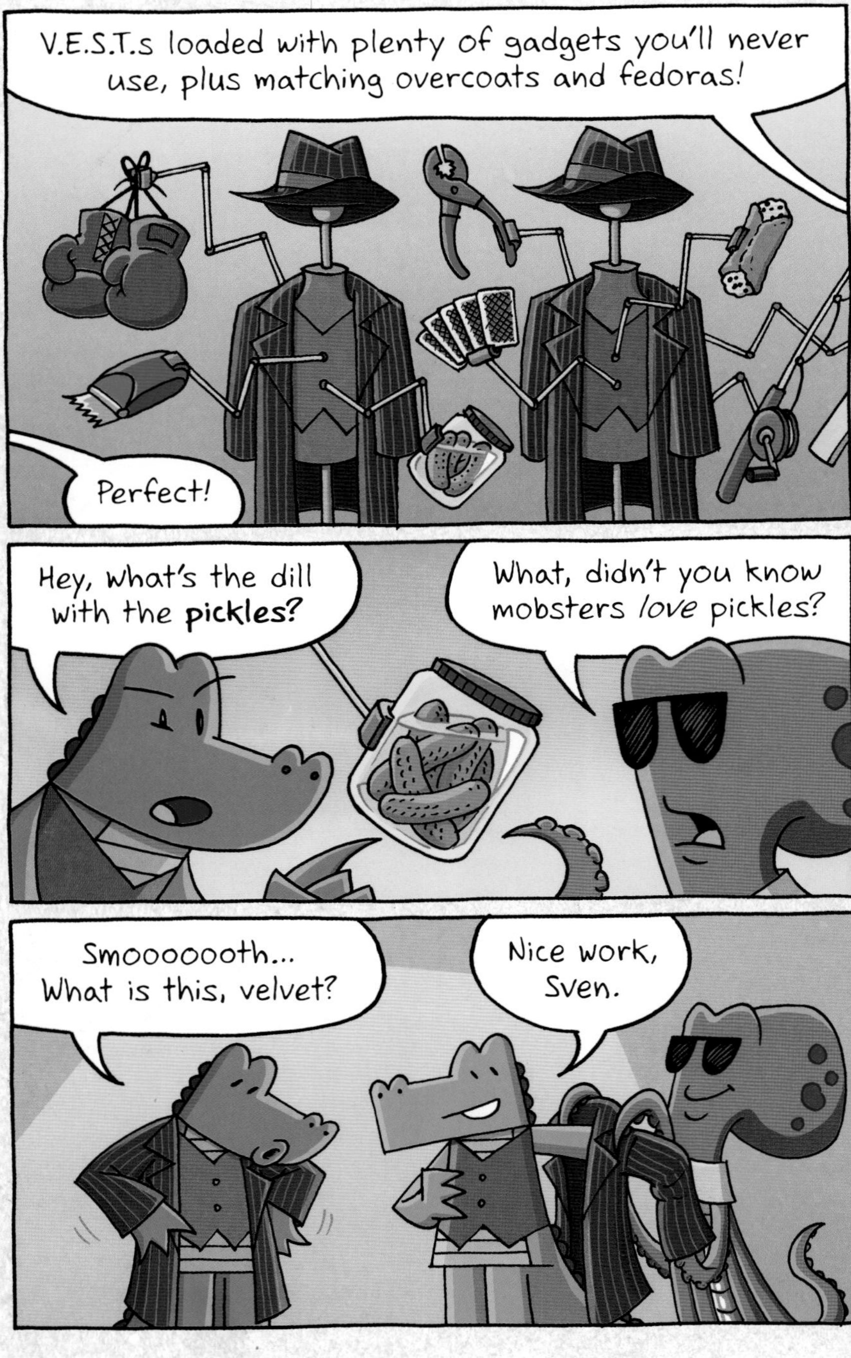
V.E.S.T.s loaded with plenty of gadgets you'll never use, plus matching overcoats and fedoras!
Perfect!
Hey, what's the dill with the **pickles?**
What, didn't you know mobsters *love* pickles?
Smooooooth... What is this, velvet?
Nice work, Sven.

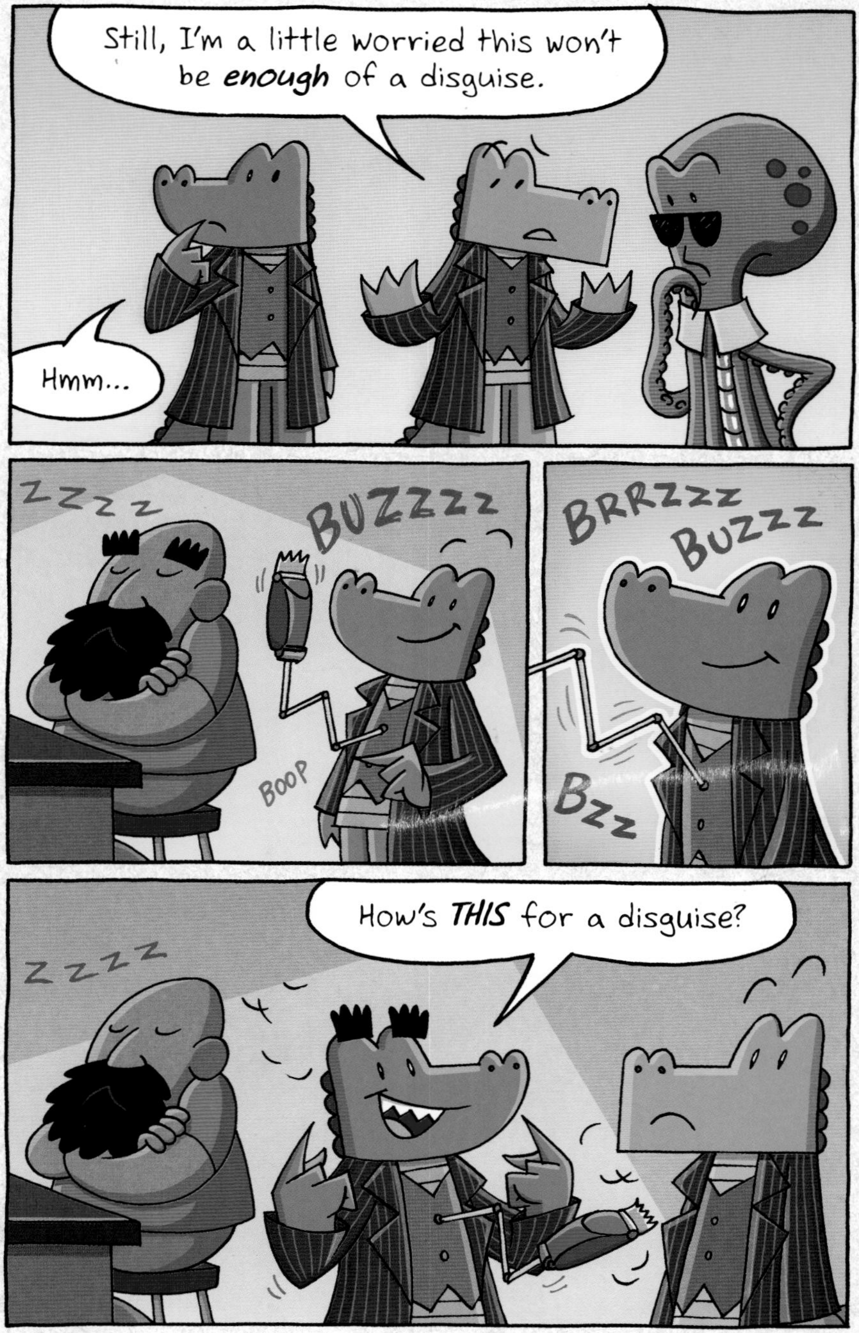
Still, I'm a little worried this won't be enough of a disguise.
Hmm...
ZZZZ
BUZZZZ
BOOP
BRRZZZ
BUZZZ
BZZ
ZZZZ
How's THIS for a disguise?

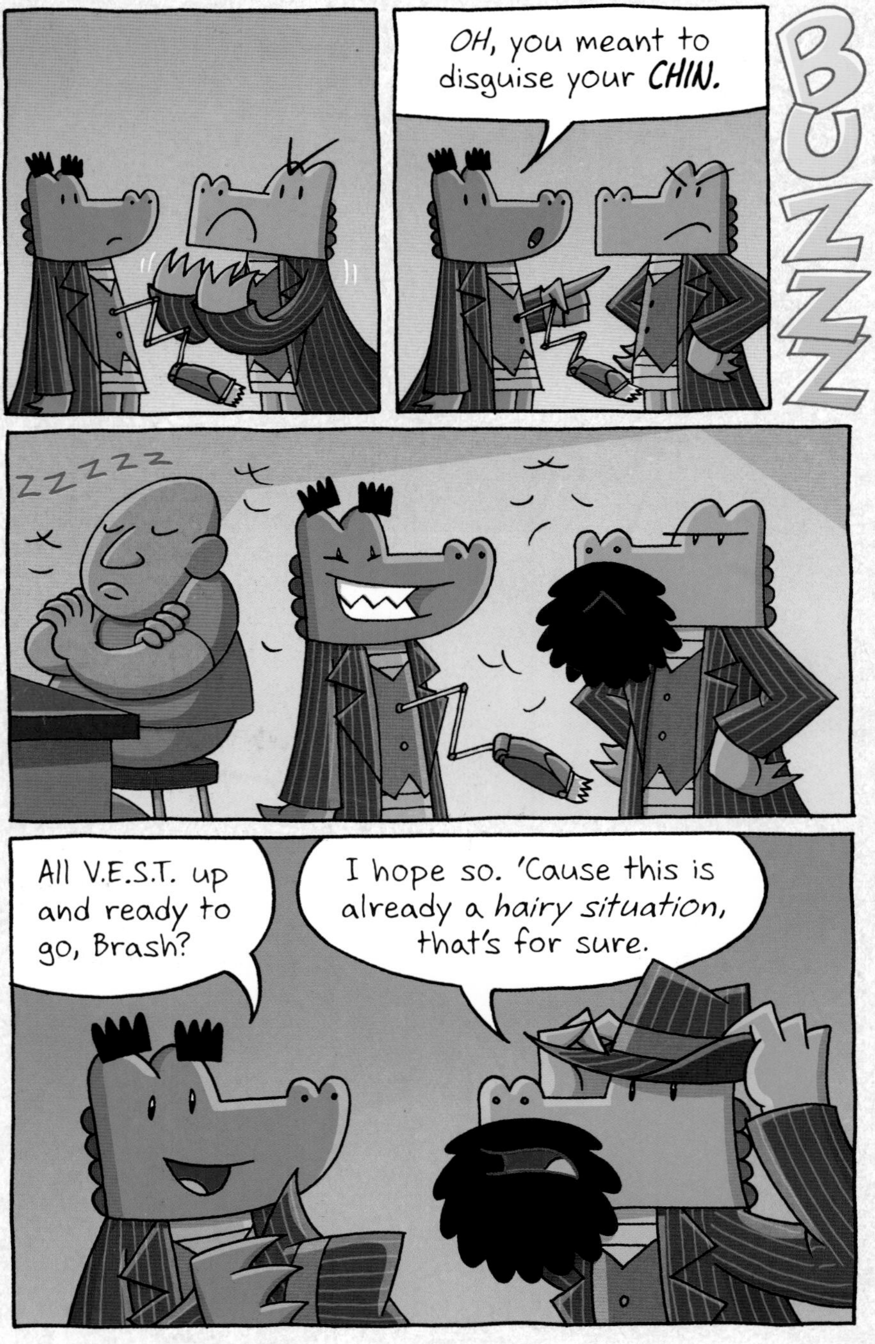
OH, you meant to disguise your CHIN.
BUZZZ
ZZZZZ
All V.E.S.T. up and ready to go, Brash?
I hope so. 'Cause this is already a hairy situation, that's for sure.

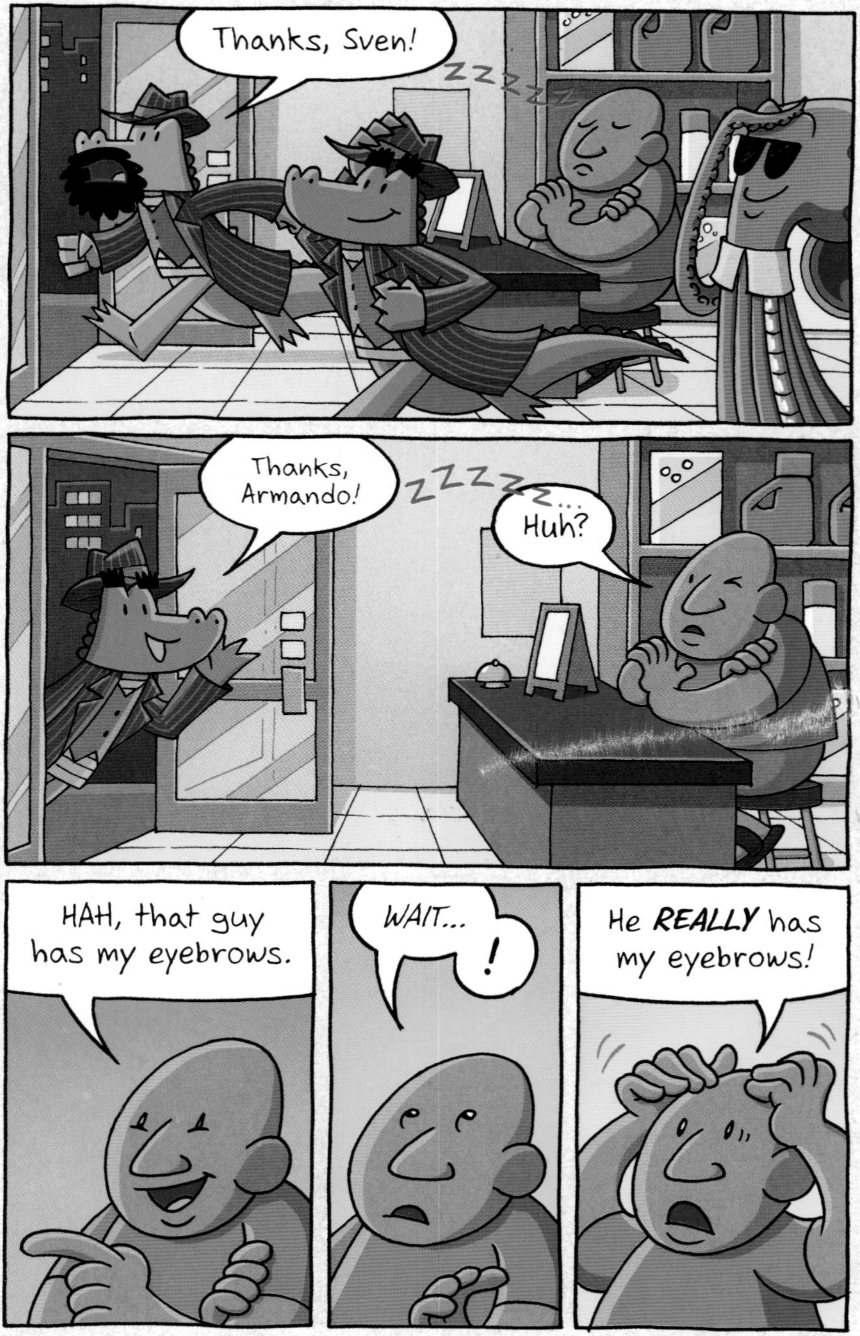
Thanks, Sven!
ZZZZZZ
Thanks, Armando!
ZZZZZZ...
Huh?
HAH, that guy has my eyebrows.
WAIT...
!
He REALLY has my eyebrows!

Chapter 8

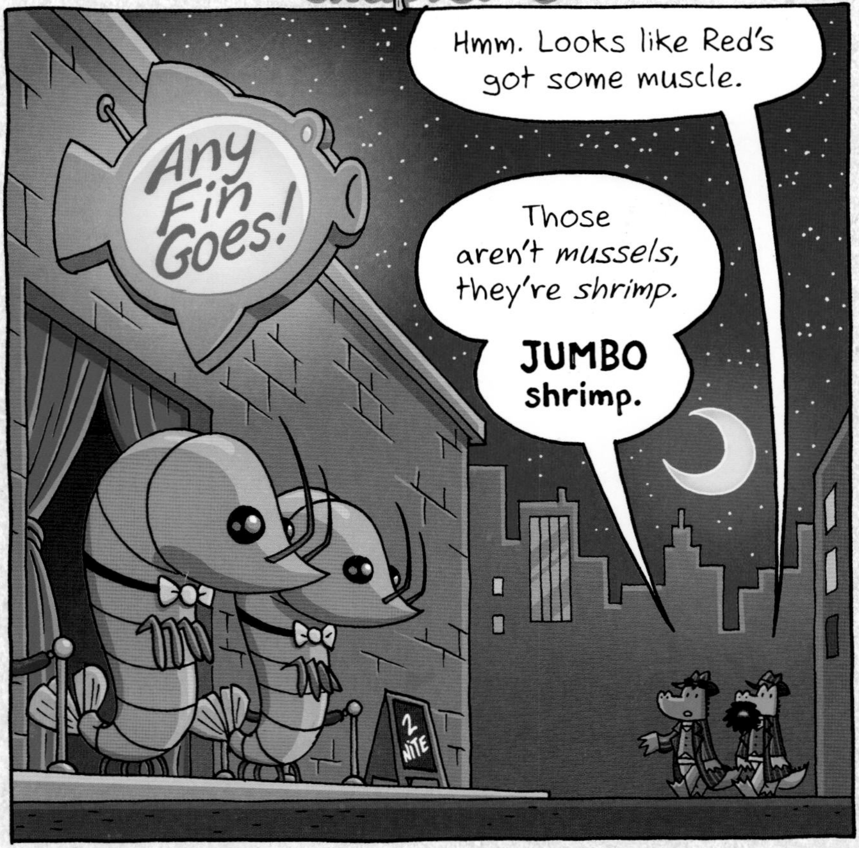
Any Fin Goes!
Hmm. Looks like Red's got some muscle.
Those aren't *mussels*, they're *shrimp*.
JUMBO shrimp.
2 NITE

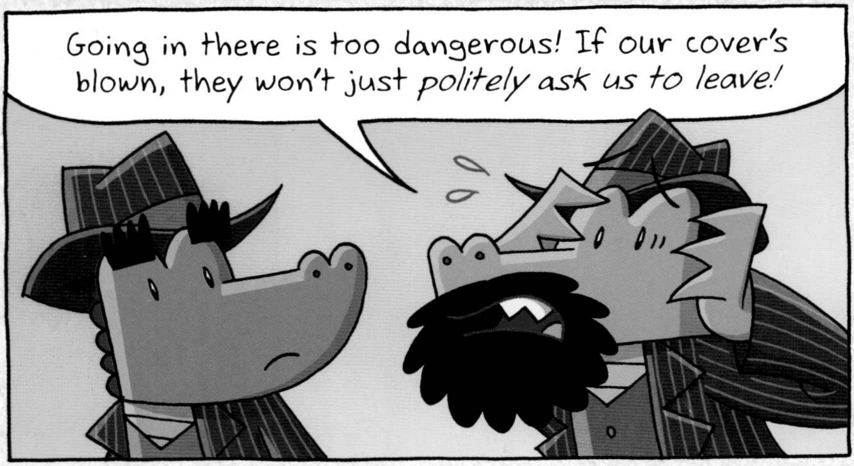
Going in there is too dangerous! If our cover's blown, they won't just *politely* ask us to leave!

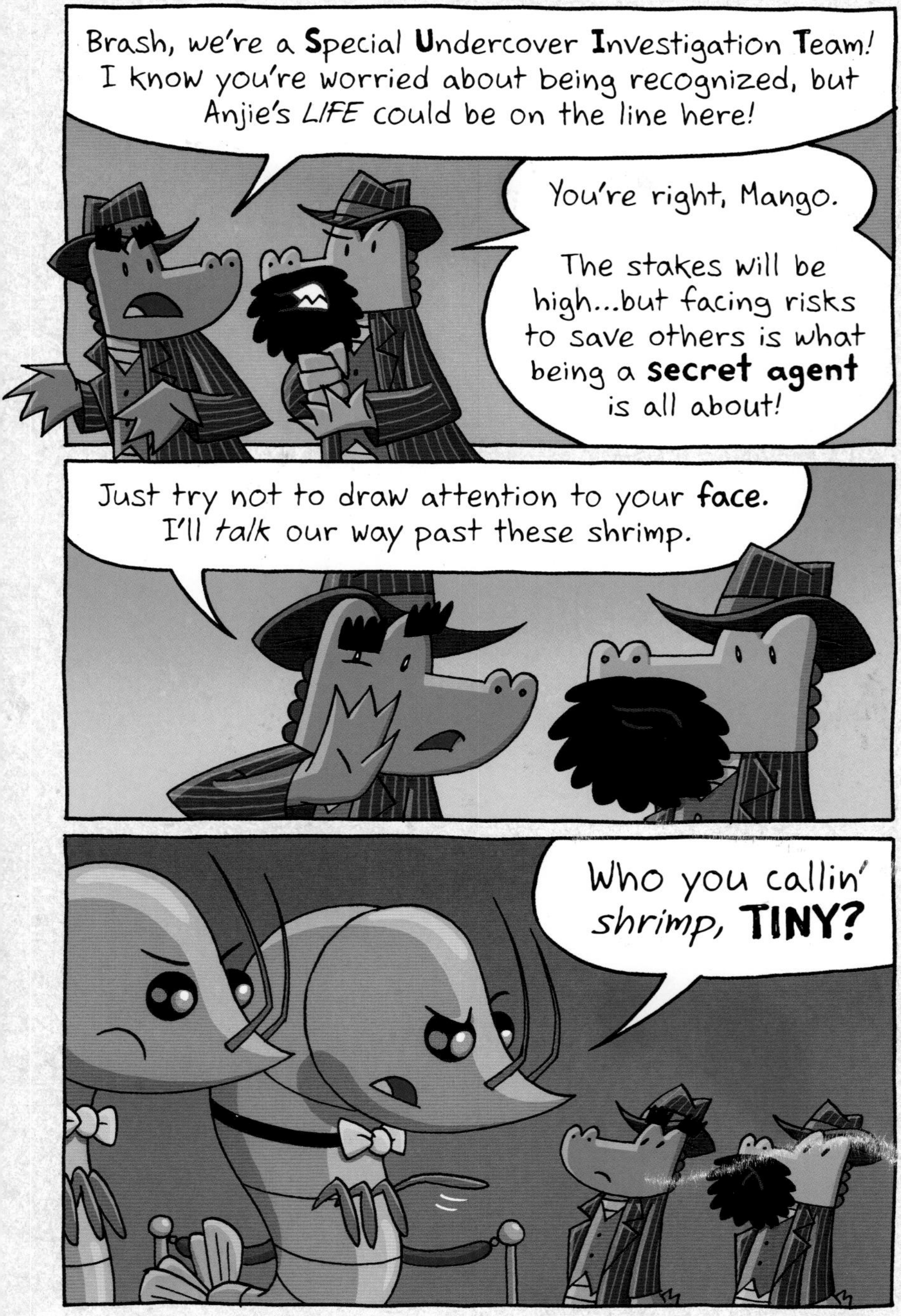
Brash, we're a Special Undercover Investigation Team! I know you're worried about being recognized, but Anjie's LIFE could be on the line here!
You're right, Mango.
The stakes will be high...but facing risks to save others is what being a secret agent is all about!
Just try not to draw attention to your face. I'll talk our way past these shrimp.
Who you callin' shrimp, TINY?

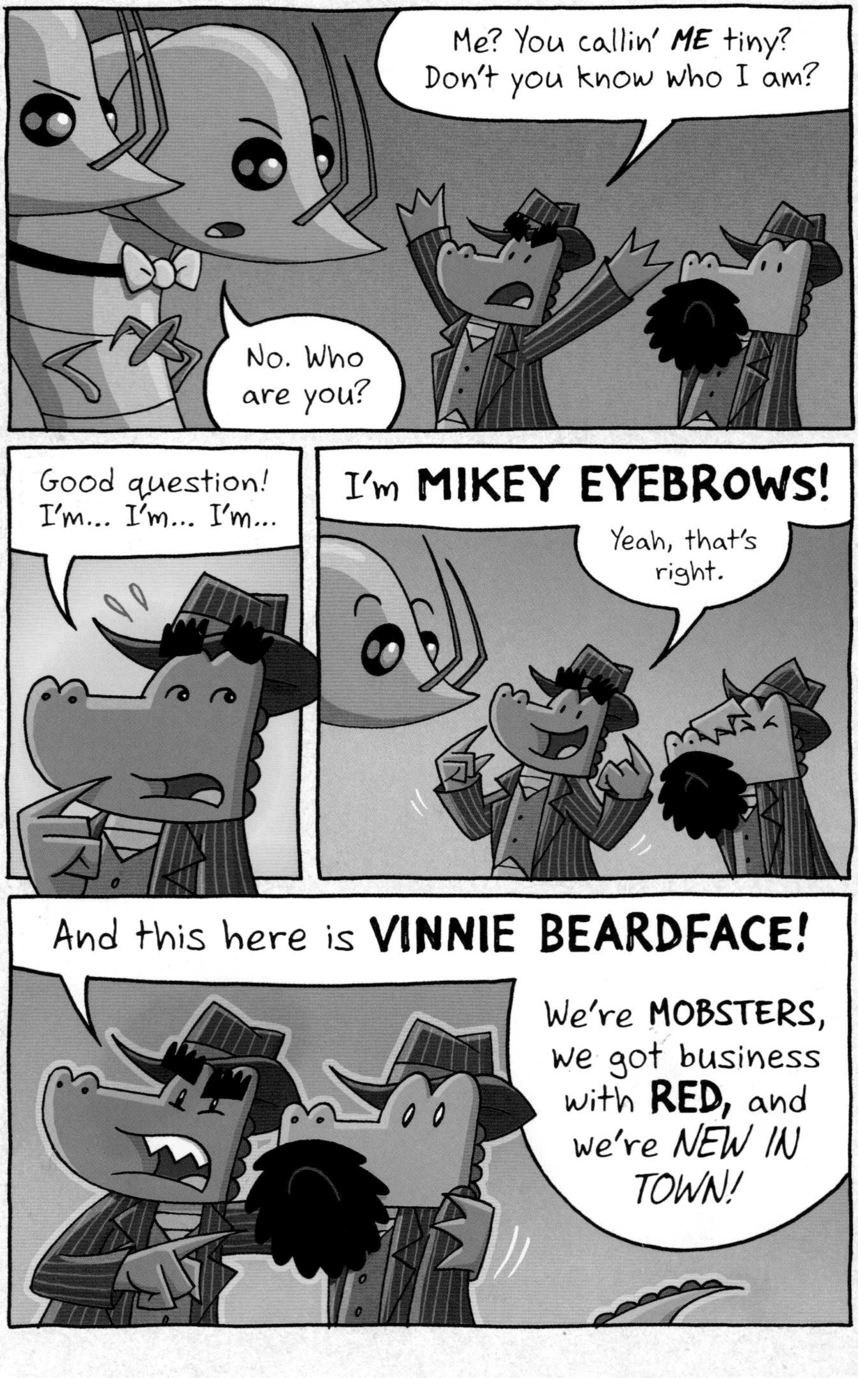
Me? You callin' ME tiny? Don't you know who I am?
No. Who are you?
Good question! I'm... I'm... I'm...
I'm MIKEY EYEBROWS!
Yeah, that's right.
And this here is VINNIE BEARDFACE!
We're MOBSTERS, we got business with RED, and we're NEW IN TOWN!

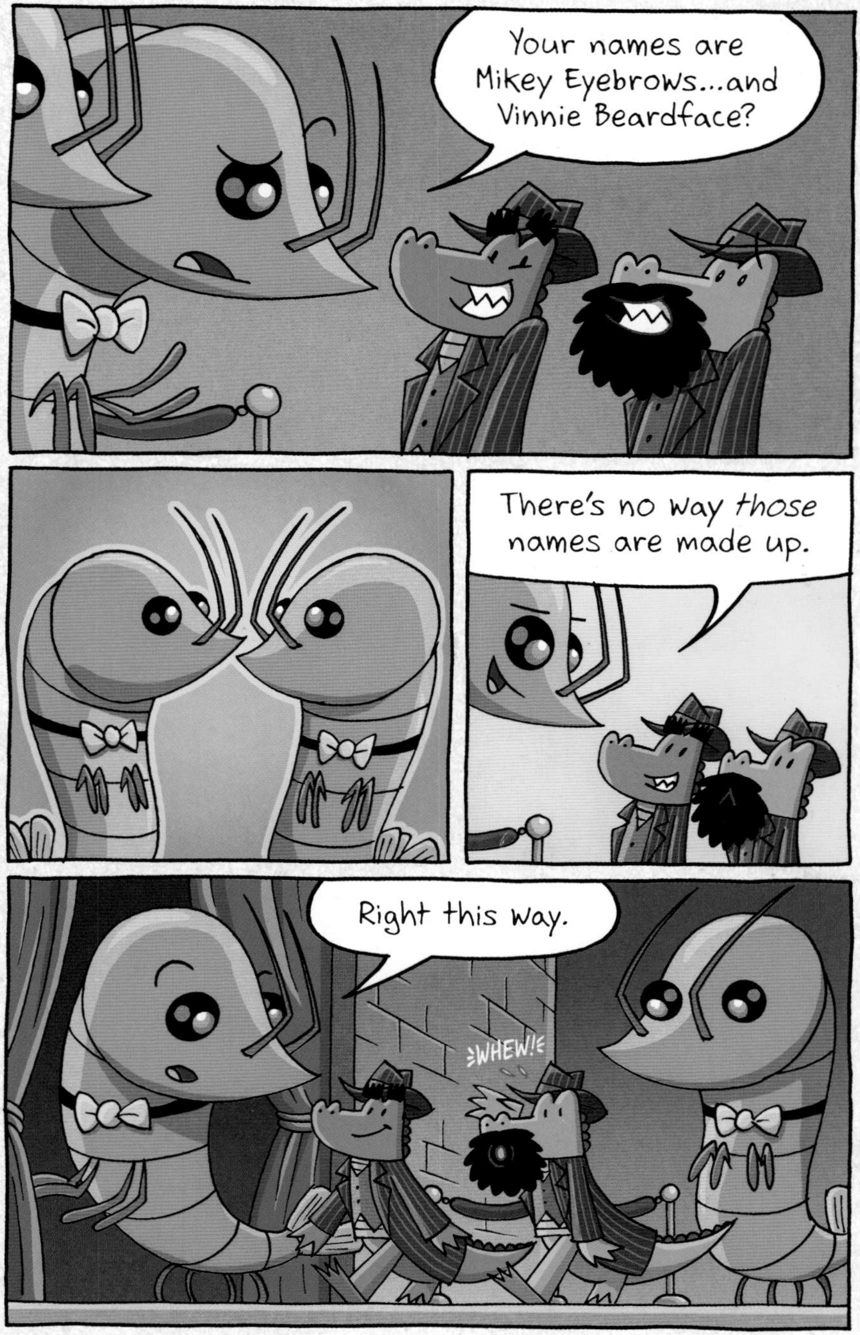
Your names are Mikey Eyebrows...and Vinnie Beardface?
There's no way *those* names are made up.
Right this way.
WHEW!

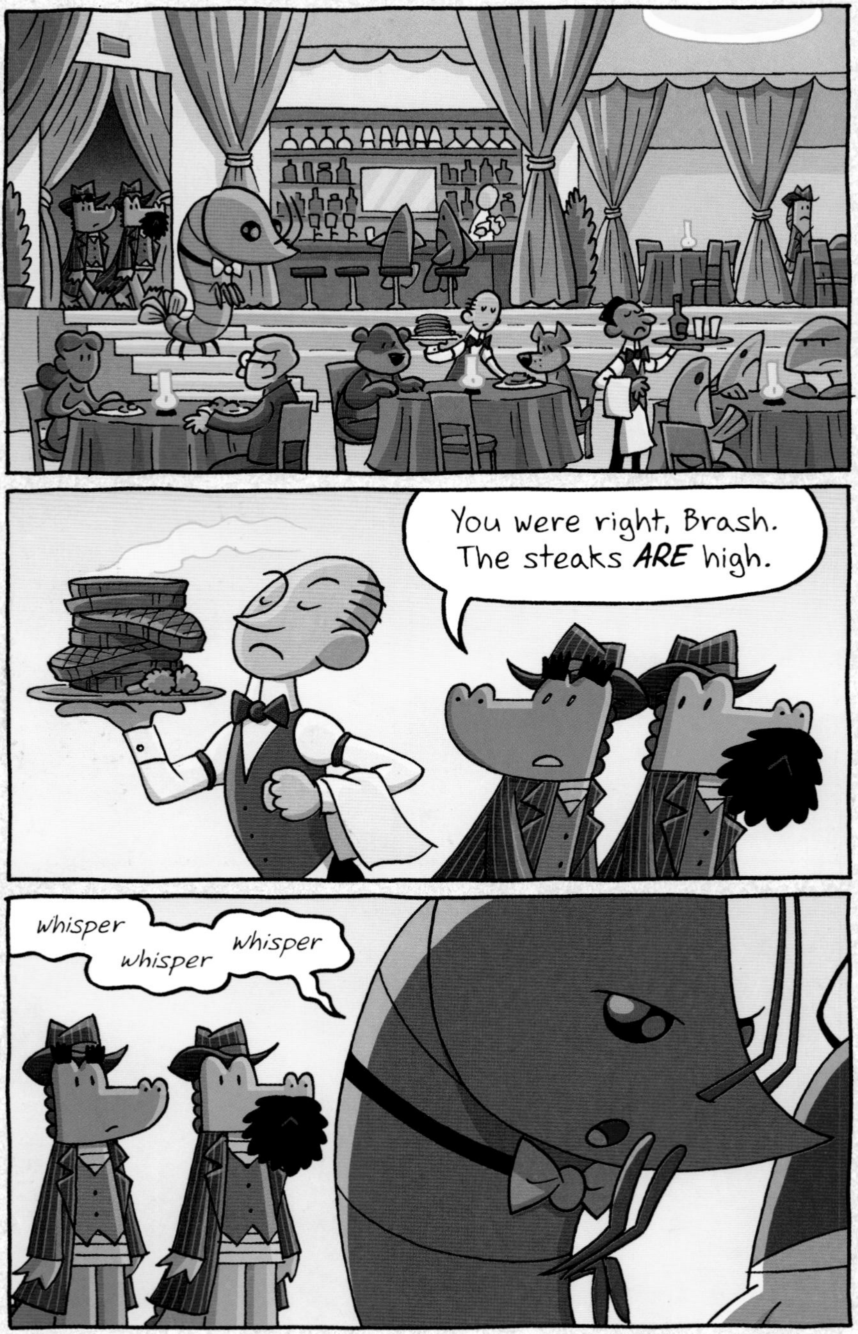
You were right, Brash.
The steaks ARE high.
whisper
whisper
whisper

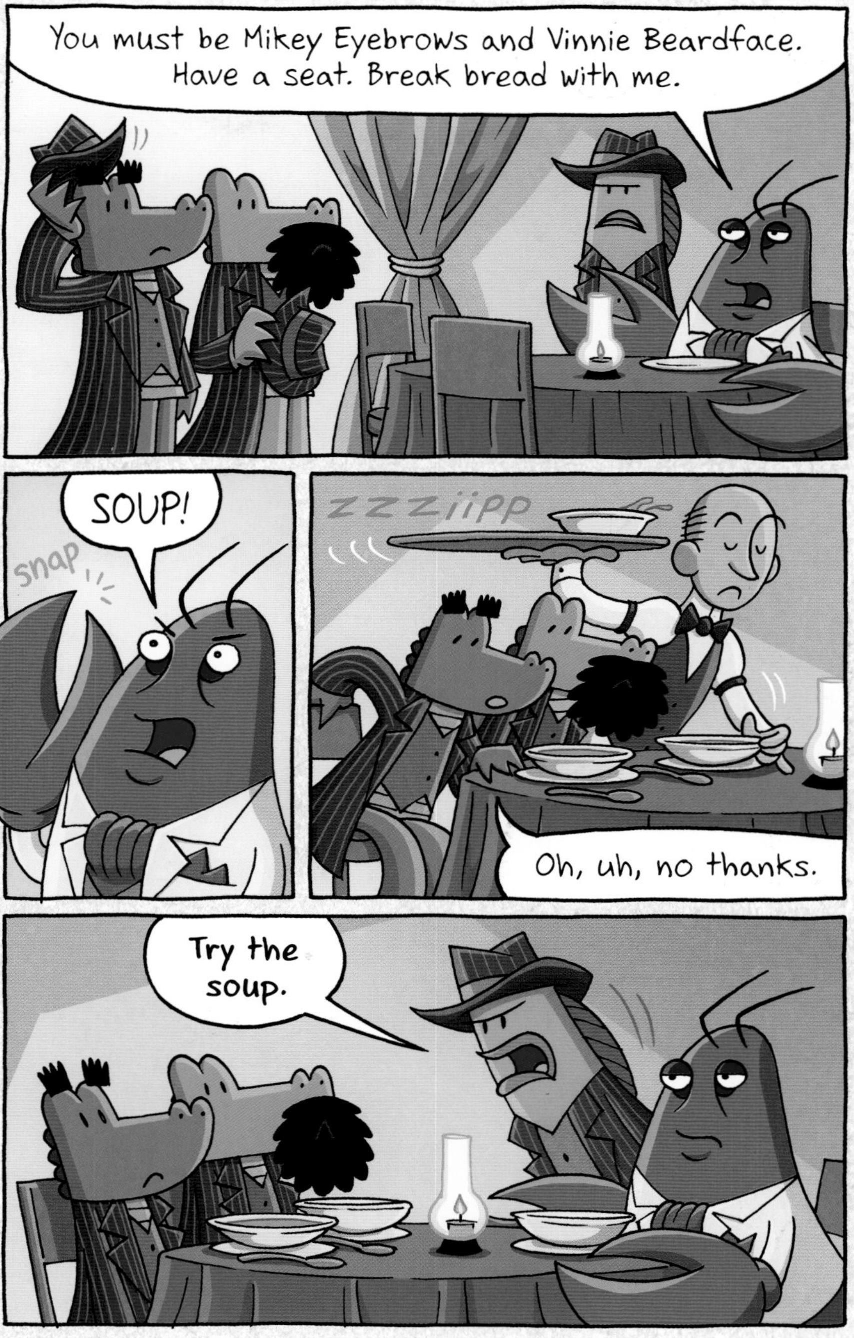

You must be Mikey Eyebrows and Vinnie Beardface. Have a seat. Break bread with me.
SOUP!
snap
zzziipp
Oh, uh, no thanks.
Try the soup.

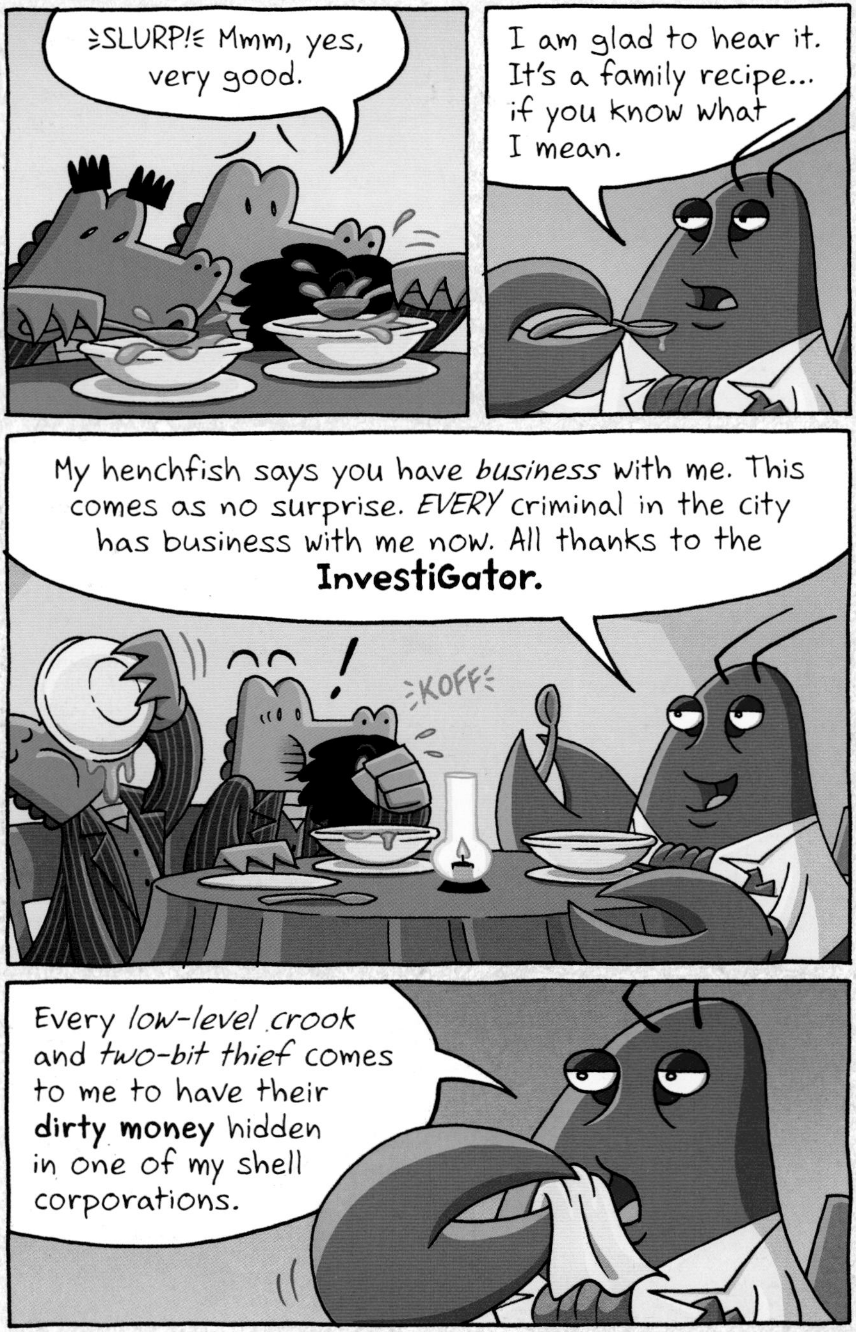

≷SLURP!≶ Mmm, yes, very good.
I am glad to hear it. It's a family recipe... if you know what I mean.
My henchfish says you have *business* with me. This comes as no surprise. *EVERY* criminal in the city has business with me now. All thanks to the **InvestiGator.**
!
≷KOFF≶
Every *low-level crook* and *two-bit thief* comes to me to have their **dirty money** hidden in one of my shell corporations.

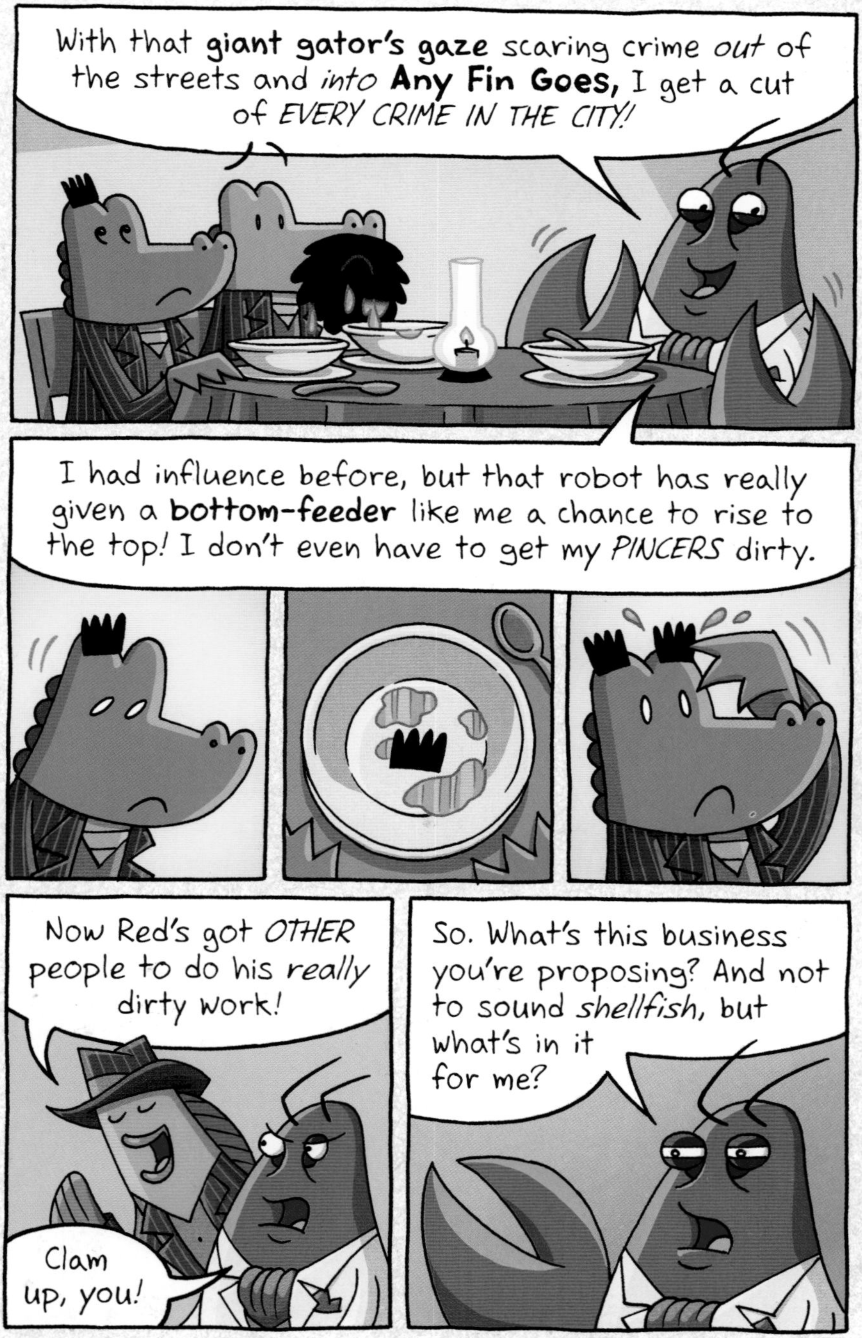
With that **giant gator's gaze** scaring crime *out* of the streets and *into* **Any Fin Goes,** I get a cut of *EVERY CRIME IN THE CITY!*
I had influence before, but that robot has really given a **bottom-feeder** like me a chance to rise to the top! I don't even have to get my *PINCERS* dirty.
Now Red's got *OTHER* people to do his *really* dirty work!
Clam up, you!
So. What's this business you're proposing? And not to sound *shellfish*, but what's in it for me?

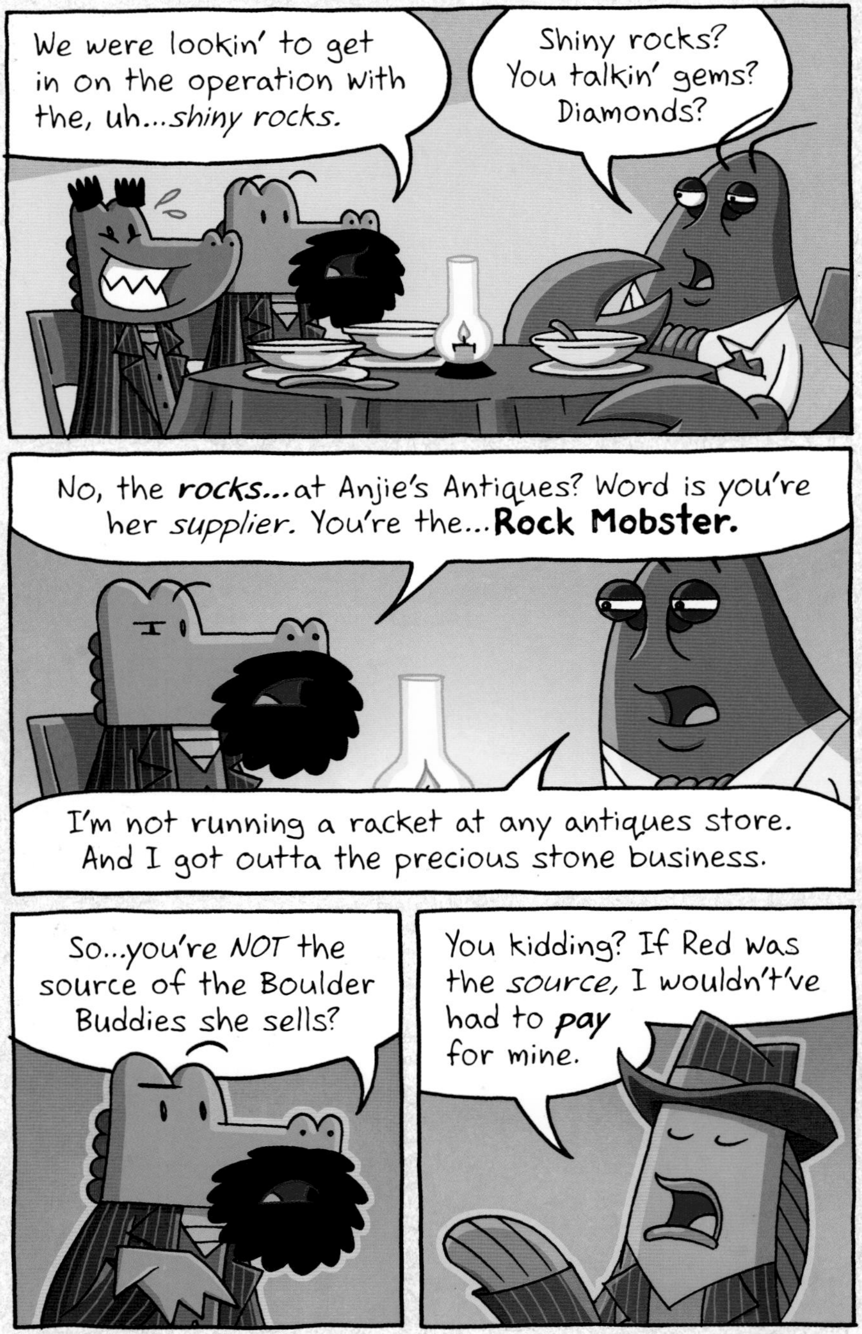
We were lookin' to get in on the operation with the, uh...*shiny rocks.*
Shiny rocks? You talkin' gems? Diamonds?
No, the **rocks...** at Anjie's Antiques? Word is you're her *supplier.* You're the...**Rock Mobster.**
I'm not running a racket at any antiques store. And I got outta the precious stone business.
So...you're *NOT* the source of the Boulder Buddies she sells?
You kidding? If Red was the *source,* I wouldn't've had to ***pay*** for mine.

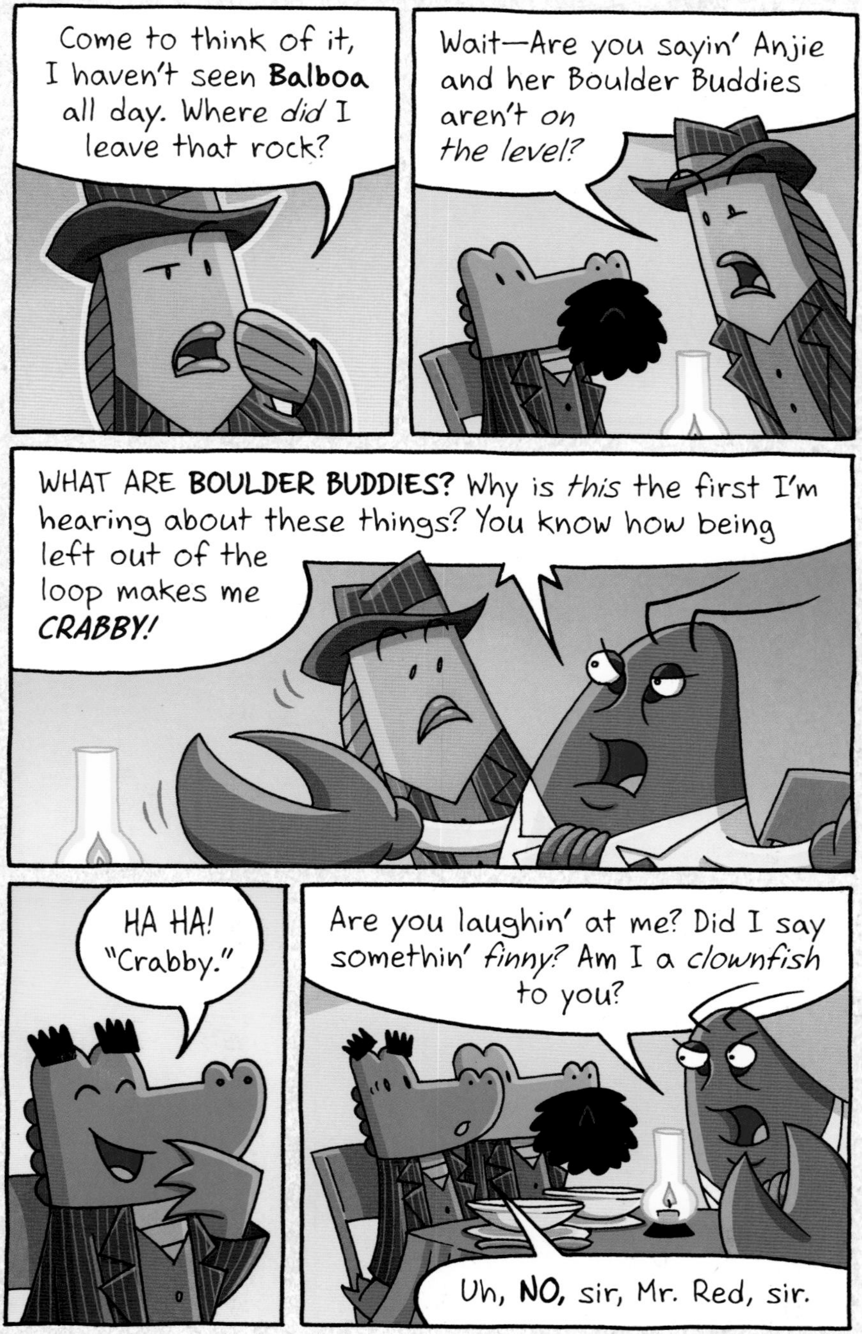

Come to think of it, I haven't seen **Balboa** all day. Where *did* I leave that rock?
Wait—Are you sayin' Anjie and her Boulder Buddies aren't on *the level?*
WHAT ARE **BOULDER BUDDIES?** Why is *this* the first I'm hearing about these things? You know how being left out of the loop makes me ***CRABBY!***
HA HA! "Crabby."
Are you laughin' at me? Did I say somethin' *finny?* Am I a *clownfish* to you?
Uh, **NO,** sir, Mr. Red, sir.

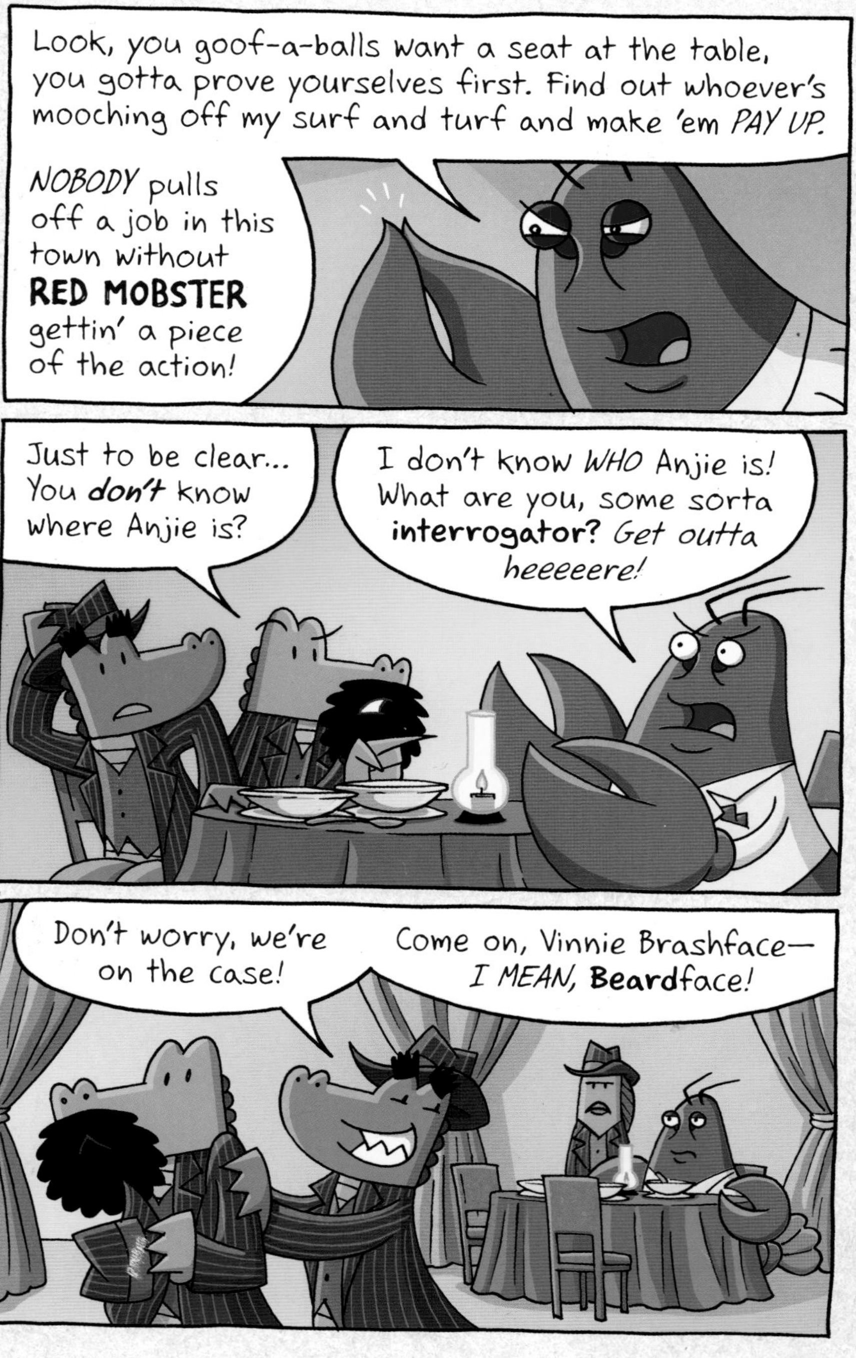
Look, you goof-a-balls want a seat at the table, you gotta prove yourselves first. Find out whoever's mooching off my surf and turf and make 'em *PAY UP.*
NOBODY pulls off a job in this town without **RED MOBSTER** gettin' a piece of the action!
Just to be clear... You ***don't*** know where Anjie is?
I don't know *WHO* Anjie is! What are you, some sorta **interrogator?** *Get outta heeeeere!*
Don't worry, we're on the case!
Come on, Vinnie Brashface— *I MEAN,* **Beard**face!

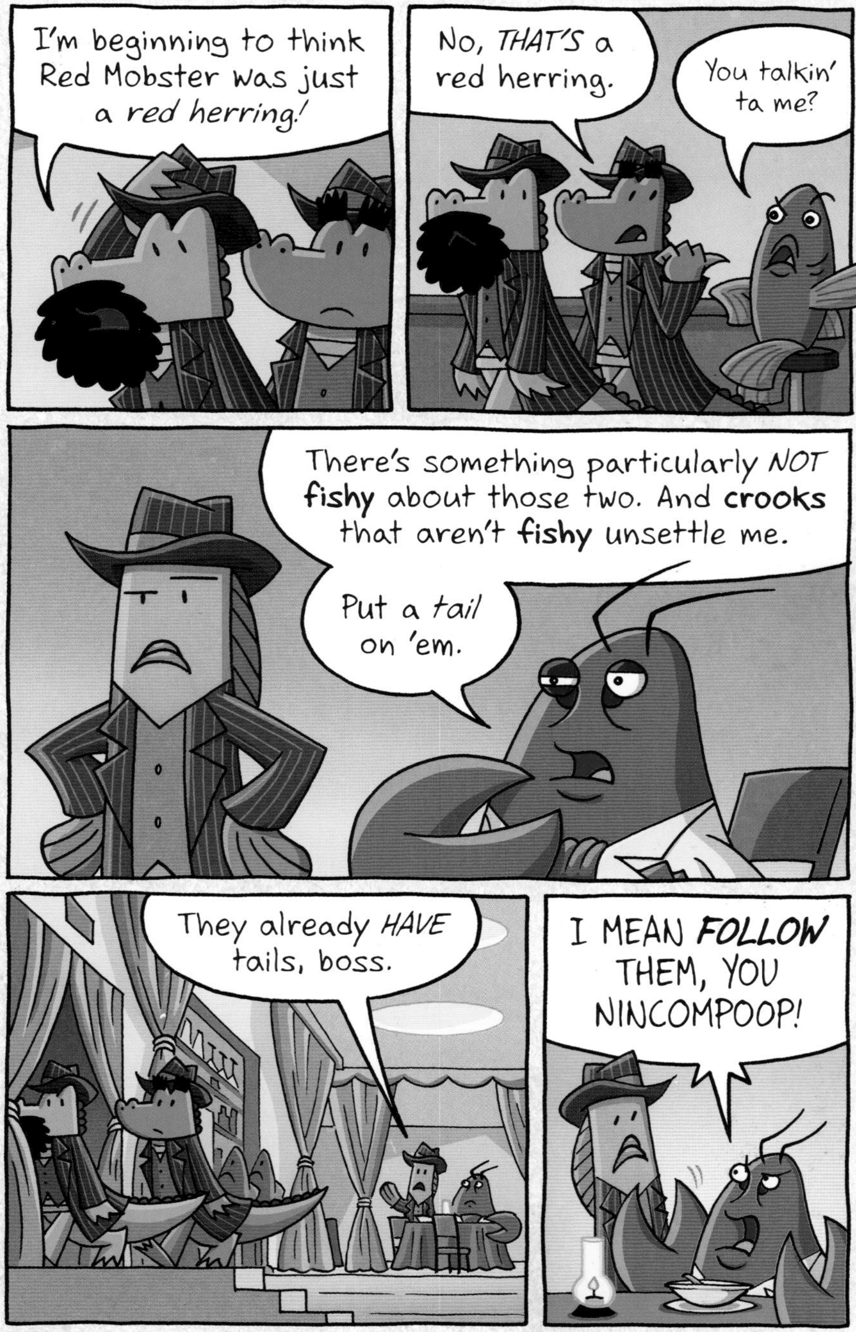
I'm beginning to think Red Mobster was just a *red herring*!
No, *THAT'S* a red herring.
You talkin' ta me?
There's something particularly *NOT* **fishy** about those two. And **crooks** that aren't **fishy** unsettle me.
Put a *tail* on 'em.
They already *HAVE* tails, boss.
I MEAN ***FOLLOW*** THEM, YOU NINCOMPOOP!

Chapter 9

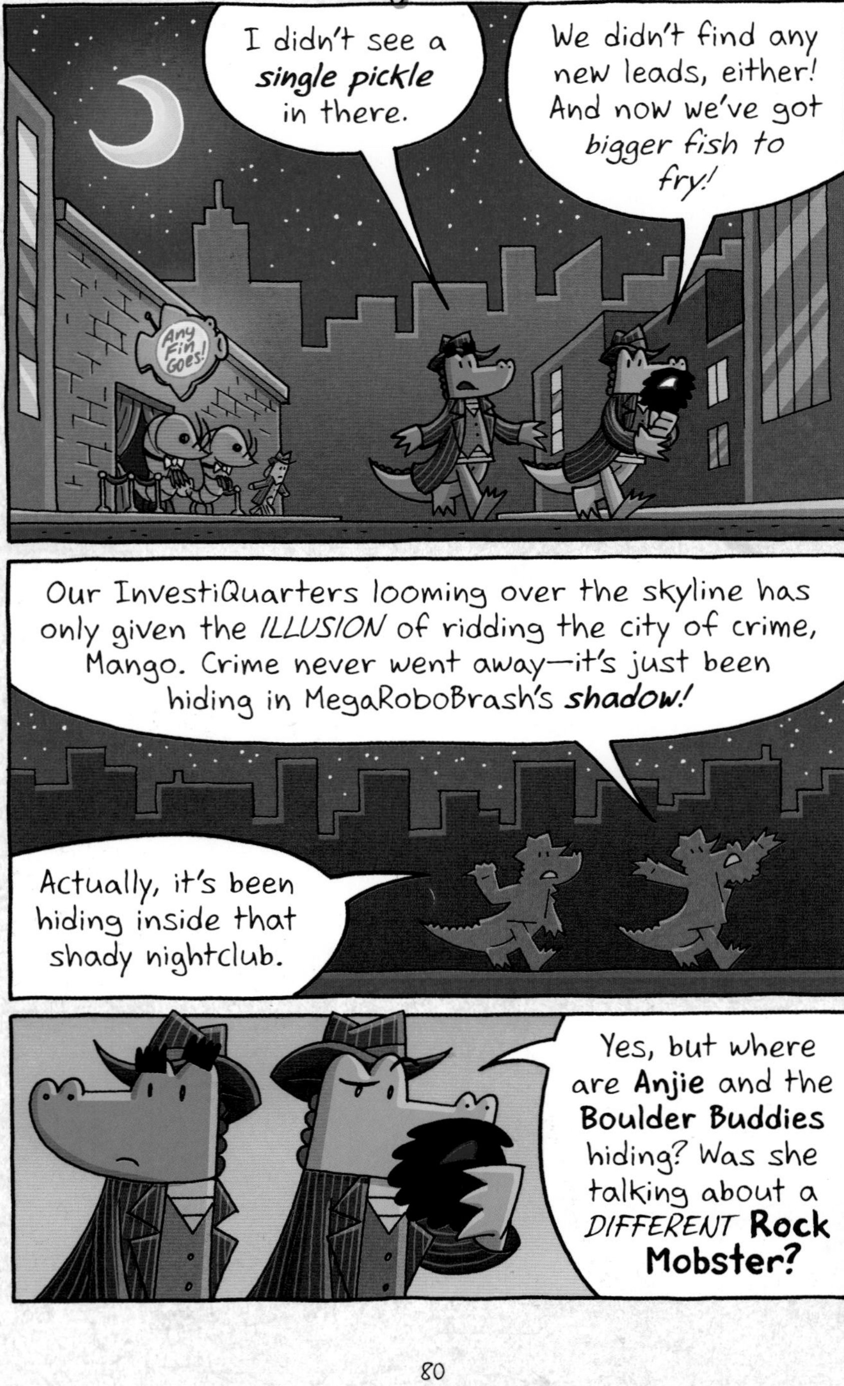
I didn't see a single pickle in there.
We didn't find any new leads, either! And now we've got bigger fish to fry!
Any Fin Goes!
Our InvestiQuarters looming over the skyline has only given the ILLUSION of ridding the city of crime, Mango. Crime never went away—it's just been hiding in MegaRoboBrash's shadow!
Actually, it's been hiding inside that shady nightclub.
Yes, but where are Anjie and the Boulder Buddies hiding? Was she talking about a DIFFERENT Rock Mobster?

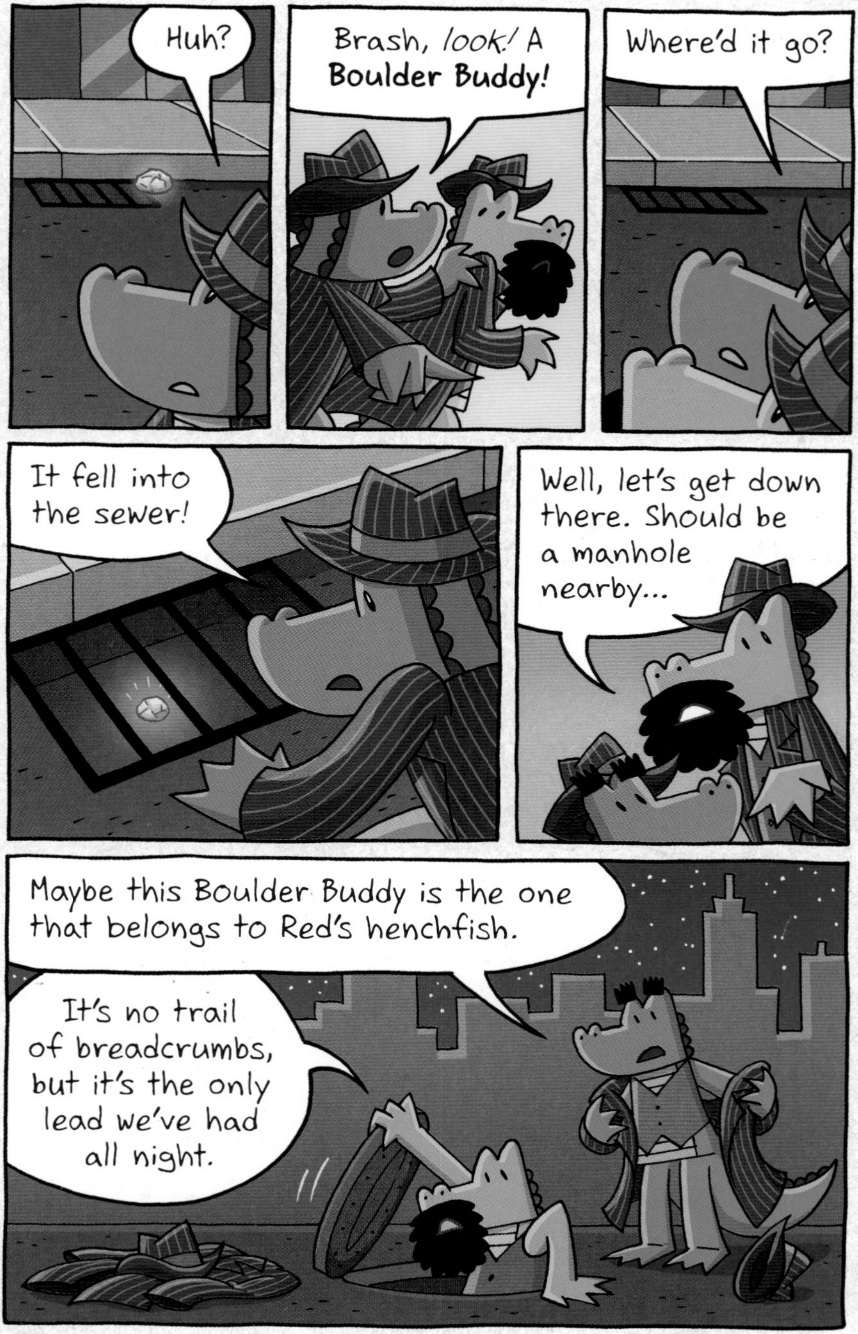
Huh?
Brash, *look!* A **Boulder Buddy!**
Where'd it go?
It fell into the sewer!
Well, let's get down there. Should be a manhole nearby...
Maybe this Boulder Buddy is the one that belongs to Red's henchfish.
It's no trail of breadcrumbs, but it's the only lead we've had all night.

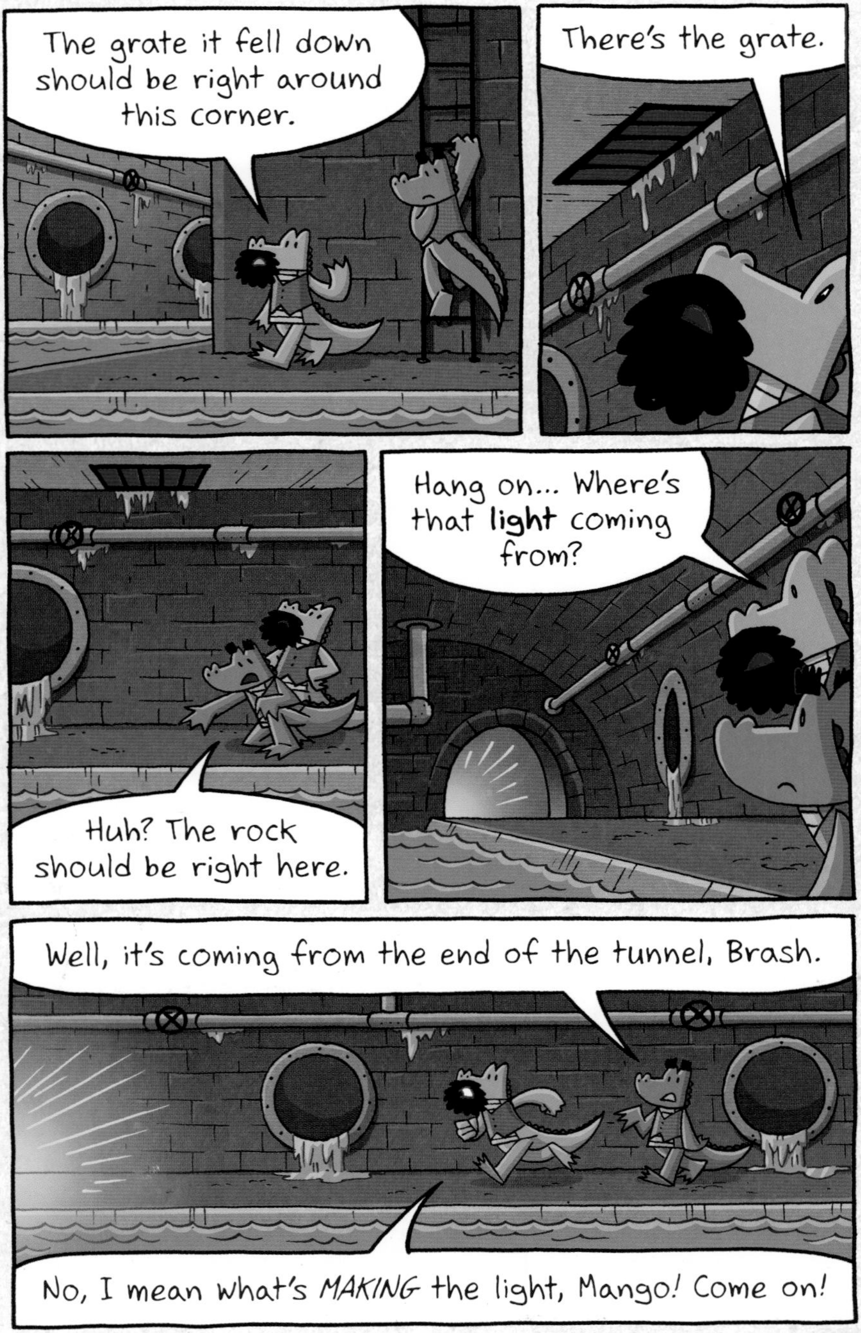

The grate it fell down should be right around this corner.
There's the grate.
Huh? The rock should be right here.
Hang on... Where's that **light** coming from?
Well, it's coming from the end of the tunnel, Brash.
No, I mean what's *MAKING* the light, Mango! Come on!

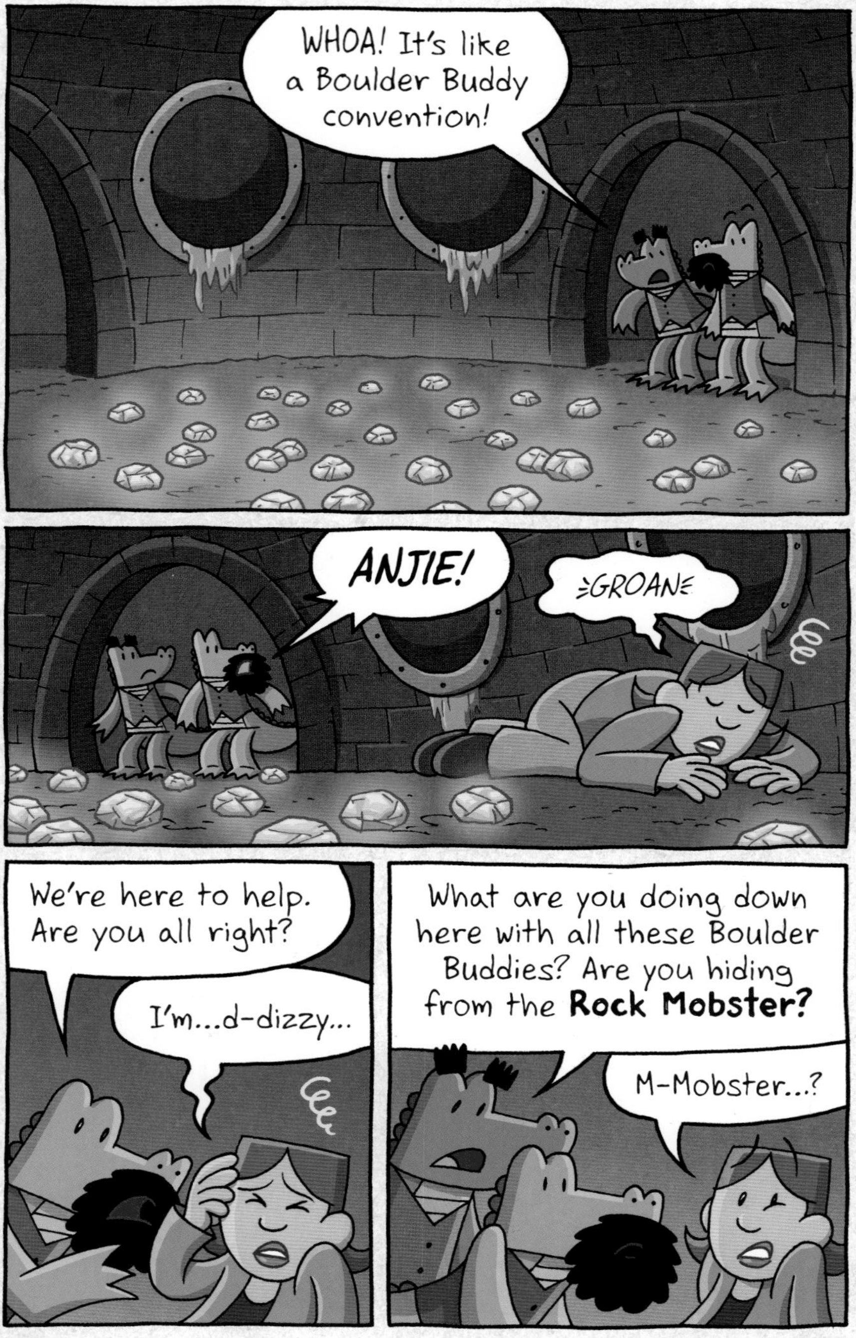
WHOA! It's like a Boulder Buddy convention!
ANJIE!
GROAN
We're here to help. Are you all right?
I'm...d-dizzy...
What are you doing down here with all these Boulder Buddies? Are you hiding from the **Rock Mobster?**
M-Mobster...?

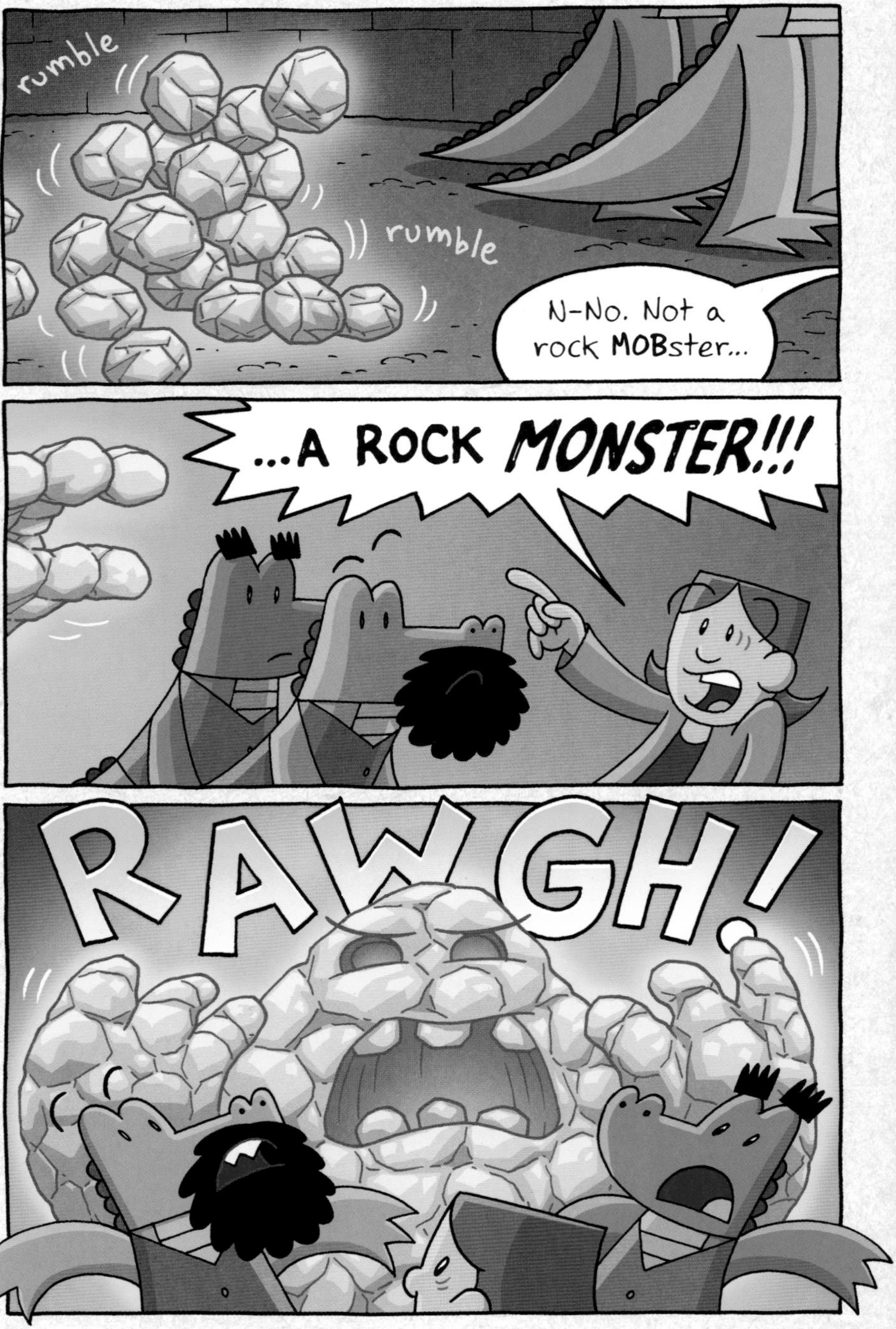
rumble
rumble
N-No. Not a rock MOBster...
...A ROCK MONSTER!!!
RAWGH!

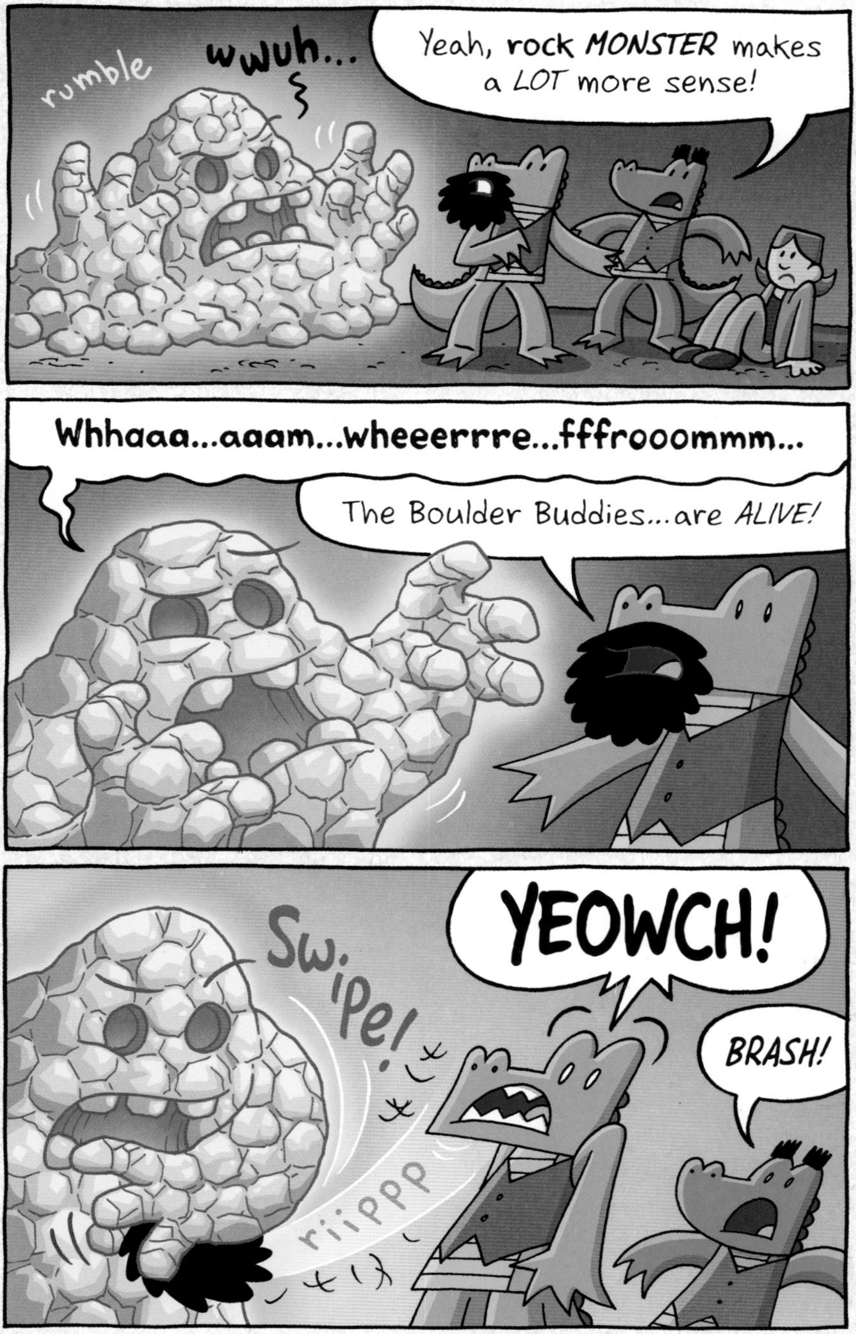
rumble
wwuh...
Yeah, rock MONSTER makes a LOT more sense!
Whhaaa...aaam...wheeerrre...fffrooommm...
The Boulder Buddies...are ALIVE!
Swipe!
riippp
YEOWCH!
BRASH!

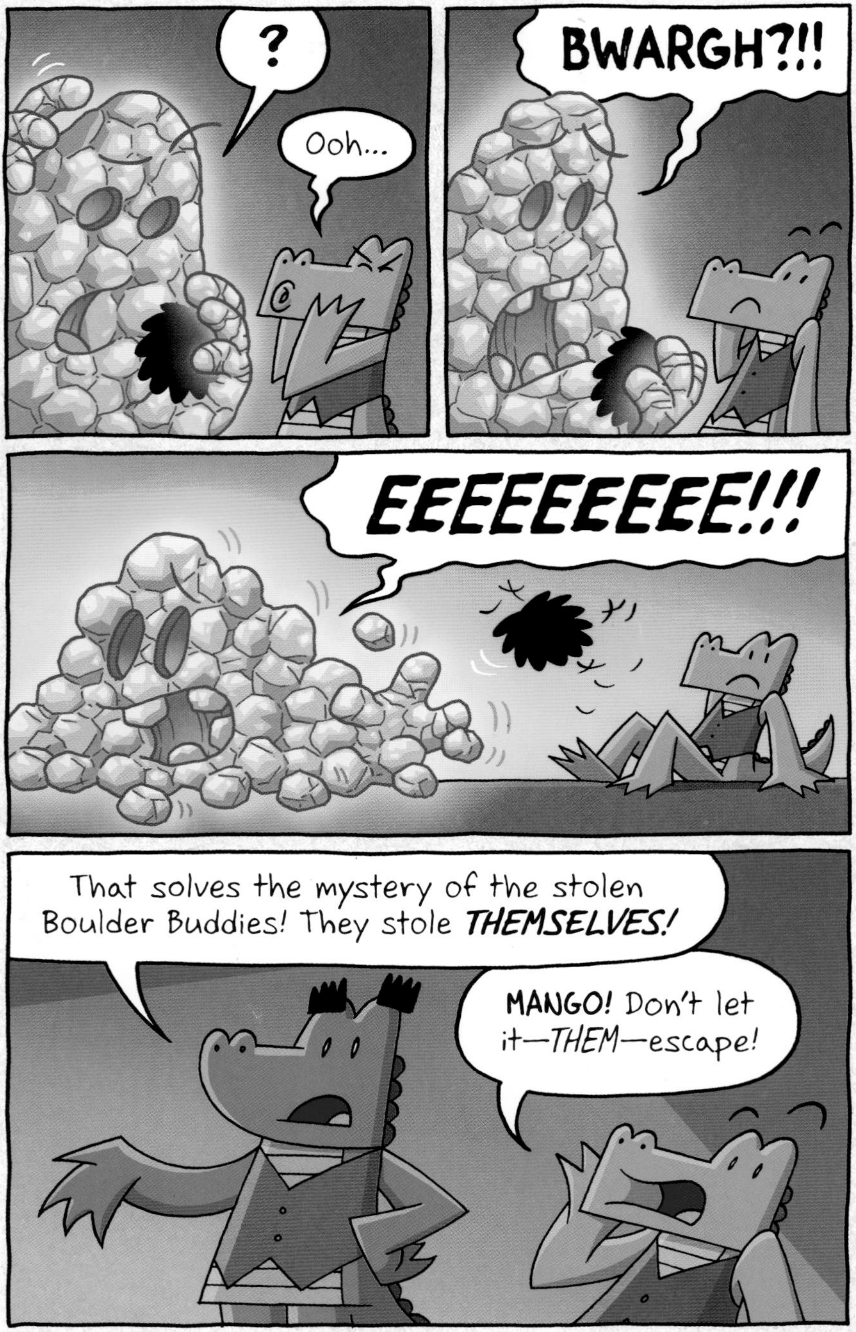
?
Ooh...
BWARGH?!!
EEEEEEEEEE!!!
That solves the mystery of the stolen Boulder Buddies! They stole **THEMSELVES!**
MANGO! Don't let it—*THEM*—escape!

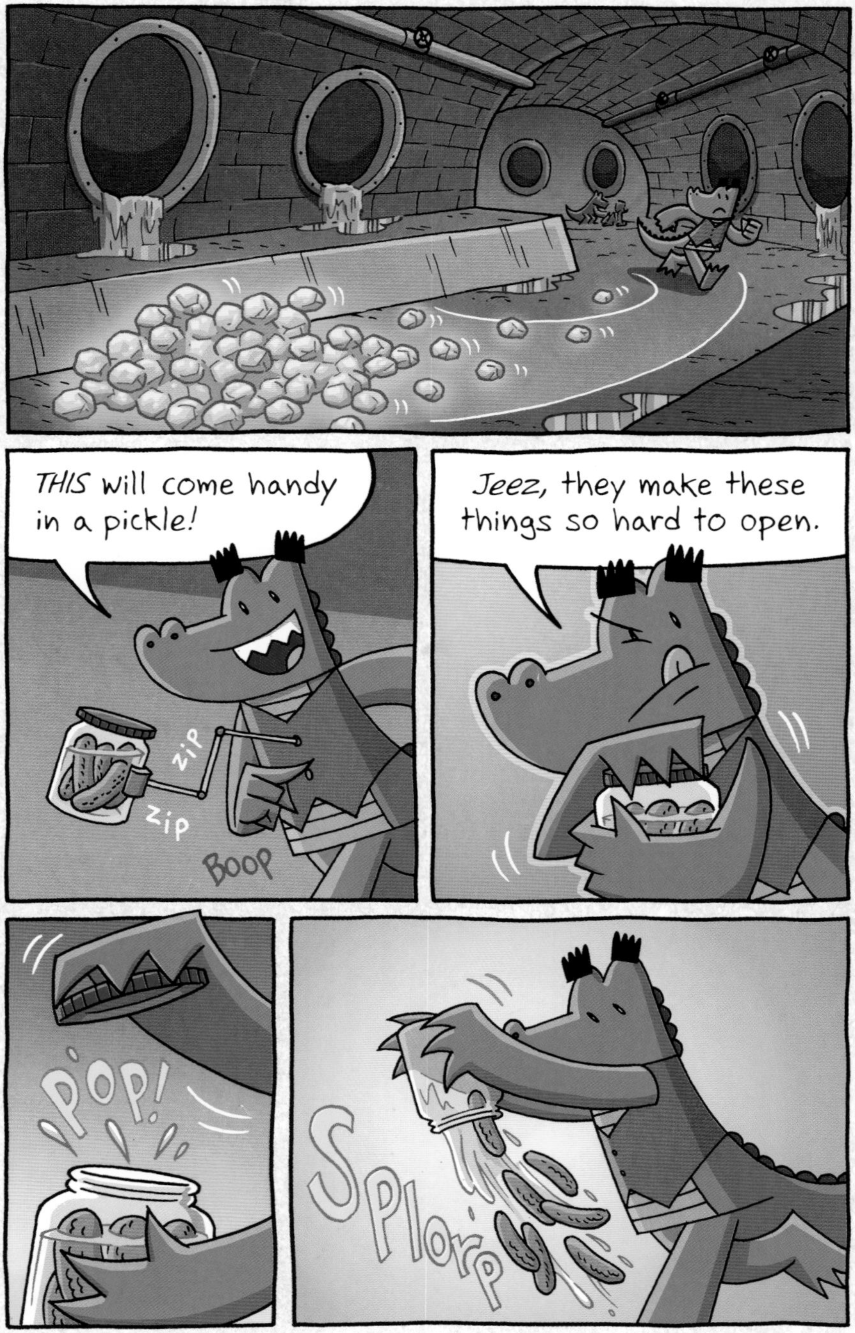
THIS will come handy in a pickle!
ZIP
ZIP
BOOP
Jeez, they make these things so hard to open.
POP!
SPLORP

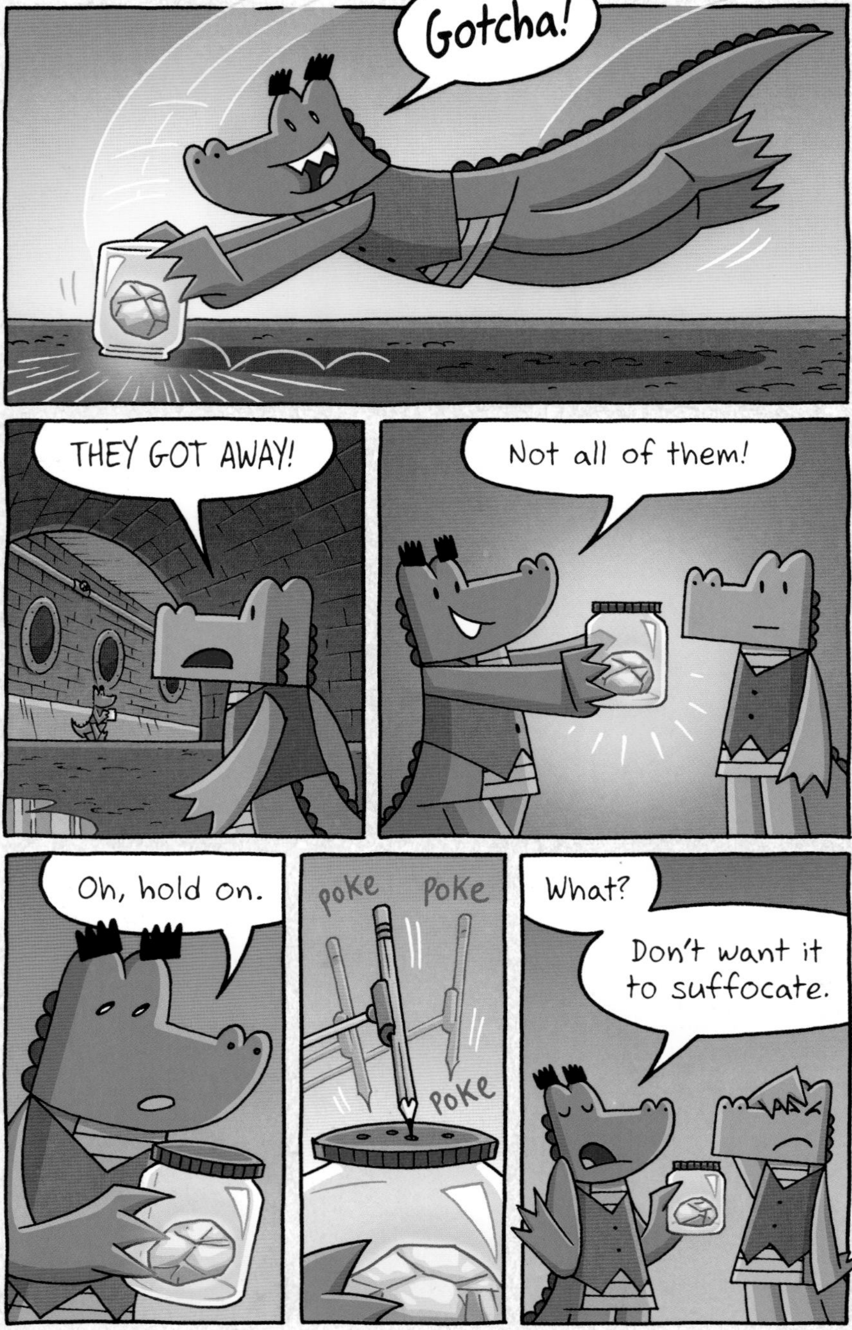
Gotcha!
THEY GOT AWAY!
Not all of them!
Oh, hold on.
poke
poke
poke
What?
Don't want it to suffocate.

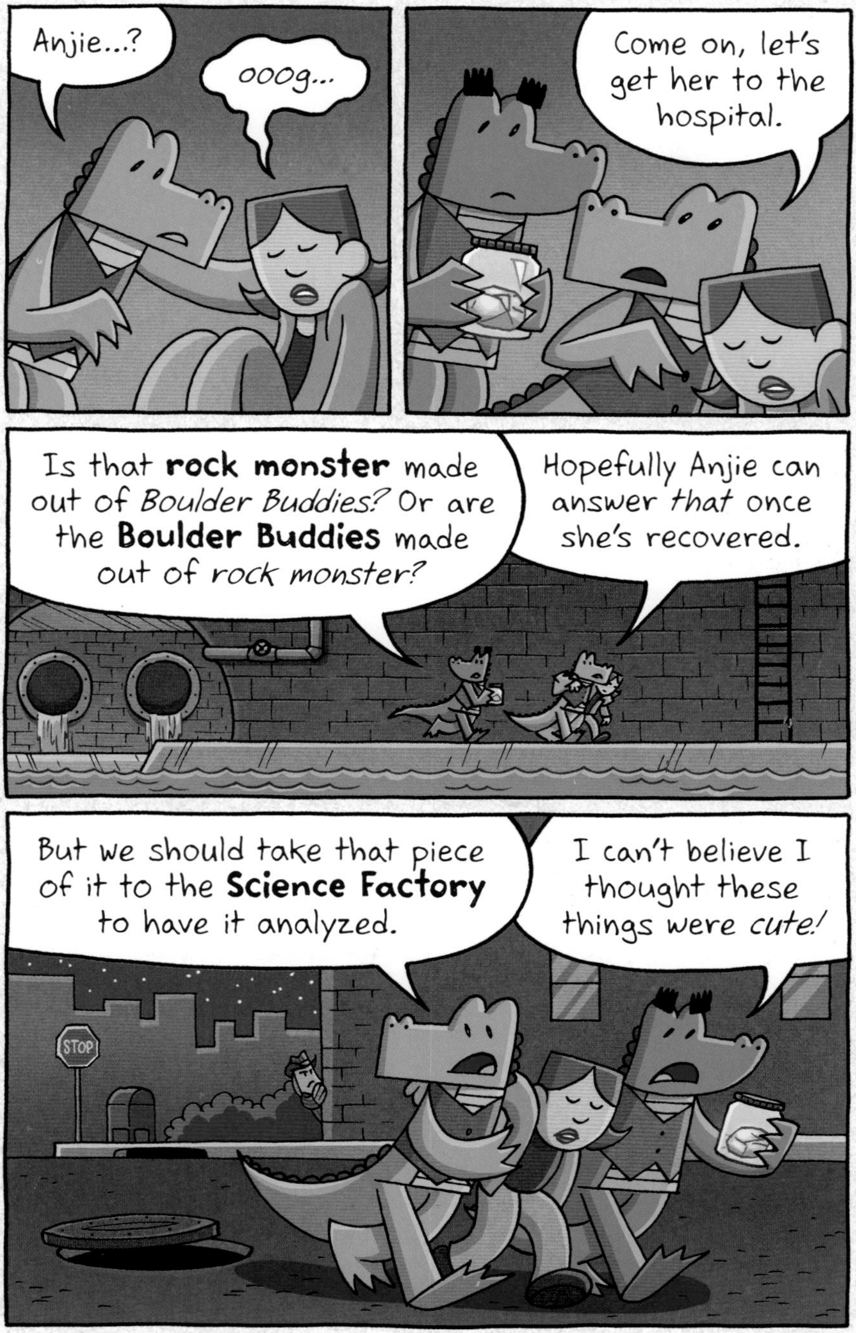
Anjie...?
ooog...
Come on, let's get her to the hospital.
Is that **rock monster** made out of *Boulder Buddies?* Or are the **Boulder Buddies** made out of *rock monster?*
Hopefully Anjie can answer *that* once she's recovered.
But we should take that piece of it to the **Science Factory** to have it analyzed.
I can't believe I thought these things were *cute!*
STOP

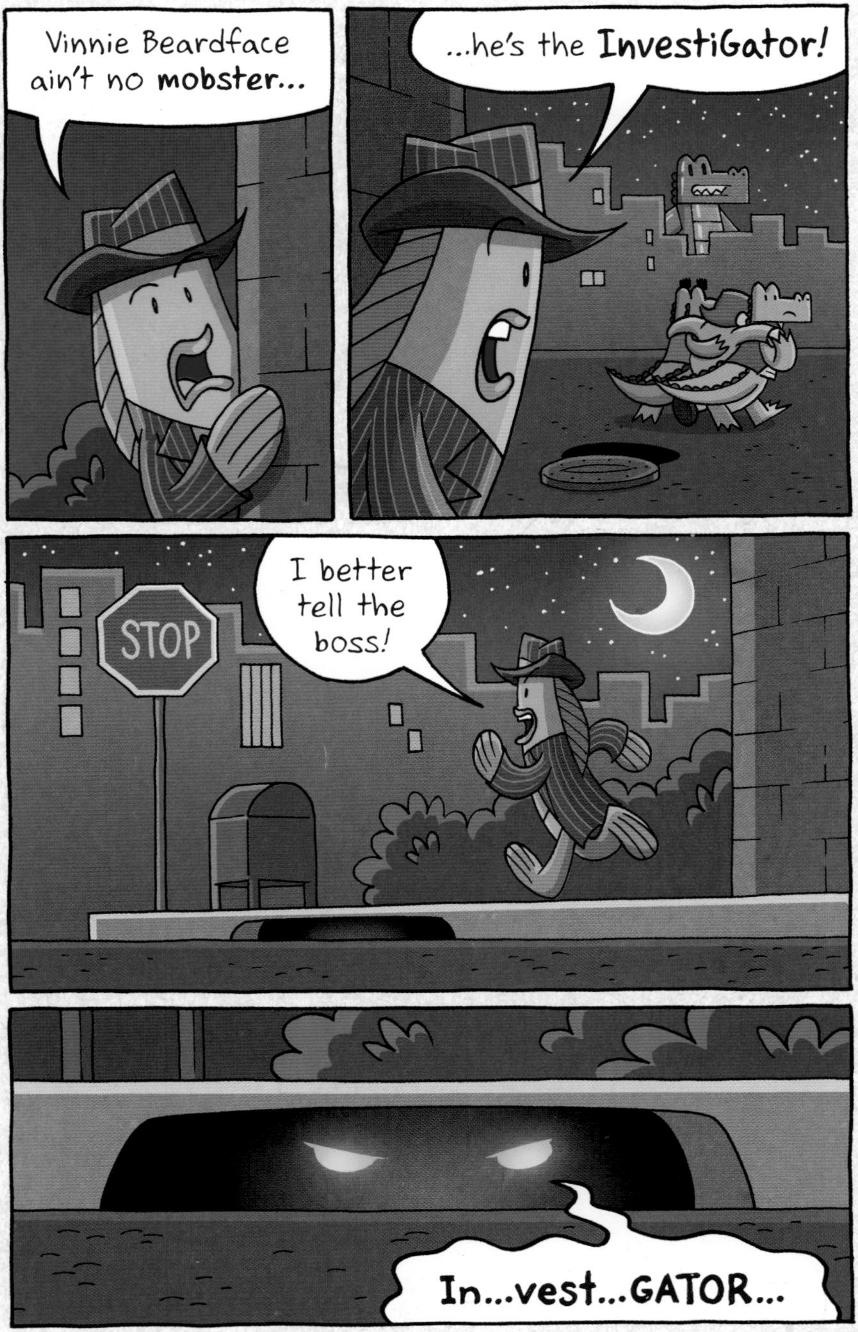
Vinnie Beardface ain't no **mobster...**
...he's the **InvestiGator!**
STOP
I better tell the boss!
In...vest...GATOR...

Chapter 10

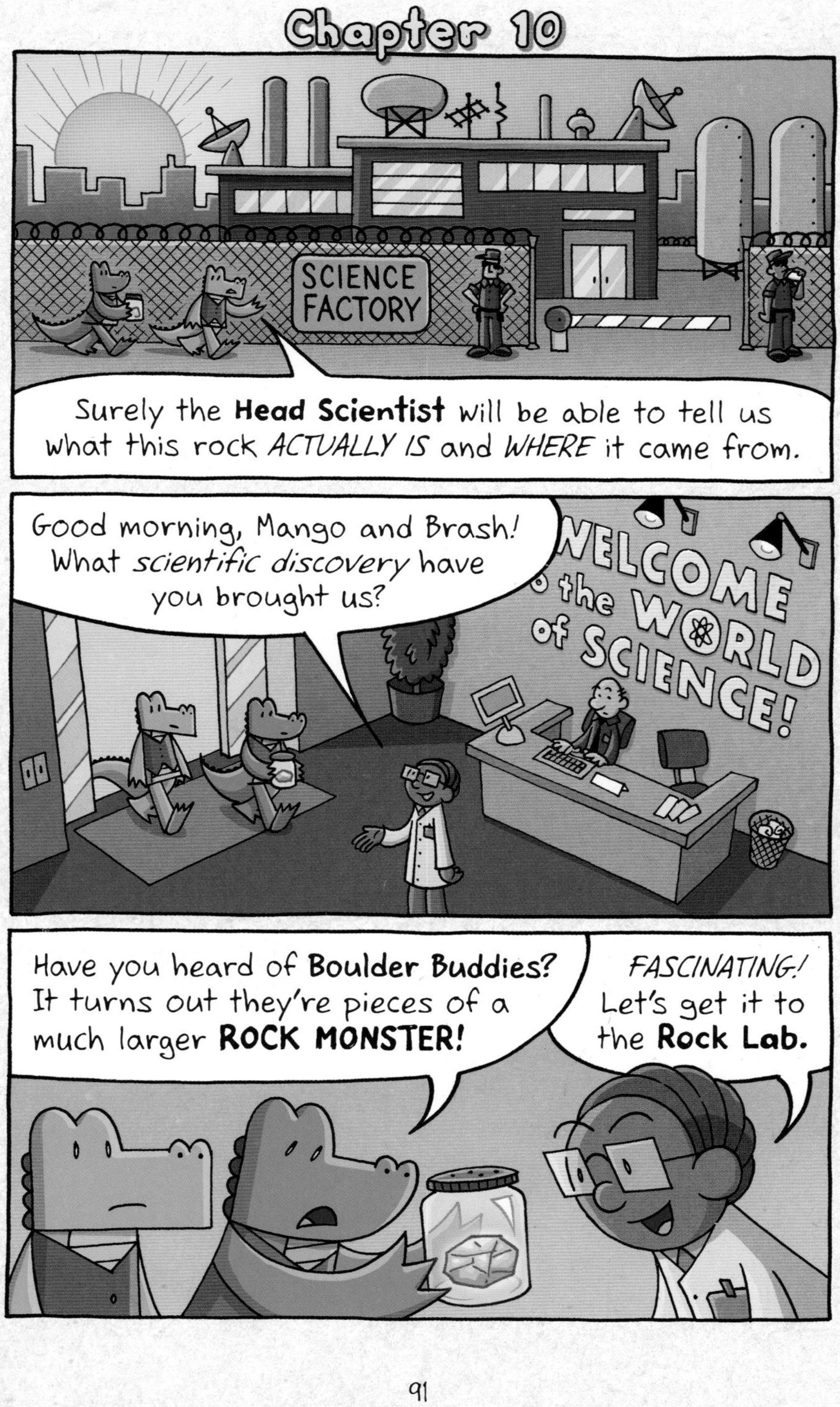

SCIENCE FACTORY
Surely the **Head Scientist** will be able to tell us what this rock *ACTUALLY IS* and *WHERE* it came from.
Good morning, Mango and Brash! What *scientific discovery* have you brought us?
WELCOME
the WORLD
of SCIENCE!
Have you heard of **Boulder Buddies?** It turns out they're pieces of a much larger **ROCK MONSTER!**
FASCINATING! Let's get it to the **Rock Lab.**

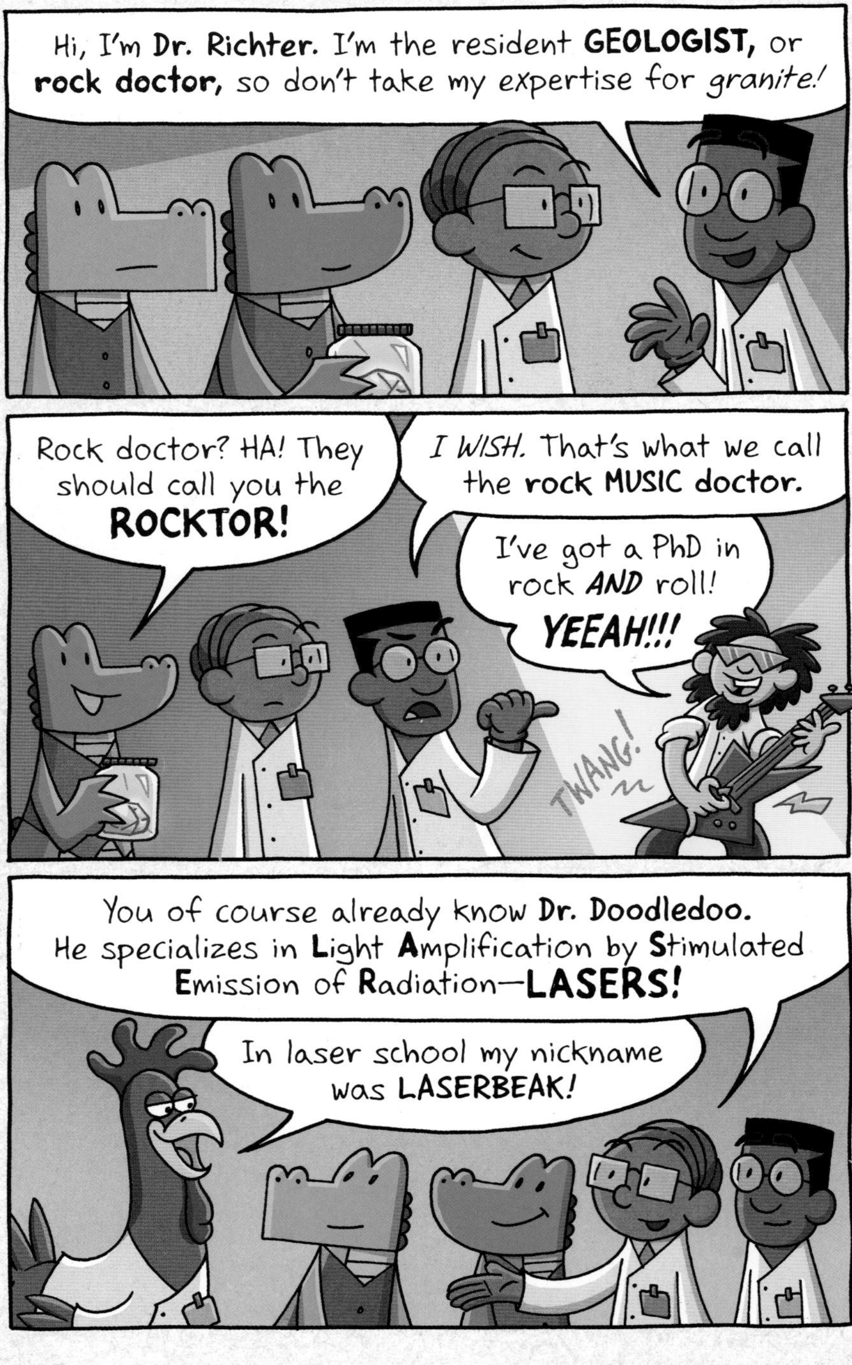
Hi, I'm Dr. Richter. I'm the resident GEOLOGIST, or rock doctor, so don't take my expertise for granite!
Rock doctor? HA! They should call you the ROCKTOR!
I WISH. That's what we call the rock MUSIC doctor.
I've got a PhD in rock AND roll! YEEAH!!!
TWANG!
You of course already know Dr. Doodledoo. He specializes in Light Amplification by Stimulated Emission of Radiation—LASERS!
In laser school my nickname was LASERBEAK!

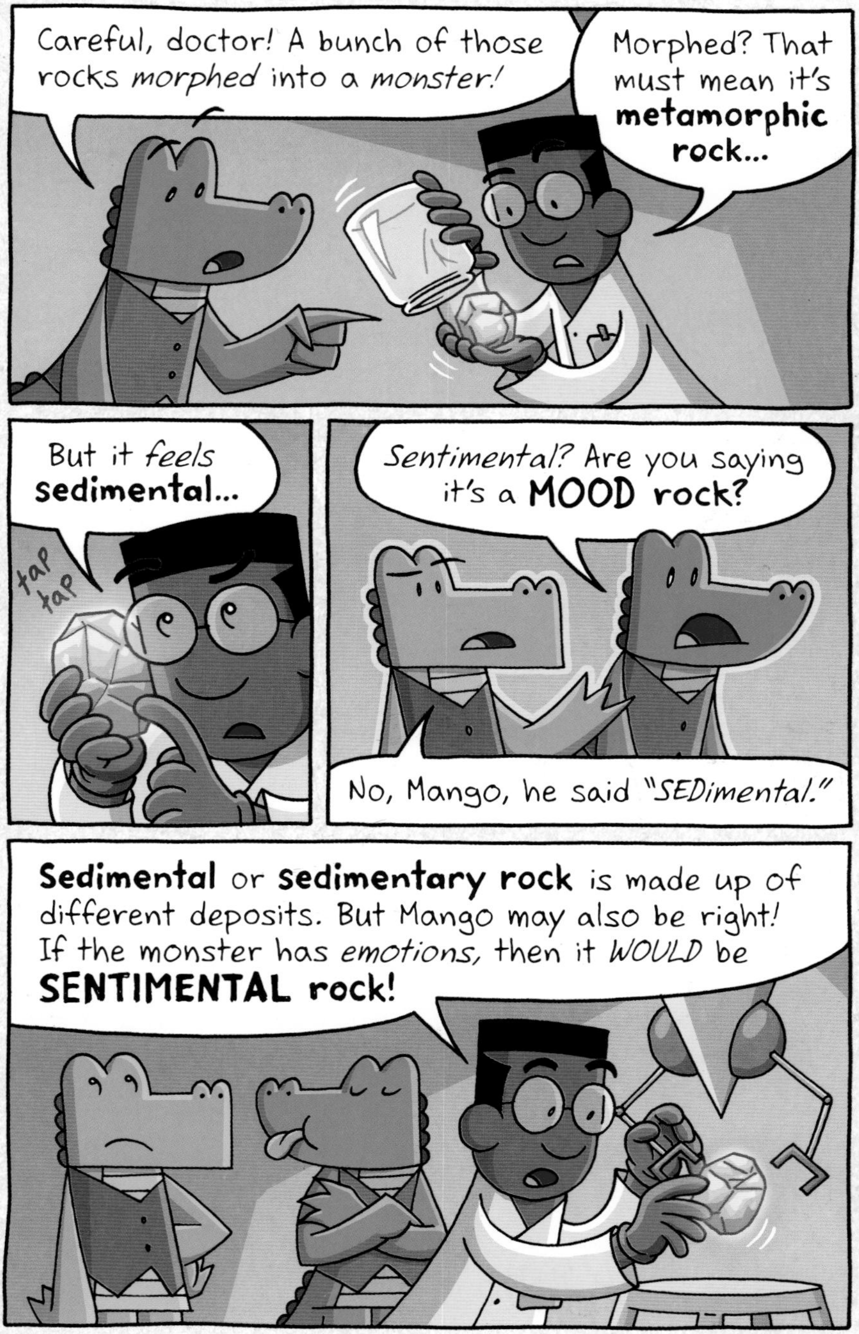
Careful, doctor! A bunch of those rocks *morphed* into a *monster!*
Morphed? That must mean it's **metamorphic rock...**
But it *feels* **sedimental...**
tap tap
Sentimental? Are you saying it's a **MOOD rock?**
No, Mango, he said "*SEDimental.*"
Sedimental or **sedimentary rock** is made up of different deposits. But Mango may also be right! If the monster has *emotions,* then it *WOULD* be **SENTIMENTAL rock!**

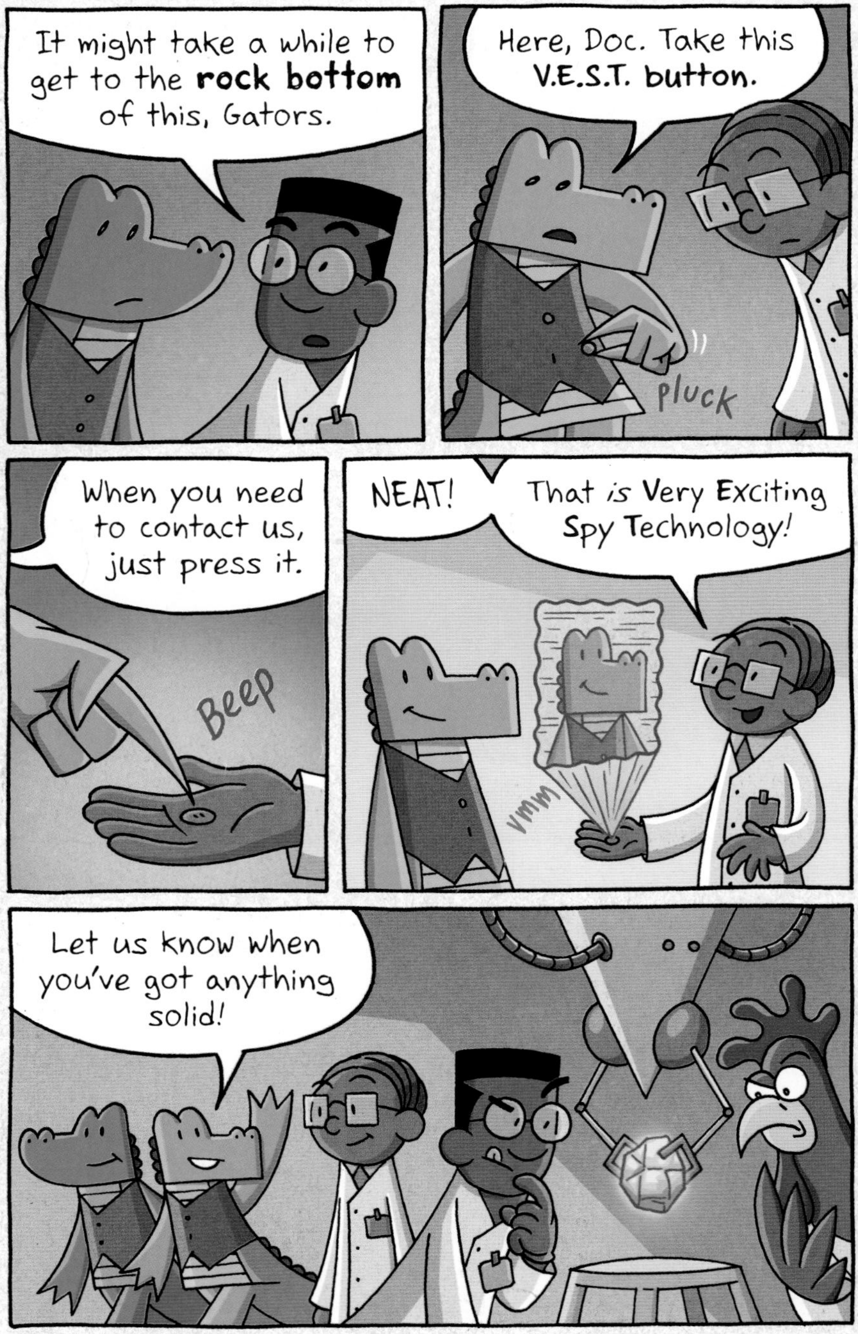
It might take a while to get to the **rock bottom** of this, Gators.
Here, Doc. Take this **V.E.S.T. button.**
pluck
When you need to contact us, just press it.
Beep
NEAT!
That *is* **V**ery **E**xciting **S**py **T**echnology!
vmm
Let us know when you've got anything solid!

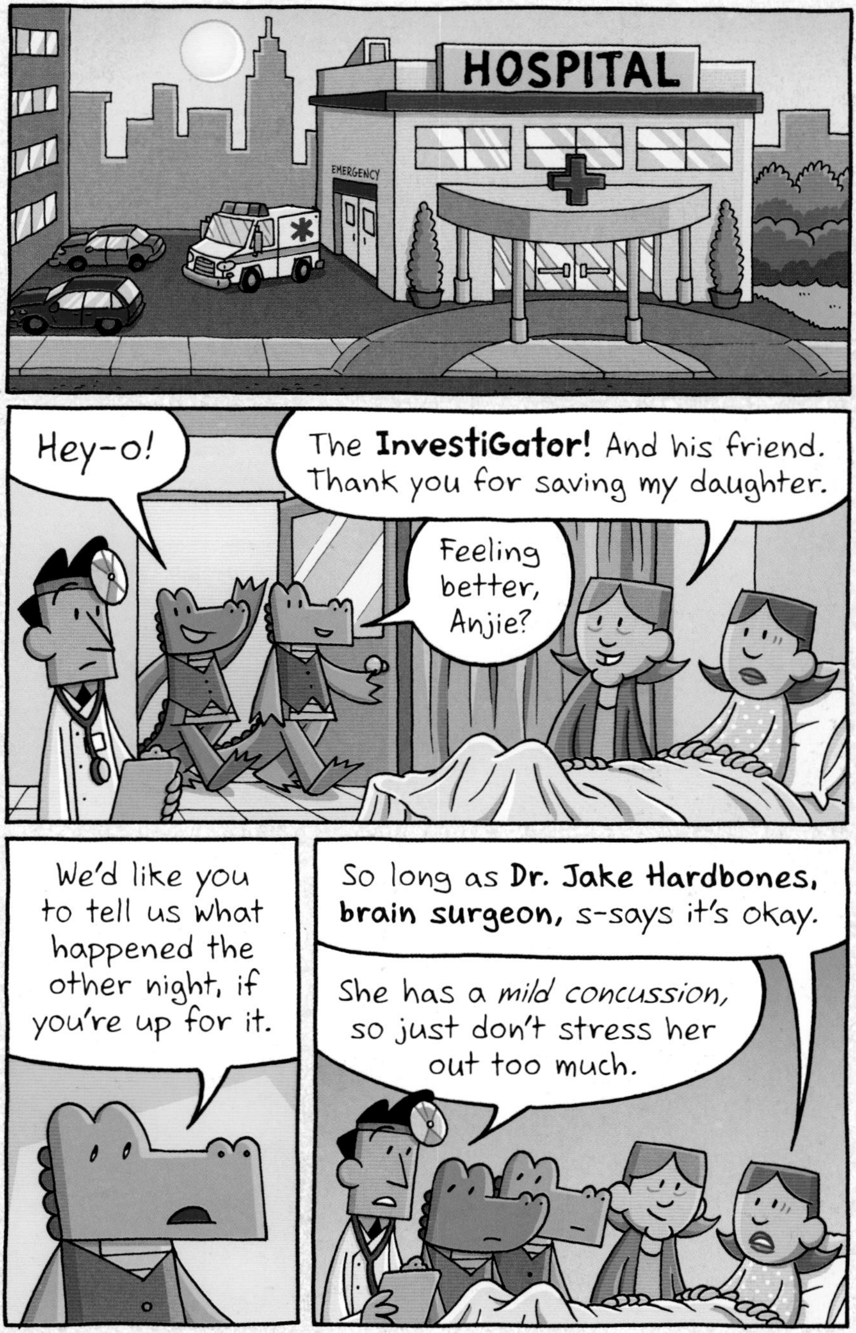
HOSPITAL
EMERGENCY
Hey-o!
The **InvestiGator!** And his friend. Thank you for saving my daughter.
Feeling better, Anjie?
We'd like you to tell us what happened the other night, if you're up for it.
So long as **Dr. Jake Hardbones, brain surgeon,** s-says it's okay.
She has a *mild concussion,* so just don't stress her out too much.

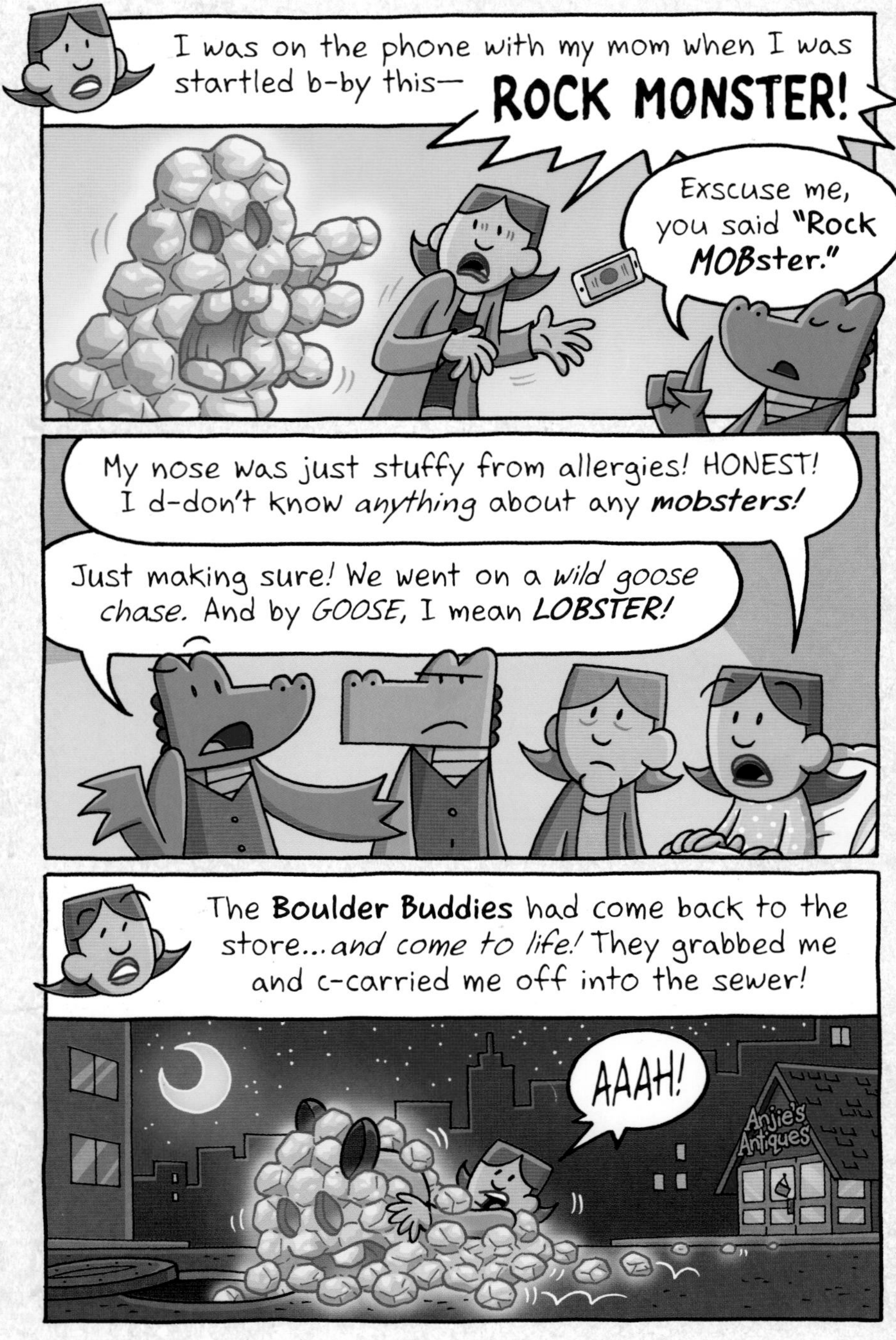
I was on the phone with my mom when I was startled b-by this—
ROCK MONSTER!
Exscuse me, you said "Rock MOBster."
My nose was just stuffy from allergies! HONEST! I d-don't know *anything* about any ***mobsters!***
Just making sure! We went on a *wild goose chase.* And by *GOOSE*, I mean ***LOBSTER!***
The **Boulder Buddies** had come back to the store... *and come to life!* They grabbed me and c-carried me off into the sewer!
AAAH!
Anjie's Antiques

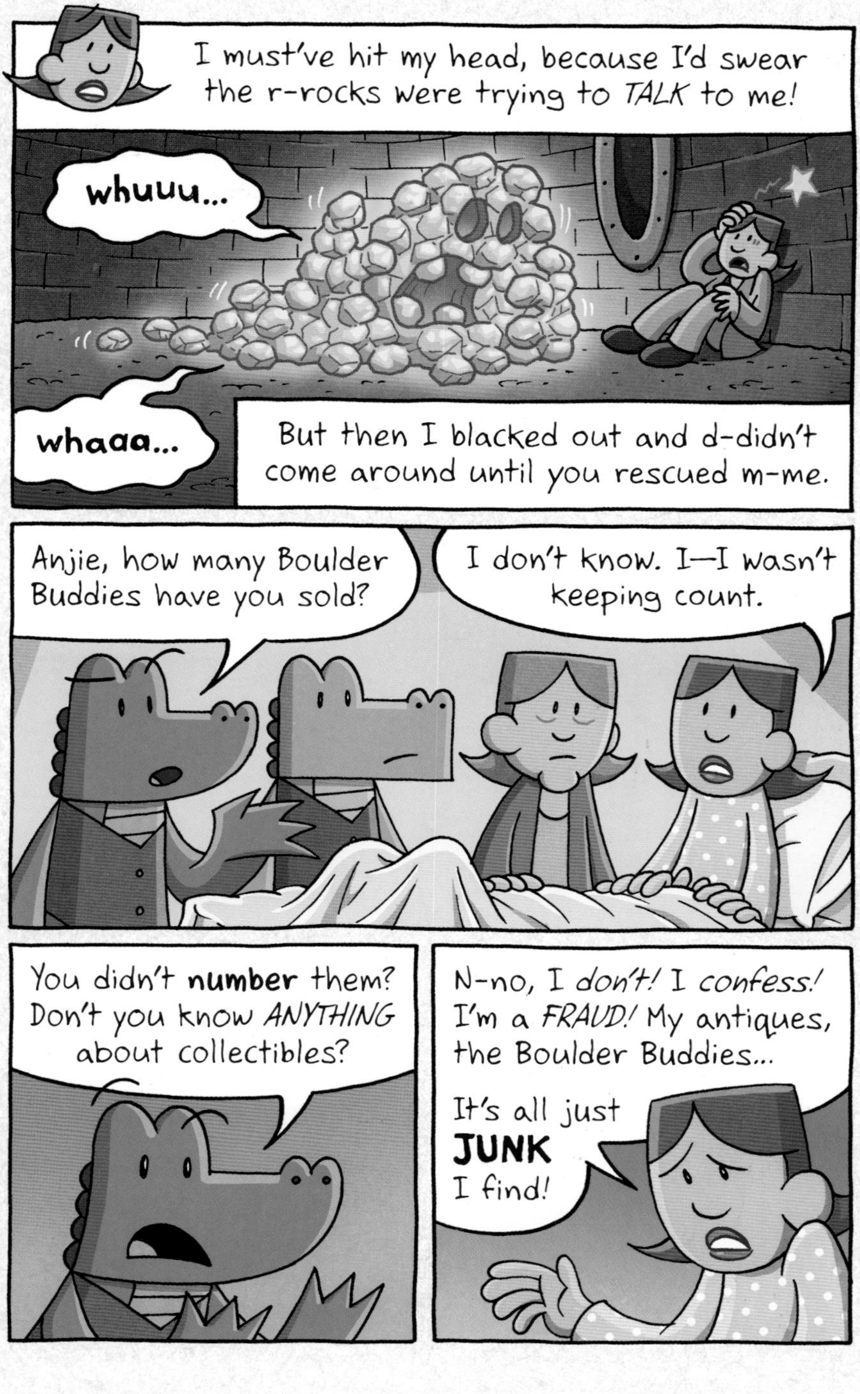
I must've hit my head, because I'd swear the r-rocks were trying to *TALK* to me!
whuuu...
whaaa...
But then I blacked out and d-didn't come around until you rescued m-me.
Anjie, how many Boulder Buddies have you sold?
I don't know. I—I wasn't keeping count.
You didn't **number** them? Don't you know *ANYTHING* about collectibles?
N-no, I *don't!* I *confess!* I'm a *FRAUD!* My antiques, the Boulder Buddies...
It's all just **JUNK** I find!

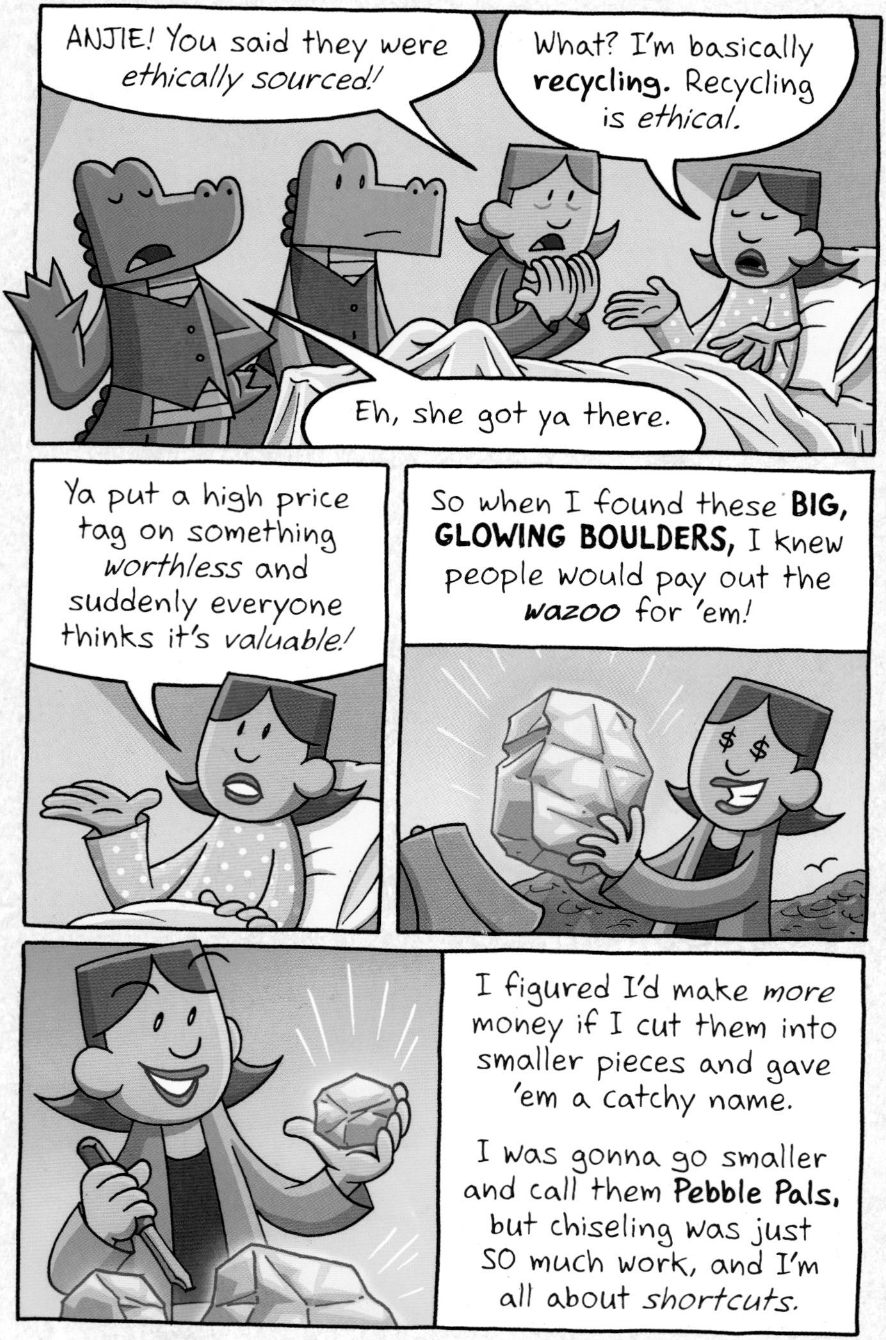
ANJIE! You said they were *ethically sourced!*
What? I'm basically **recycling.** Recycling is *ethical.*
Eh, she got ya there.
Ya put a high price tag on something *worthless* and suddenly everyone thinks it's *valuable!*
So when I found these **BIG, GLOWING BOULDERS,** I knew people would pay out the ***wazoo*** for 'em!
I figured I'd make *more* money if I cut them into smaller pieces and gave 'em a catchy name.
I was gonna go smaller and call them **Pebble Pals,** but chiseling was just SO much work, and I'm all about *shortcuts.*

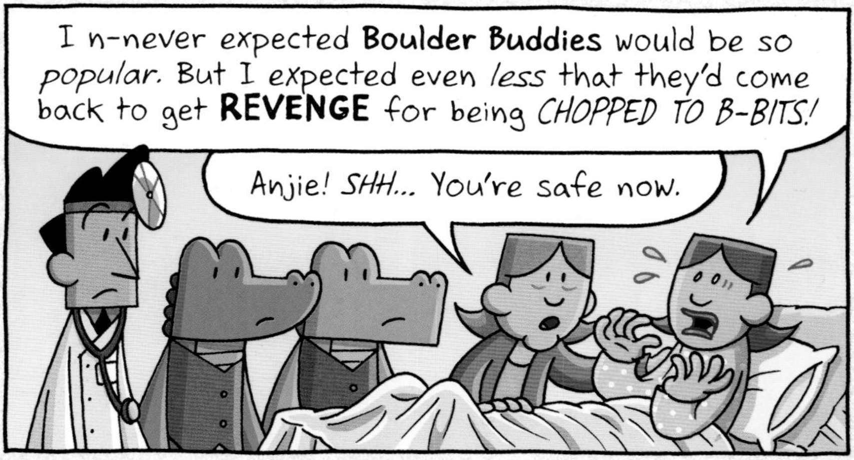
I n-never expected **Boulder Buddies** would be so *popular.* But I expected even *less* that they'd come back to get **REVENGE** for being *CHOPPED TO B-BITS!*
Anjie! *SHH...* You're safe now.

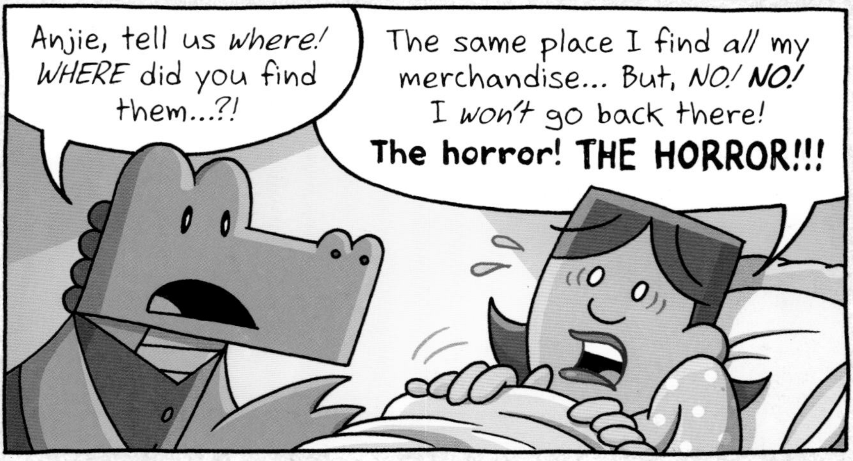
Anjie, tell us *where!* *WHERE* did you find them...?!
The same place I find *all* my merchandise... But, *NO!* ***NO!*** I *won't* go back there! **The horror! THE HORROR!!!**

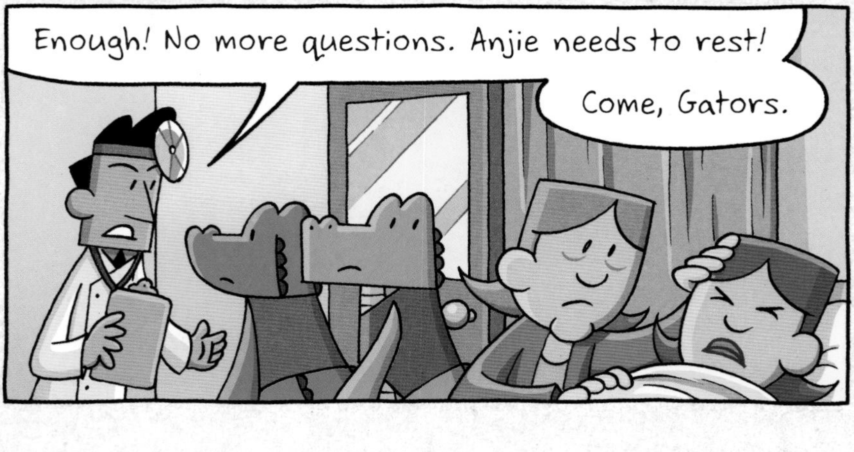
Enough! No more questions. Anjie needs to rest!
Come, Gators.

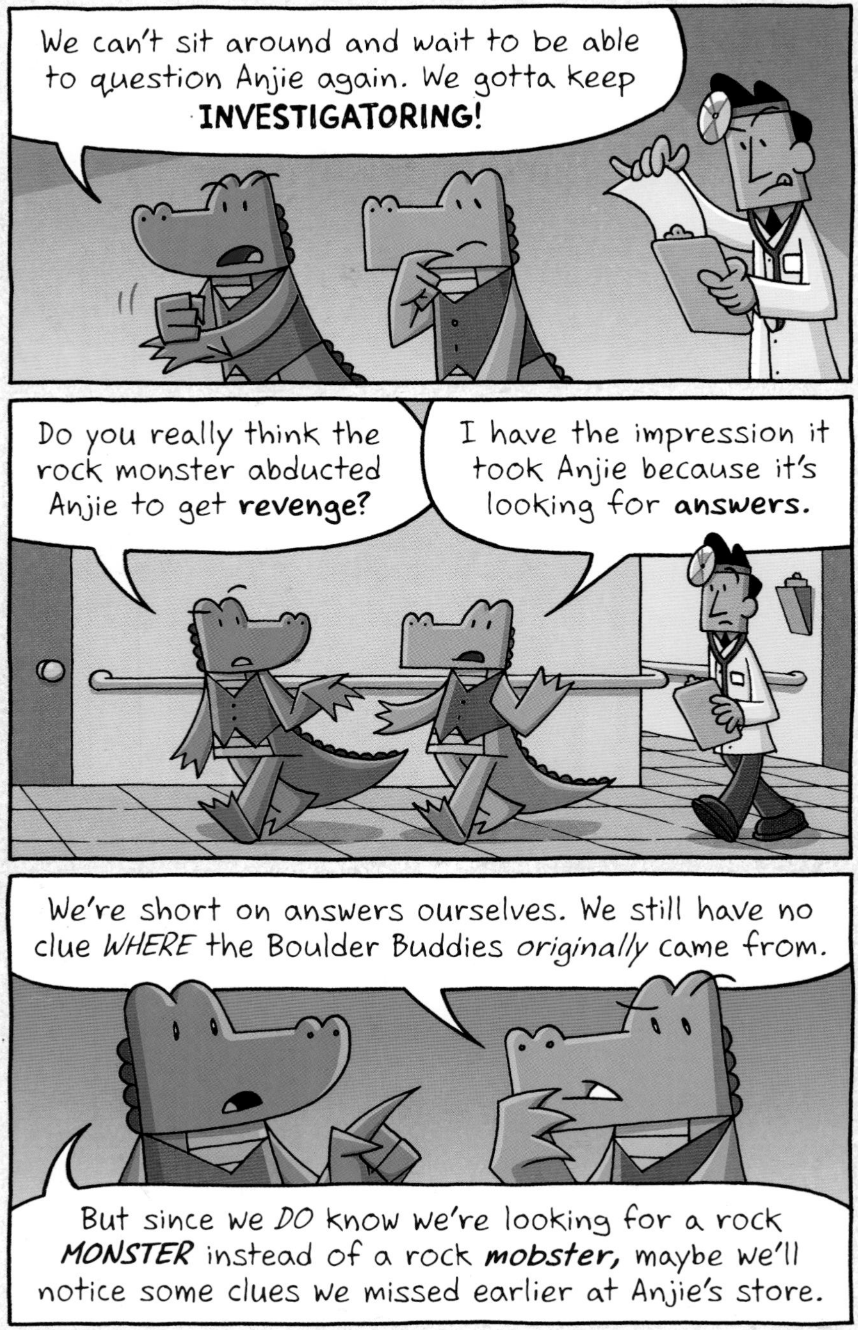
We can't sit around and wait to be able to question Anjie again. We gotta keep **INVESTIGATORING!**
Do you really think the rock monster abducted Anjie to get **revenge?**
I have the impression it took Anjie because it's looking for **answers.**
We're short on answers ourselves. We still have no clue *WHERE* the Boulder Buddies *originally* came from.
But since we *DO* know we're looking for a rock ***MONSTER*** instead of a rock ***mobster,*** maybe we'll notice some clues we missed earlier at Anjie's store.

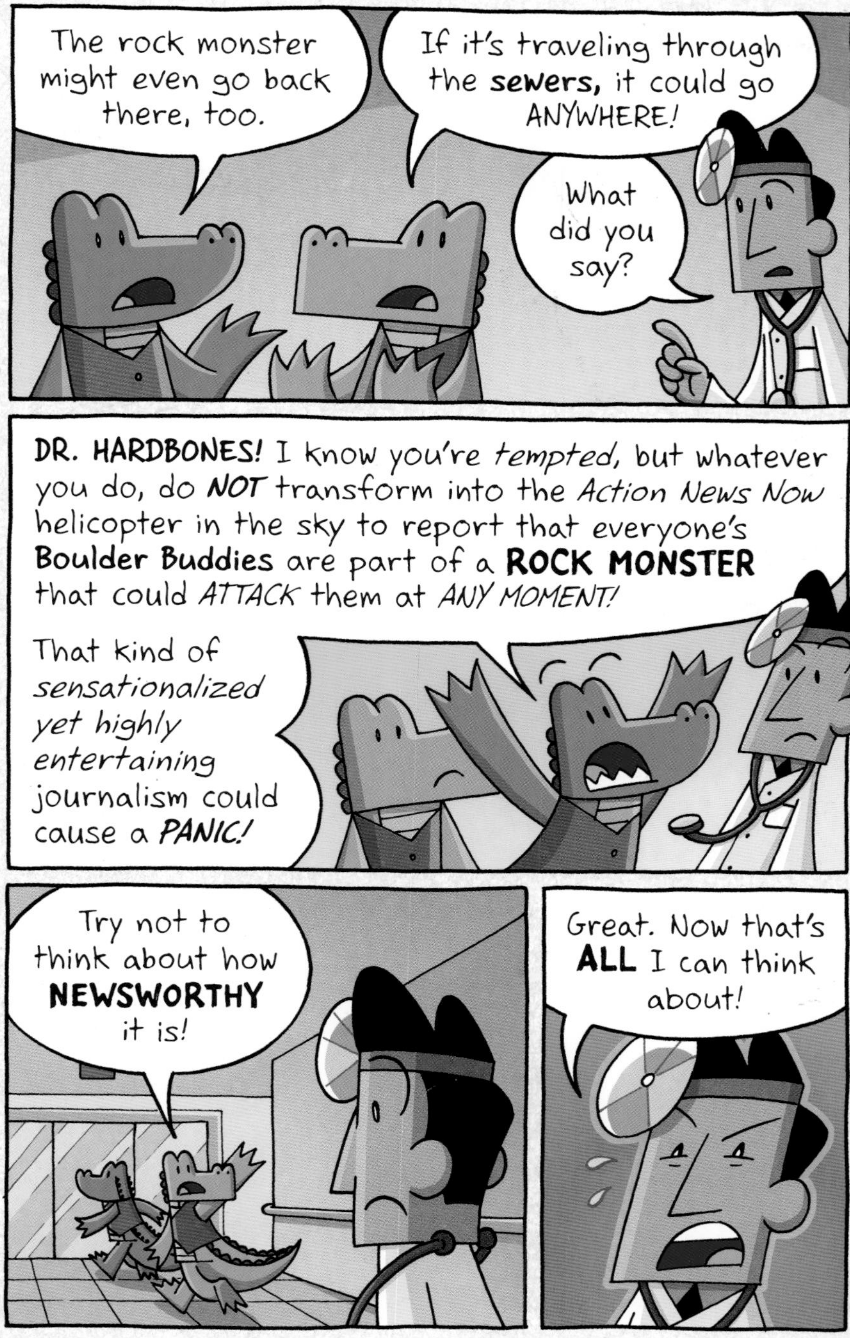
The rock monster might even go back there, too.
If it's traveling through the **sewers,** it could go ANYWHERE!
What did you say?
DR. HARDBONES! I know you're *tempted*, but whatever you do, do ***NOT*** transform into the *Action News Now* helicopter in the sky to report that everyone's **Boulder Buddies** are part of a **ROCK MONSTER** that could *ATTACK* them at *ANY MOMENT!*
That kind of *sensationalized yet highly entertaining* journalism could cause a *PANIC!*
Try not to think about how **NEWSWORTHY** it is!
Great. Now that's **ALL** I can think about!

Chapter 11

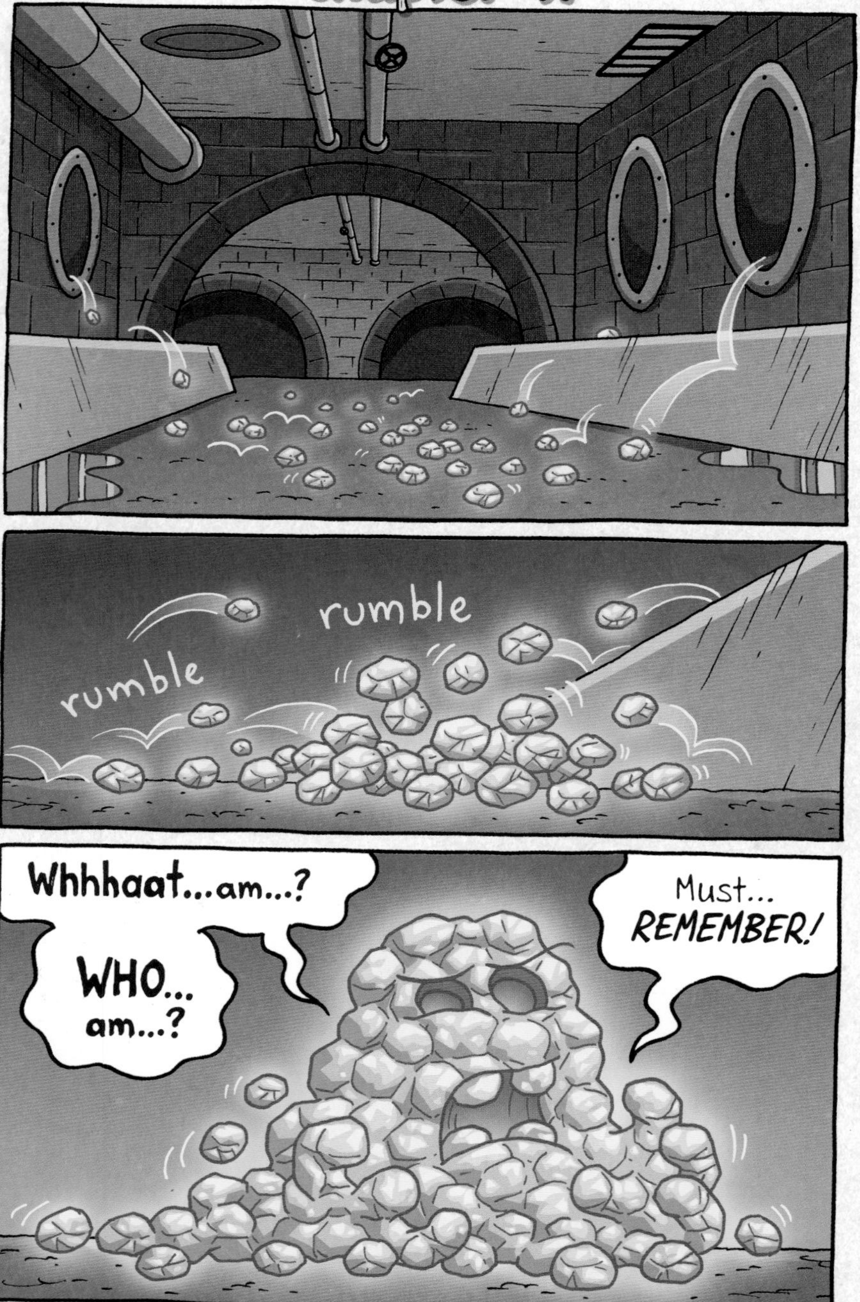

rumble
rumble
Whhhaat...am...?
WHO... am...?
Must... REMEMBER!

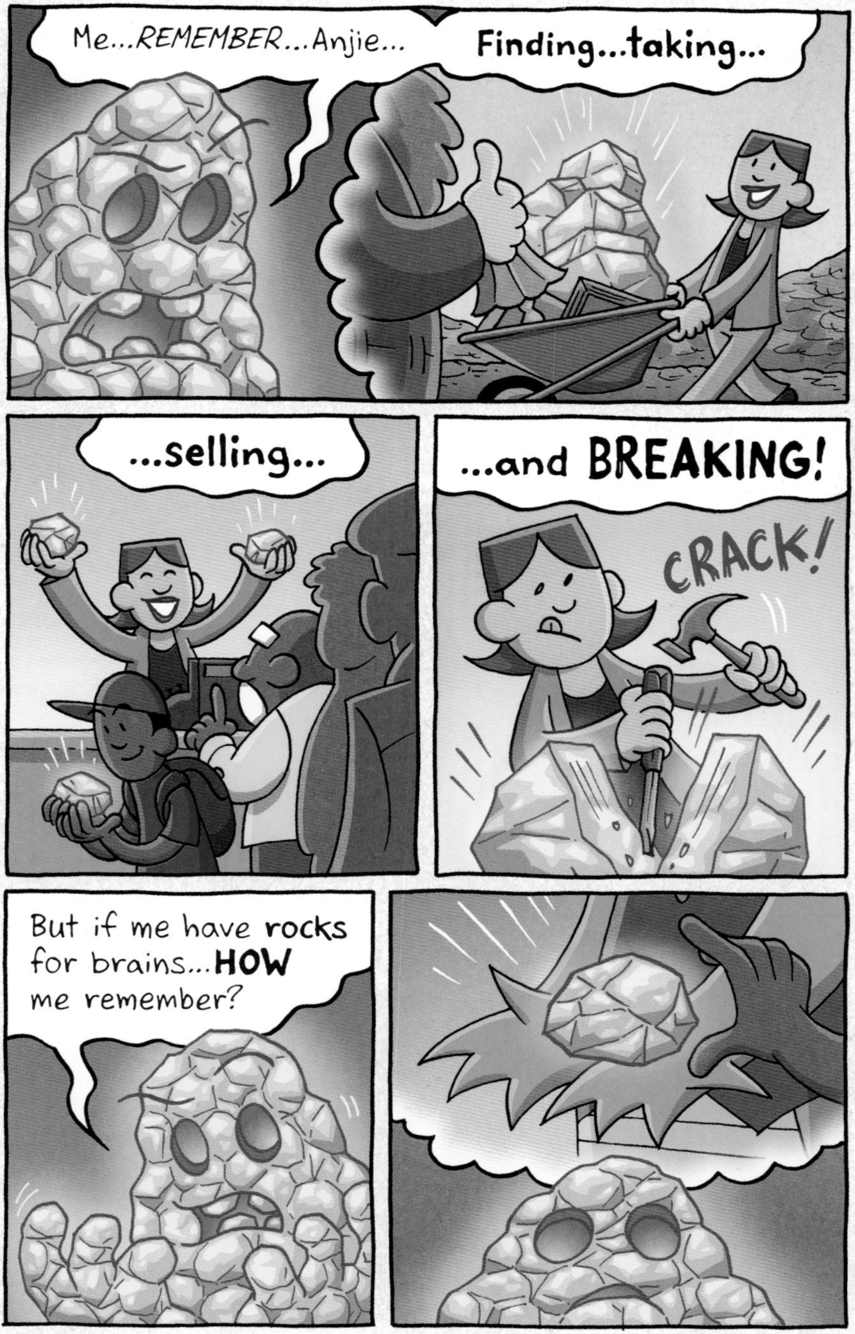
Me...*REMEMBER*...Anjie...
Finding...taking...
...selling...
...and BREAKING!
CRACK!
But if me have **rocks** for brains...**HOW** me remember?

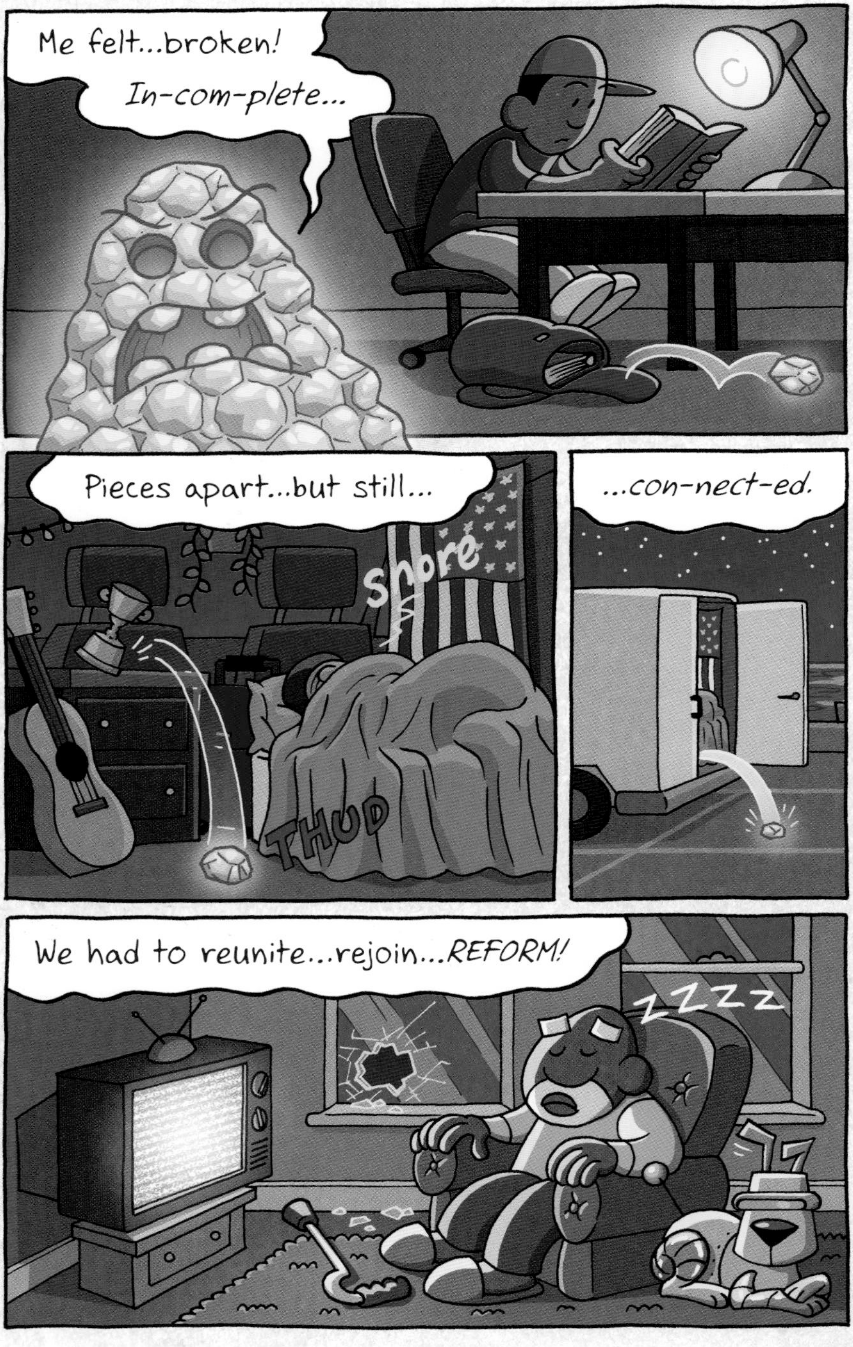
Me felt...broken!
In-com-plete...
Pieces apart...but still...
SNORE
THUD
...con-nect-ed.
We had to reunite...rejoin...REFORM!
ZZZZ

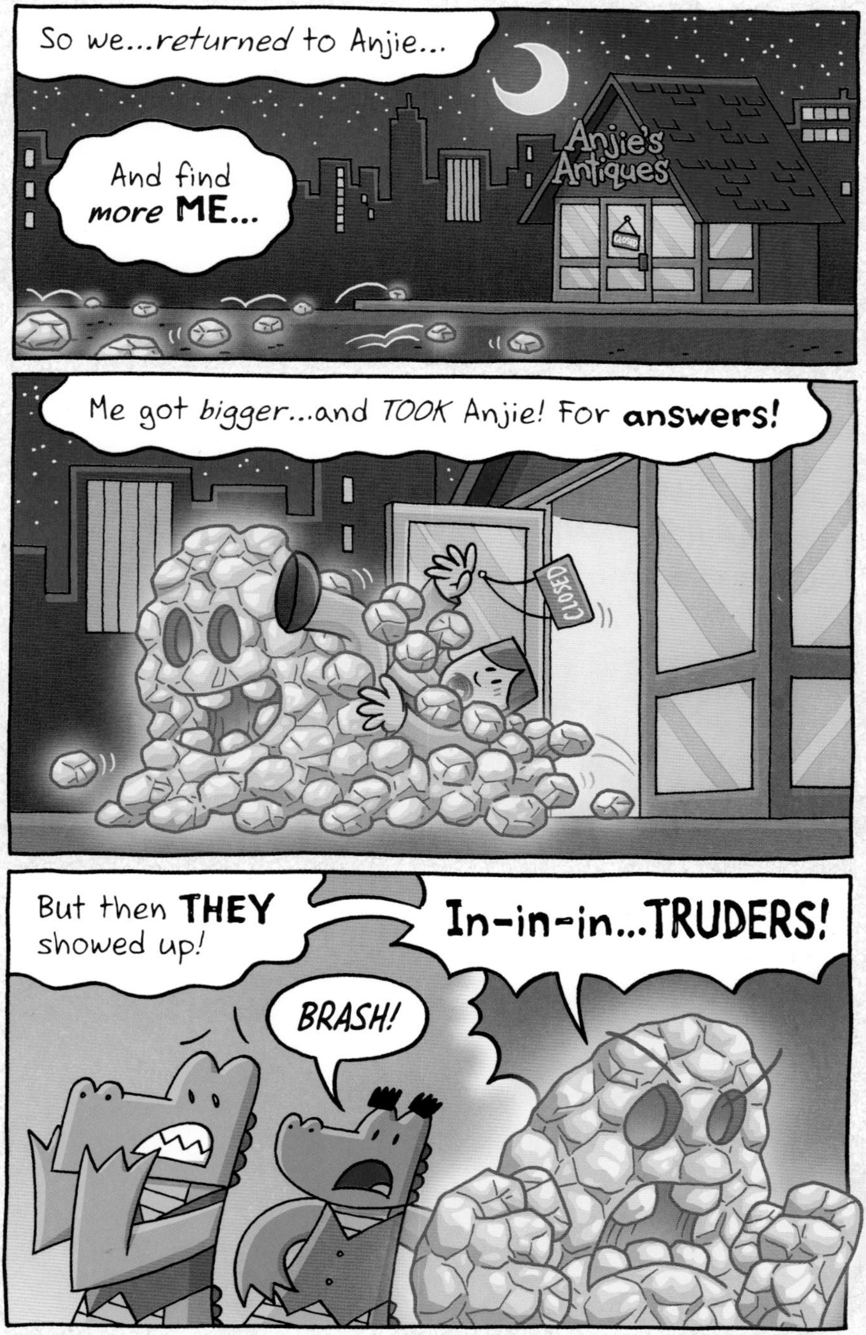
So we...returned to Anjie...
And find more ME...
Anjie's Antiques
CLOSED
Me got bigger...and TOOK Anjie! For answers!
CLOSED
But then THEY showed up!
In-in-in...TRUDERS!
BRASH!

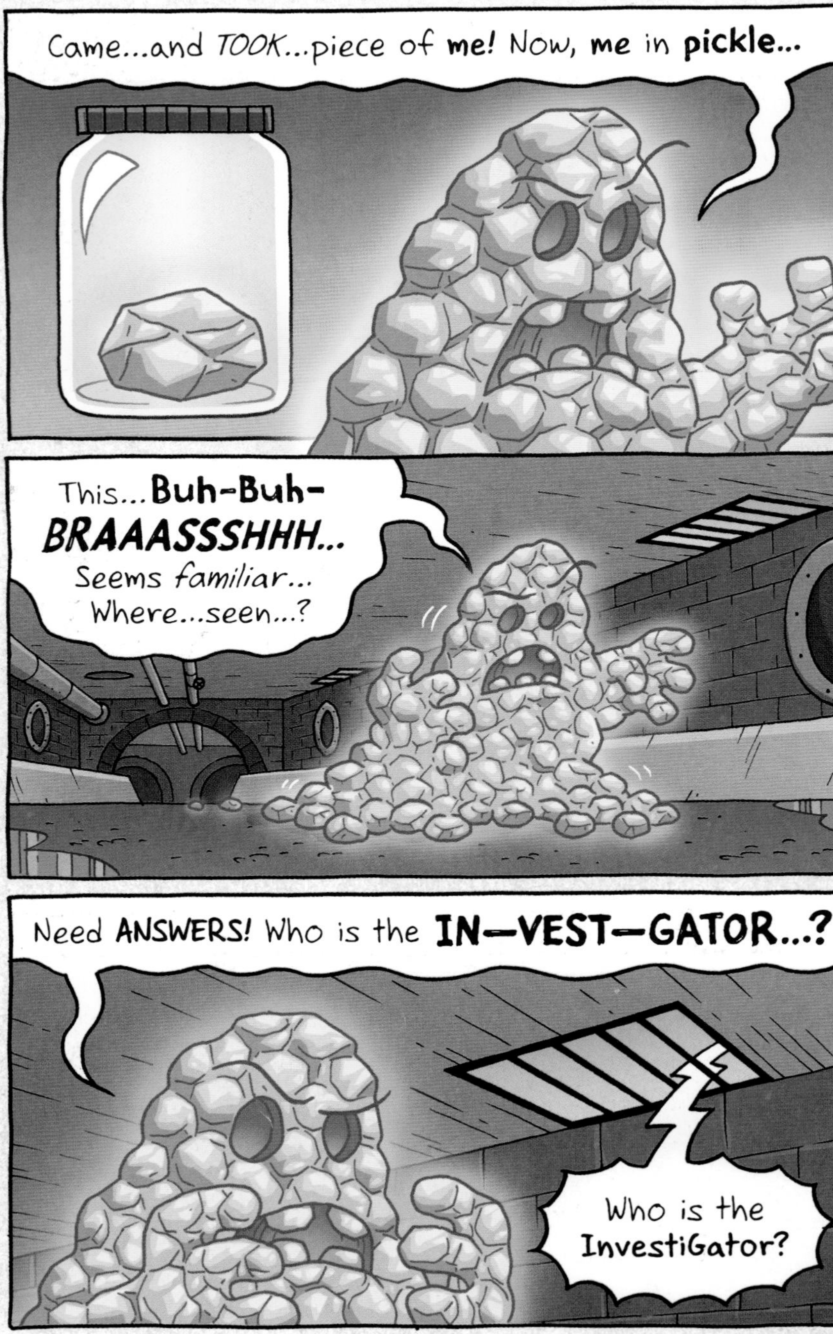
Came...and TOOK...piece of **me!** Now, **me** in **pickle...**
This...**Buh-Buh-**
BRAAASSSHHH...
Seems familiar...
Where...seen...?
Need **ANSWERS!** Who is the **IN—VEST—GATOR...?**
Who is the
InvestiGator?

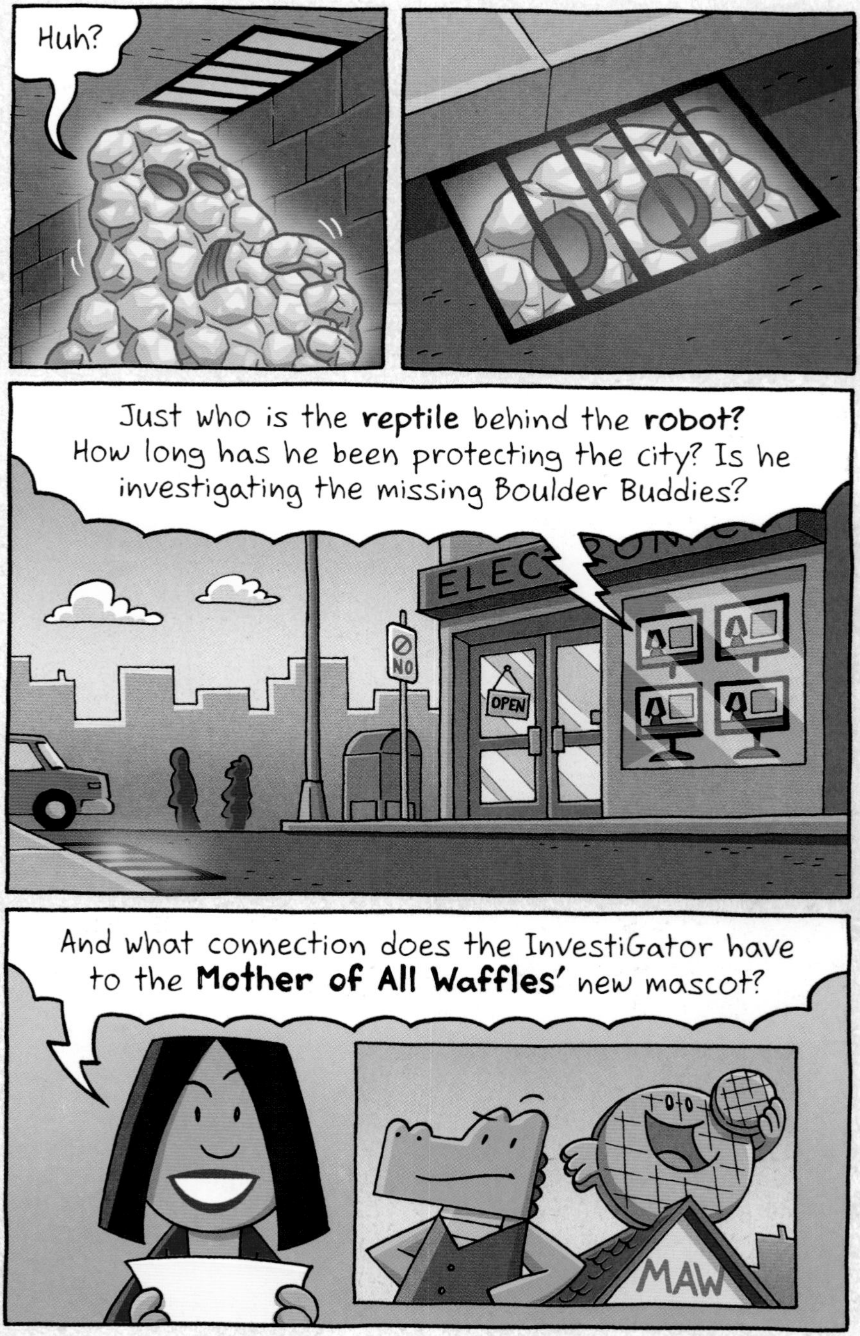
Huh?
Just who is the **reptile** behind the **robot?** How long has he been protecting the city? Is he investigating the missing Boulder Buddies?
ELEC
NO
OPEN
And what connection does the InvestiGator have to the **Mother of All Waffles'** new mascot?
MAW

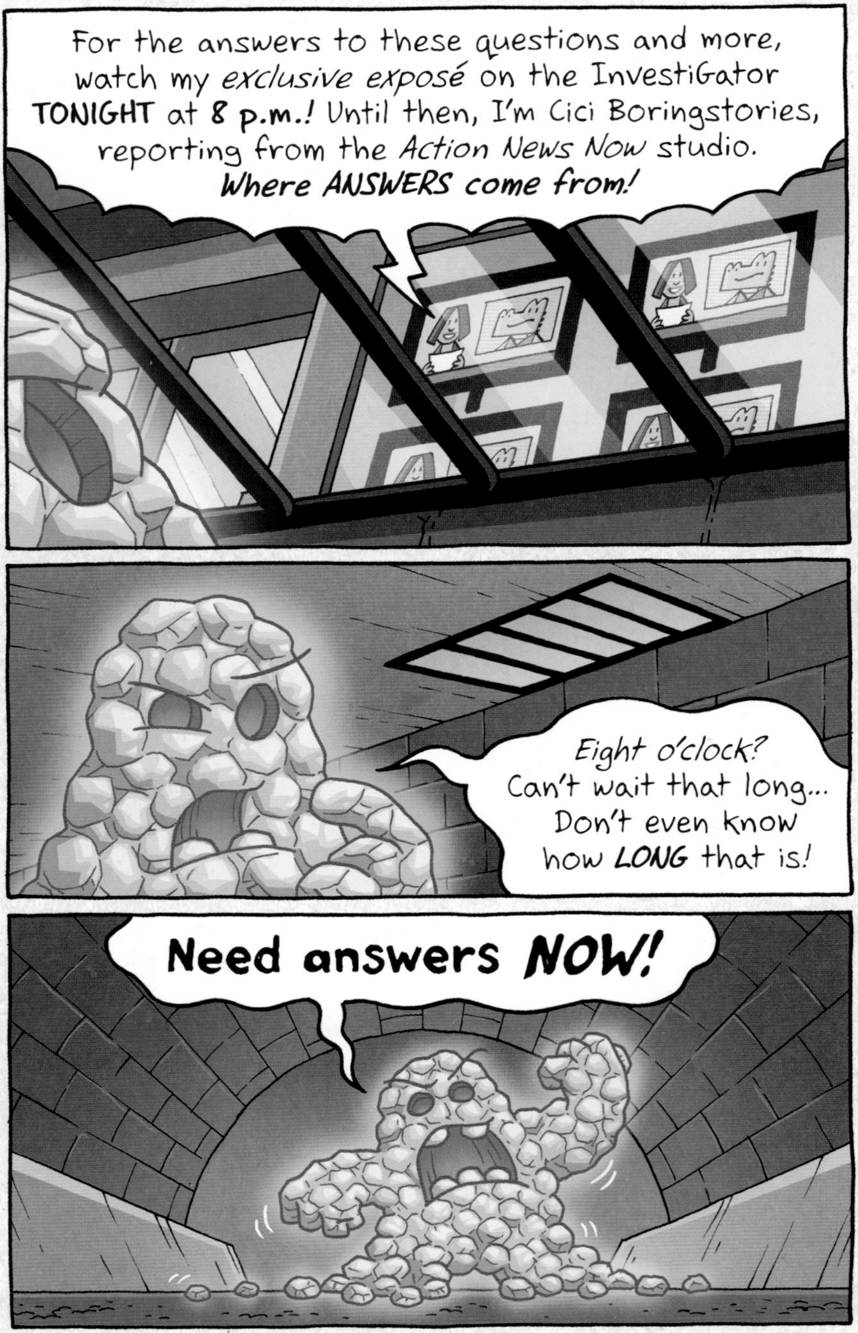
For the answers to these questions and more, watch my *exclusive exposé* on the InvestiGator **TONIGHT** at **8 p.m.**! Until then, I'm Cici Boringstories, reporting from the *Action News Now* studio. ***Where ANSWERS come from!***
Eight o'clock? Can't wait that long... Don't even know how ***LONG*** that is!
Need answers *NOW!*

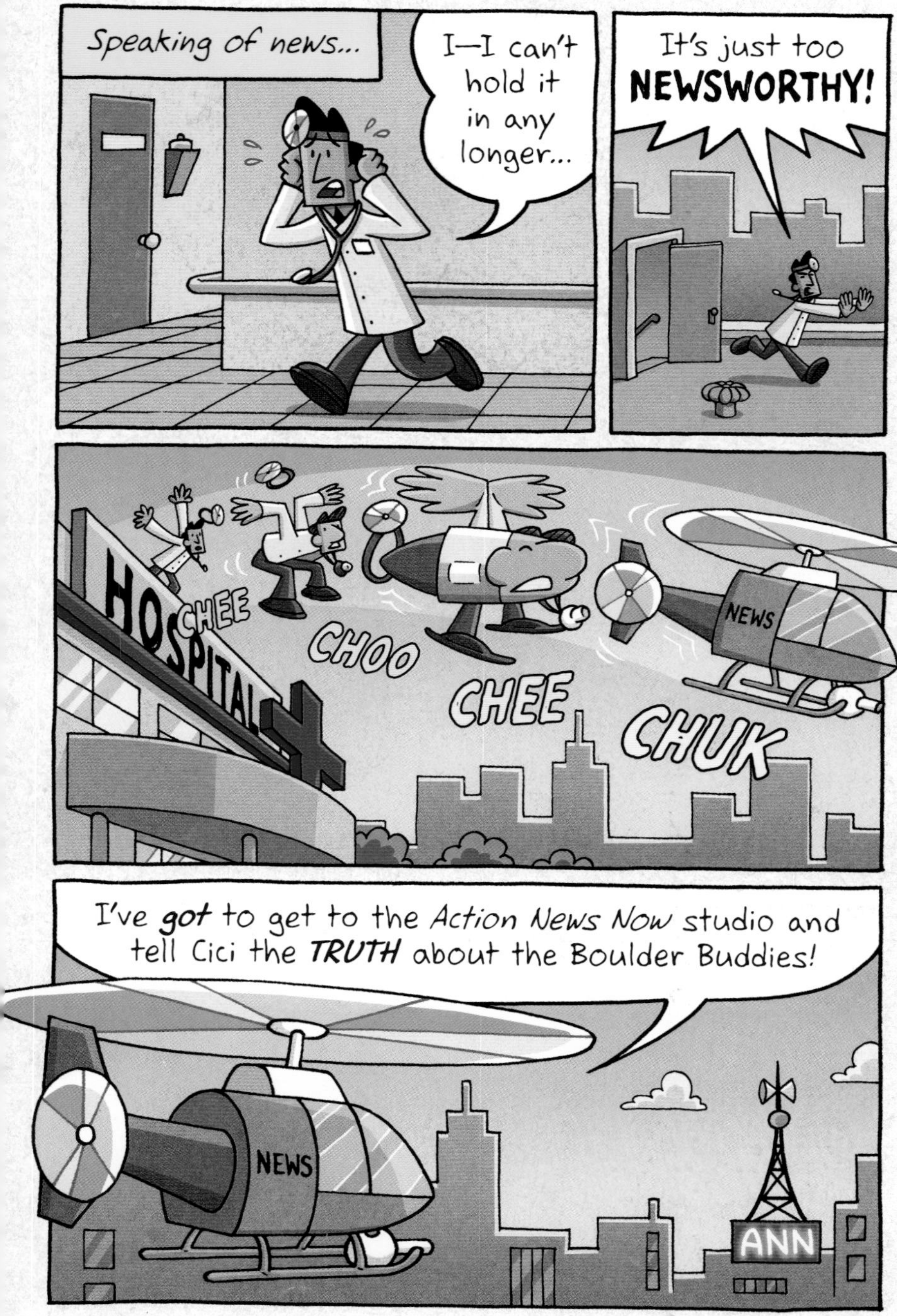
Speaking of news...
I—I can't hold it in any longer...
It's just too NEWSWORTHY!
HOSPITAL
CHEE
CHOO
CHEE
CHUK
NEWS
I've *got* to get to the *Action News Now* studio and tell Cici the ***TRUTH*** about the Boulder Buddies!
NEWS
ANN

Chapter 12

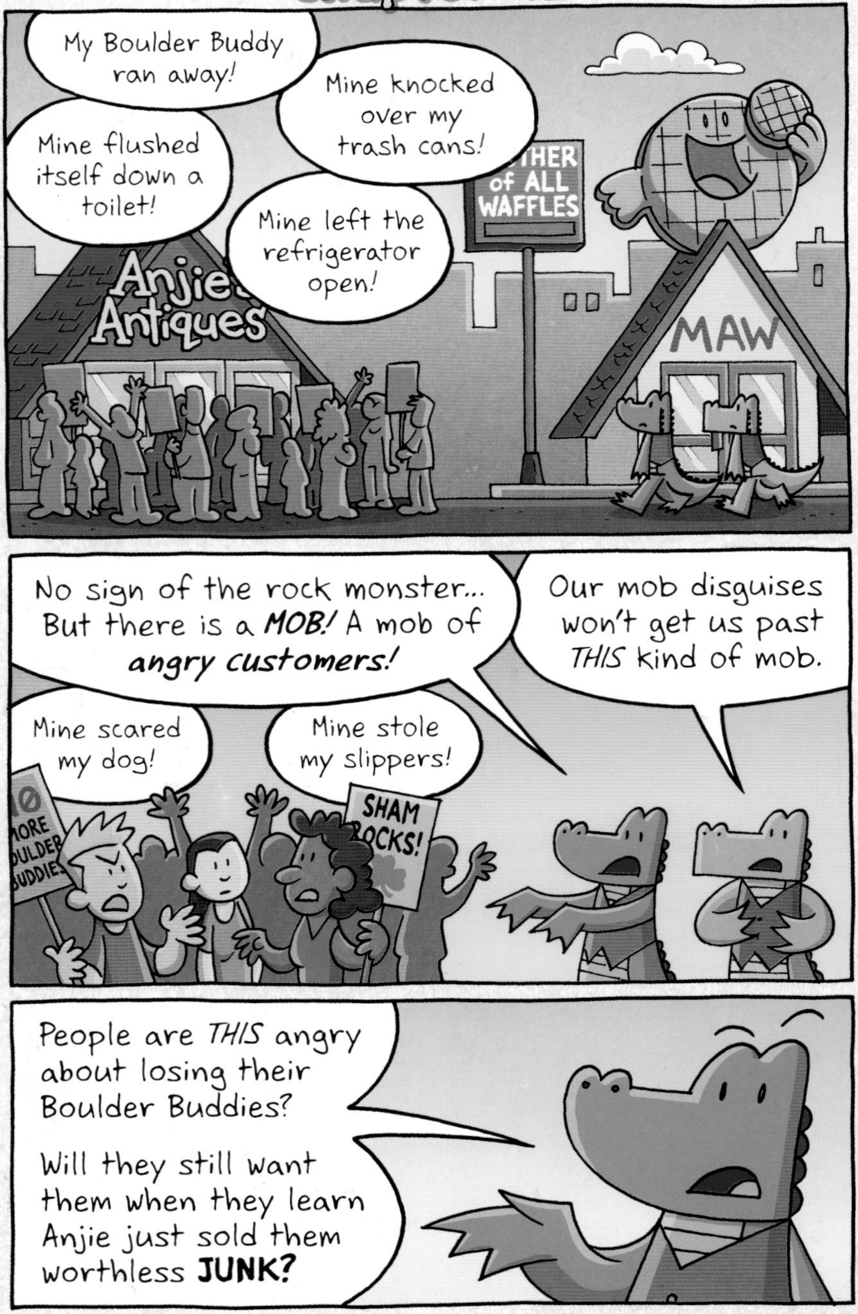

My Boulder Buddy ran away!
Mine knocked over my trash cans!
Mine flushed itself down a toilet!
Mine left the refrigerator open!
OTHER of ALL WAFFLES
Anjie's Antiques
MAW
No sign of the rock monster... But there is a *MOB!* A mob of **angry customers!**
Our mob disguises won't get us past *THIS* kind of mob.
Mine scared my dog!
Mine stole my slippers!
NO MORE BOULDER BUDDIES
SHAM ROCKS!
People are *THIS* angry about losing their Boulder Buddies?
Will they still want them when they learn Anjie just sold them worthless **JUNK?**

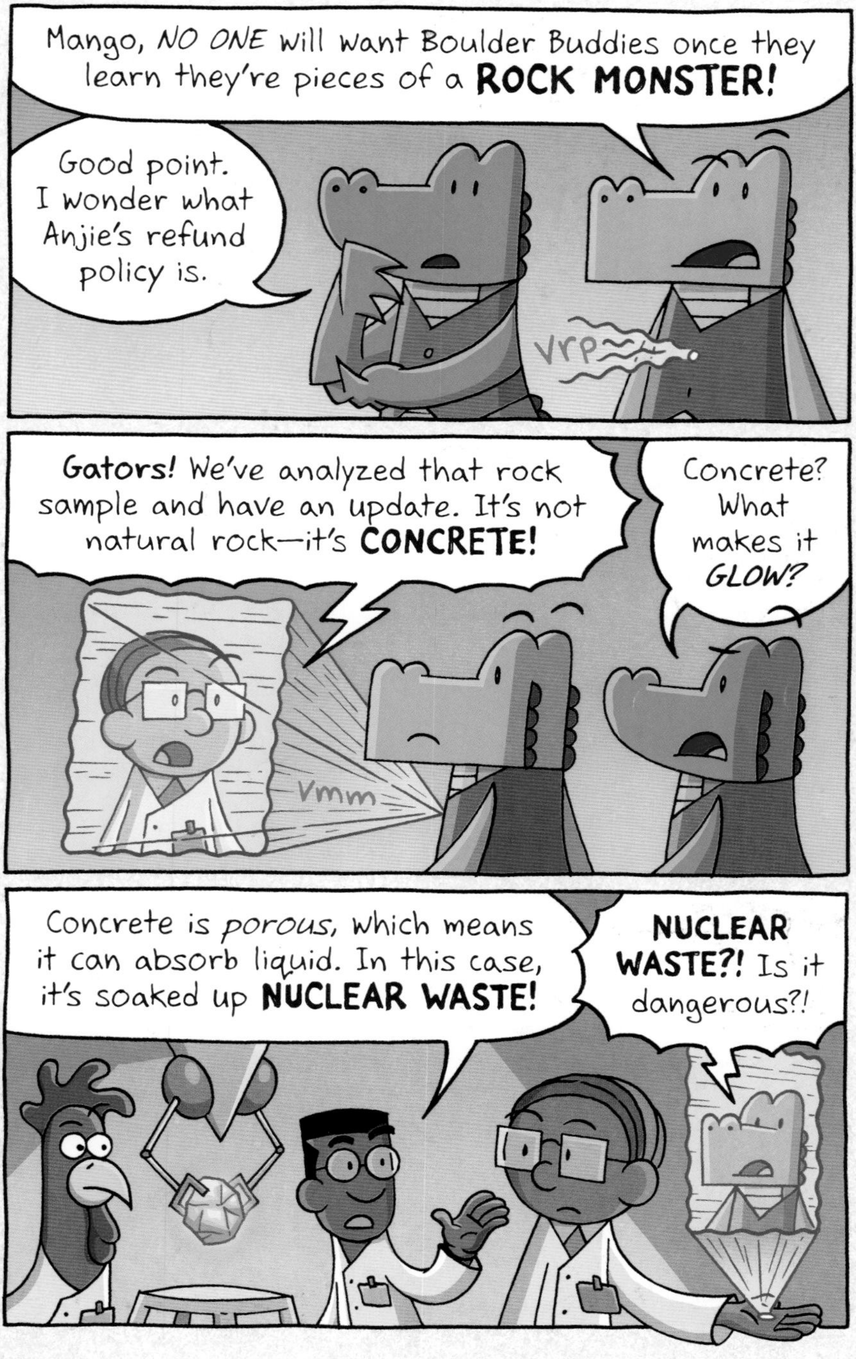
Mango, *NO ONE* will want Boulder Buddies once they learn they're pieces of a **ROCK MONSTER!**
Good point. I wonder what Anjie's refund policy is.
VRP
Gators! We've analyzed that rock sample and have an update. It's not natural rock—it's **CONCRETE!**
Concrete? What makes it *GLOW?*
VMM
Concrete is *porous,* which means it can absorb liquid. In this case, it's soaked up **NUCLEAR WASTE!**
NUCLEAR WASTE?! Is it dangerous?!

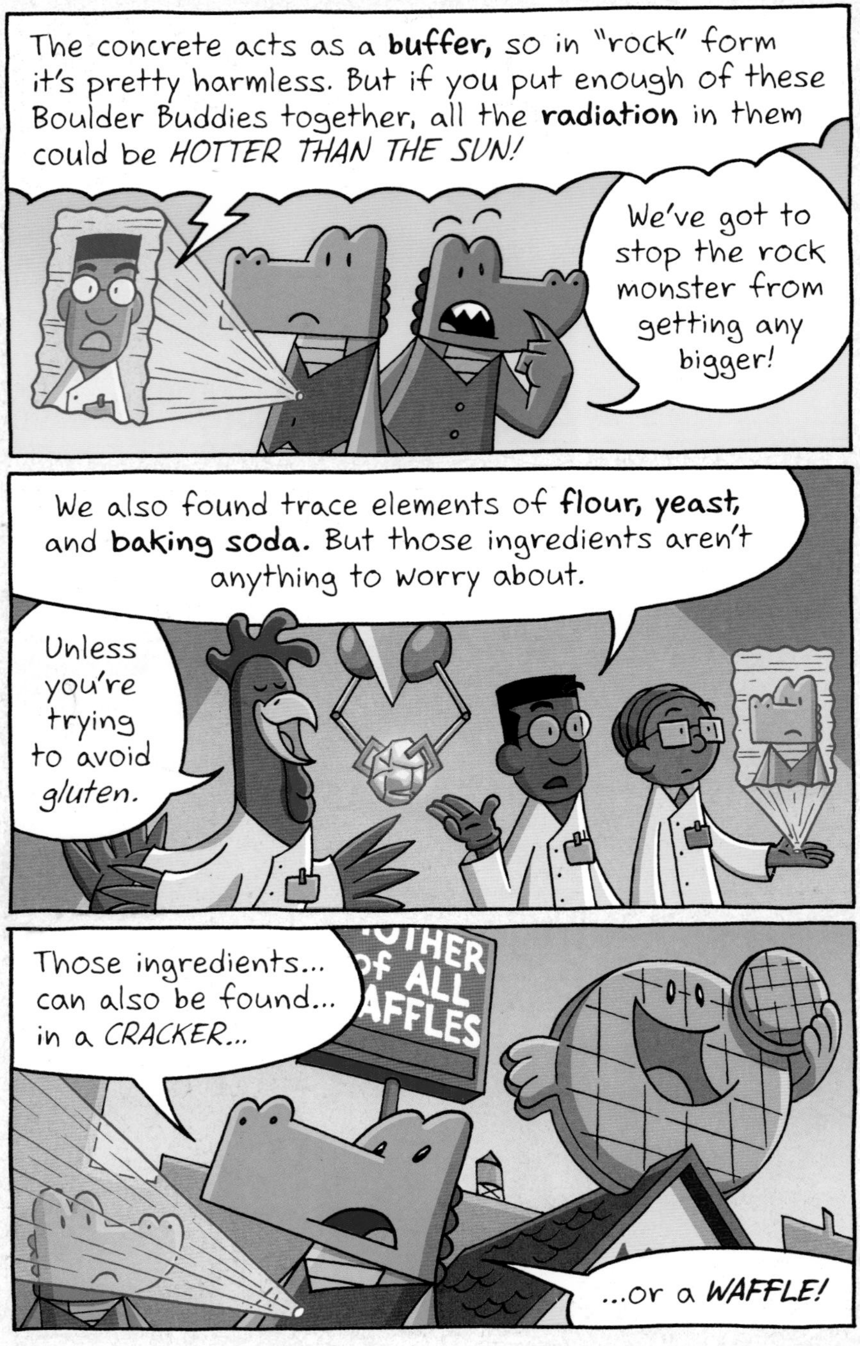
The concrete acts as a **buffer,** so in "rock" form it's pretty harmless. But if you put enough of these Boulder Buddies together, all the **radiation** in them could be *HOTTER THAN THE SUN!*
We've got to stop the rock monster from getting any bigger!
We also found trace elements of **flour, yeast,** and **baking soda.** But those ingredients aren't anything to worry about.
Unless you're trying to avoid *gluten.*
Those ingredients... can also be found... in a *CRACKER*...
OTHER OF ALL AFFLES
...or a ***WAFFLE!***

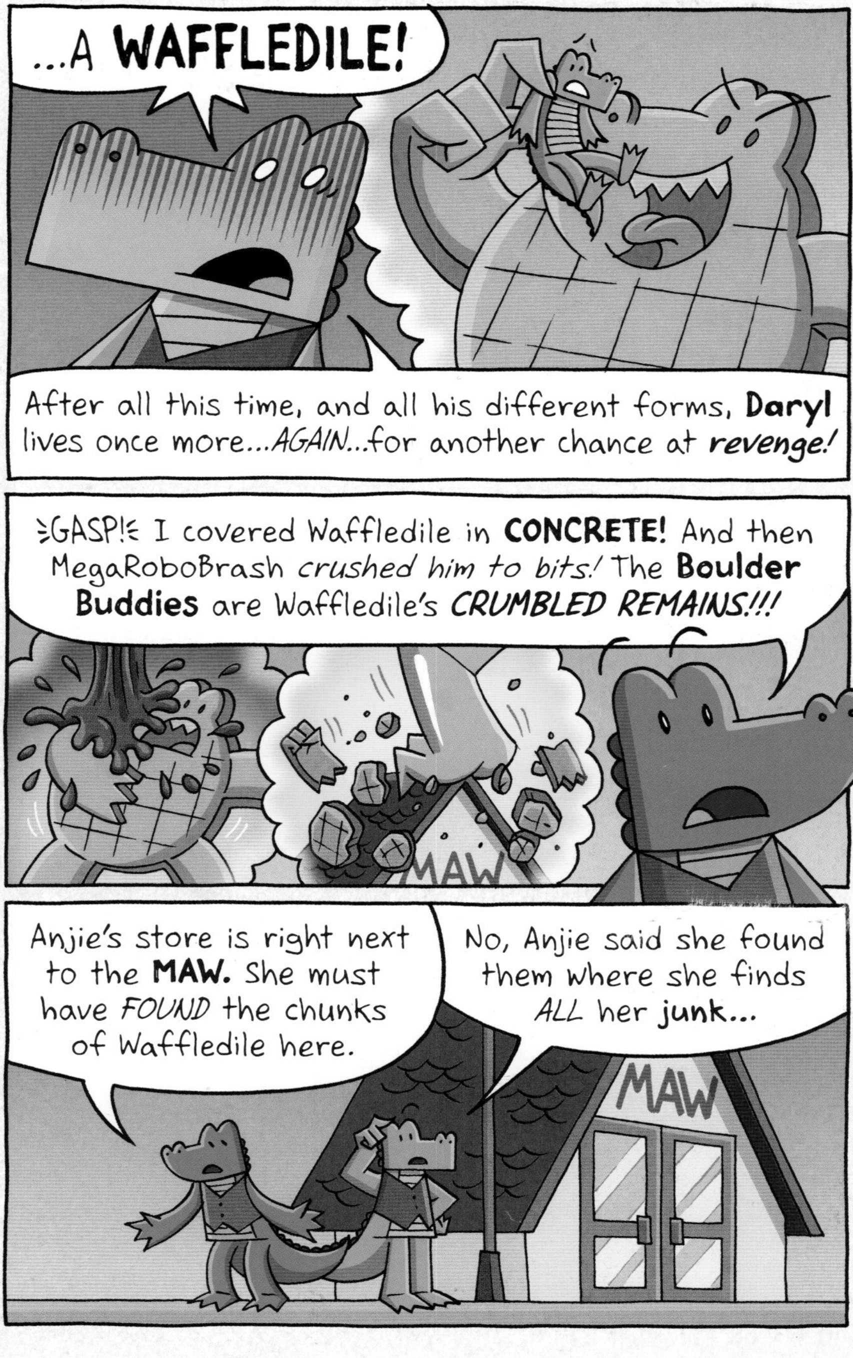
...A WAFFLEDILE!
After all this time, and all his different forms, Daryl lives once more...AGAIN...for another chance at revenge!
GASP! I covered Waffledile in CONCRETE! And then MegaRoboBrash crushed him to bits! The Boulder Buddies are Waffledile's CRUMBLED REMAINS!!!
MAW
Anjie's store is right next to the MAW. She must have FOUND the chunks of Waffledile here.
No, Anjie said she found them where she finds ALL her junk...
MAW

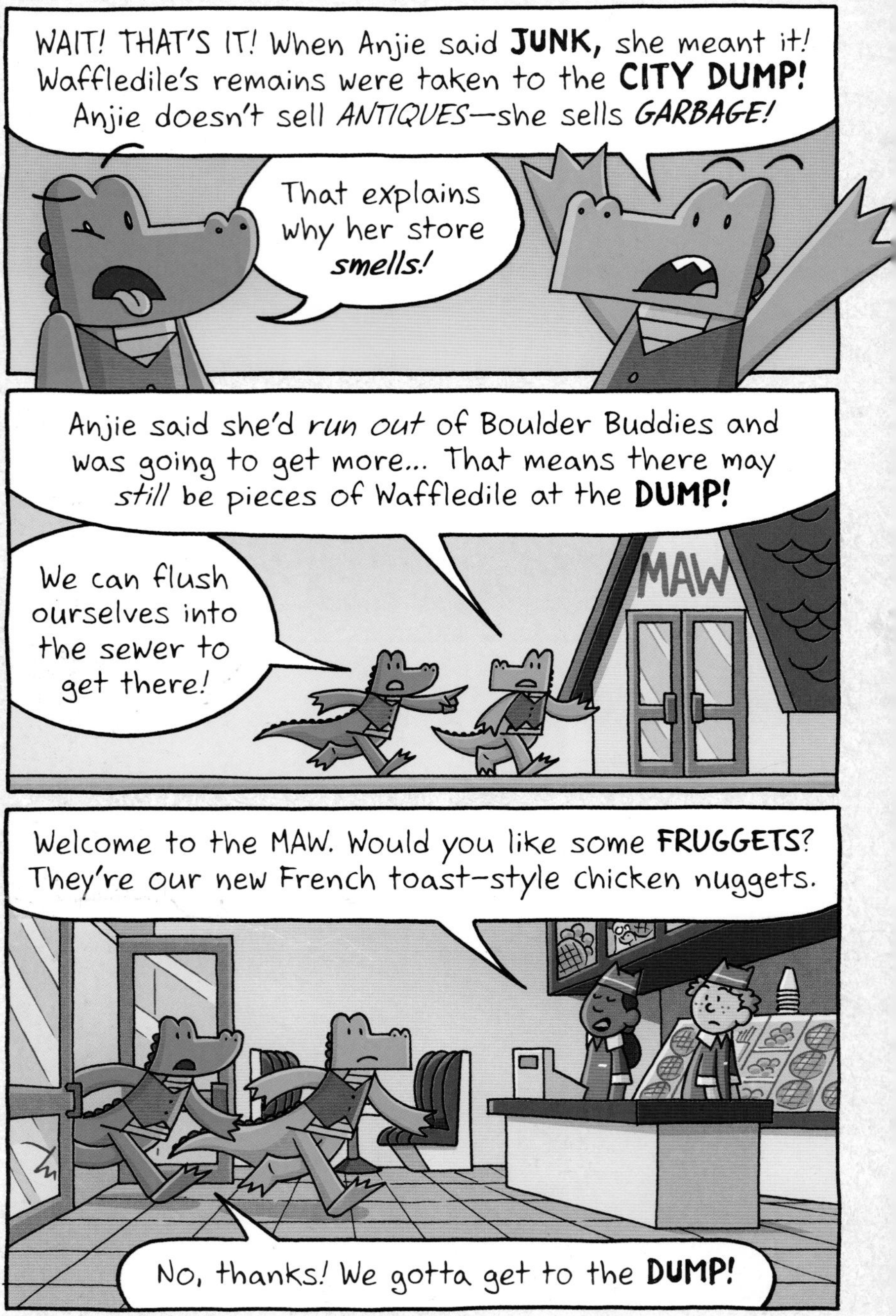
WAIT! THAT'S IT! When Anjie said **JUNK,** she meant it! Waffledile's remains were taken to the **CITY DUMP!** Anjie doesn't sell *ANTIQUES*—she sells *GARBAGE!*
That explains why her store ***smells!***
Anjie said she'd *run out* of Boulder Buddies and was going to get more... That means there may *still* be pieces of Waffledile at the **DUMP!**
We can flush ourselves into the sewer to get there!
MAW
Welcome to the MAW. Would you like some **FRUGGETS**? They're our new French toast-style chicken nuggets.
No, thanks! We gotta get to the **DUMP!**

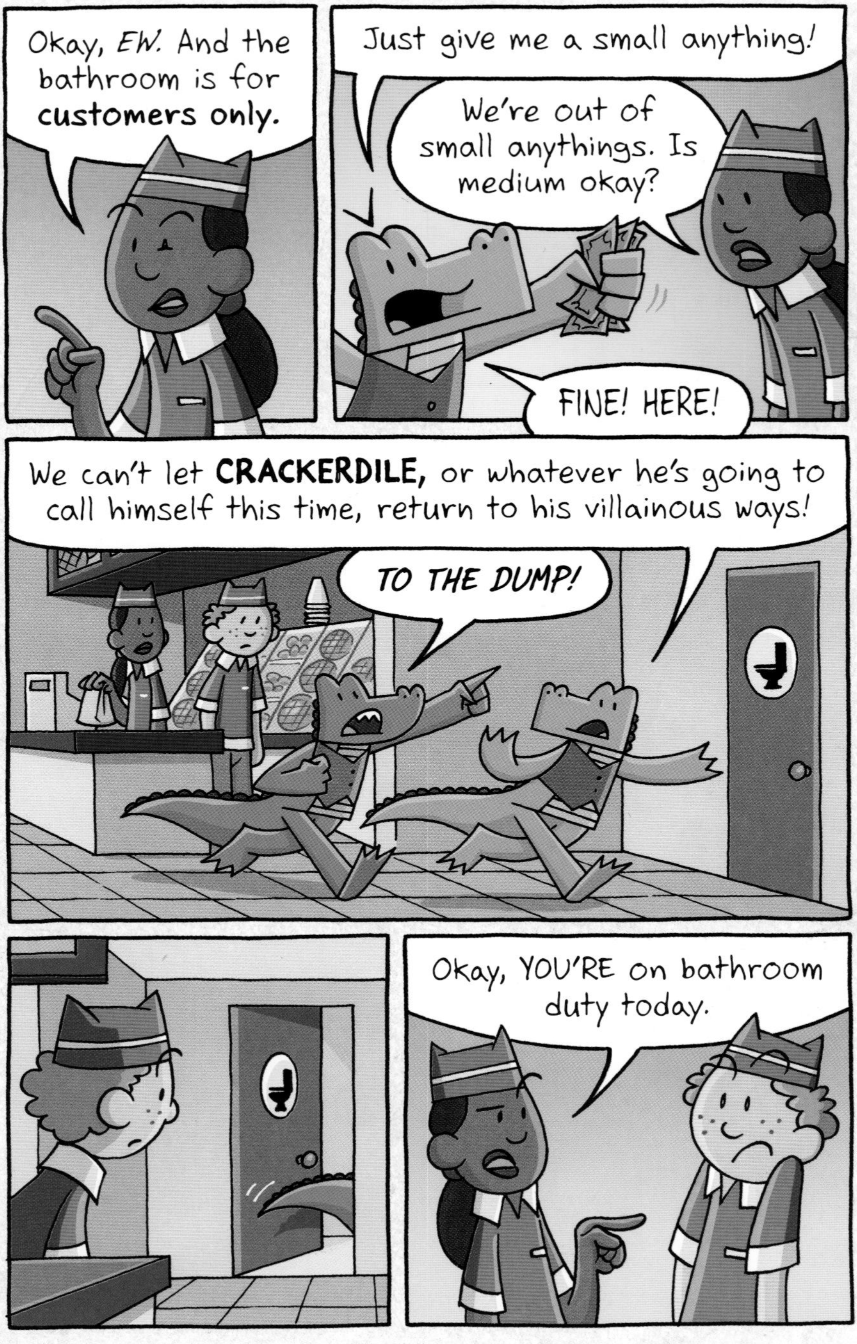
Okay, *EW.* And the bathroom is for **customers only.**
Just give me a small anything!
We're out of small anythings. Is medium okay?
FINE! HERE!
We can't let **CRACKERDILE,** or whatever he's going to call himself this time, return to his villainous ways!
TO THE DUMP!
Okay, YOU'RE on bathroom duty today.

Chapter 13

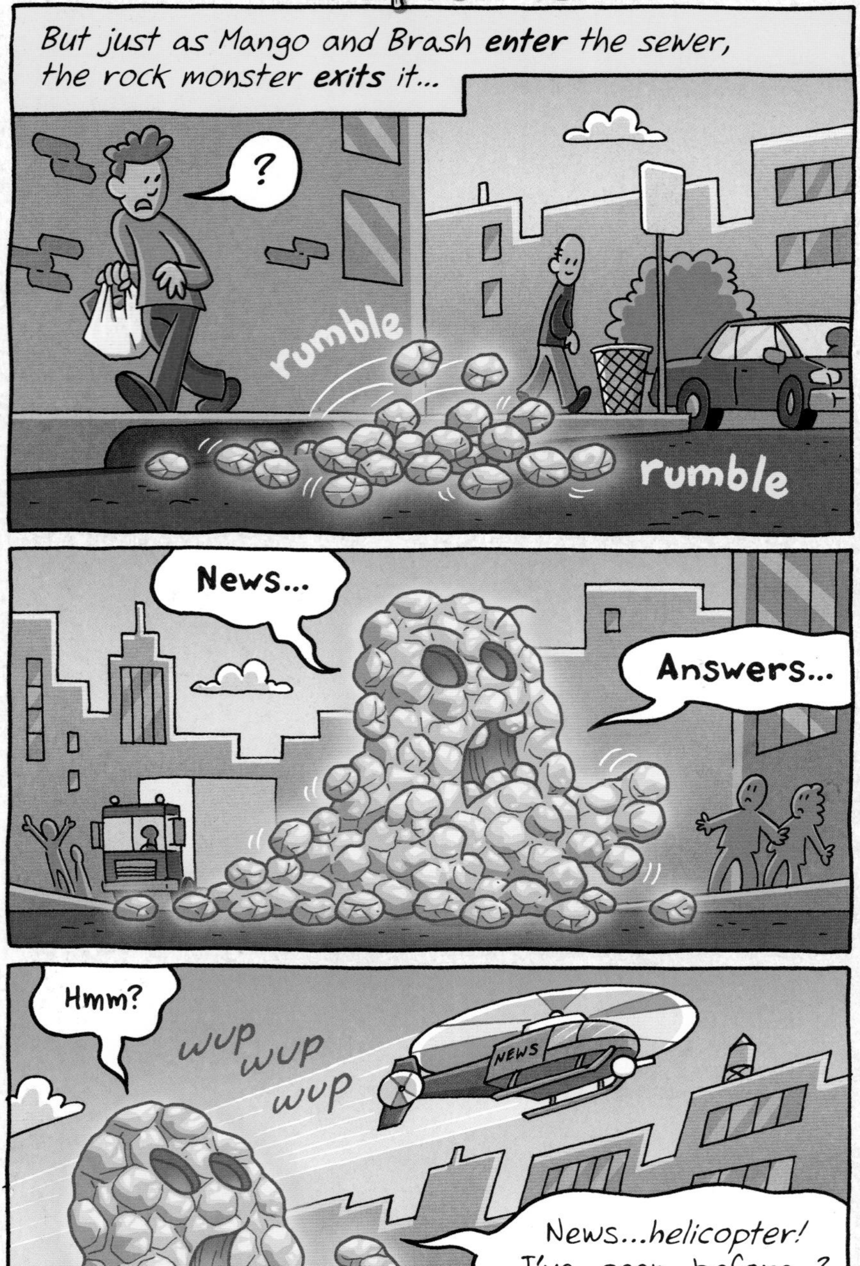

But just as Mango and Brash **enter** the sewer, the rock monster **exits** it...
?
rumble
rumble
News...
Answers...
Hmm?
wup wup wup
NEWS
News...helicopter! I've...seen...before...?

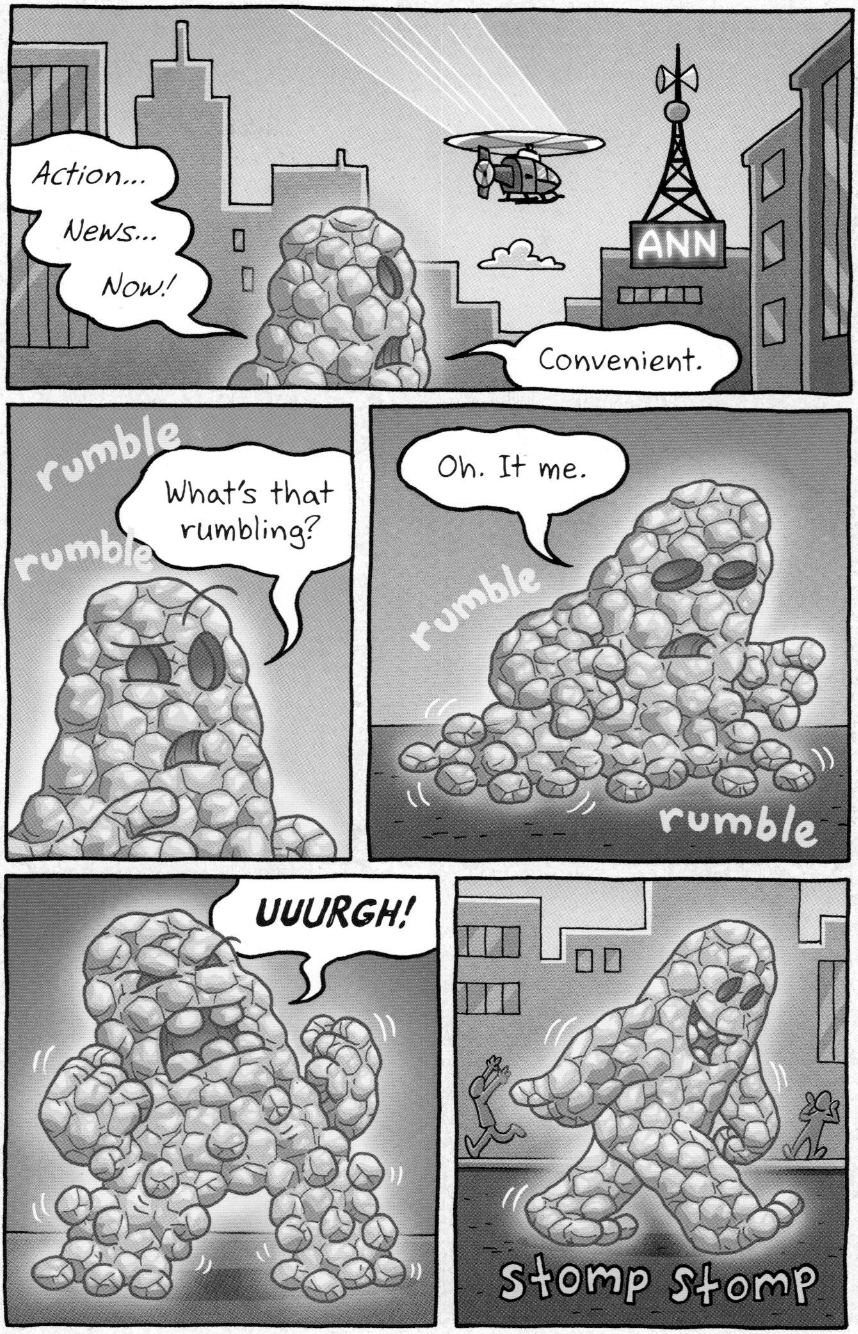

Action... News... Now!
ANN
Convenient.
rumble
rumble
What's that rumbling?
Oh. It me.
rumble
rumble
UUURGH!
stomp stomp

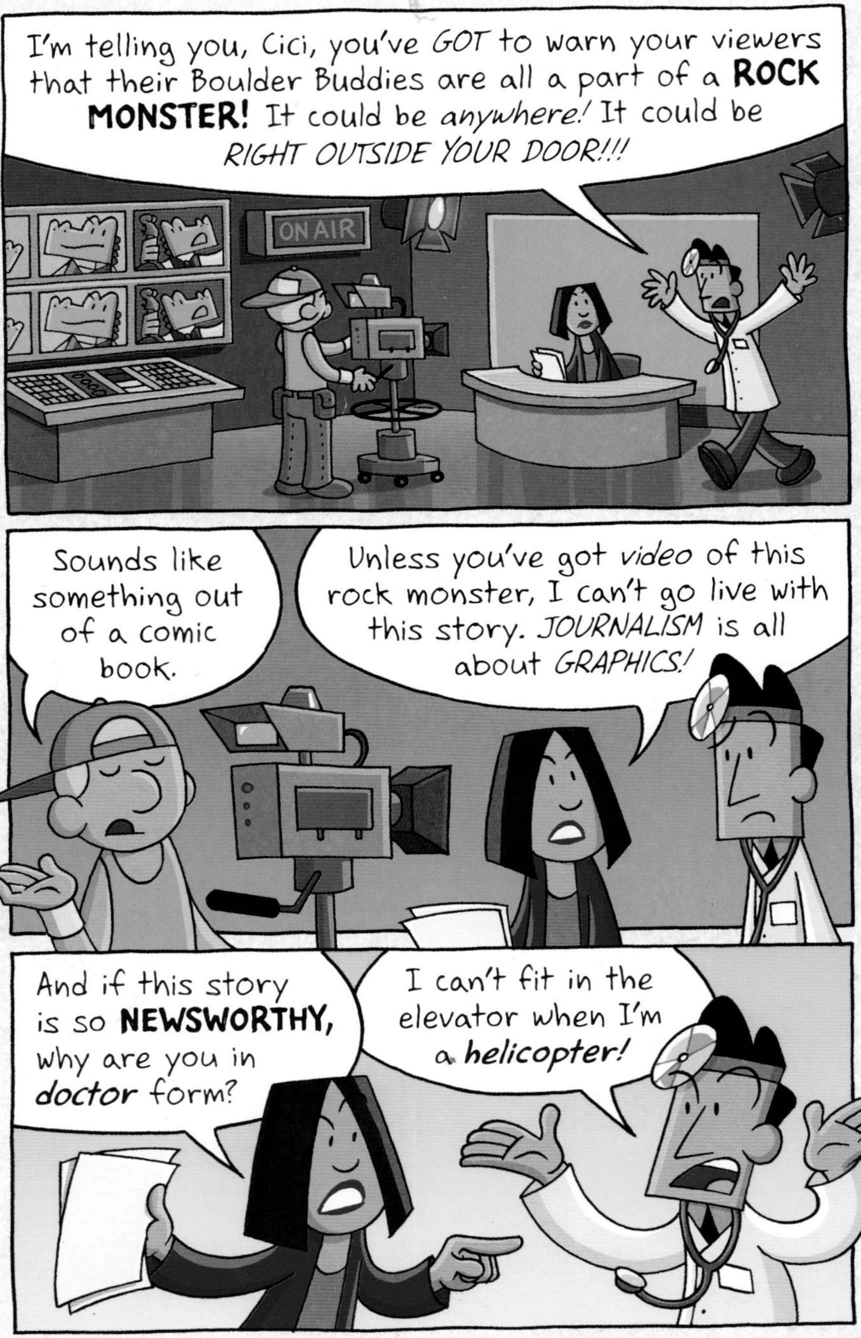
I'm telling you, Cici, you've *GOT* to warn your viewers that their Boulder Buddies are all a part of a **ROCK MONSTER!** It could be *anywhere!* It could be *RIGHT OUTSIDE YOUR DOOR!!!*
ON AIR
Sounds like something out of a comic book.
Unless you've got *video* of this rock monster, I can't go live with this story. *JOURNALISM* is all about *GRAPHICS!*
And if this story is so **NEWSWORTHY,** why are you in ***doctor*** form?
I can't fit in the elevator when I'm a ***helicopter!***

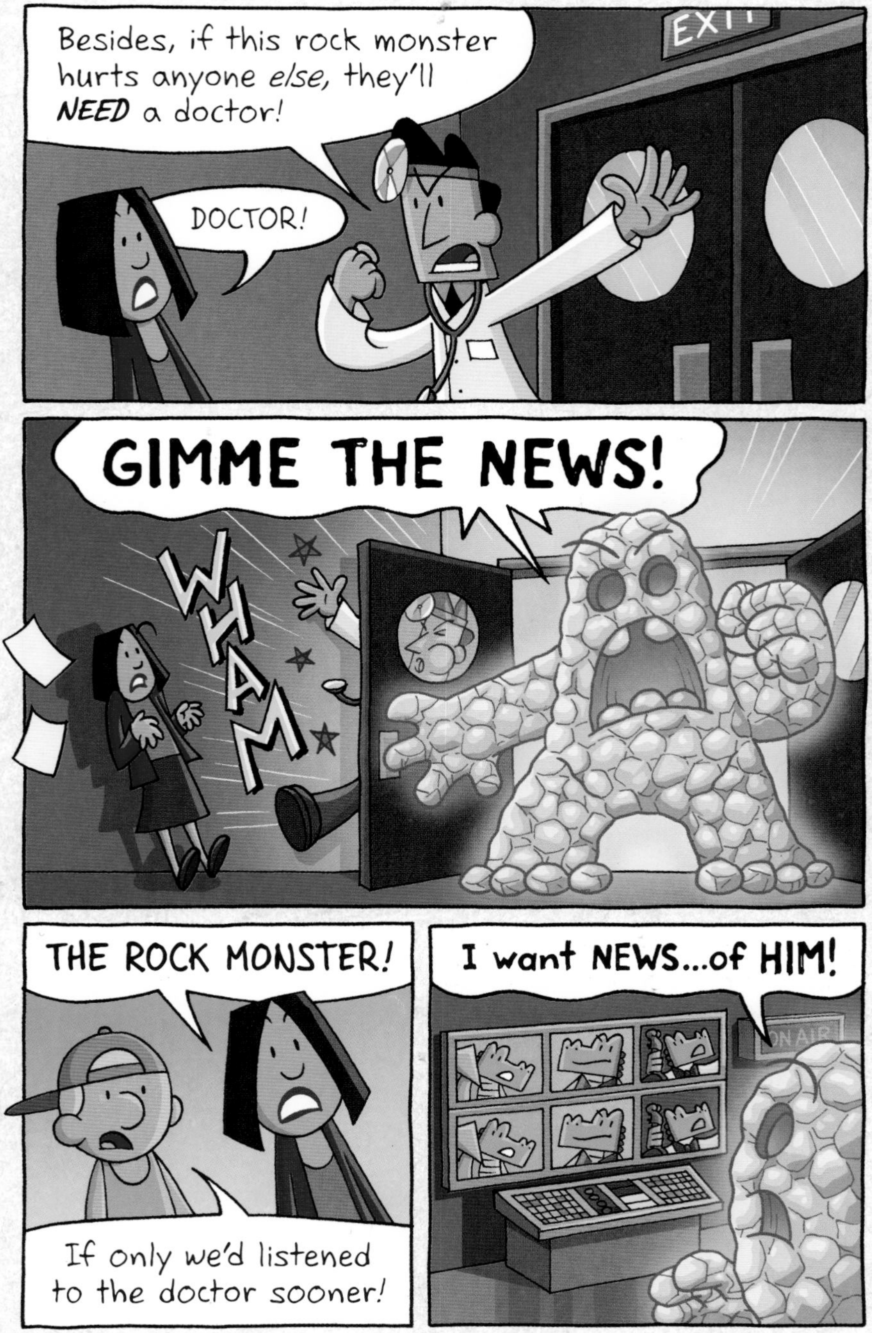
Besides, if this rock monster hurts anyone else, they'll NEED a doctor!
EXIT
DOCTOR!
GIMME THE NEWS!
WHAM
THE ROCK MONSTER!
If only we'd listened to the doctor sooner!
I want NEWS...of HIM!
ON AIR

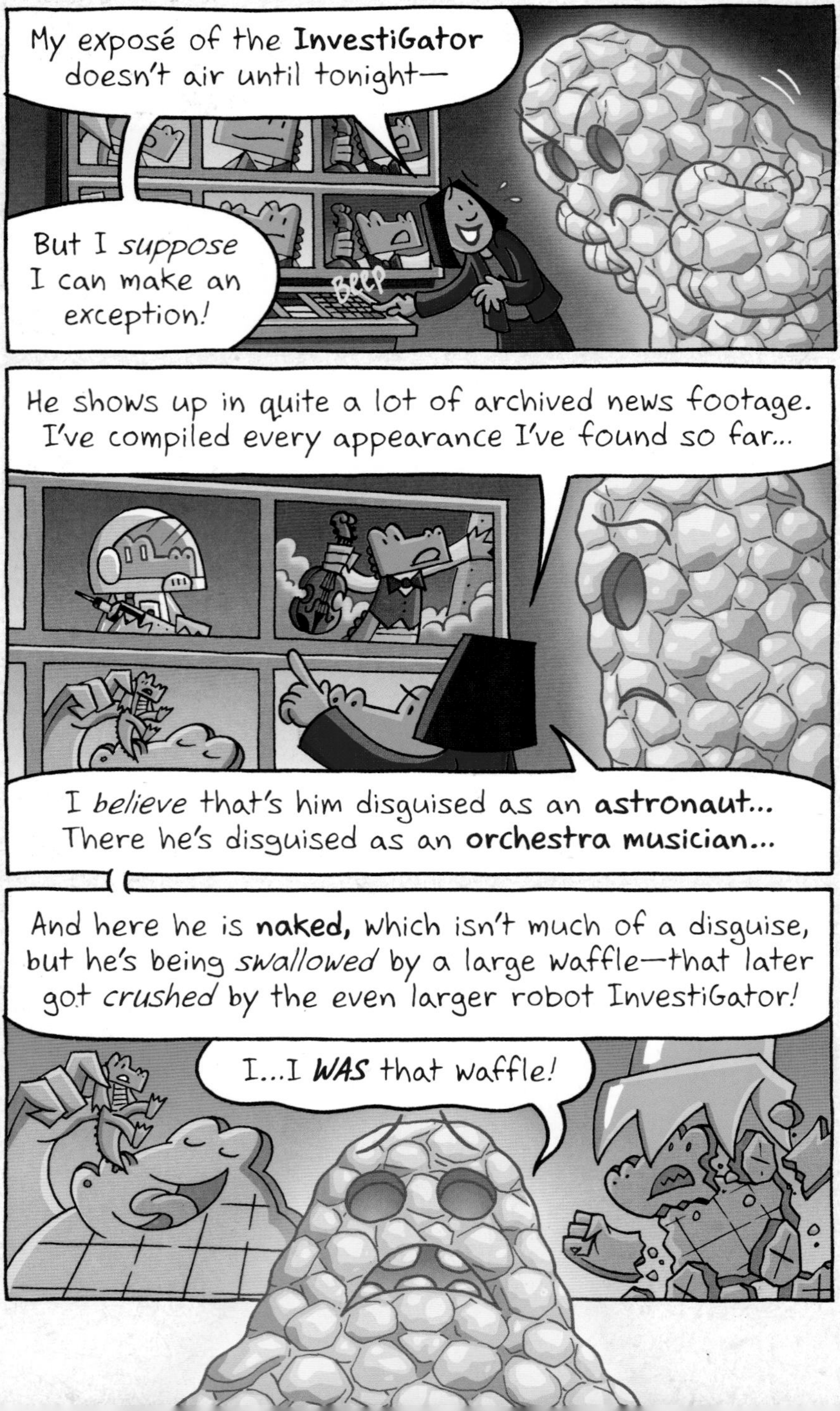
My exposé of the **InvestiGator** doesn't air until tonight—
But I *suppose* I can make an exception!
BEEP
He shows up in quite a lot of archived news footage. I've compiled every appearance I've found so far...
I *believe* that's him disguised as an **astronaut**... There he's disguised as an **orchestra musician**...
And here he is **naked,** which isn't much of a disguise, but he's being *swallowed* by a large waffle—that later got *crushed* by the even larger robot InvestiGator!
I...I ***WAS*** that waffle!

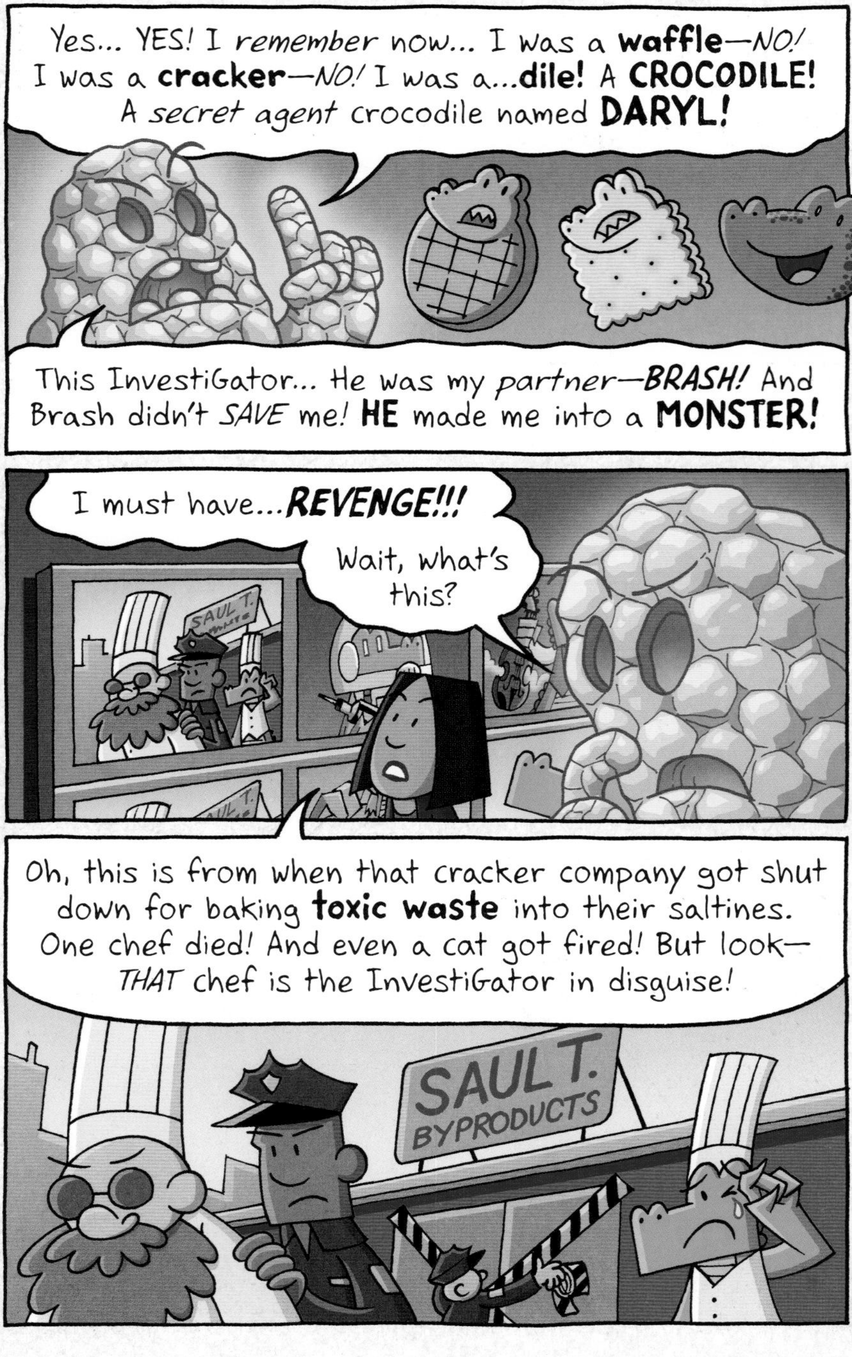
Yes... YES! I *remember* now... I was a **waffle**—*NO!* I was a **cracker**—*NO!* I was a...**dile!** A **CROCODILE!** A *secret agent* crocodile named **DARYL!**
This InvestiGator... He was my *partner*—***BRASH!*** And Brash didn't *SAVE* me! **HE** made me into a **MONSTER!**
I must have...***REVENGE!!!***
Wait, what's this?
SAUL T.
Oh, this is from when that cracker company got shut down for baking **toxic waste** into their saltines. One chef died! And even a cat got fired! But look—*THAT* chef is the InvestiGator in disguise!
SAUL T. BYPRODUCTS

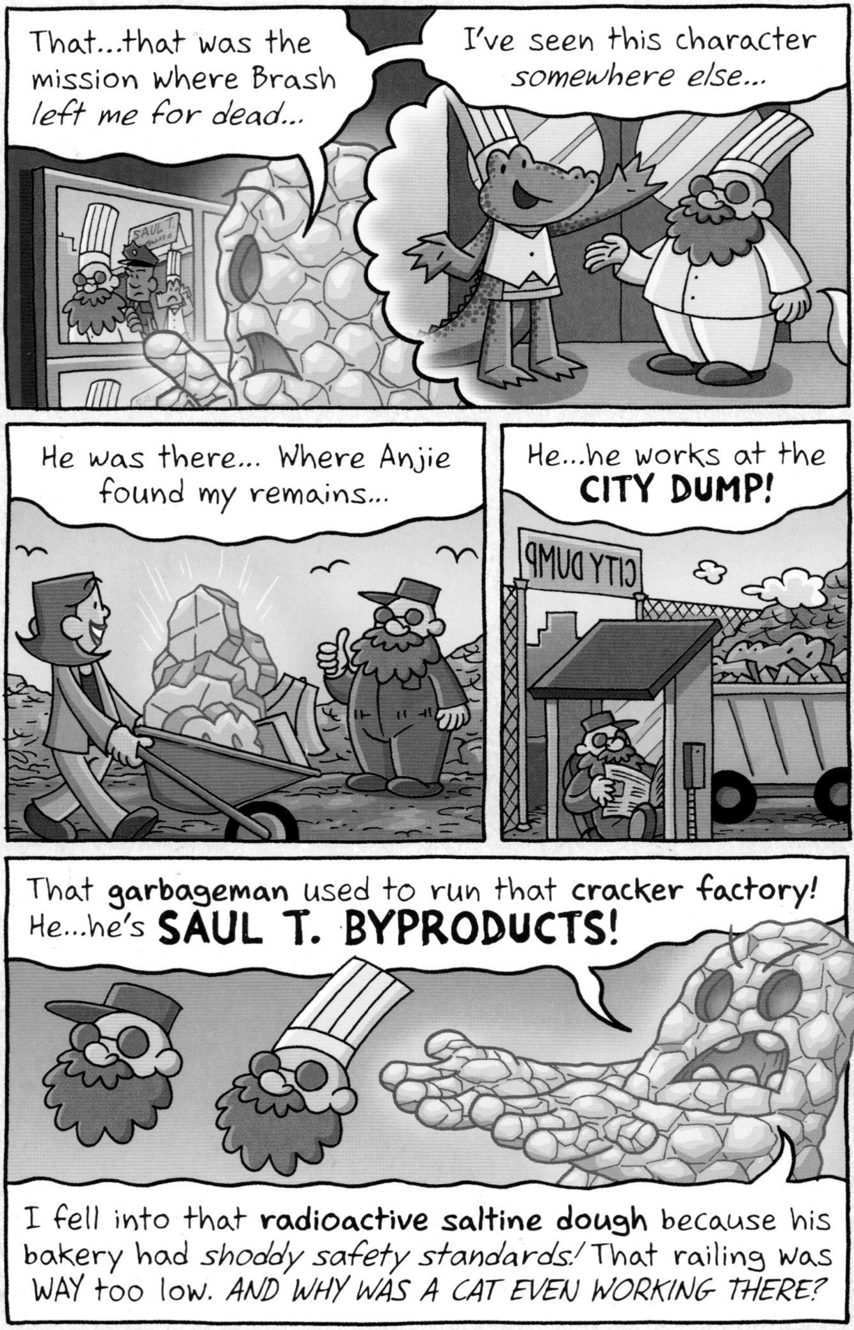
That...that was the mission where Brash *left me for dead...*
I've seen this character *somewhere else...*
SAUL T.
He was there... Where Anjie found my remains...
He...he works at the **CITY DUMP!**
CITY DUMP
That **garbageman** used to run that **cracker factory!** He...he's **SAUL T. BYPRODUCTS!**
I fell into that **radioactive saltine dough** because his bakery had *shoddy safety standards!* That railing was WAY too low. *AND WHY WAS A CAT EVEN WORKING THERE?*

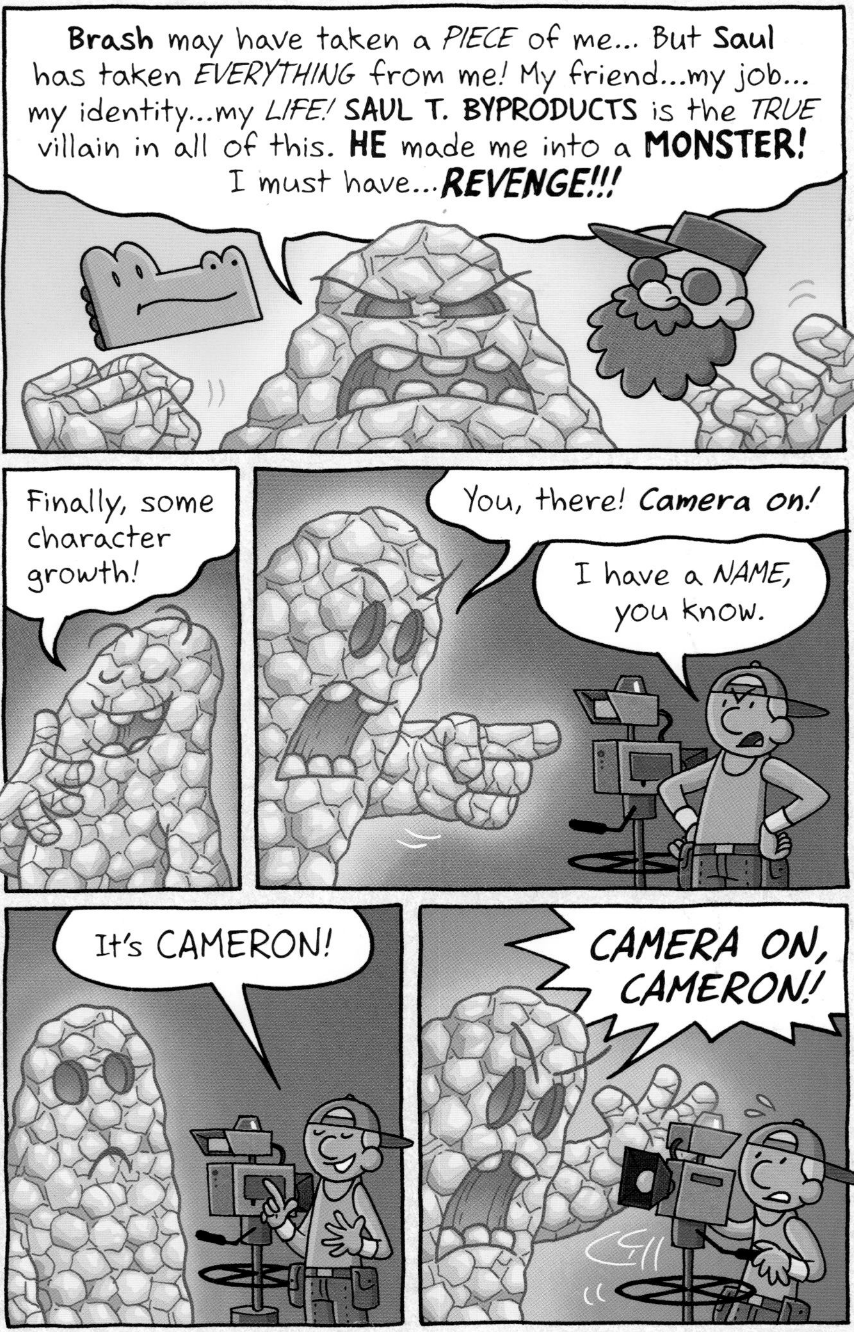
Brash may have taken a PIECE of me... But Saul has taken EVERYTHING from me! My friend...my job... my identity...my LIFE! SAUL T. BYPRODUCTS is the TRUE villain in all of this. HE made me into a MONSTER! I must have...REVENGE!!!
Finally, some character growth!
You, there! Camera on!
I have a NAME, you know.
It's CAMERON!
CAMERA ON, CAMERON!

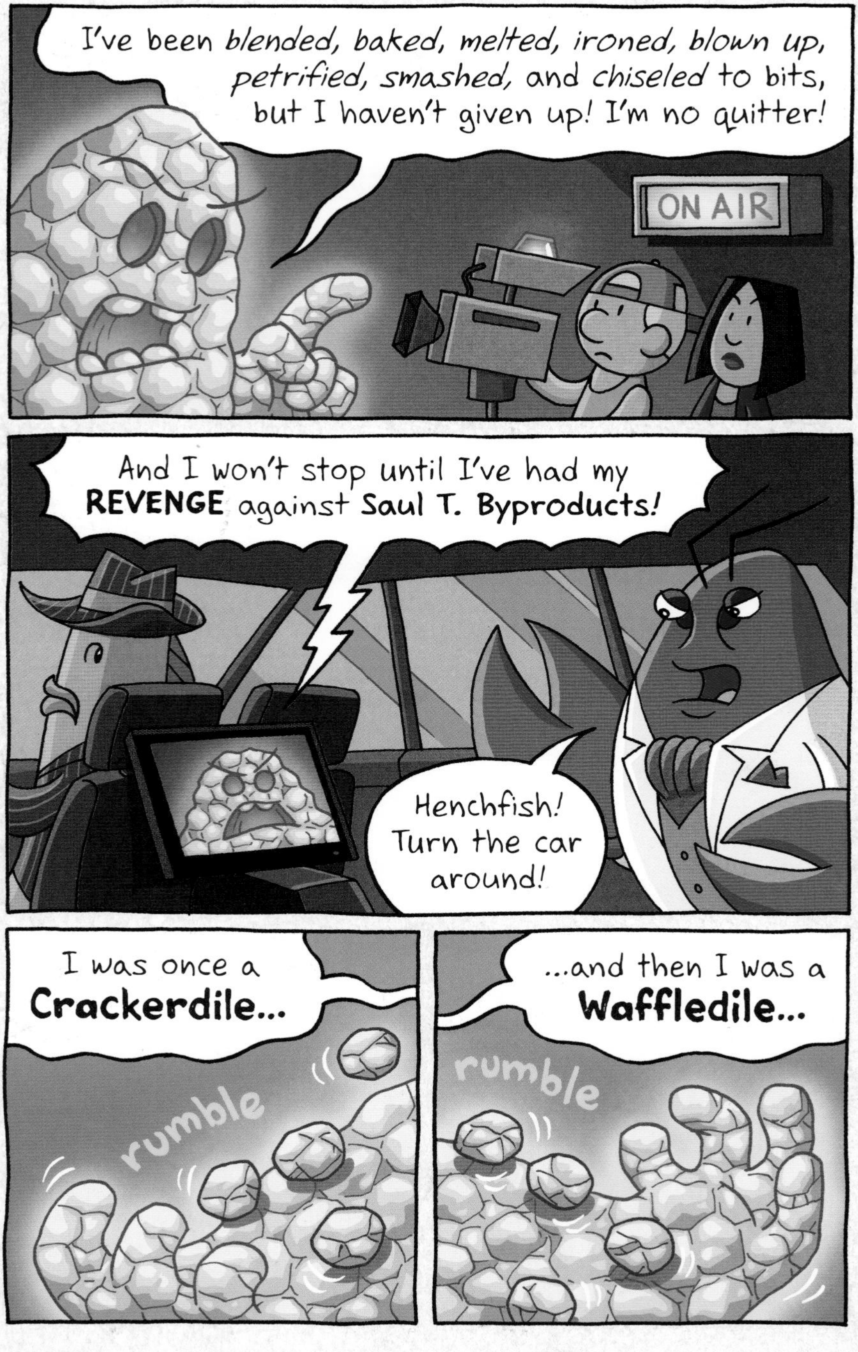
I've been *blended*, *baked*, *melted*, *ironed*, *blown up*, *petrified*, *smashed*, and *chiseled* to bits, but I haven't given up! I'm no quitter!
ON AIR
And I won't stop until I've had my **REVENGE** against **Saul T. Byproducts!**
Henchfish! Turn the car around!
I was once a **Crackerdile...**
rumble
...and then I was a **Waffledile...**
rumble

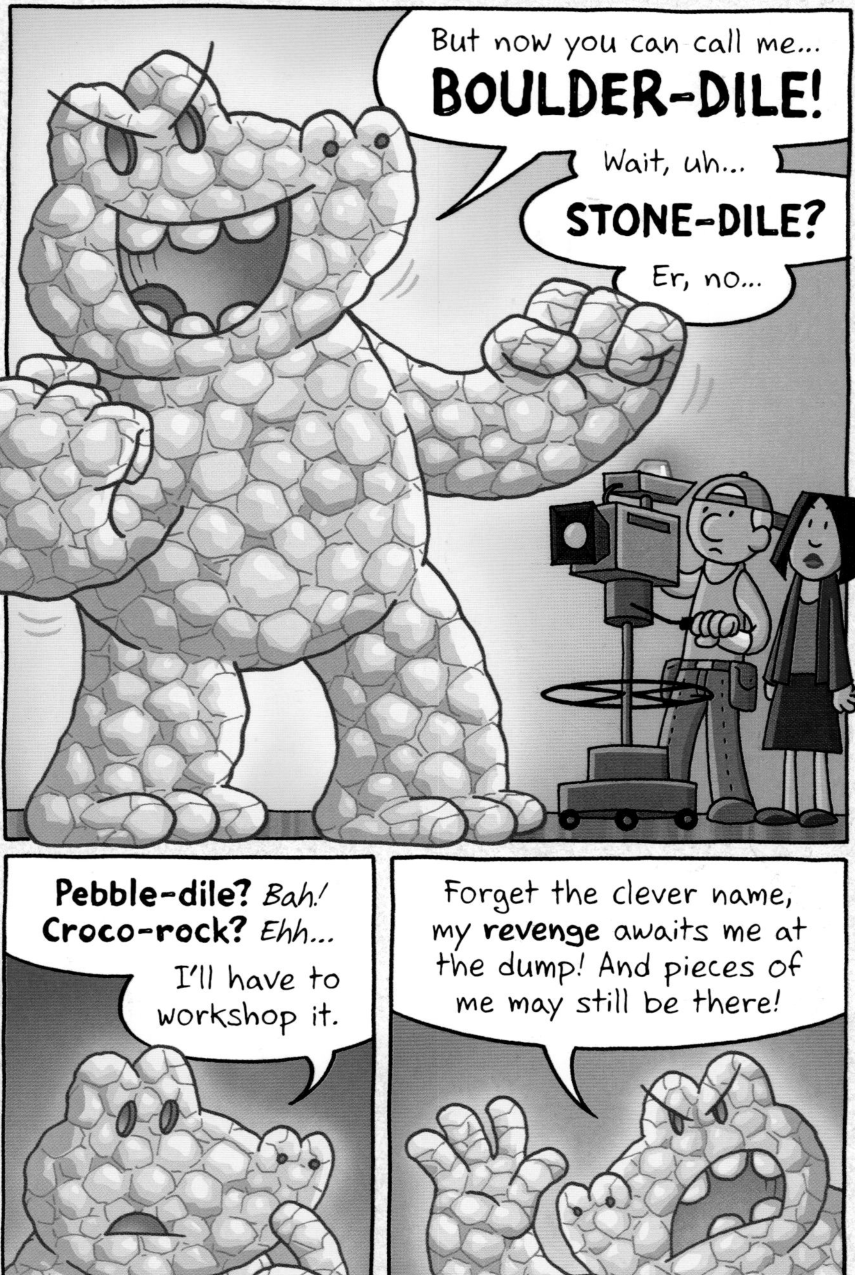
But now you can call me... BOULDER-DILE!
Wait, uh... STONE-DILE?
Er, no...
Pebble-dile? Bah! Croco-rock? Ehh...
I'll have to workshop it.
Forget the clever name, my revenge awaits me at the dump! And pieces of me may still be there!

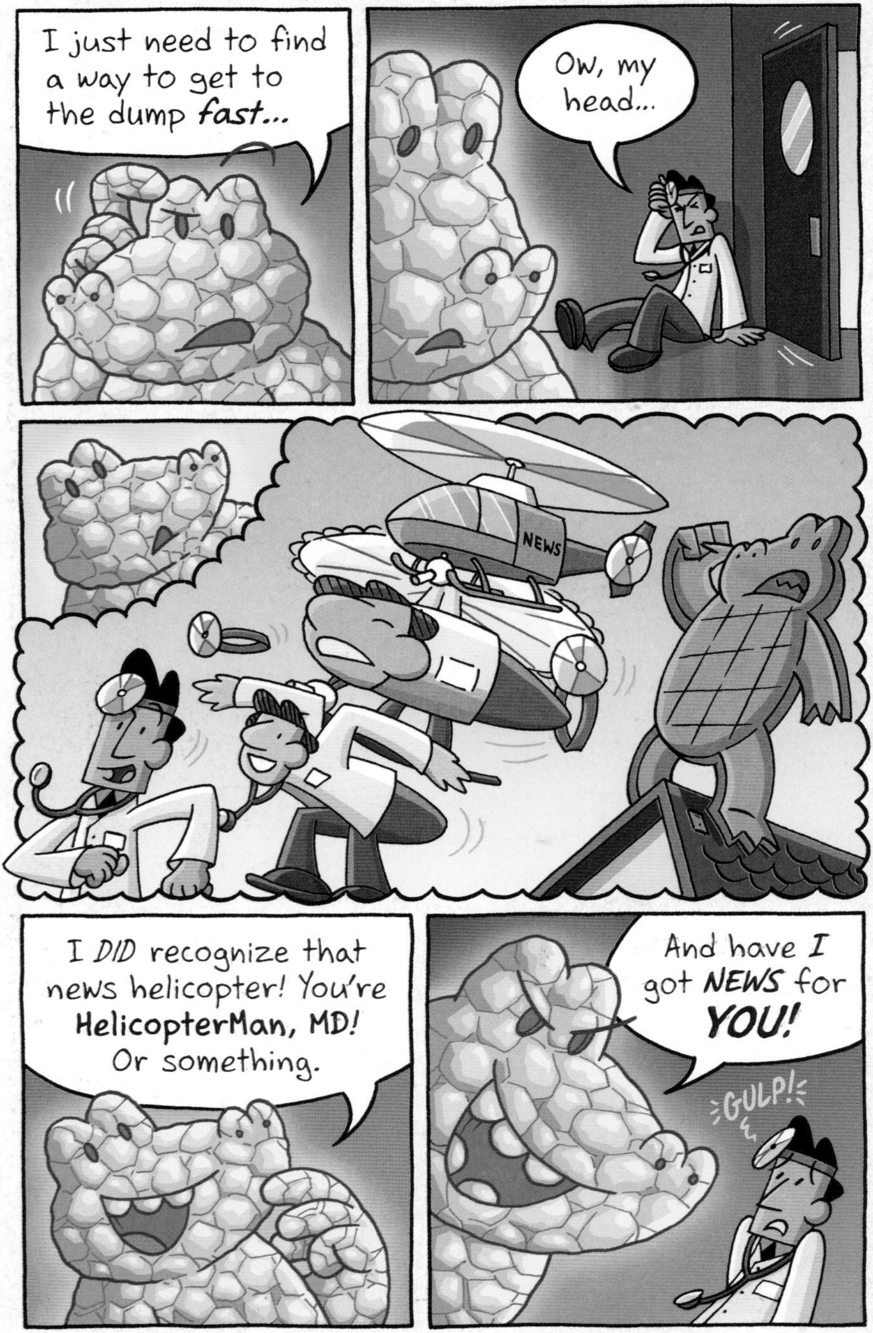
I just need to find a way to get to the dump *fast...*
Ow, my head...
NEWS
I *DID* recognize that news helicopter! You're **HelicopterMan, MD!** Or something.
And have *I* got **NEWS** for ***YOU!***
GULP!

Chapter 14

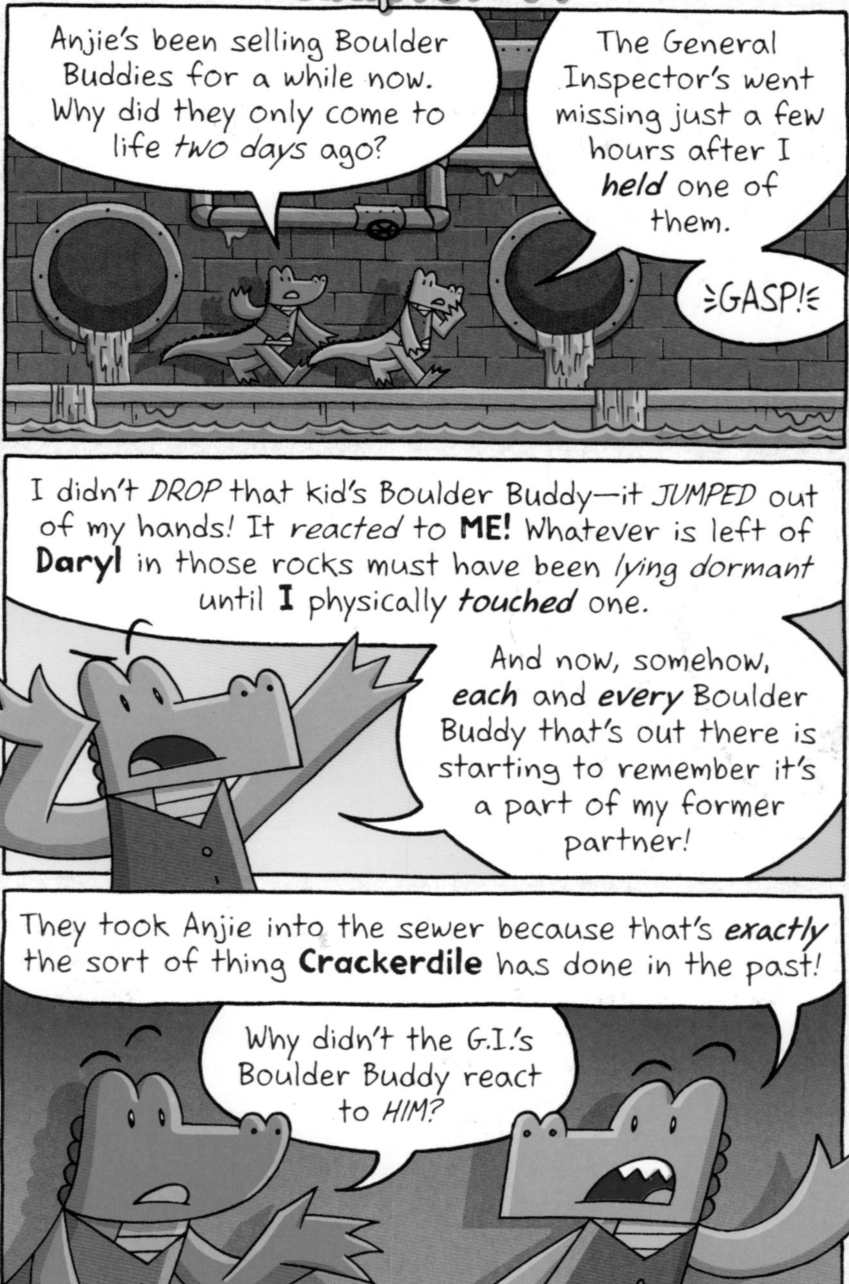
Anjie's been selling Boulder Buddies for a while now. Why did they only come to life *two days* ago?
The General Inspector's went missing just a few hours after I **held** one of them.
GASP!
I didn't *DROP* that kid's Boulder Buddy—it *JUMPED* out of my hands! It *reacted* to **ME!** Whatever is left of **Daryl** in those rocks must have been *lying dormant* until **I** physically ***touched*** one.
And now, somehow, ***each*** and ***every*** Boulder Buddy that's out there is starting to remember it's a part of my former partner!
They took Anjie into the sewer because that's ***exactly*** the sort of thing **Crackerdile** has done in the past!
Why didn't the G.I.'s Boulder Buddy react to *HIM*?

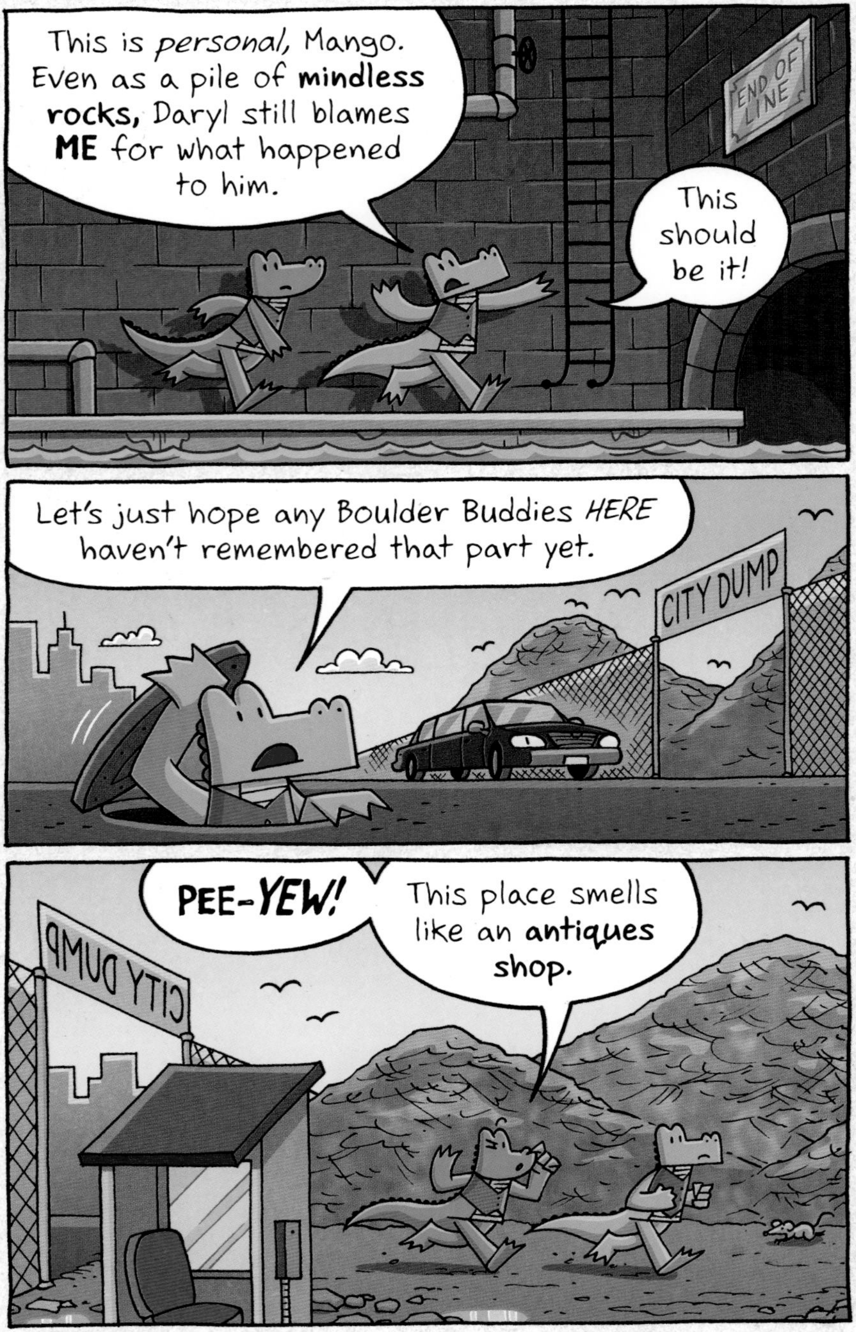

This is *personal,* Mango. Even as a pile of **mindless rocks,** Daryl still blames **ME** for what happened to him.
END OF LINE
This should be it!
Let's just hope any Boulder Buddies *HERE* haven't remembered that part yet.
CITY DUMP
CITY DUMP
PEE-*YEW!*
This place smells like an **antiques shop.**

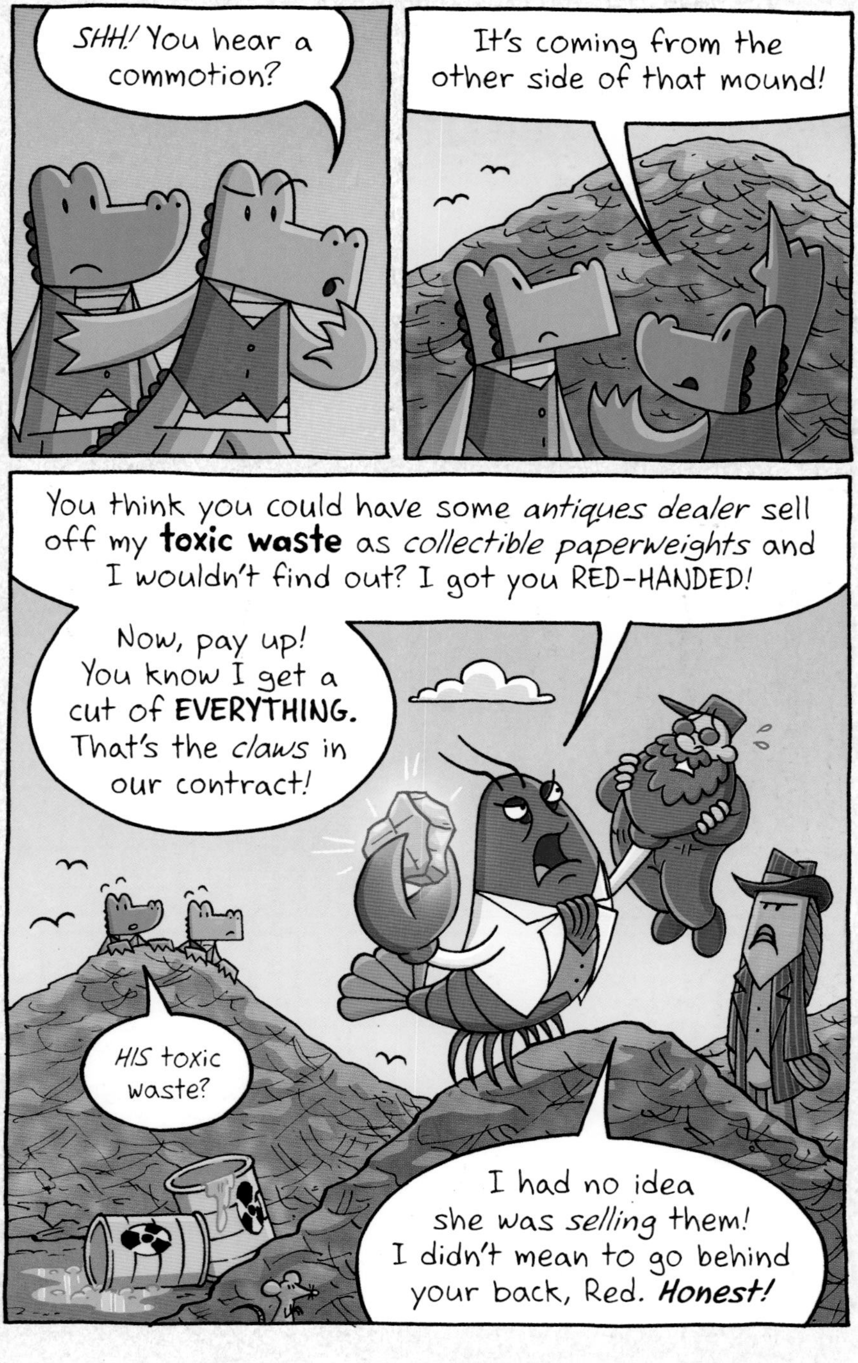

SHH! You hear a commotion?
It's coming from the other side of that mound!
You think you could have some *antiques dealer* sell off my **toxic waste** as *collectible paperweights* and I wouldn't find out? I got you RED-HANDED!
Now, pay up! You know I get a cut of **EVERYTHING.** That's the *claws* in our contract!
HIS toxic waste?
I had no idea she was *selling* them! I didn't mean to go behind your back, Red. ***Honest!***

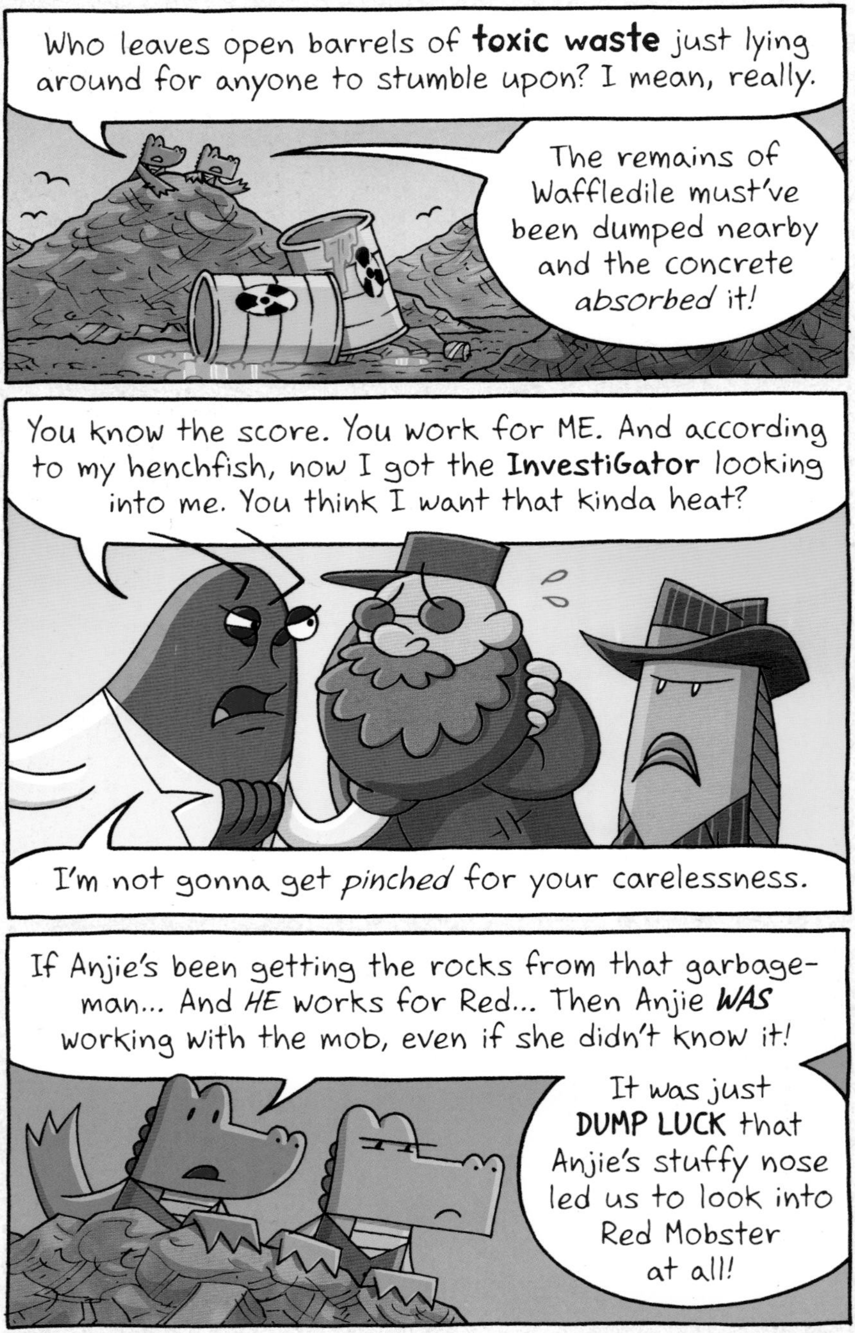

Who leaves open barrels of **toxic waste** just lying around for anyone to stumble upon? I mean, really.
The remains of Waffledile must've been dumped nearby and the concrete *absorbed* it!
You know the score. You work for ME. And according to my henchfish, now I got the **InvestiGator** looking into me. You think I want that kinda heat?
I'm not gonna get *pinched* for your carelessness.
If Anjie's been getting the rocks from that garbage-man... And *HE* works for Red... Then Anjie ***WAS*** working with the mob, even if she didn't know it!
It was just **DUMP LUCK** that Anjie's stuffy nose led us to look into Red Mobster at all!

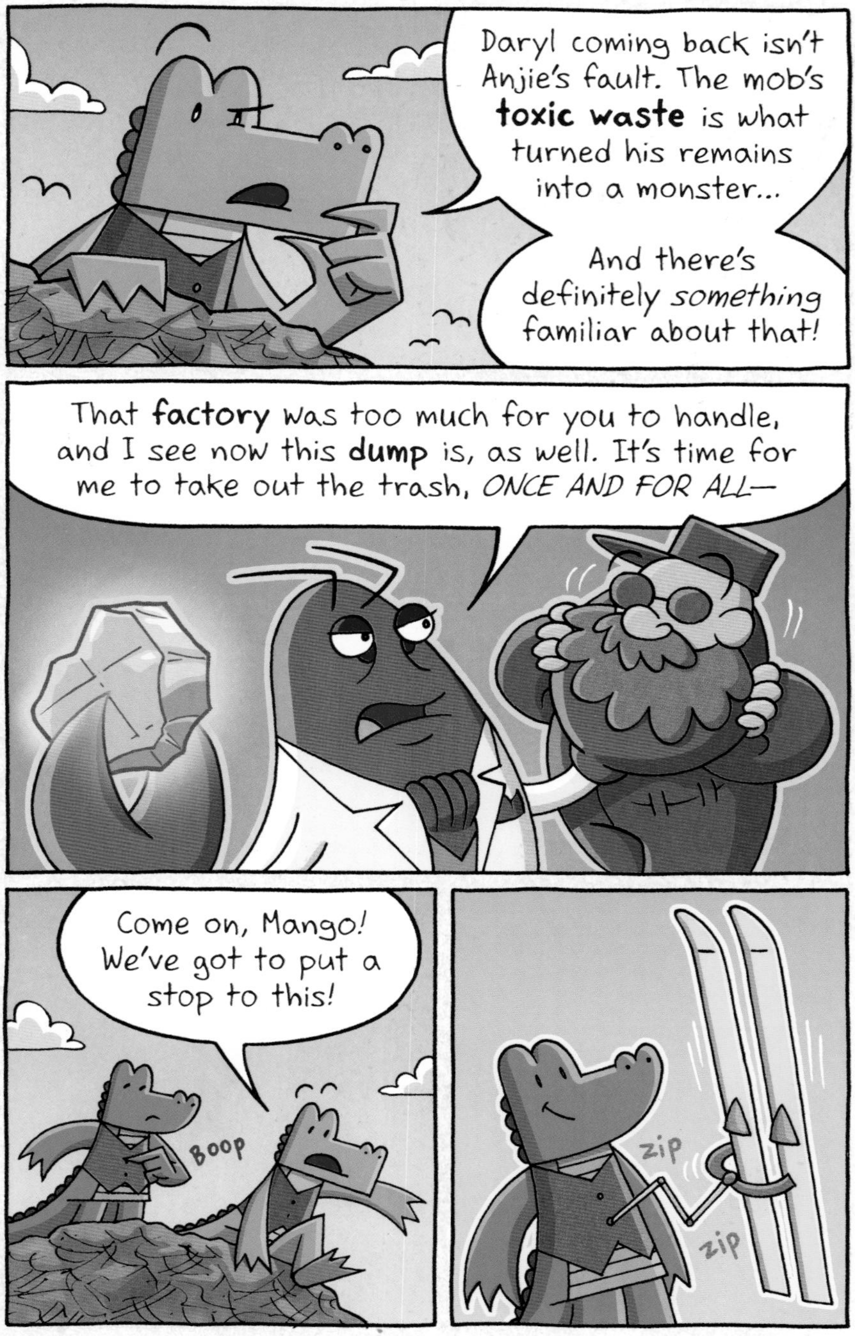

Daryl coming back isn't Anjie's fault. The mob's **toxic waste** is what turned his remains into a monster...
And there's definitely *something* familiar about that!
That **factory** was too much for you to handle, and I see now this **dump** is, as well. It's time for me to take out the trash, *ONCE AND FOR ALL—*
Come on, Mango! We've got to put a stop to this!
BOOP
zip
zip

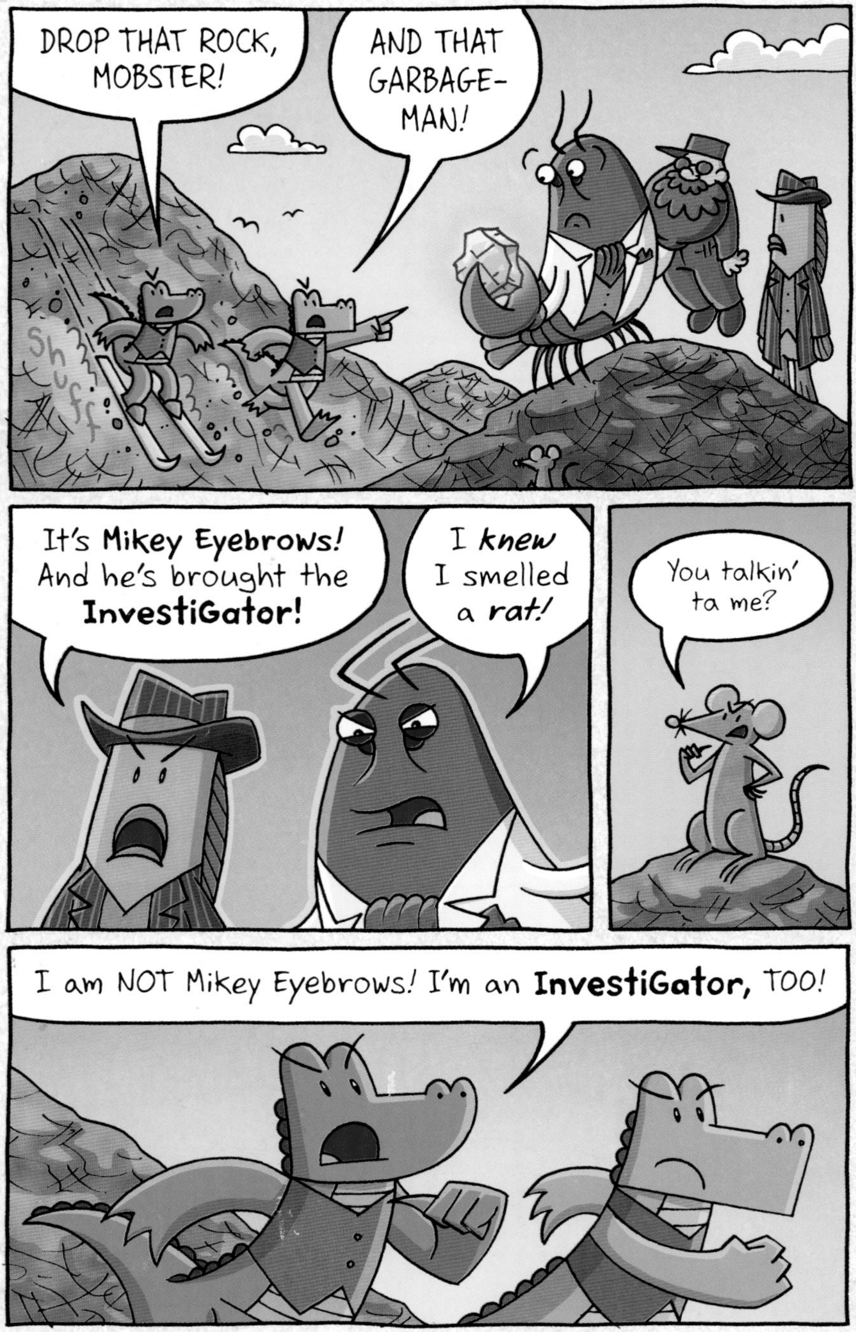
DROP THAT ROCK, MOBSTER!
AND THAT GARBAGE-MAN!
Shuff
It's **Mikey Eyebrows!** And he's brought the **InvestiGator!**
I *knew* I smelled a *rat!*
You talkin' ta me?
I am NOT Mikey Eyebrows! I'm an **InvestiGator,** TOO!

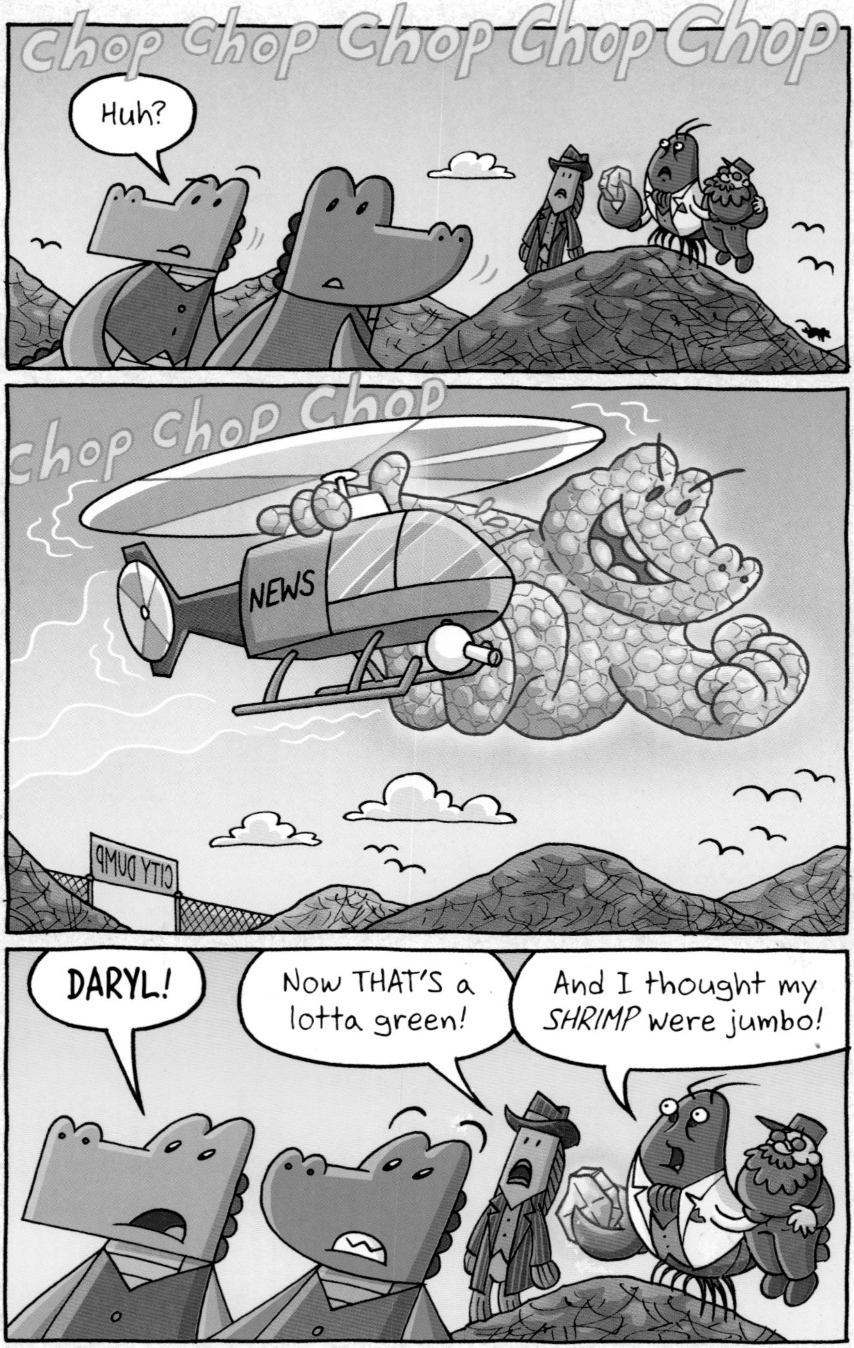
Chop Chop Chop Chop Chop
Huh?
Chop Chop Chop
NEWS
CITY DUMP
DARYL!
Now THAT'S a lotta green!
And I thought my *SHRIMP* were jumbo!

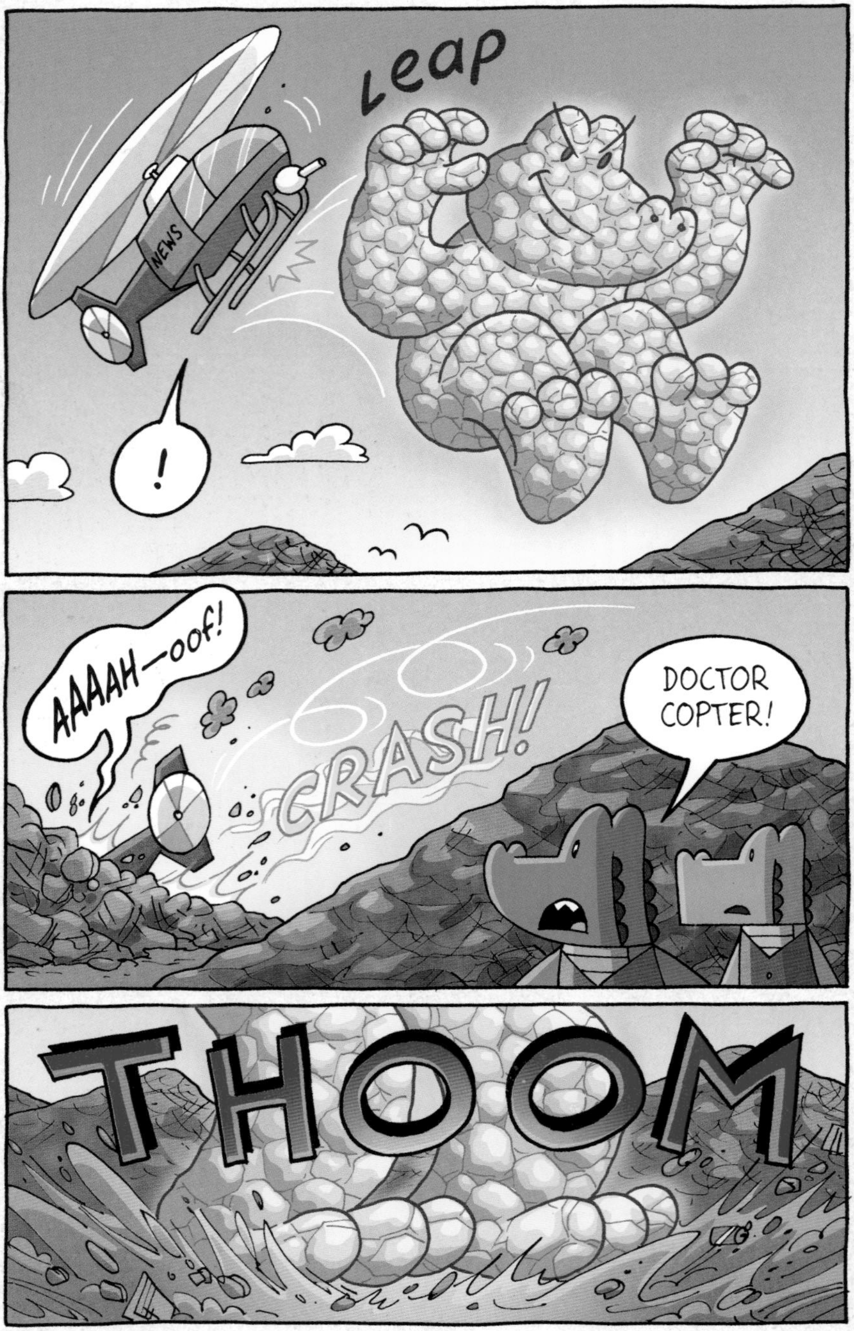
LEAP
NEWS
!
AAAAH—OOF!
CRASH!
DOCTOR COPTER!
THOOM

Chapter 15

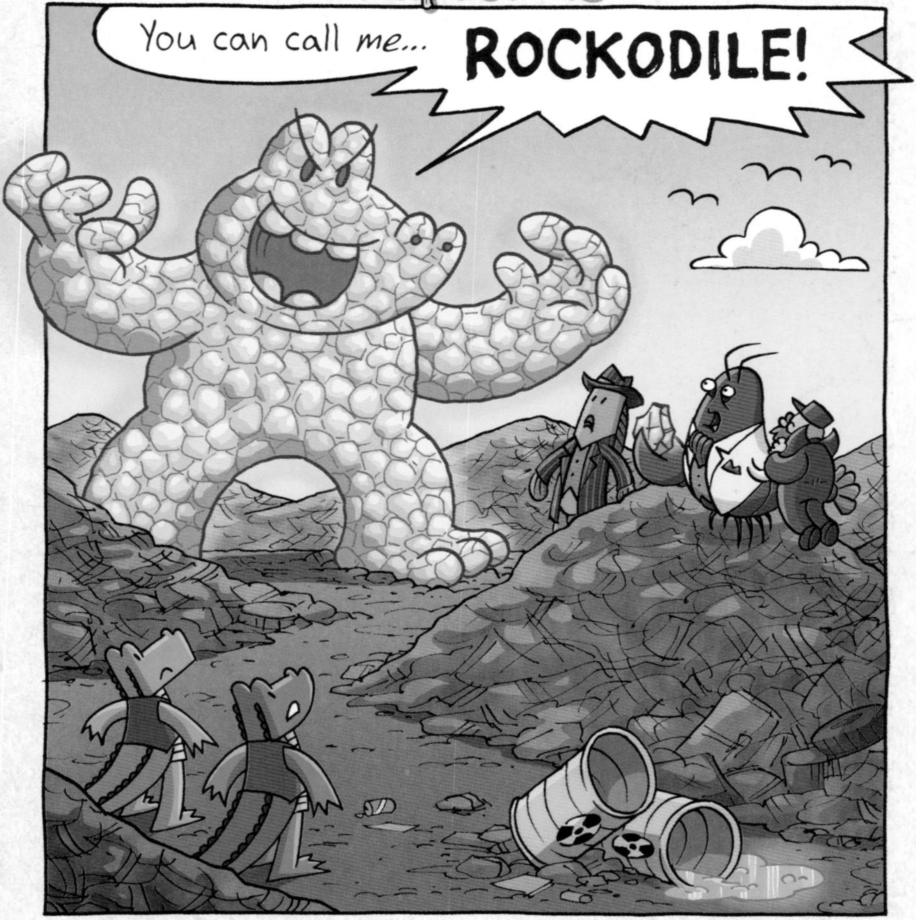
You can call me... ROCKODILE!

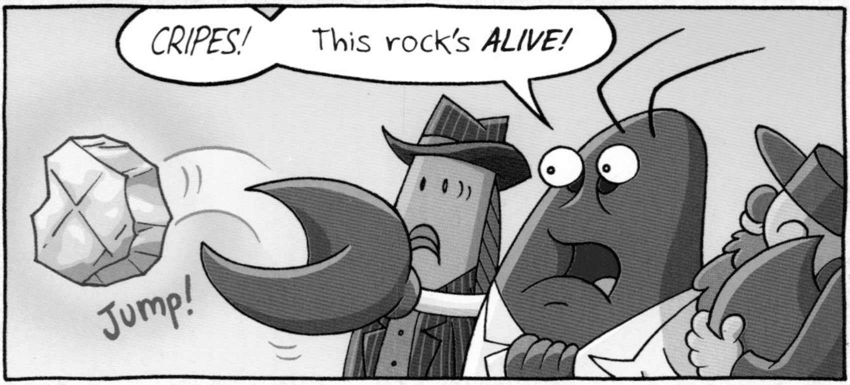
CRIPES! This rock's ALIVE!
Jump!

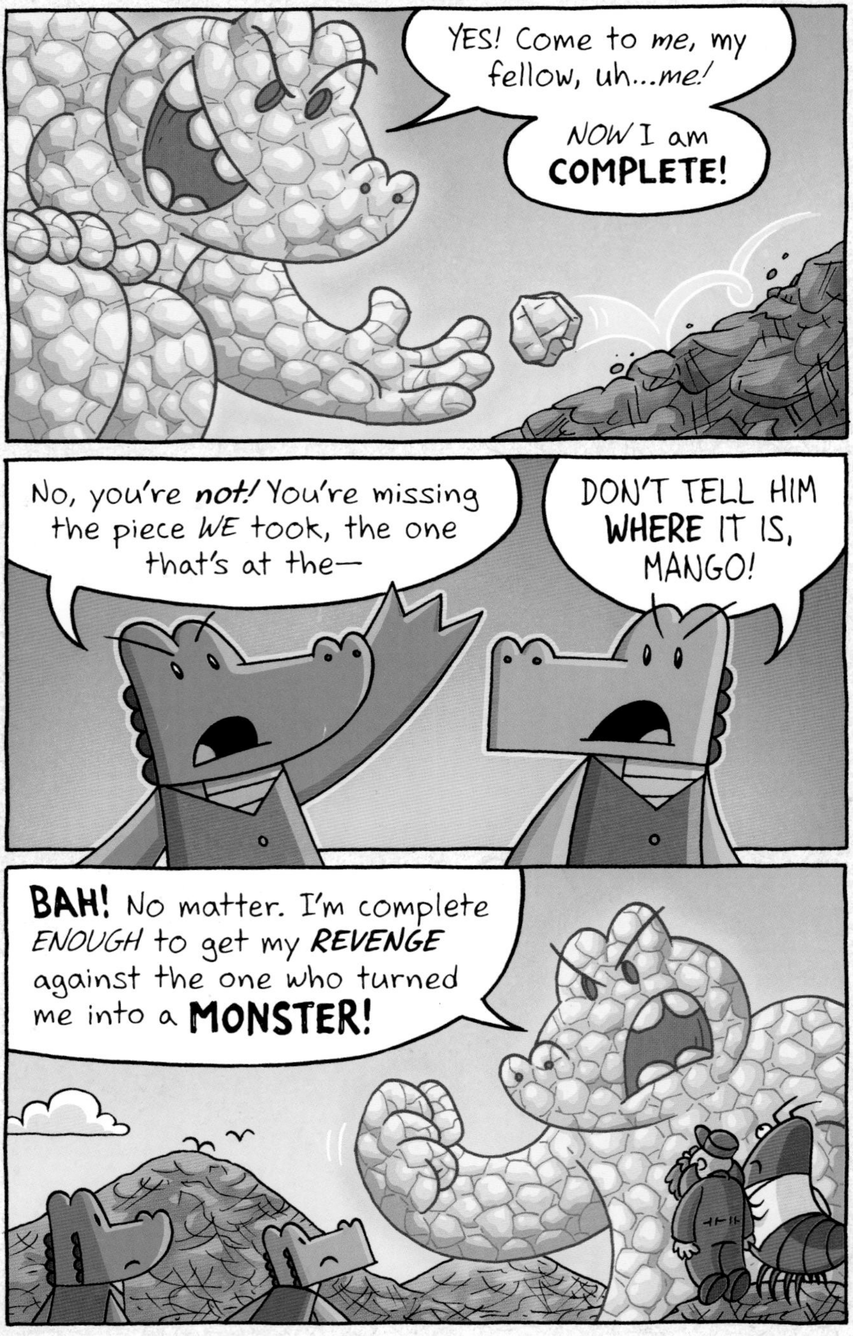
YES! Come to *me*, my fellow, uh...*me!*
NOW I am **COMPLETE!**
No, you're ***not!*** You're missing the piece *WE* took, the one that's at the—
DON'T TELL HIM **WHERE** IT IS, MANGO!
BAH! No matter. I'm complete *ENOUGH* to get my ***REVENGE*** against the one who turned me into a **MONSTER!**

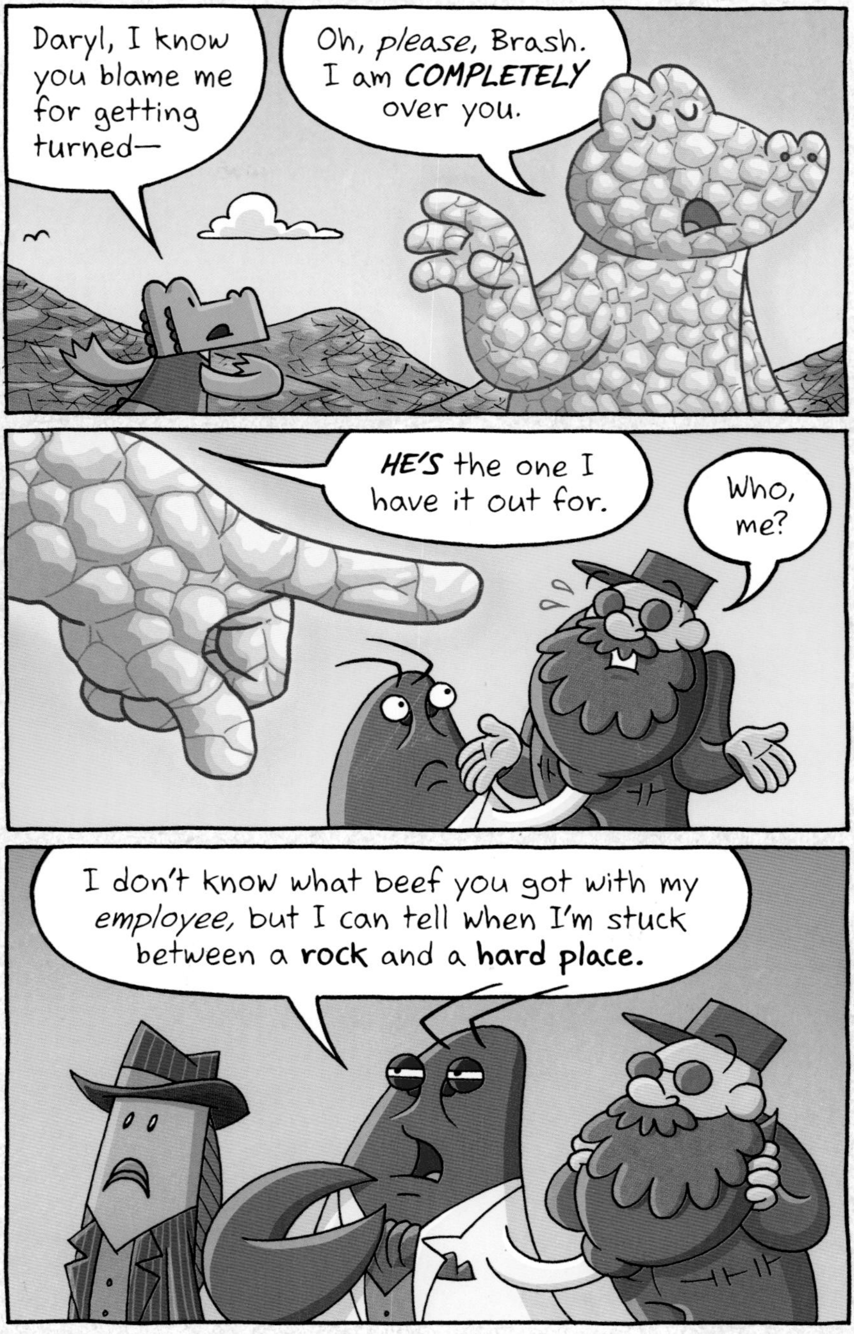
Daryl, I know you blame me for getting turned—
Oh, *please,* Brash. I am **COMPLETELY** over you.
HE'S the one I have it out for.
Who, me?
I don't know what beef you got with my *employee,* but I can tell when I'm stuck between a **rock** and a **hard place.**

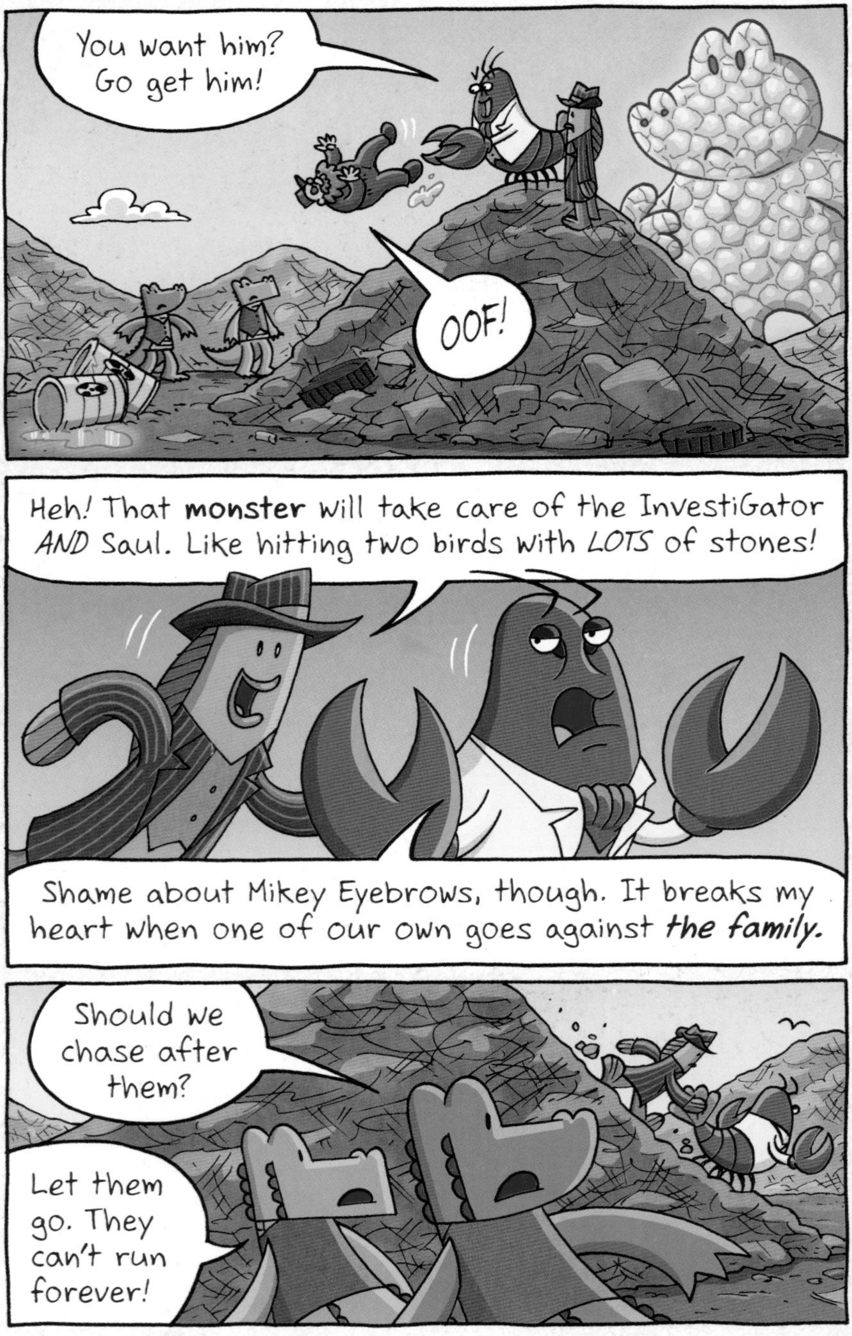
You want him? Go get him!
OOF!
Heh! That **monster** will take care of the InvestiGator *AND* Saul. Like hitting two birds with *LOTS* of stones!
Shame about Mikey Eyebrows, though. It breaks my heart when one of our own goes against ***the family.***
Should we chase after them?
Let them go. They can't run forever!

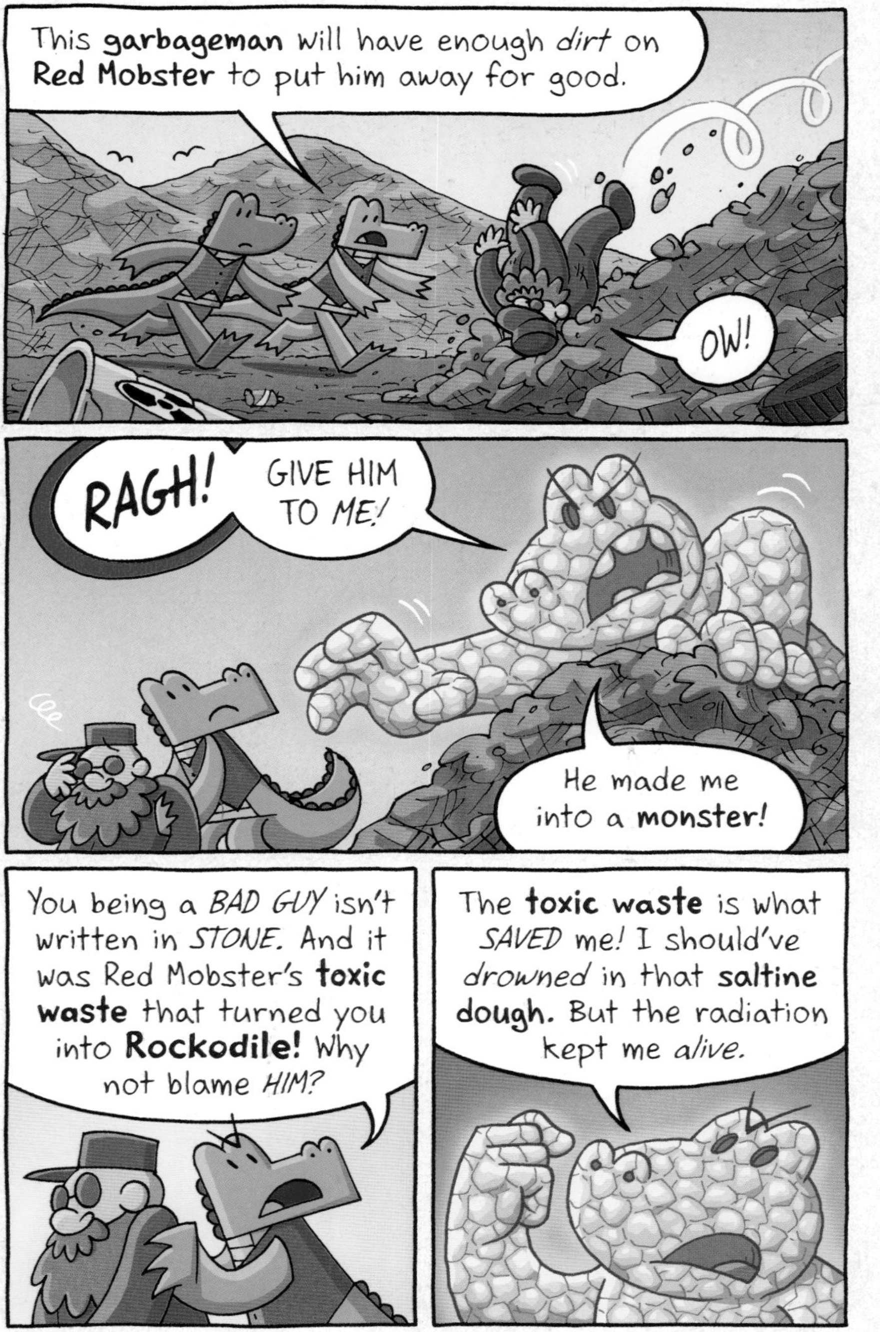
This garbageman will have enough dirt on Red Mobster to put him away for good.
OW!
RAGH!
GIVE HIM TO ME!
He made me into a monster!
You being a BAD GUY isn't written in STONE. And it was Red Mobster's toxic waste that turned you into Rockodile! Why not blame HIM?
The toxic waste is what SAVED me! I should've drowned in that saltine dough. But the radiation kept me alive.

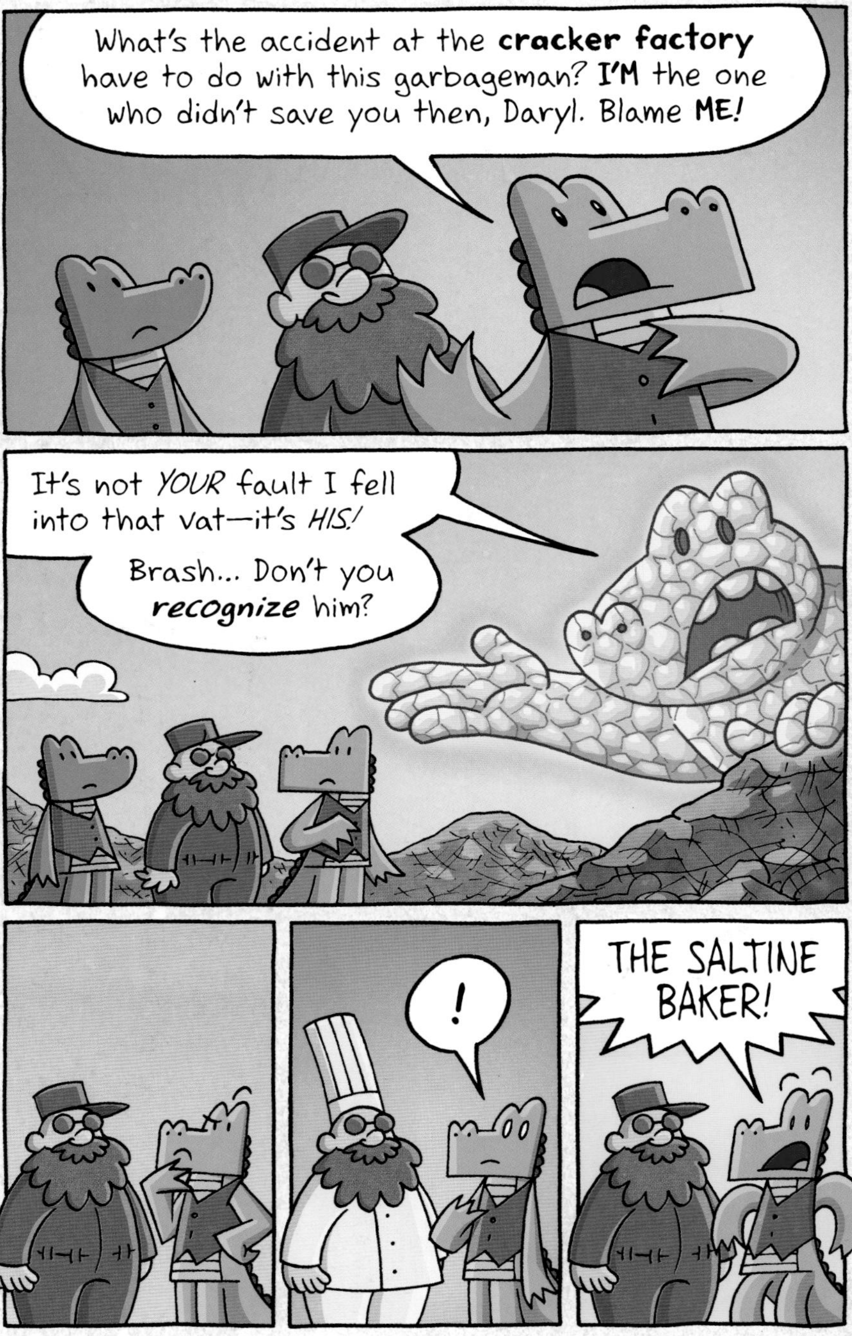
What's the accident at the **cracker factory** have to do with this garbageman? **I'M** the one who didn't save you then, Daryl. Blame **ME!**
It's not *YOUR* fault I fell into that vat—it's *HIS!*
Brash... Don't you **recognize** him?
!
THE SALTINE BAKER!

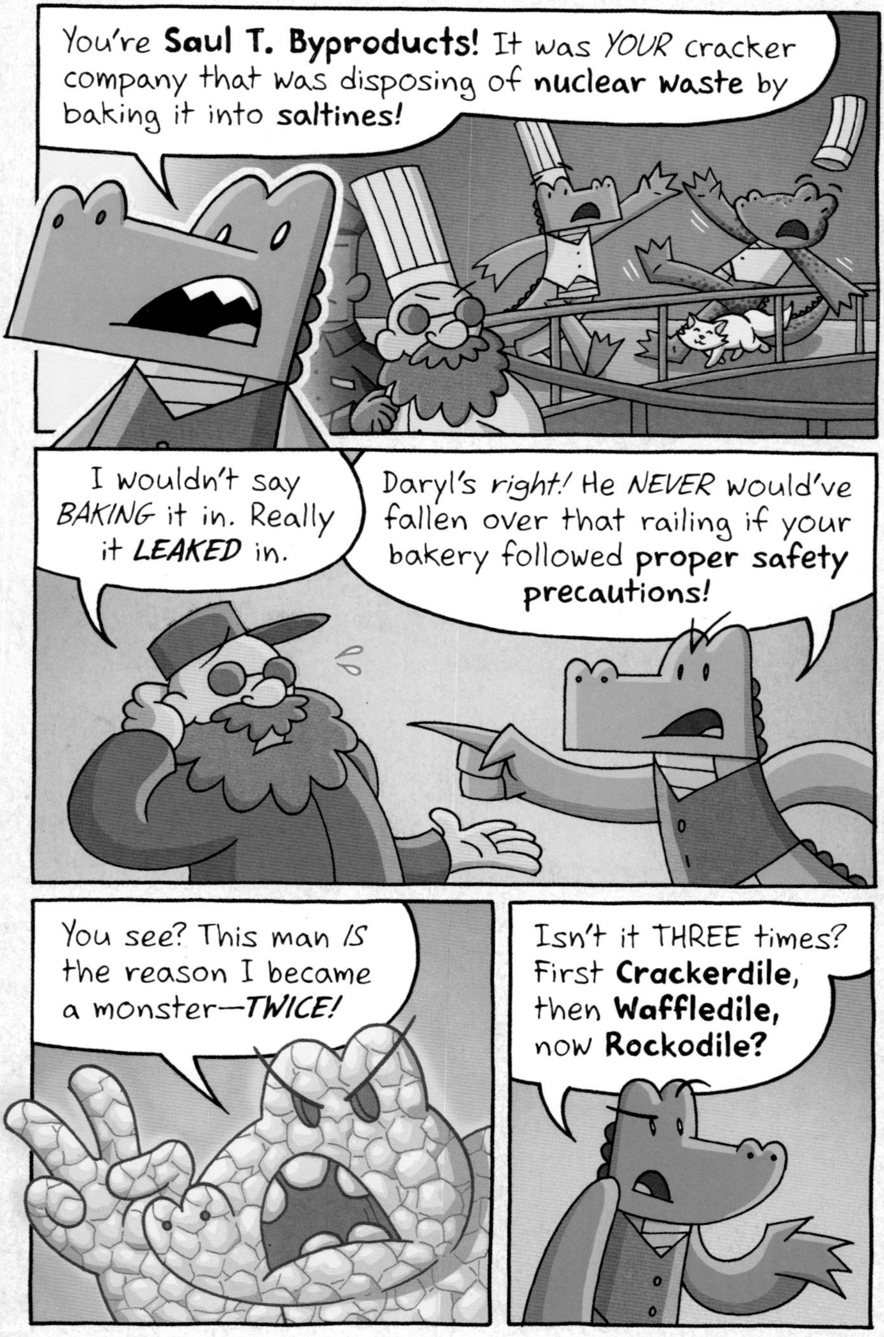
You're **Saul T. Byproducts!** It was *YOUR* cracker company that was disposing of **nuclear waste** by baking it into **saltines!**
I wouldn't say *BAKING* it in. Really it ***LEAKED*** in.
Daryl's *right!* He *NEVER* would've fallen over that railing if your bakery followed **proper safety precautions!**
You see? This man *IS* the reason I became a monster—***TWICE!***
Isn't it THREE times? First **Crackerdile,** then **Waffledile,** now **Rockodile?**

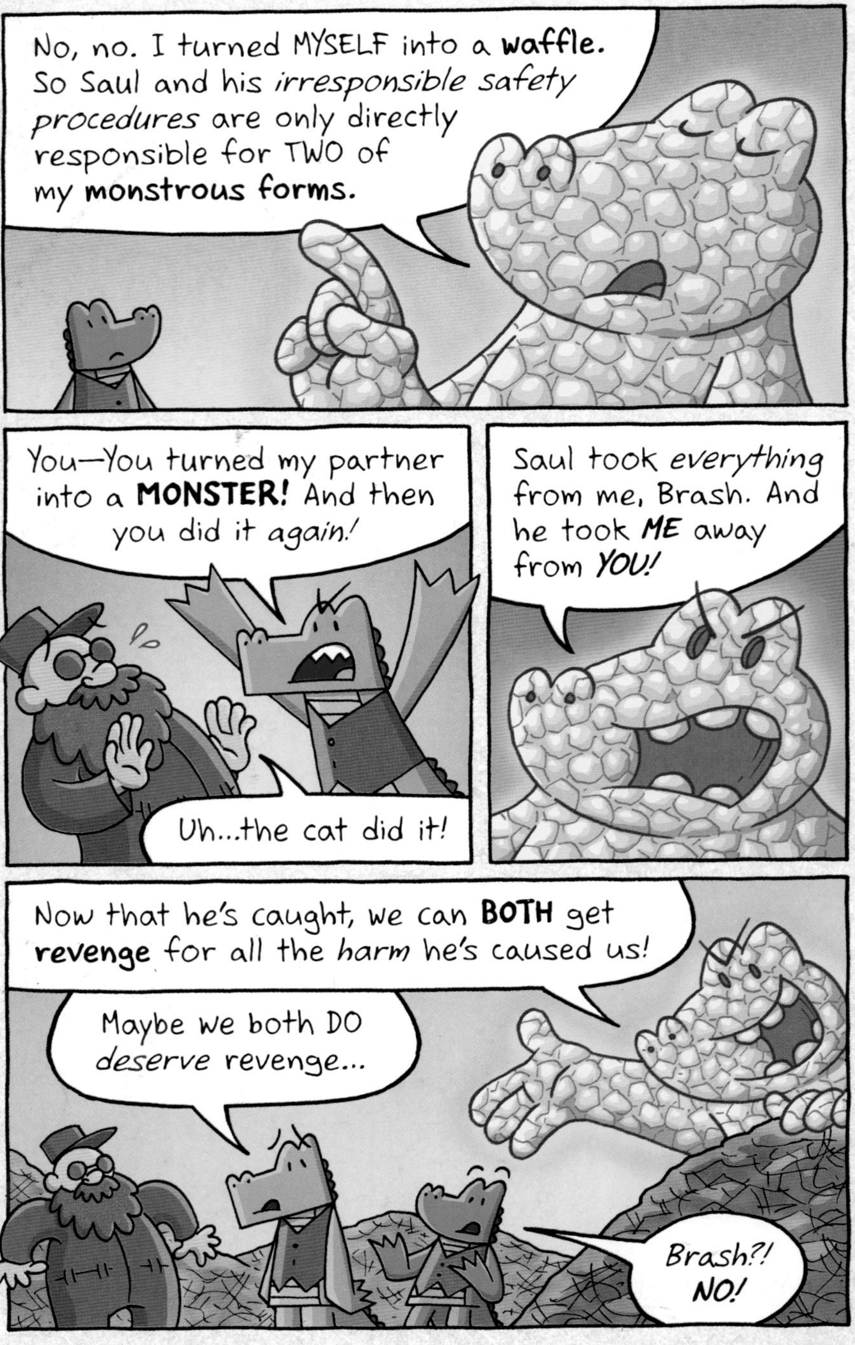
No, no. I turned MYSELF into a **waffle.** So Saul and his *irresponsible safety procedures* are only directly responsible for TWO of my **monstrous forms.**
You—You turned my partner into a **MONSTER!** And then you did it *again!*
Uh...the cat did it!
Saul took *everything* from me, Brash. And he took **ME** away from **YOU!**
Now that he's caught, we can **BOTH** get **revenge** for all the *harm* he's caused us!
Maybe we both DO *deserve* revenge...
Brash?! NO!

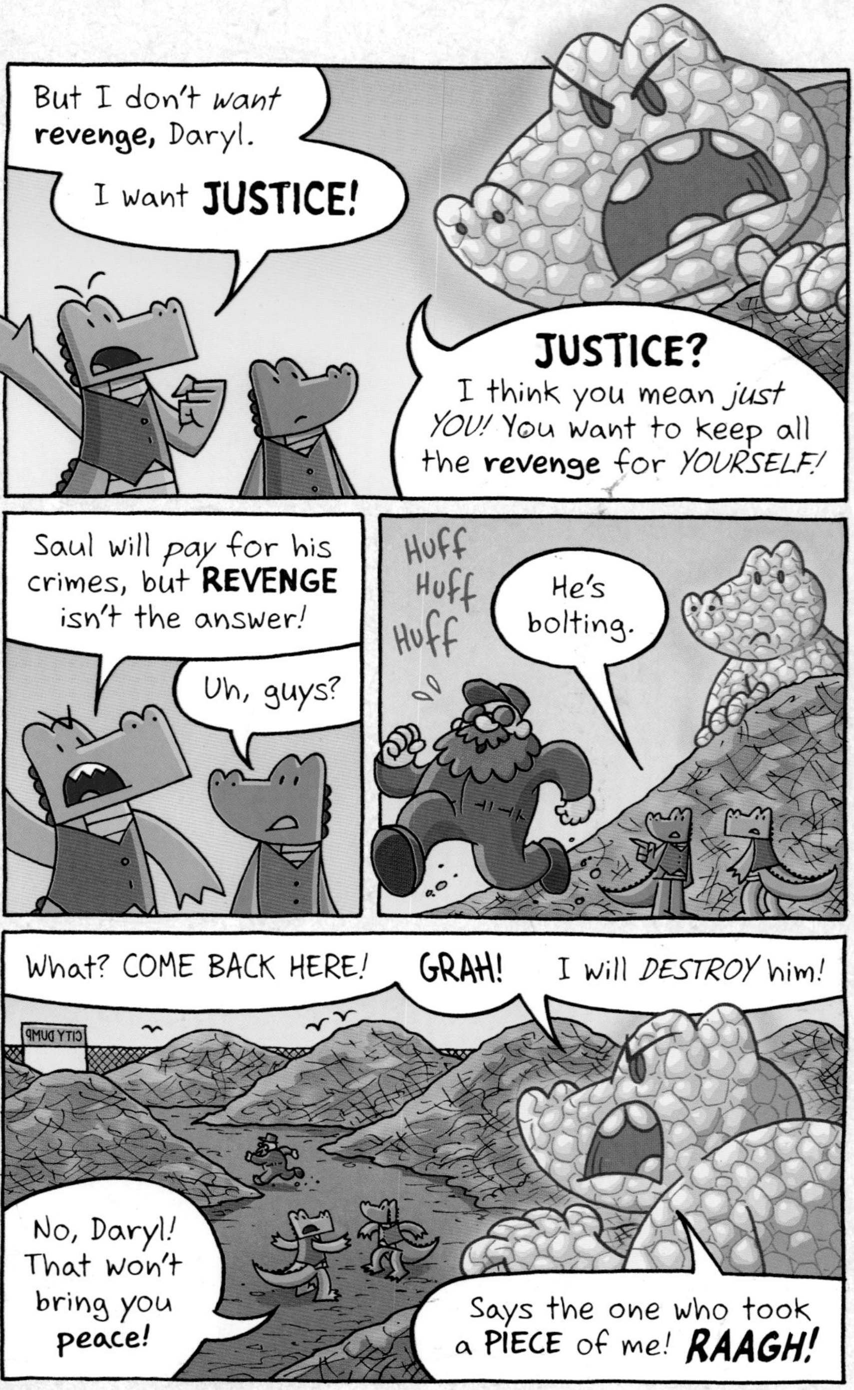
But I don't *want* **revenge,** Daryl.
I want **JUSTICE!**
JUSTICE? I think you mean *just YOU!* You want to keep all the **revenge** for *YOURSELF!*
Saul will *pay* for his crimes, but **REVENGE** isn't the answer!
Uh, guys?
HUFF HUFF HUFF
He's bolting.
What? COME BACK HERE! **GRAH!** I will *DESTROY* him!
CITY DUMP
No, Daryl! That won't bring you **peace!**
Says the one who took a **PIECE** of me! ***RAAGH!***

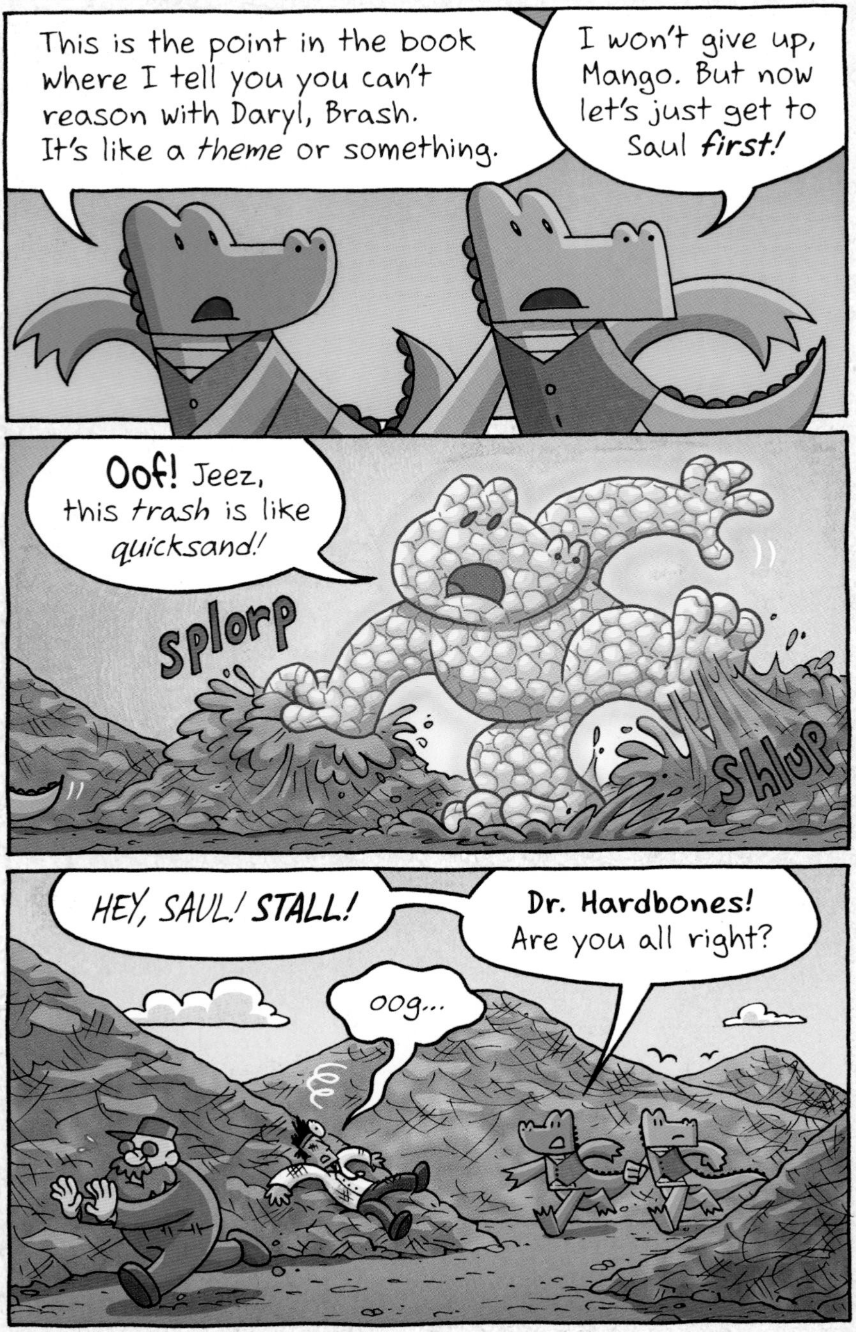
This is the point in the book where I tell you you can't reason with Daryl, Brash. It's like a *theme* or something.
I won't give up, Mango. But now let's just get to Saul ***first!***
Oof! Jeez, this *trash* is like *quicksand!*
splorp
SHLUP
HEY, SAUL! ***STALL!***
Dr. Hardbones! Are you all right?
oog...

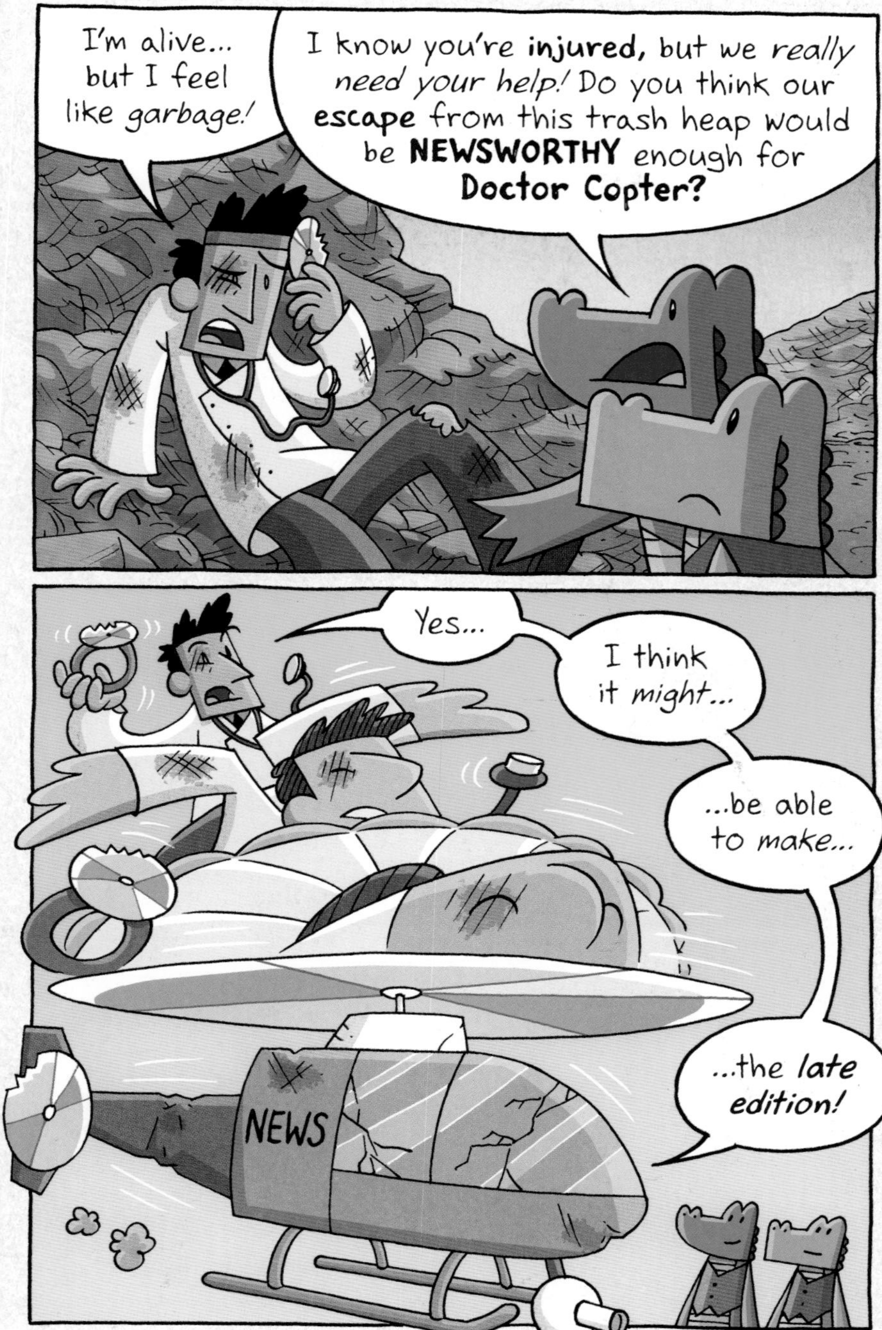
I'm alive... but I feel like *garbage!*
I know you're **injured,** but we *really need your help!* Do you think our **escape** from this trash heap would be **NEWSWORTHY** enough for **Doctor Copter?**
Yes...
I think it *might...*
...be able to *make...*
...the *late* **edition!**
NEWS

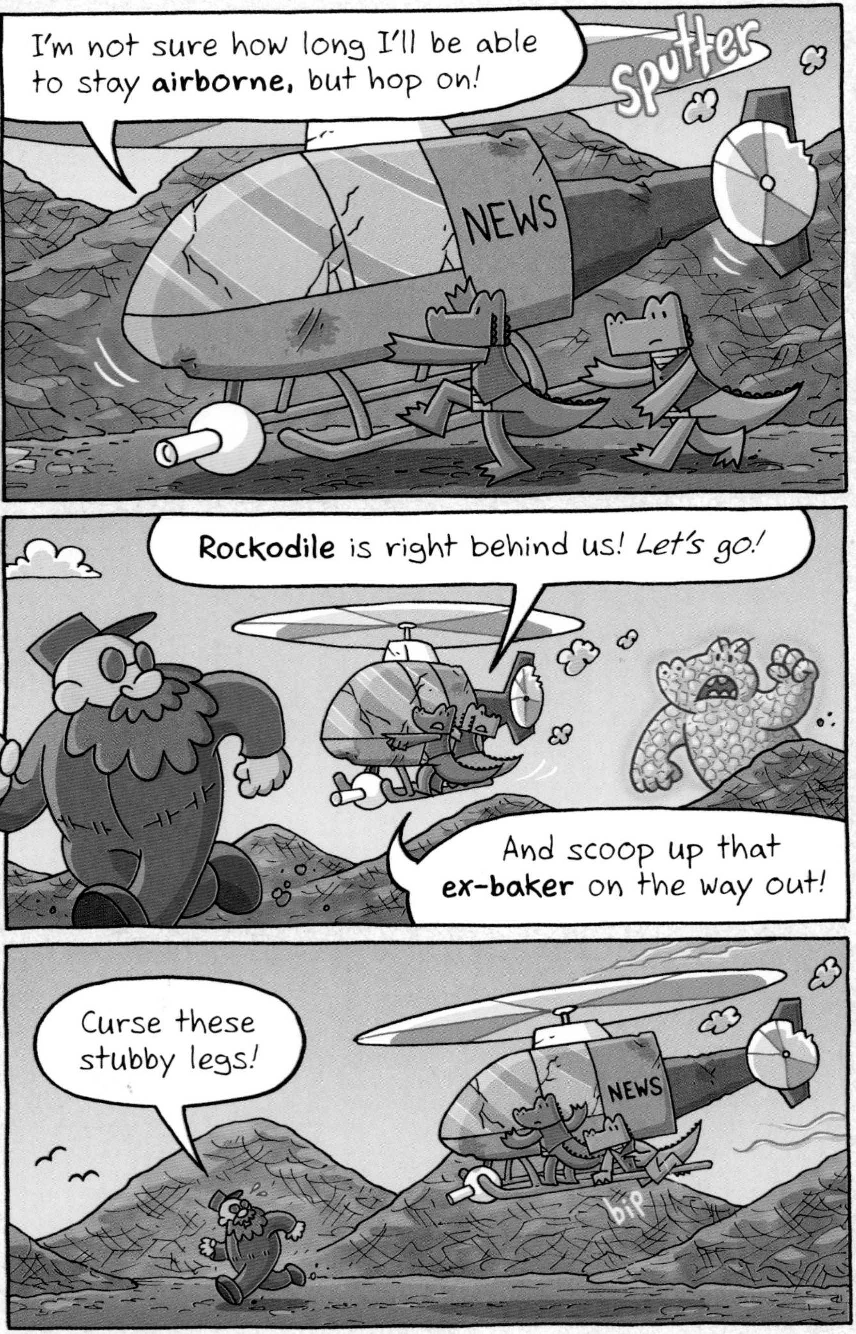
I'm not sure how long I'll be able to stay **airborne**, but hop on!
Sputter
NEWS
Rockodile is right behind us! *Let's go!*
And scoop up that **ex-baker** on the way out!
Curse these stubby legs!
NEWS
bip

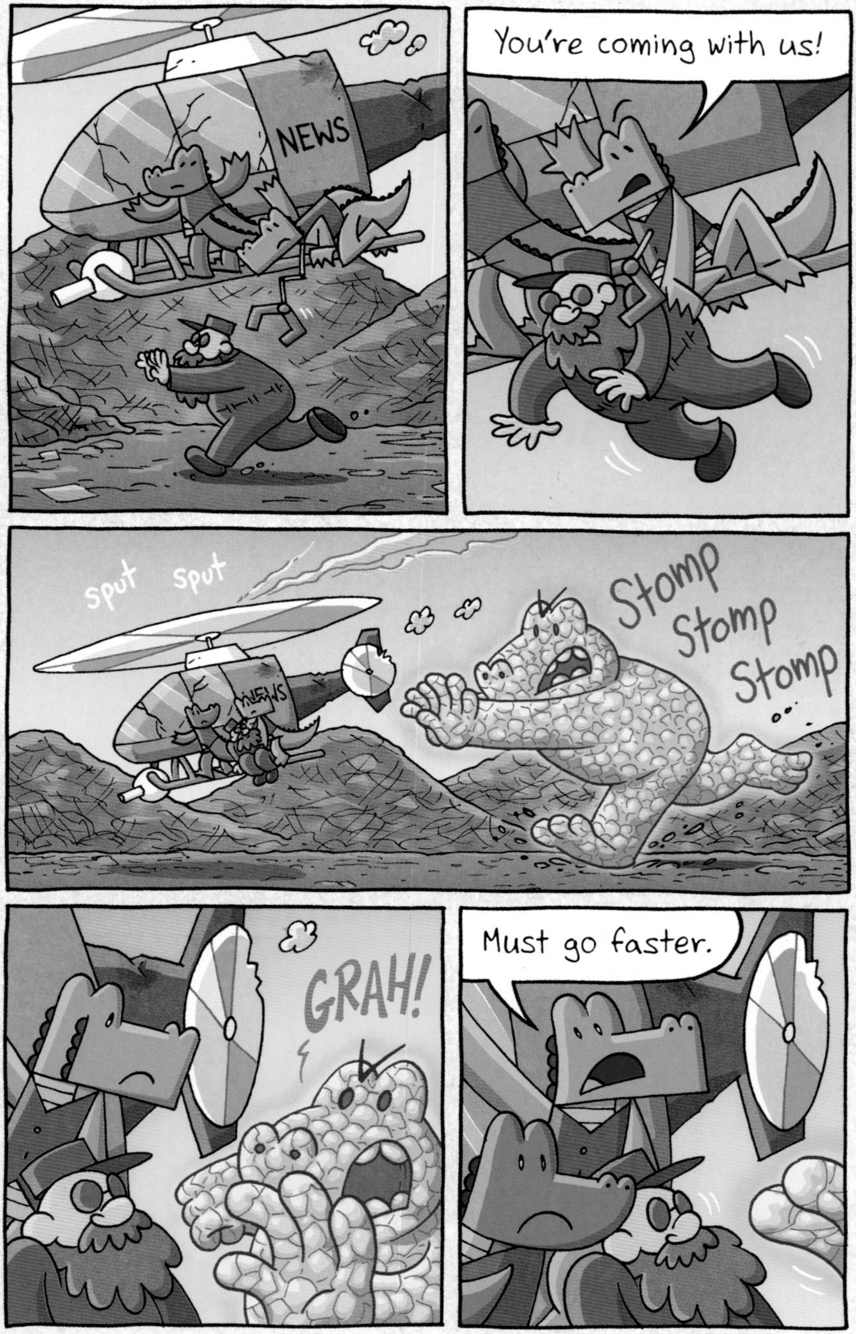
NEWS
You're coming with us!
sput sput
Stomp
Stomp
Stomp
GRAH!
Must go faster.

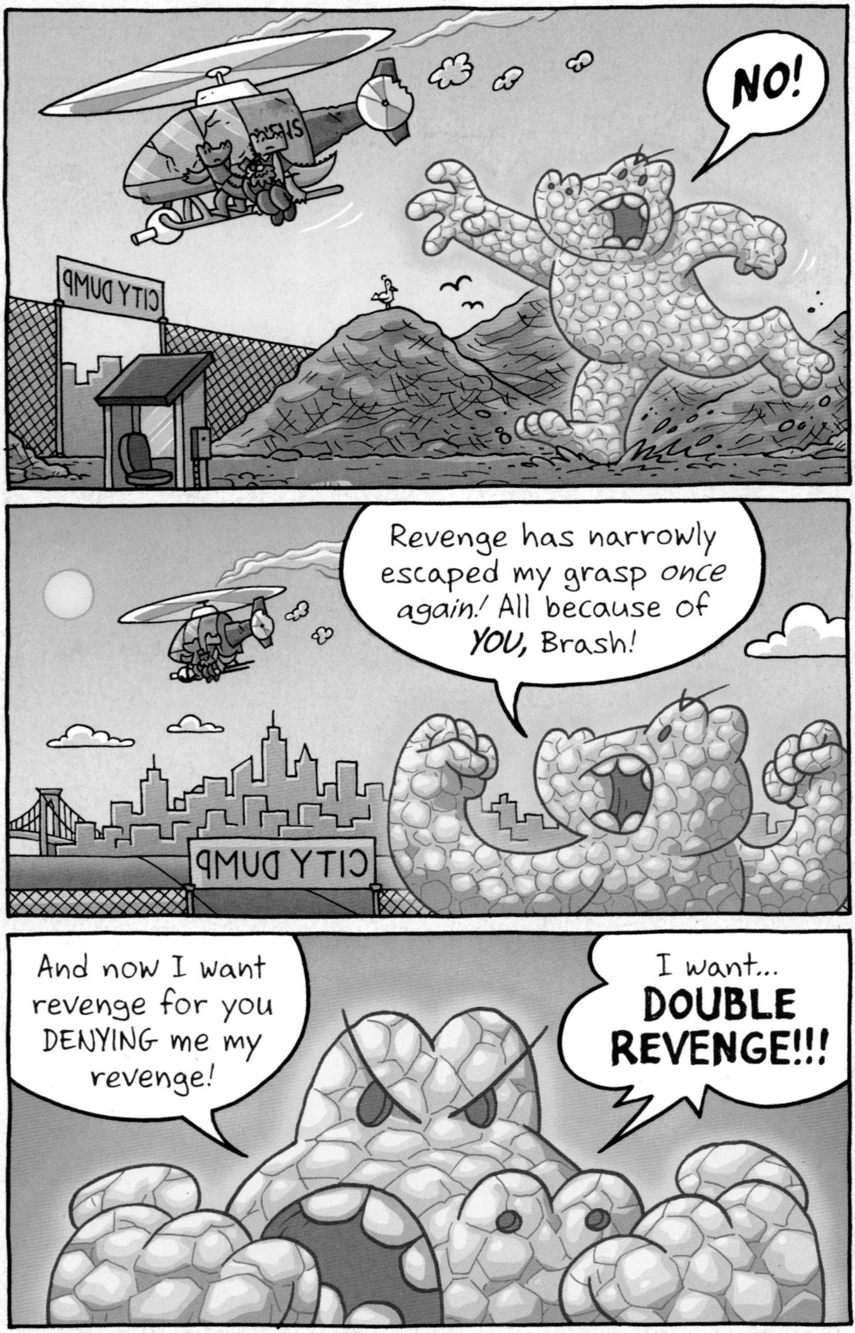
NO!
Revenge has narrowly escaped my grasp once again! All because of YOU, Brash!
And now I want revenge for you DENYING me my revenge!
I want... DOUBLE REVENGE!!!

Chapter 16

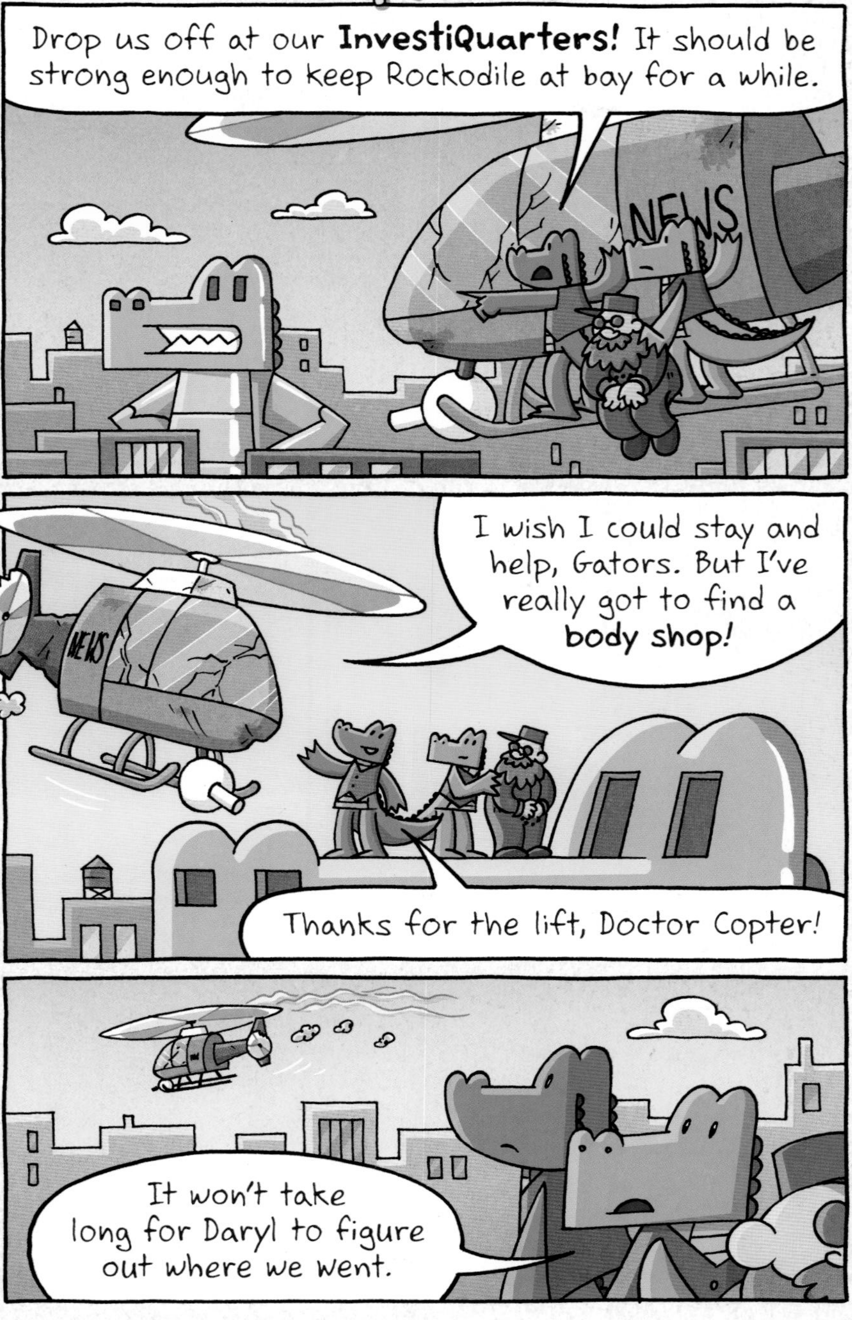
Drop us off at our **InvestiQuarters!** It should be strong enough to keep Rockodile at bay for a while.
NEWS
I wish I could stay and help, Gators. But I've really got to find a **body shop!**
NEWS
Thanks for the lift, Doctor Copter!
It won't take long for Daryl to figure out where we went.

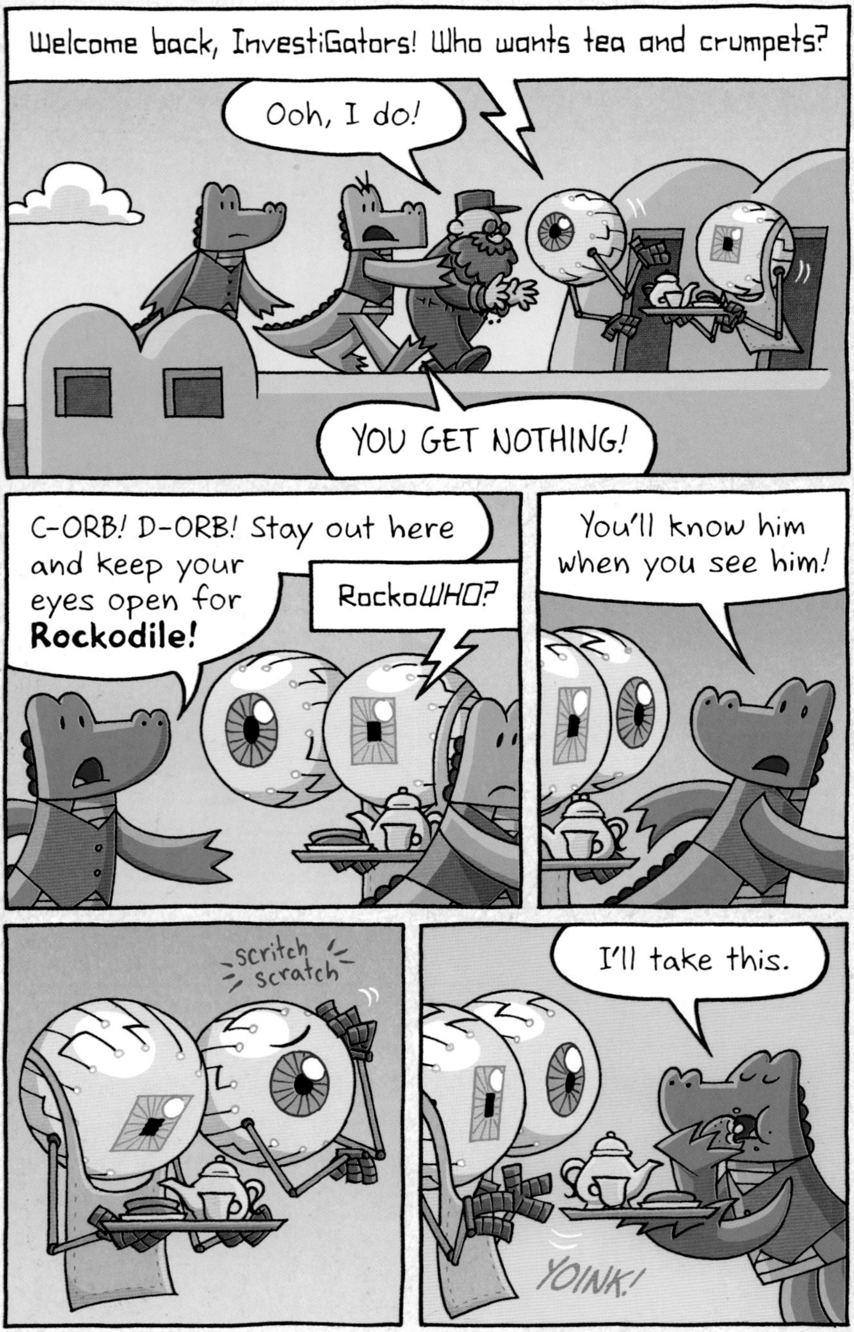
Welcome back, InvestiGators! Who wants tea and crumpets?
Ooh, I do!
YOU GET NOTHING!
C-ORB! D-ORB! Stay out here and keep your eyes open for **Rockodile!**
RockoWHO?
You'll know him when you see him!
scritch scratch
I'll take this.
YOINK!

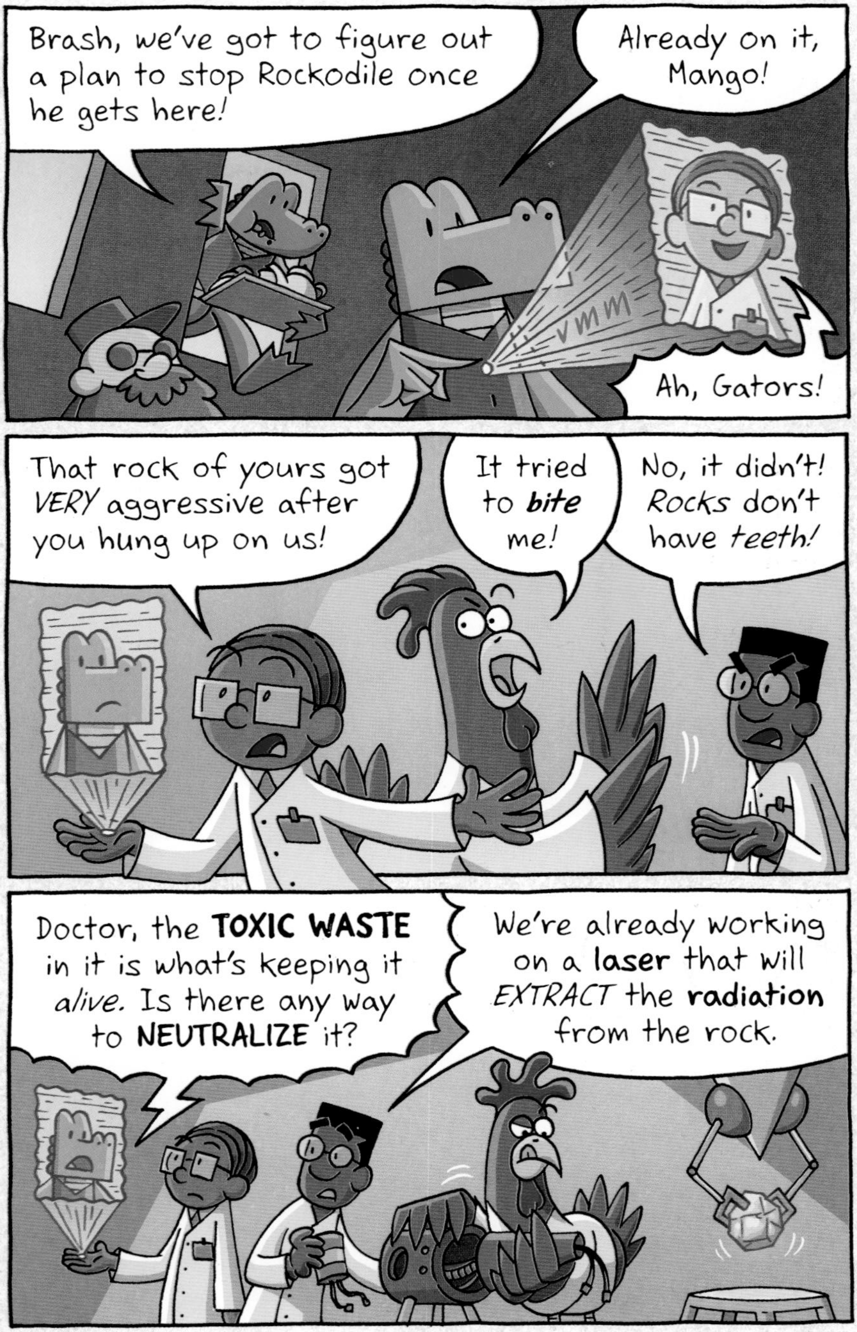
Brash, we've got to figure out a plan to stop Rockodile once he gets here!
Already on it, Mango!
VMM
Ah, Gators!
That rock of yours got *VERY* aggressive after you hung up on us!
It tried to **bite** me!
No, it didn't! *Rocks* don't have *teeth!*
Doctor, the **TOXIC WASTE** in it is what's keeping it *alive.* Is there any way to **NEUTRALIZE** it?
We're already working on a **laser** that will *EXTRACT* the **radiation** from the rock.

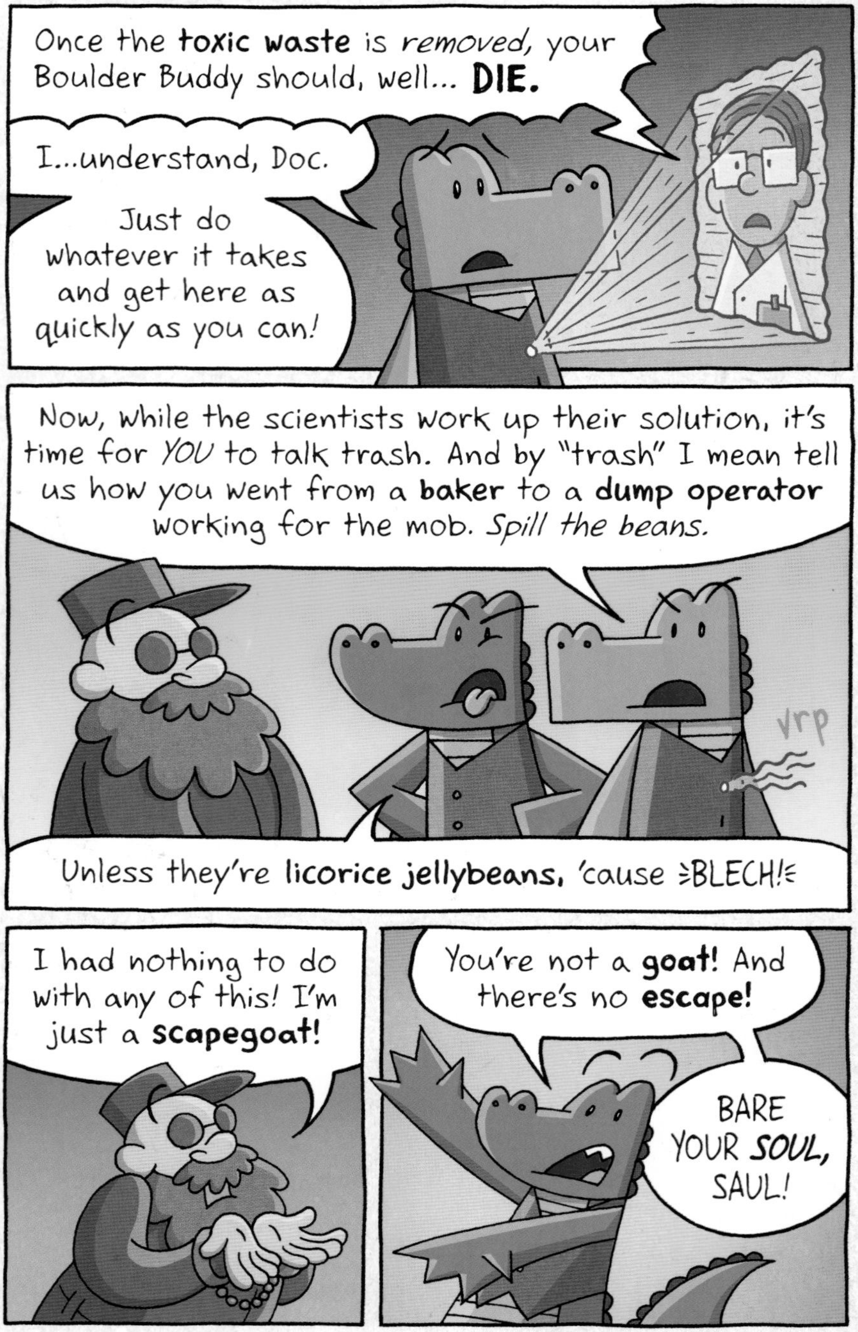
Once the **toxic waste** is *removed*, your Boulder Buddy should, well... **DIE.**
I...understand, Doc.
Just do whatever it takes and get here as quickly as you can!
Now, while the scientists work up their solution, it's time for *YOU* to talk trash. And by "trash" I mean tell us how you went from a **baker** to a **dump operator** working for the mob. *Spill the beans.*
vrp
Unless they're **licorice jellybeans**, 'cause BLECH!
I had nothing to do with any of this! I'm just a **scapegoat!**
You're not a **goat!** And there's no **escape!**
BARE YOUR *SOUL*, SAUL!

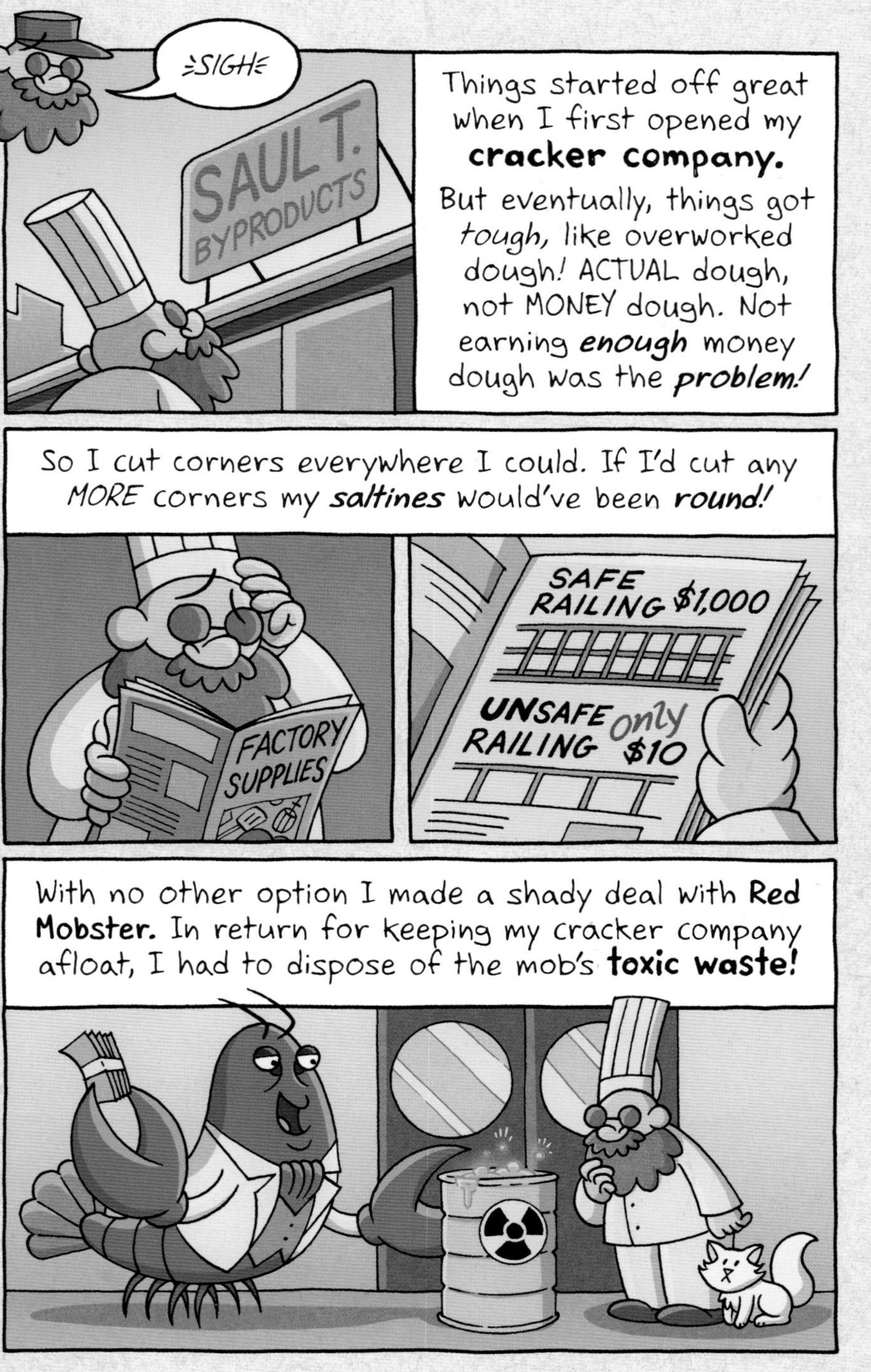
≈SIGH≈
SAUL T. BYPRODUCTS
Things started off great when I first opened my **cracker company.**
But eventually, things got *tough,* like overworked dough! ACTUAL dough, not MONEY dough. Not earning ***enough*** money dough was the ***problem!***
So I cut corners everywhere I could. If I'd cut any *MORE* corners my ***saltines*** would've been ***round!***
FACTORY SUPPLIES
SAFE RAILING $1,000
UNSAFE RAILING only $10
With no other option I made a shady deal with **Red Mobster.** In return for keeping my cracker company afloat, I had to dispose of the mob's **toxic waste!**

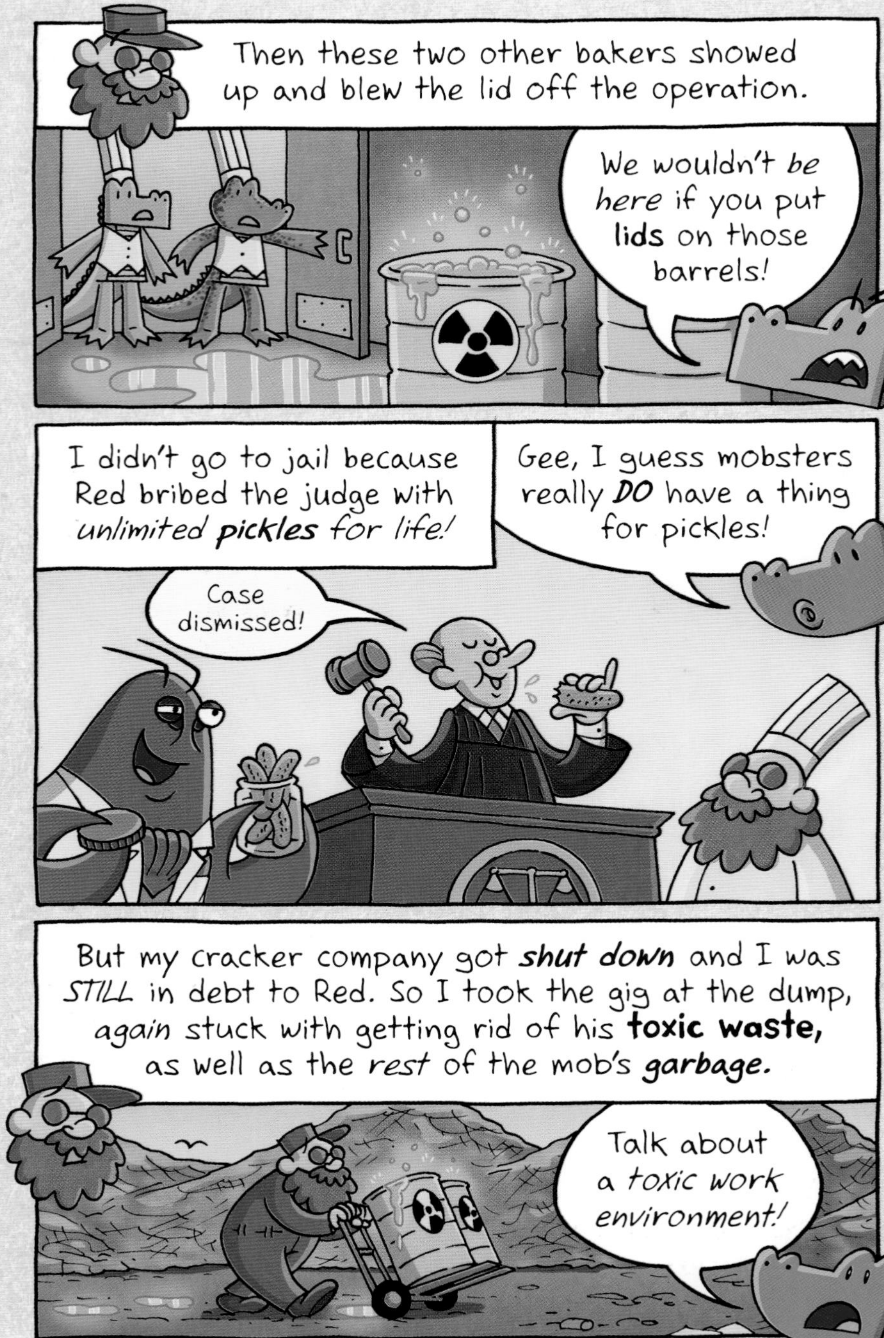

Then these two other bakers showed up and blew the lid off the operation.
We wouldn't *be here* if you put **lids** on those barrels!
I didn't go to jail because Red bribed the judge with *unlimited* ***pickles*** *for life!*
Gee, I guess mobsters really ***DO*** have a thing for pickles!
Case dismissed!
But my cracker company got ***shut down*** and I was *STILL* in debt to Red. So I took the gig at the dump, *again* stuck with getting rid of his **toxic waste,** as well as the *rest* of the mob's ***garbage.***
Talk about a *toxic work environment!*

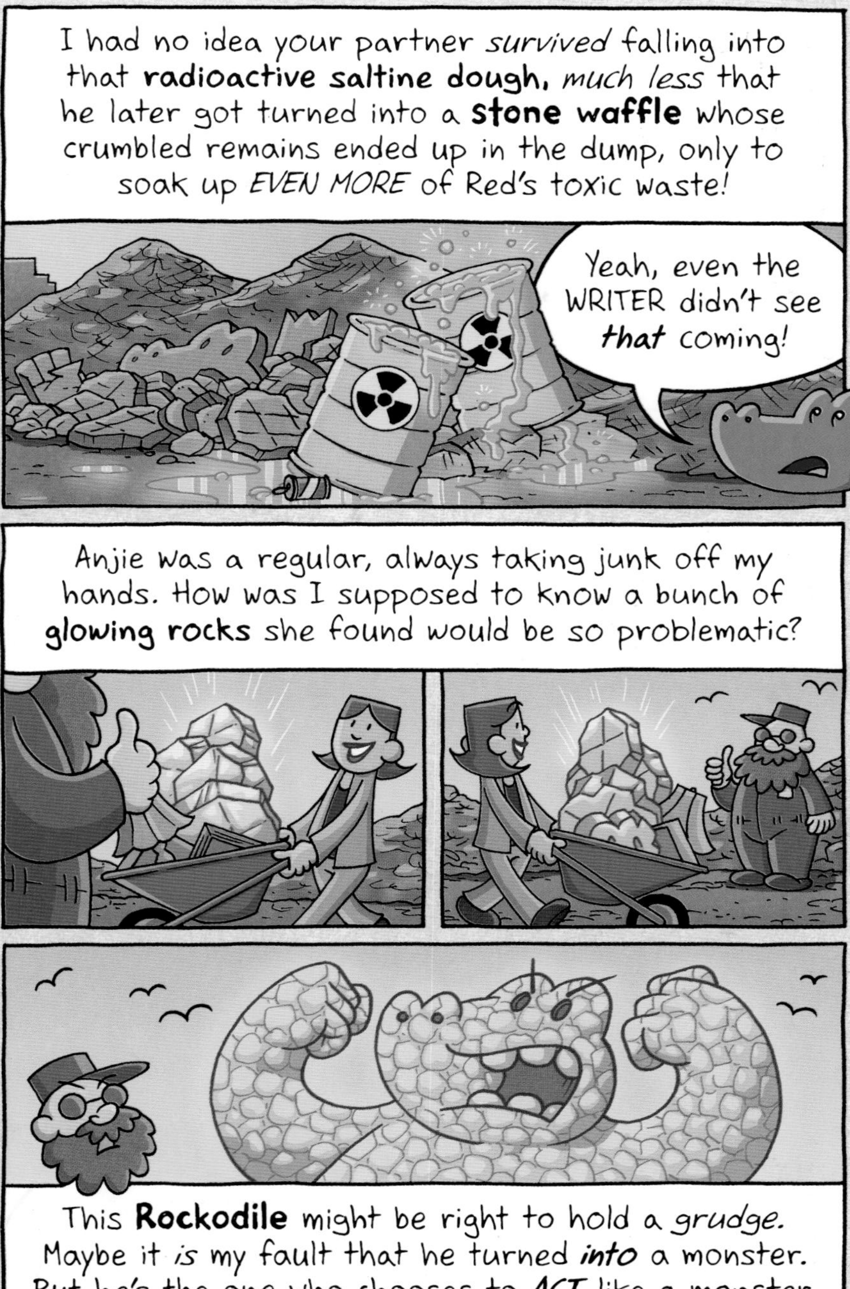
I had no idea your partner *survived* falling into that **radioactive saltine dough,** *much less* that he later got turned into a **stone waffle** whose crumbled remains ended up in the dump, only to soak up *EVEN MORE* of Red's toxic waste!
Yeah, even the WRITER didn't see ***that*** coming!
Anjie was a regular, always taking junk off my hands. How was I supposed to know a bunch of **glowing rocks** she found would be so problematic?
This **Rockodile** might be right to hold a *grudge.* Maybe it *is* my fault that he turned ***into*** a monster. But he's the one who chooses to ***ACT*** like a monster.

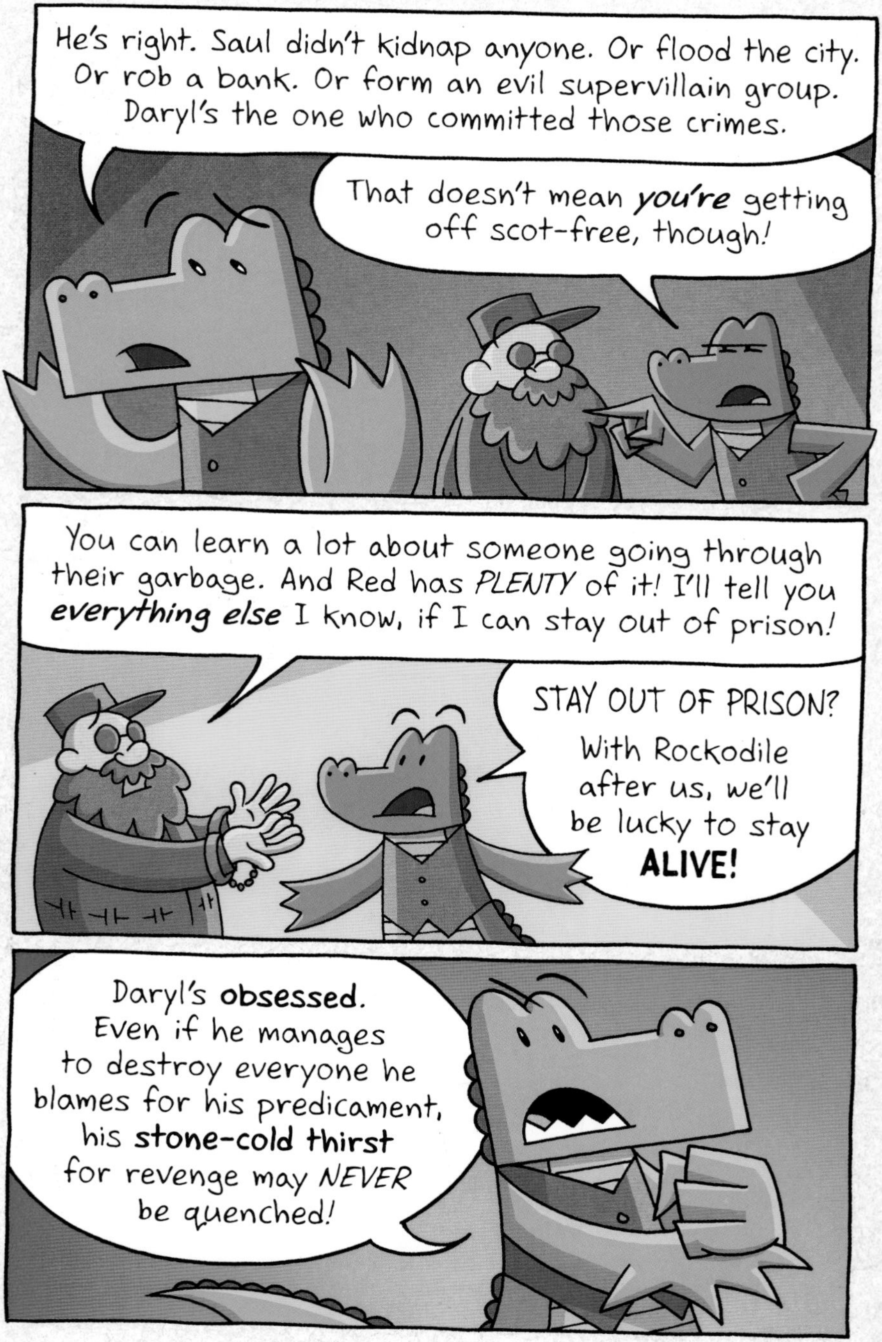
He's right. Saul didn't kidnap anyone. Or flood the city. Or rob a bank. Or form an evil supervillain group. Daryl's the one who committed those crimes.
That doesn't mean *you're* getting off scot-free, though!
You can learn a lot about someone going through their garbage. And Red has *PLENTY* of it! I'll tell you ***everything else*** I know, if I can stay out of prison!
STAY OUT OF PRISON?
With Rockodile after us, we'll be lucky to stay **ALIVE!**
Daryl's **obsessed.** Even if he manages to destroy everyone he blames for his predicament, his **stone-cold thirst** for revenge may *NEVER* be quenched!

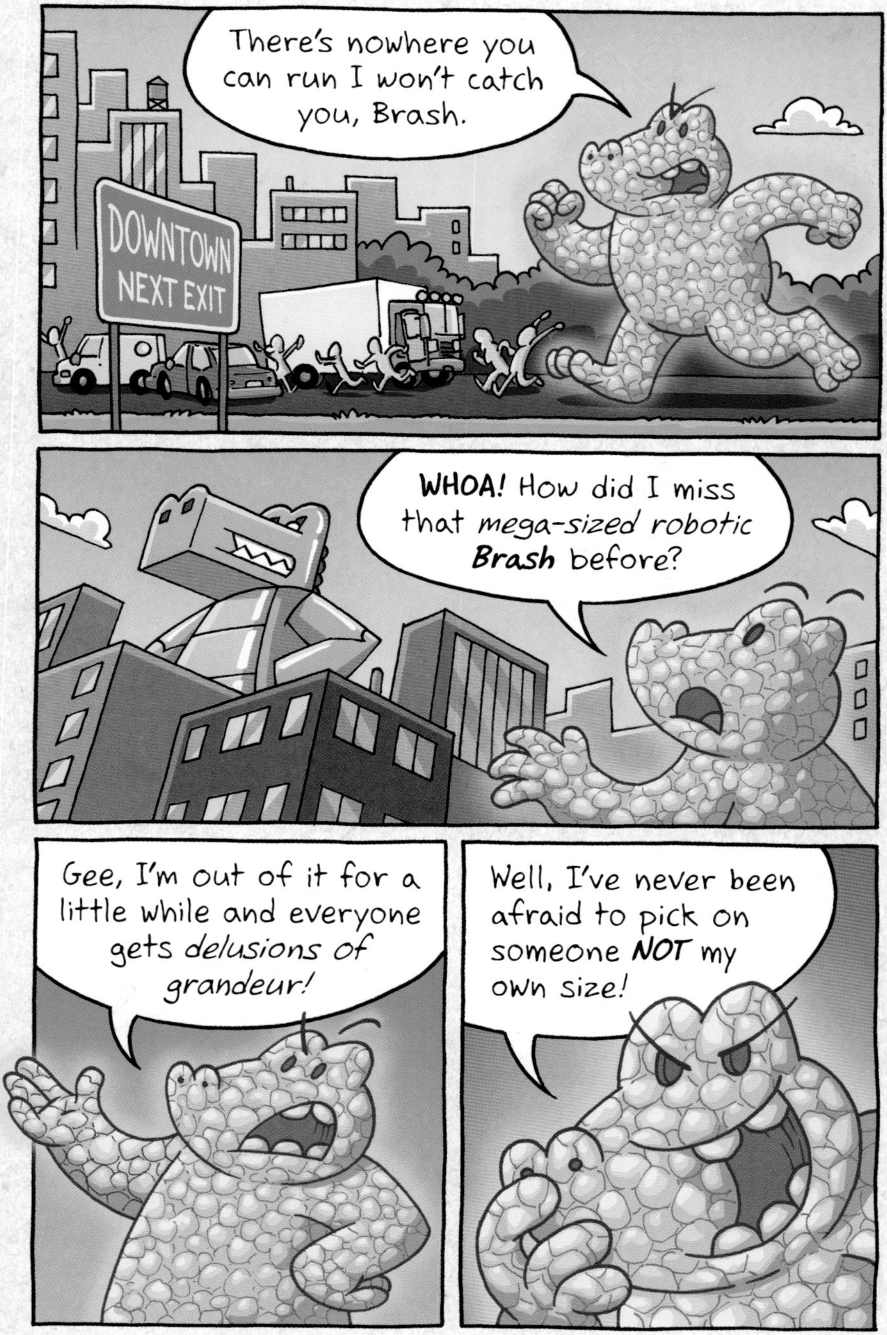
There's nowhere you can run I won't catch you, Brash.
DOWNTOWN NEXT EXIT
WHOA! How did I miss that *mega-sized robotic* **Brash** before?
Gee, I'm out of it for a little while and everyone gets *delusions of grandeur!*
Well, I've never been afraid to pick on someone **NOT** my own size!

Chapter 17

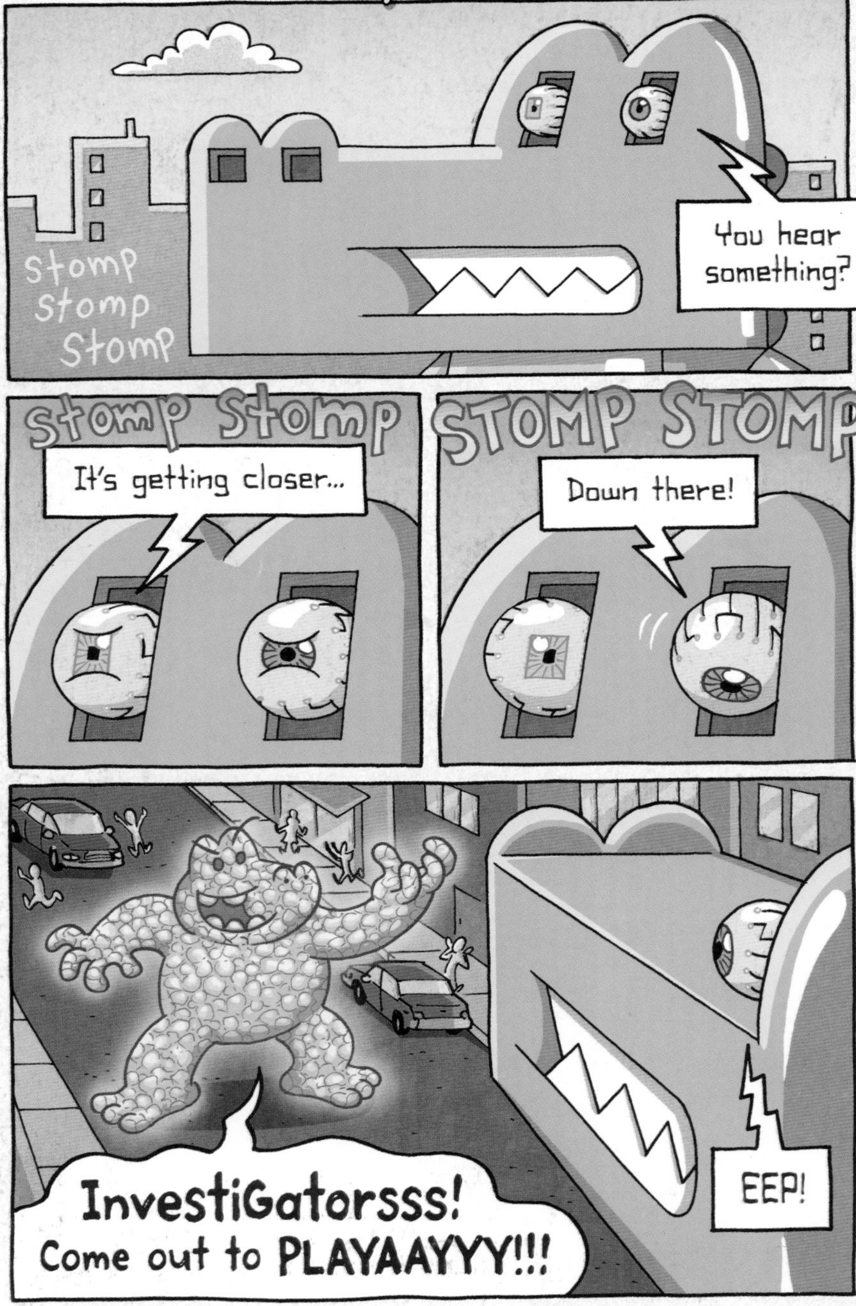
stomp
stomp
stomp
You hear something?
stomp Stomp
It's getting closer...
STOMP STOMP
Down there!
InvestiGatorsss! Come out to PLAYAAYYY!!!
EEP!

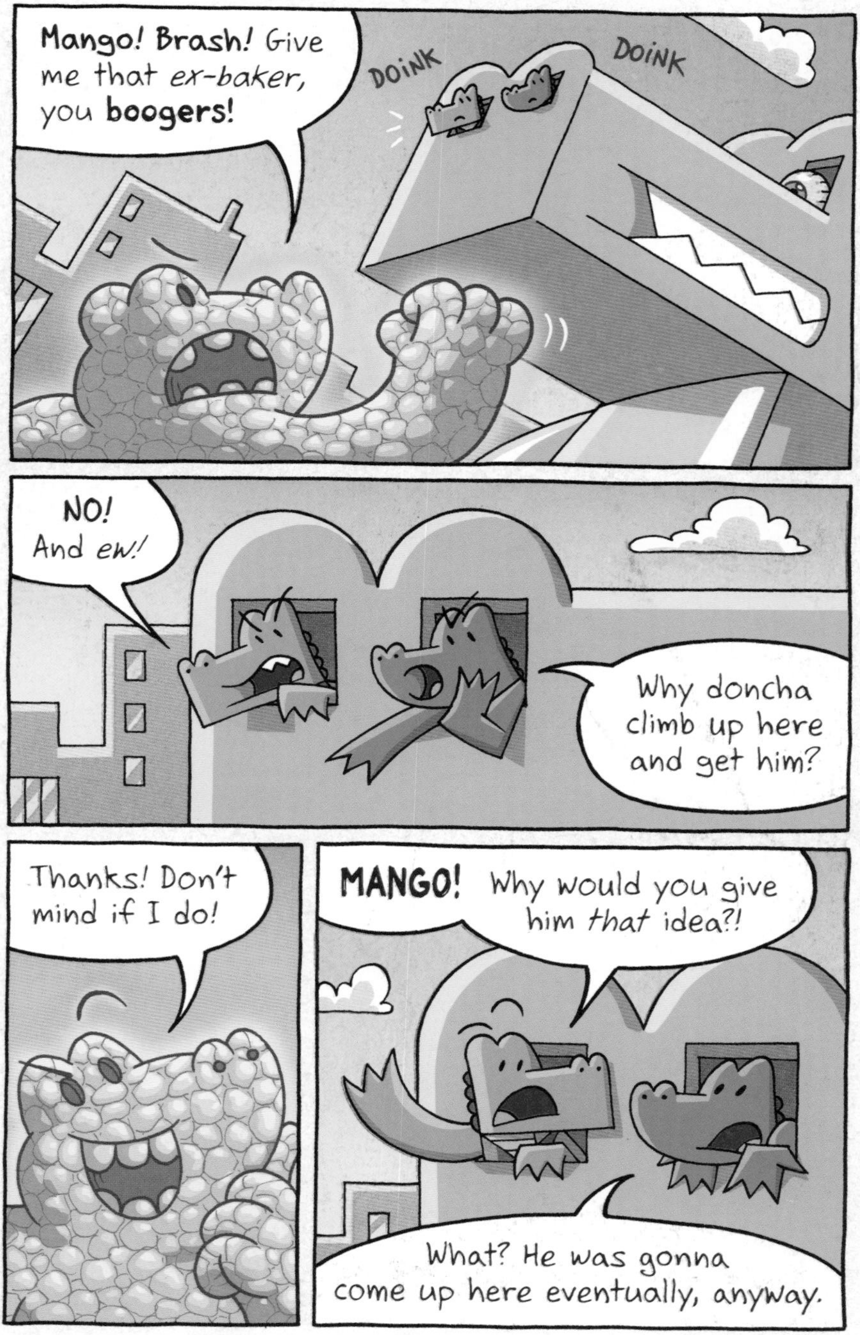

Mango! Brash! Give me that *ex-baker,* you **boogers!**
DOINK
DOINK
NO! And *ew!*
Why doncha climb up here and get him?
Thanks! Don't mind if I do!
MANGO! Why would you give him *that* idea?!
What? He was gonna come up here eventually, anyway.

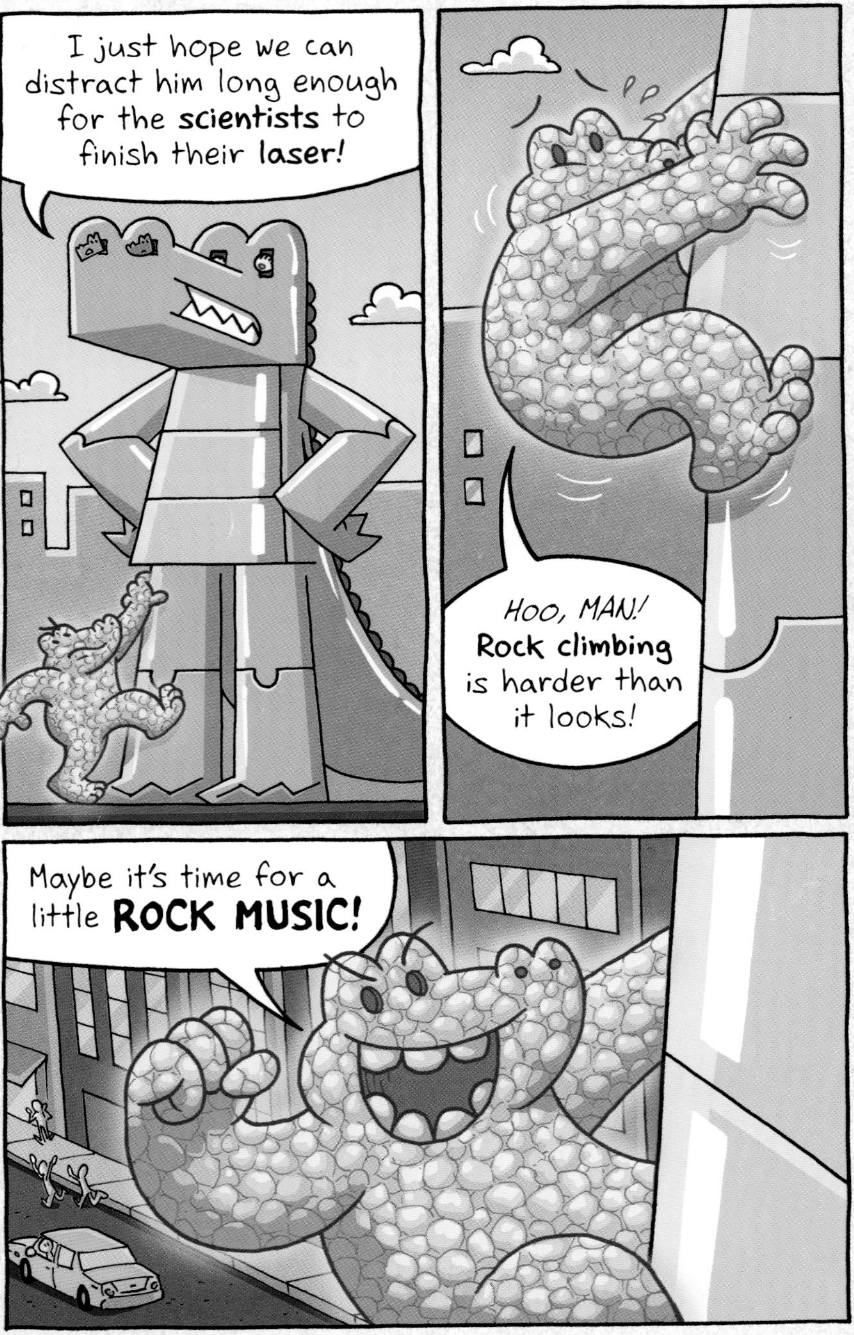
I just hope we can distract him long enough for the **scientists** to finish their **laser**!
HOO, MAN! **Rock climbing** is harder than it looks!
Maybe it's time for a little **ROCK MUSIC!**

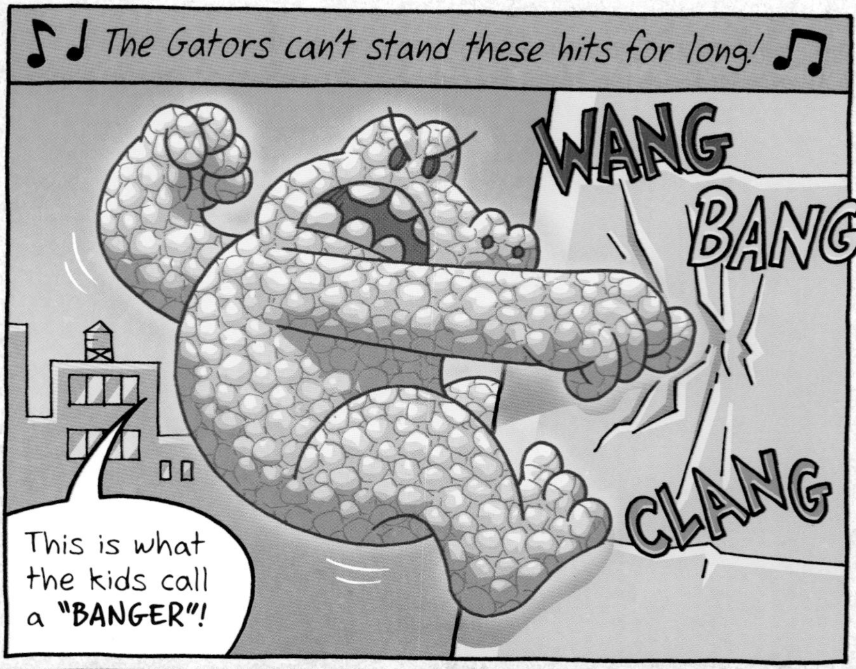
The Gators can't stand these hits for long!
WANG
BANG
CLANG
This is what the kids call a "BANGER"!

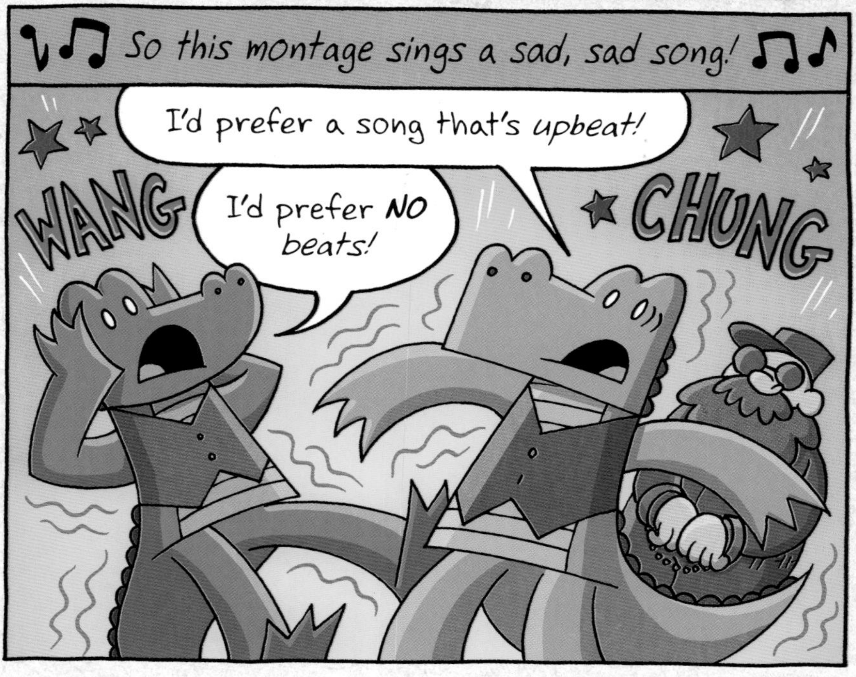
So this montage sings a sad, sad song!
I'd prefer a song that's upbeat!
I'd prefer NO beats!
WANG
CHUNG

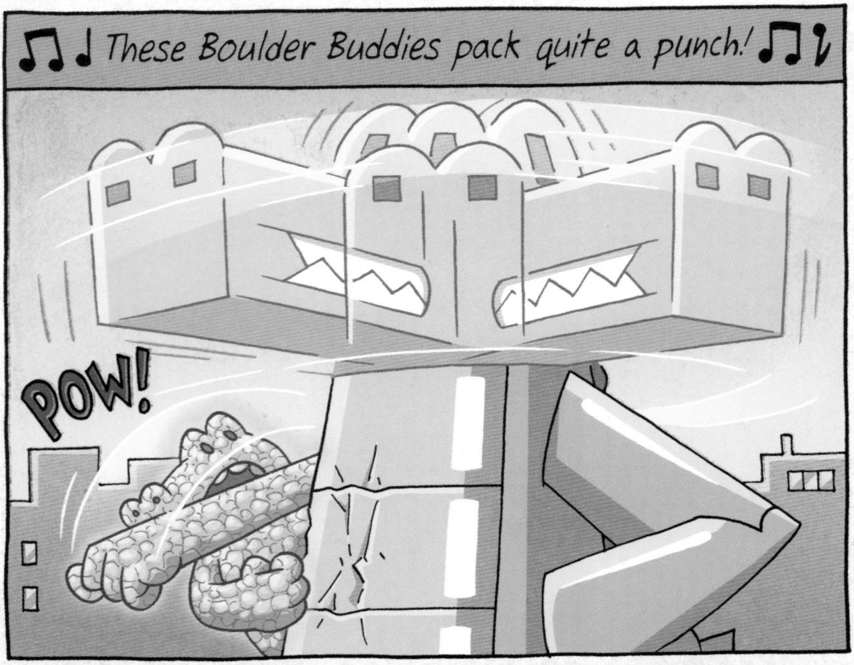
These Boulder Buddies pack quite a punch!
POW!

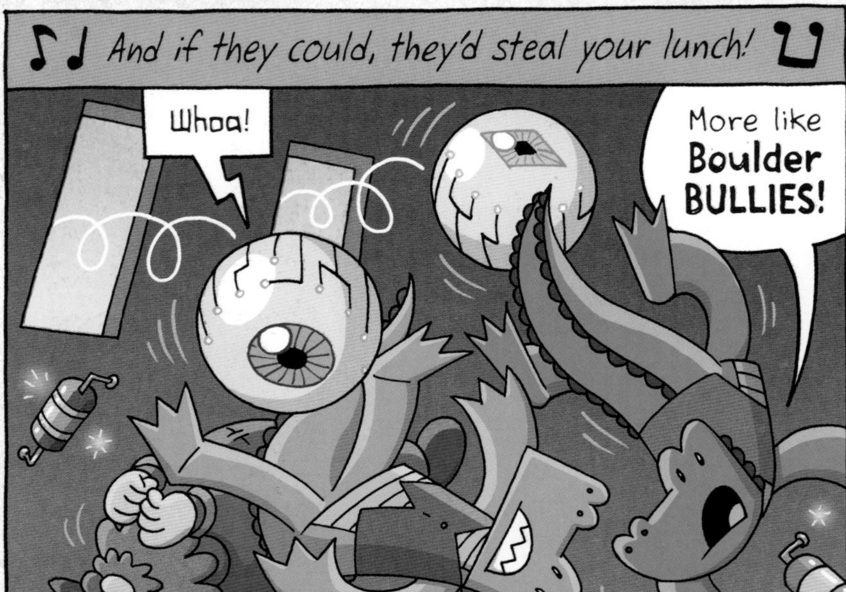
And if they could, they'd steal your lunch!
Whoa!
More like **Boulder BULLIES!**

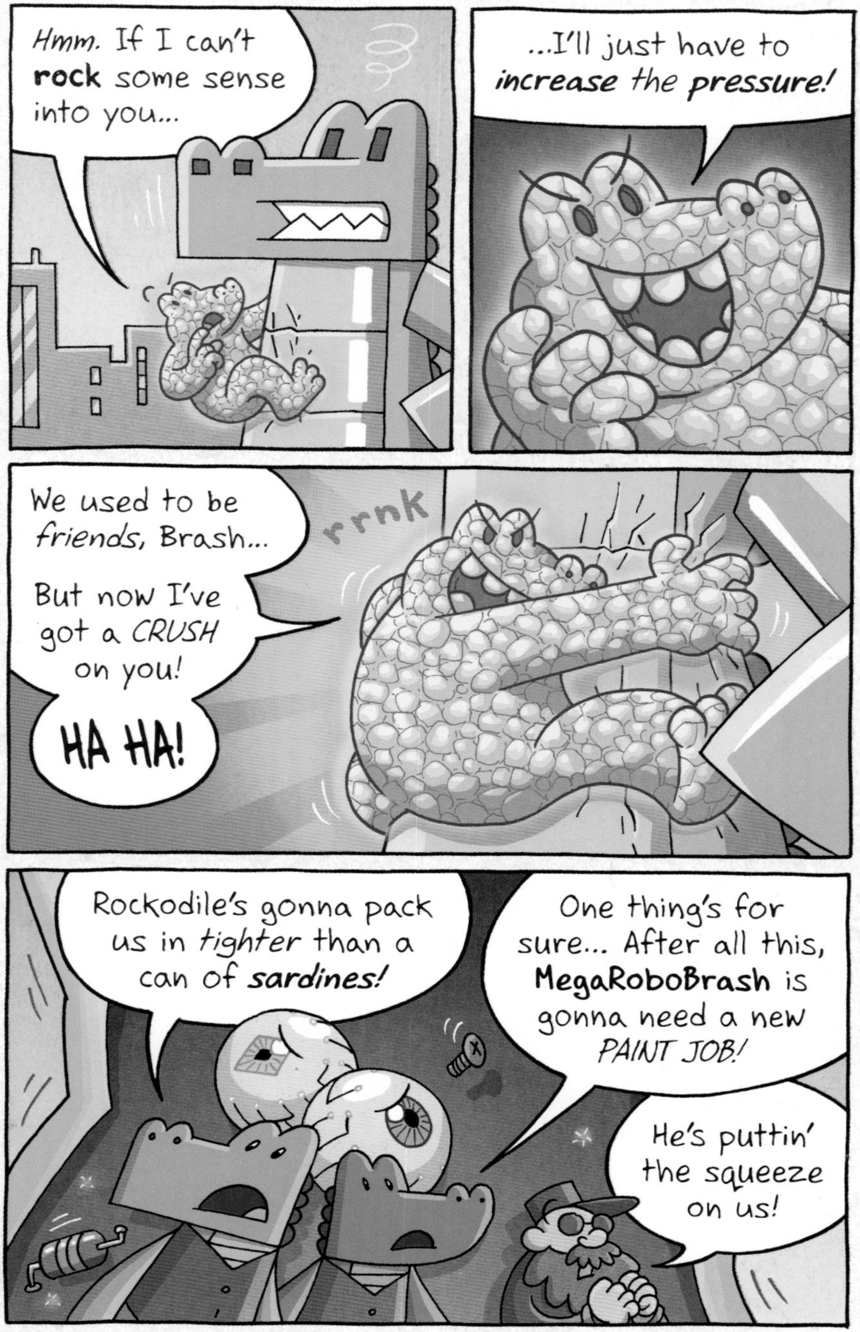
Hmm. If I can't **rock** some sense into you...
...I'll just have to *increase the* ***pressure!***
rrnK
We used to be *friends,* Brash...
But now I've got a *CRUSH* on you!
HA HA!
Rockodile's gonna pack us in *tighter* than a can of ***sardines!***
One thing's for sure... After all this, **MegaRoboBrash** is gonna need a new *PAINT JOB!*
He's puttin' the squeeze on us!

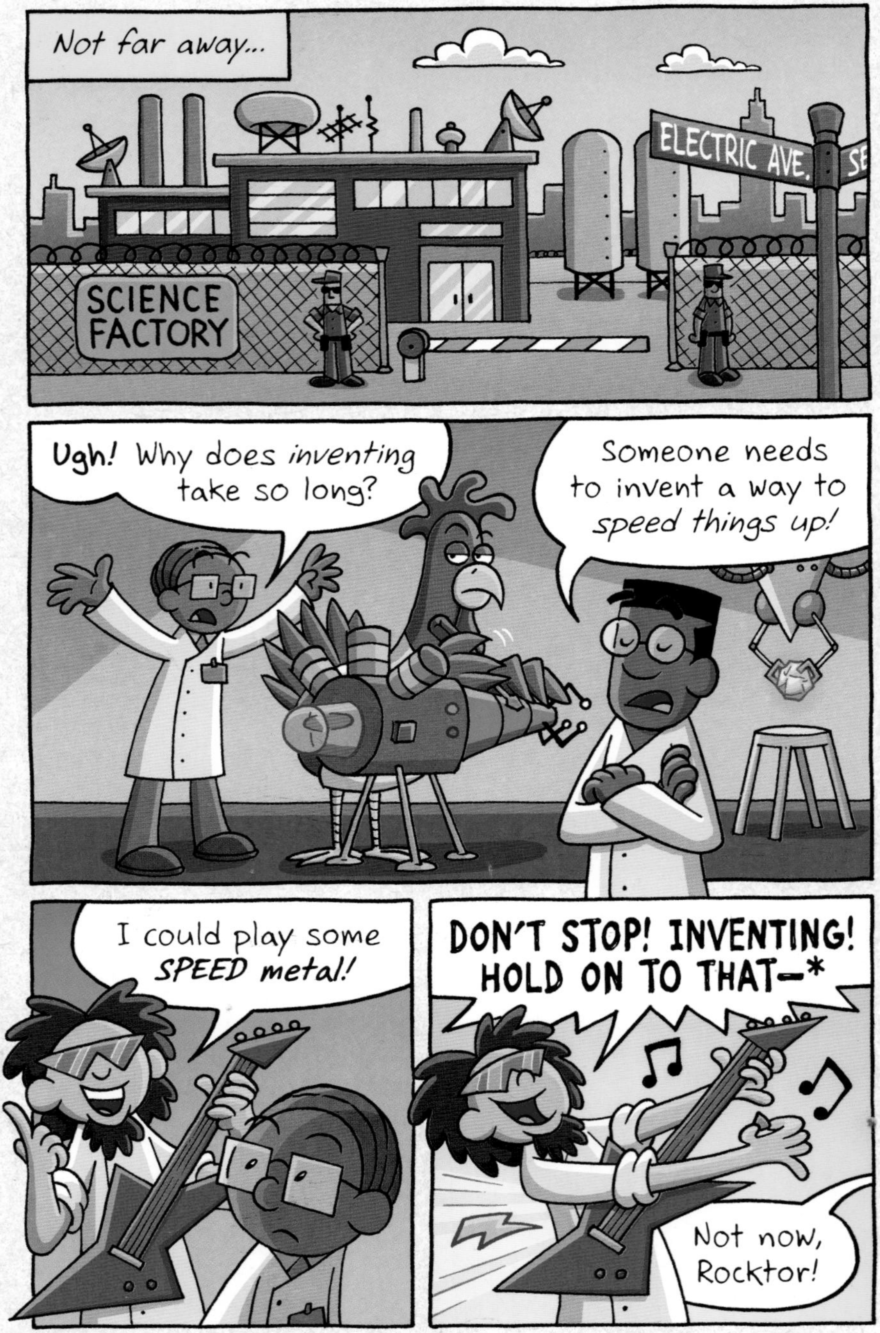
Not far away...
ELECTRIC AVE.
SCIENCE FACTORY
Ugh! Why does inventing take so long?
Someone needs to invent a way to speed things up!
I could play some SPEED metal!
DON'T STOP! INVENTING! HOLD ON TO THAT—*
Not now, Rocktor!

*Any song can be speed metal if you play it fast enough!

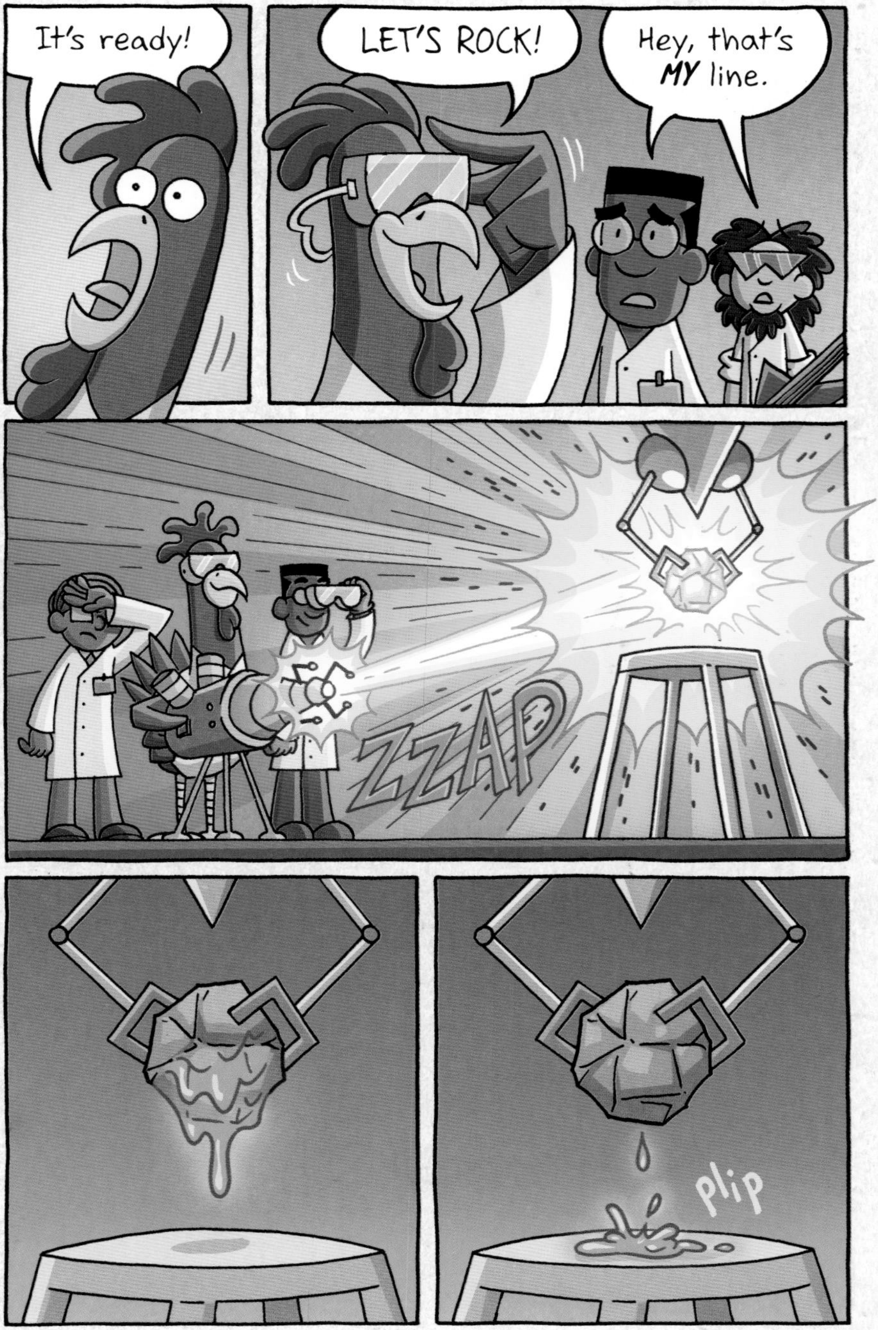
It's ready!
LET'S ROCK!
Hey, that's *MY* line.
ZZAP
plip

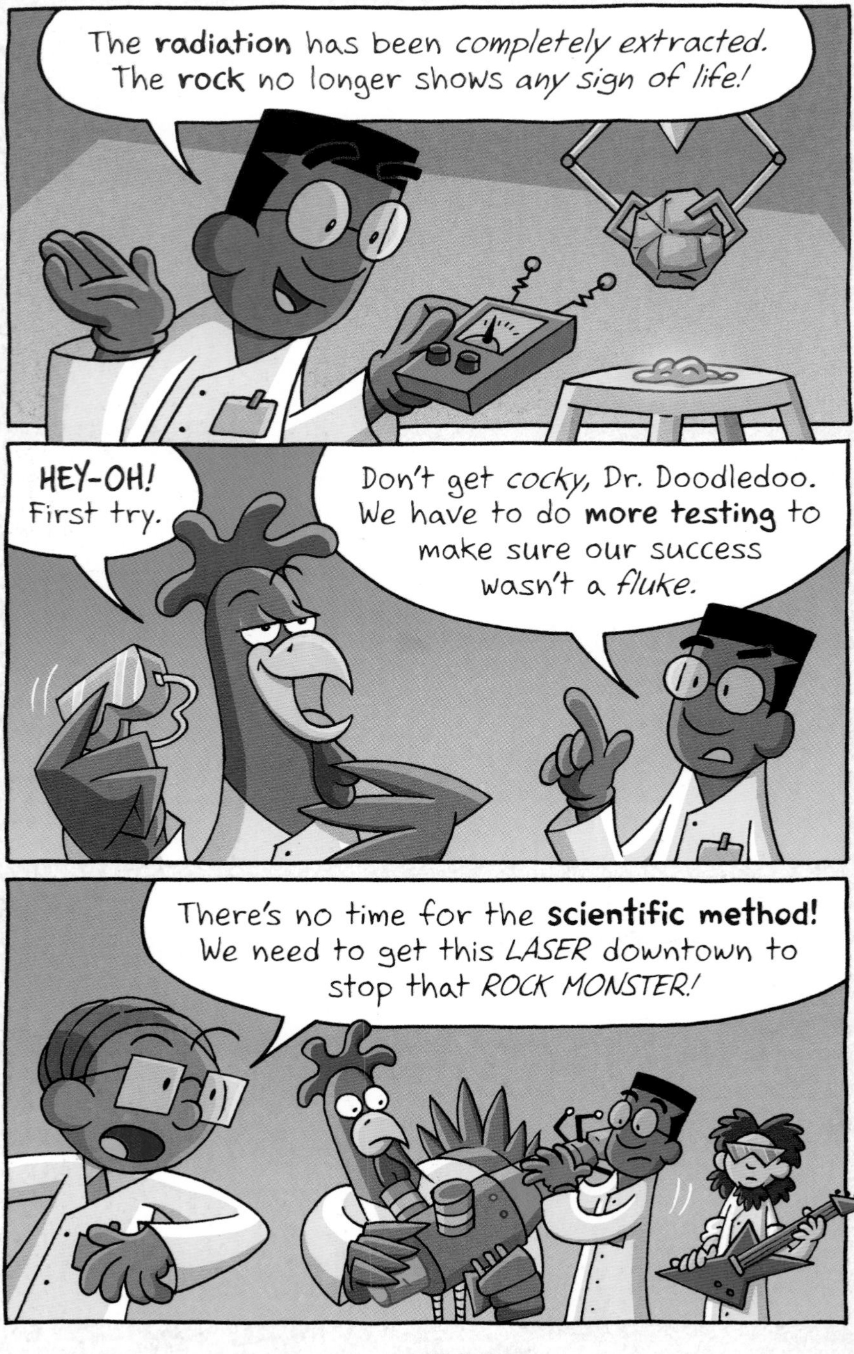
The **radiation** has been *completely extracted.* The **rock** no longer shows *any sign of life!*
HEY-OH! First try.
Don't get *cocky,* Dr. Doodledoo. We have to do **more testing** to make sure our success wasn't a *fluke.*
There's no time for the **scientific method!** We need to get this *LASER* downtown to stop that *ROCK MONSTER!*

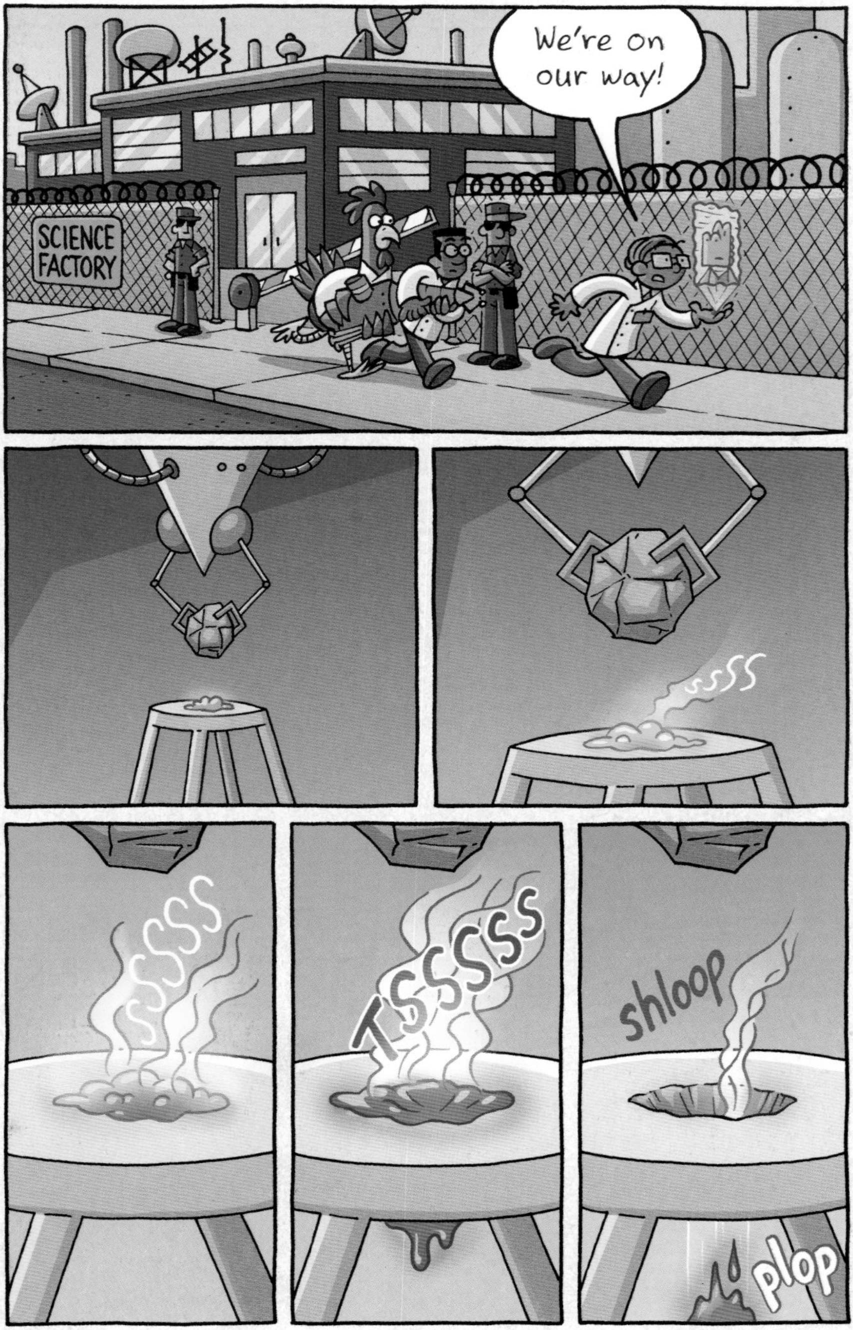
We're on our way!
SCIENCE FACTORY
SSSS
SSSSS
TSSSSSS
shloop
plop

Chapter 18

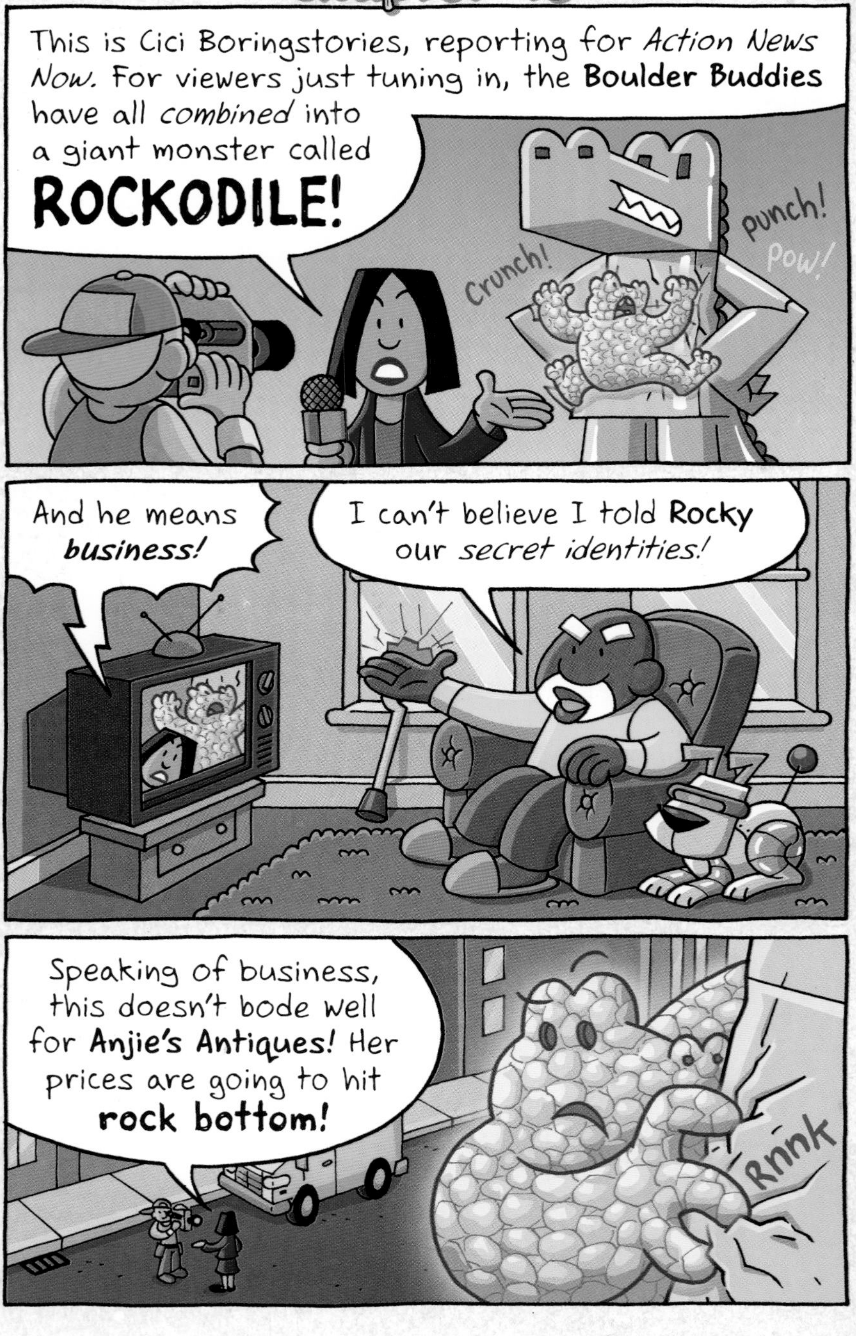
This is Cici Boringstories, reporting for *Action News Now*. For viewers just tuning in, the **Boulder Buddies** have all *combined* into a giant monster called **ROCKODILE!**
Crunch!
punch!
Pow!
And he means ***business!***
I can't believe I told **Rocky** our *secret identities!*
Speaking of business, this doesn't bode well for **Anjie's Antiques!** Her prices are going to hit **rock bottom!**
Rnnk

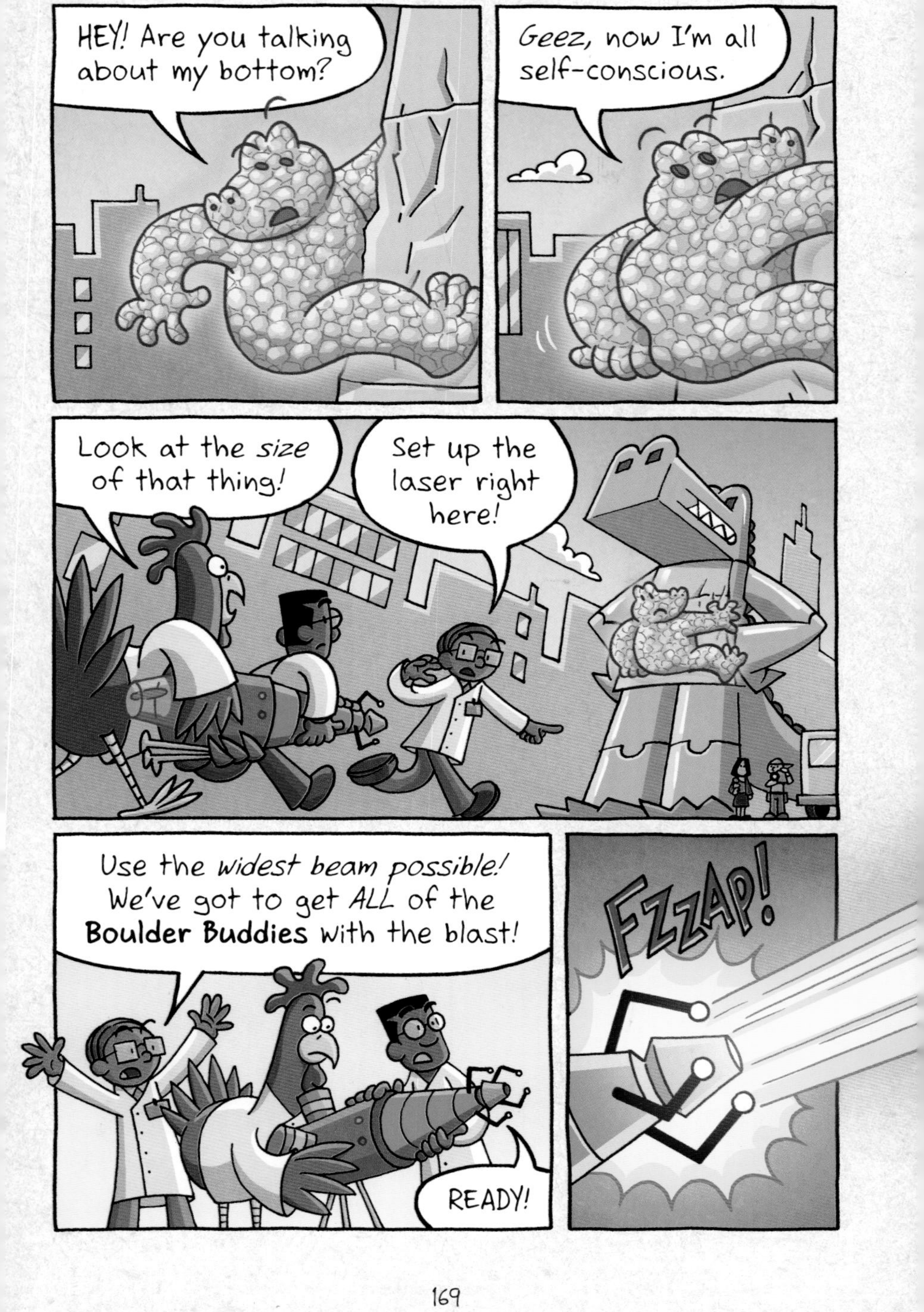
HEY! Are you talking about my bottom?
Geez, now I'm all self-conscious.
Look at the *size* of that thing!
Set up the laser right here!
Use the *widest beam possible!* We've got to get *ALL* of the **Boulder Buddies** with the blast!
READY!
FZZAP!

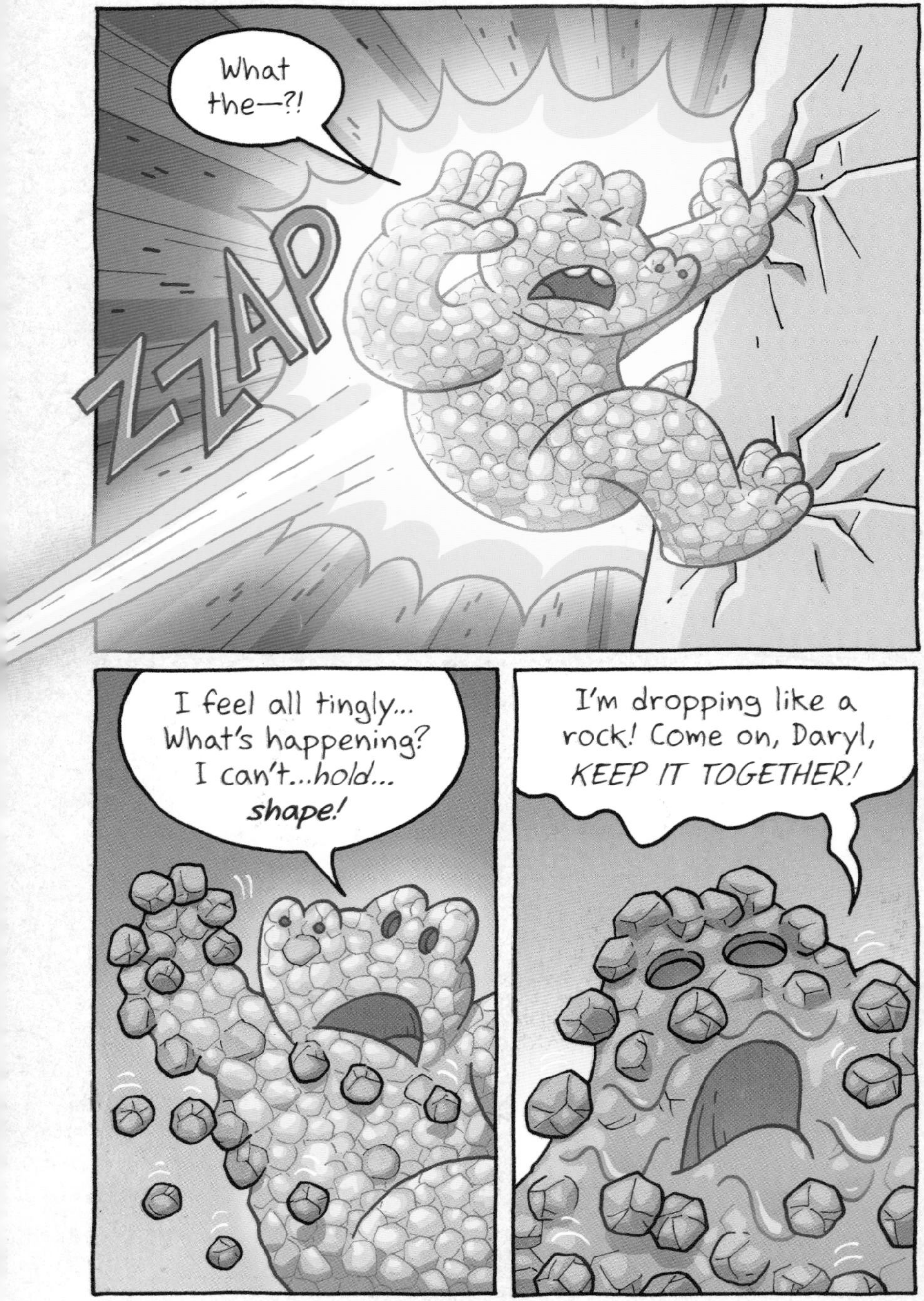
What the—?!
ZZAP
I feel all tingly... What's happening? I can't...hold... *shape!*
I'm dropping like a rock! Come on, Daryl, *KEEP IT TOGETHER!*

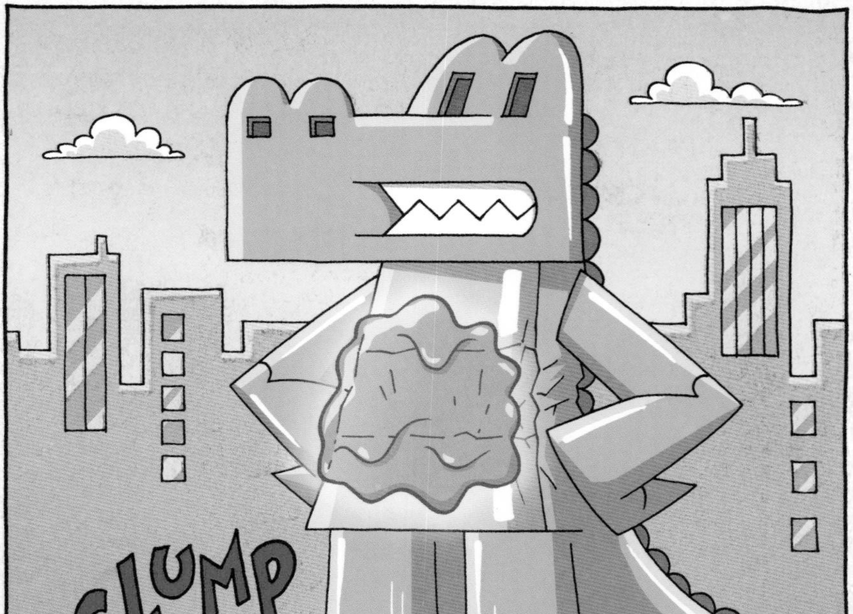
CLUMP

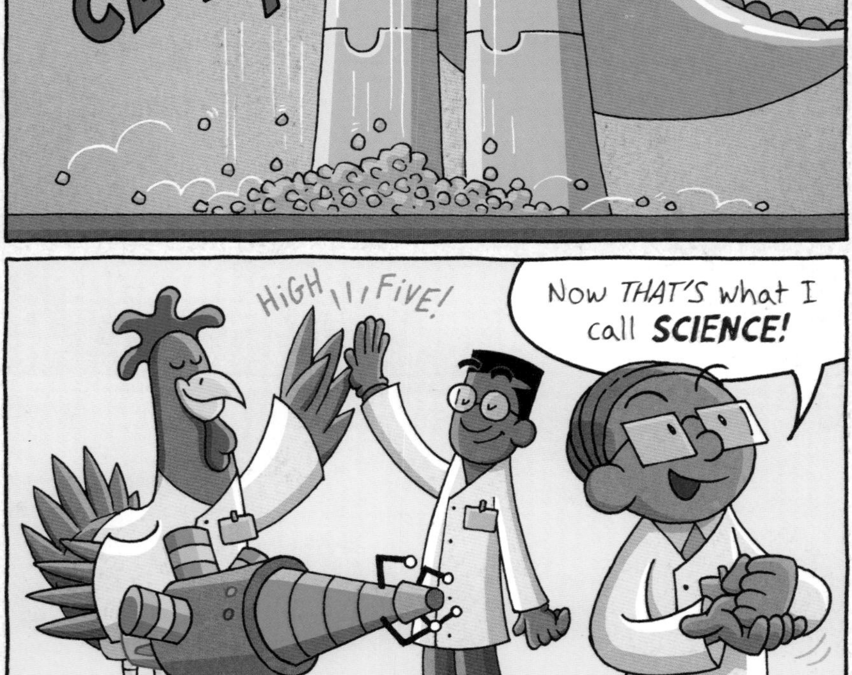
HIGH FIVE!
Now THAT'S what I call **SCIENCE!**

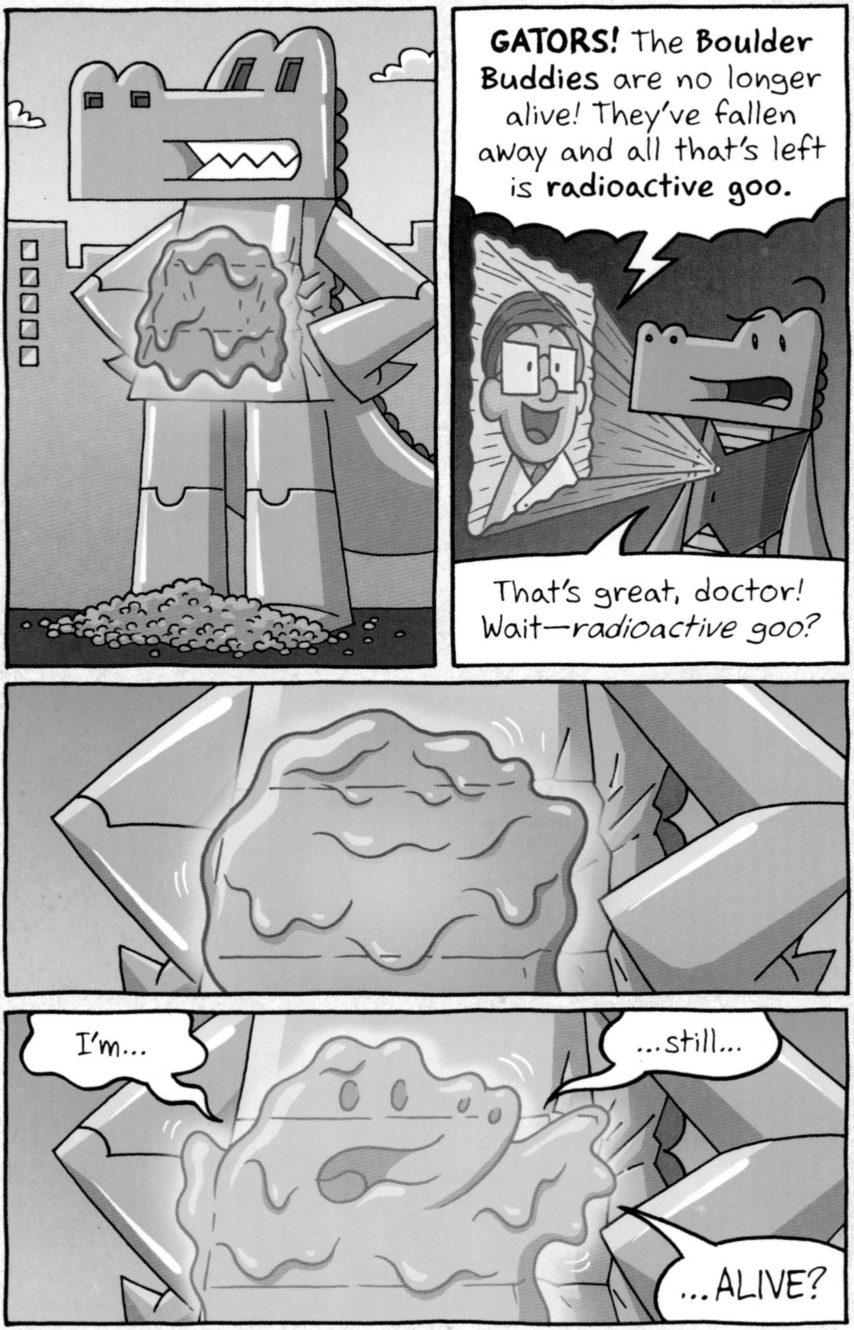
GATORS! The **Boulder Buddies** are no longer alive! They've fallen away and all that's left is **radioactive goo.**
That's great, doctor! Wait—*radioactive goo?*
I'm...
...still...
...ALIVE?

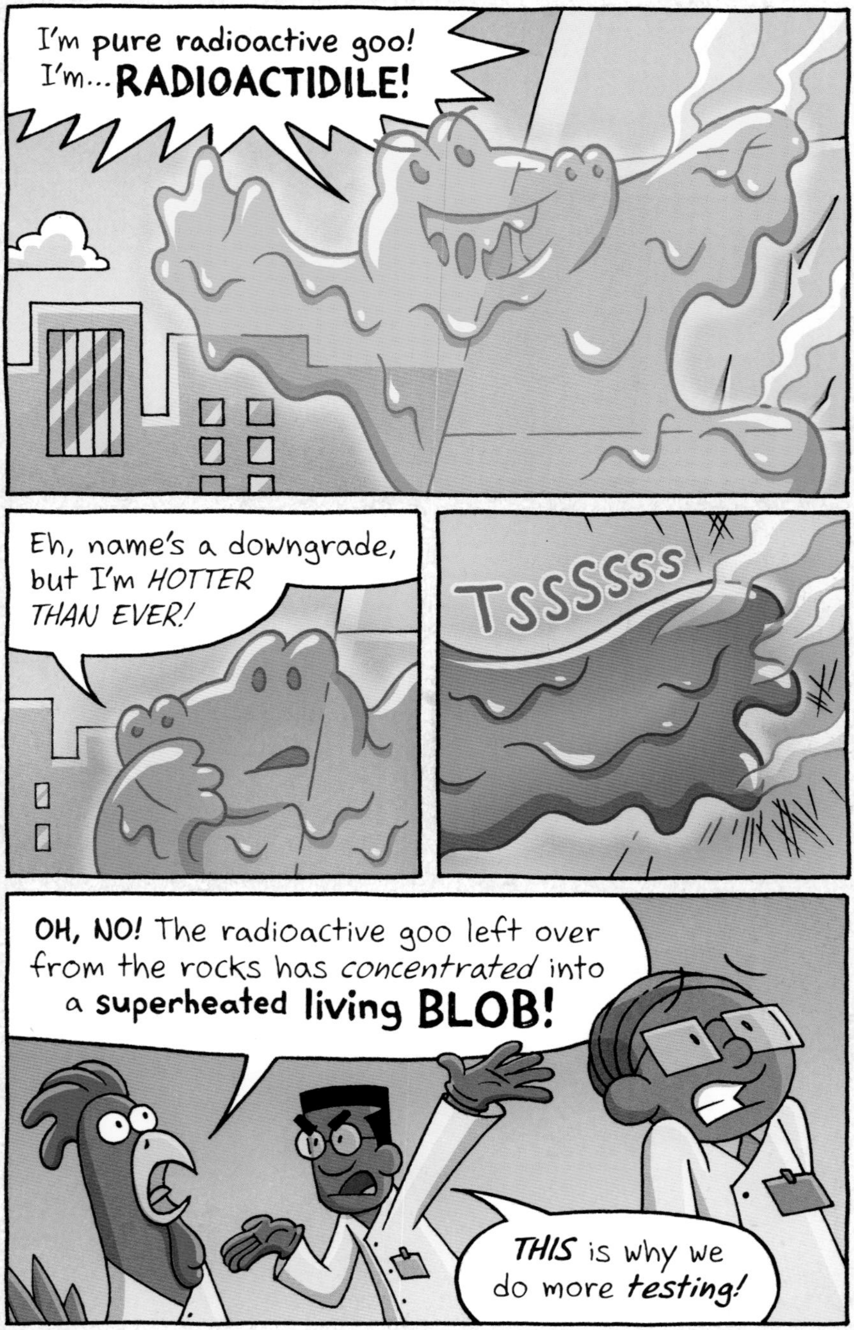
I'm pure radioactive goo!
I'm... RADIOACTIDILE!
Eh, name's a downgrade, but I'm HOTTER THAN EVER!
TSSSSSS
OH, NO! The radioactive goo left over from the rocks has concentrated into a superheated living BLOB!
THIS is why we do more testing!

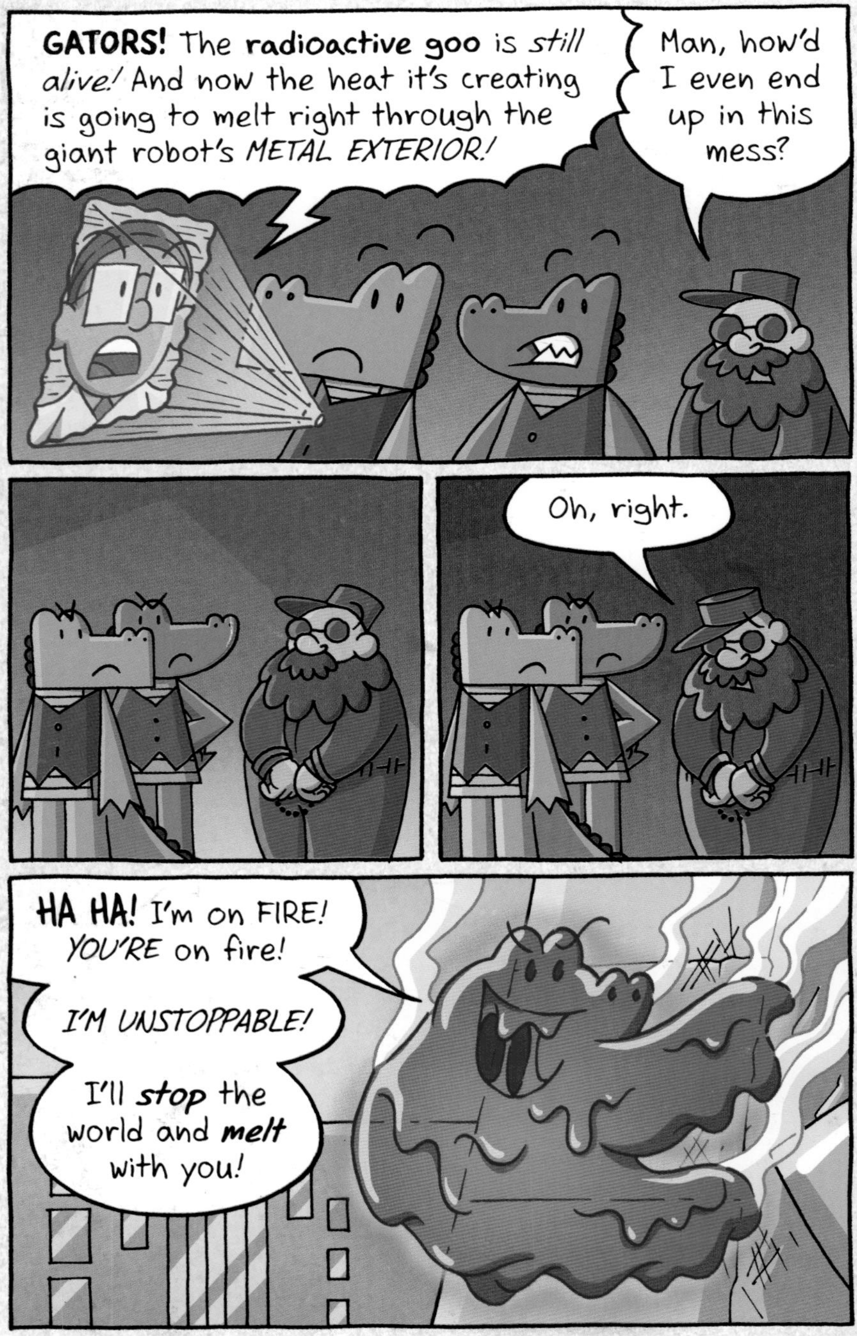
GATORS! The radioactive goo is still alive! And now the heat it's creating is going to melt right through the giant robot's METAL EXTERIOR!
Man, how'd I even end up in this mess?
Oh, right.
HA HA! I'm on FIRE! YOU'RE on fire!
I'M UNSTOPPABLE!
I'll stop the world and melt with you!

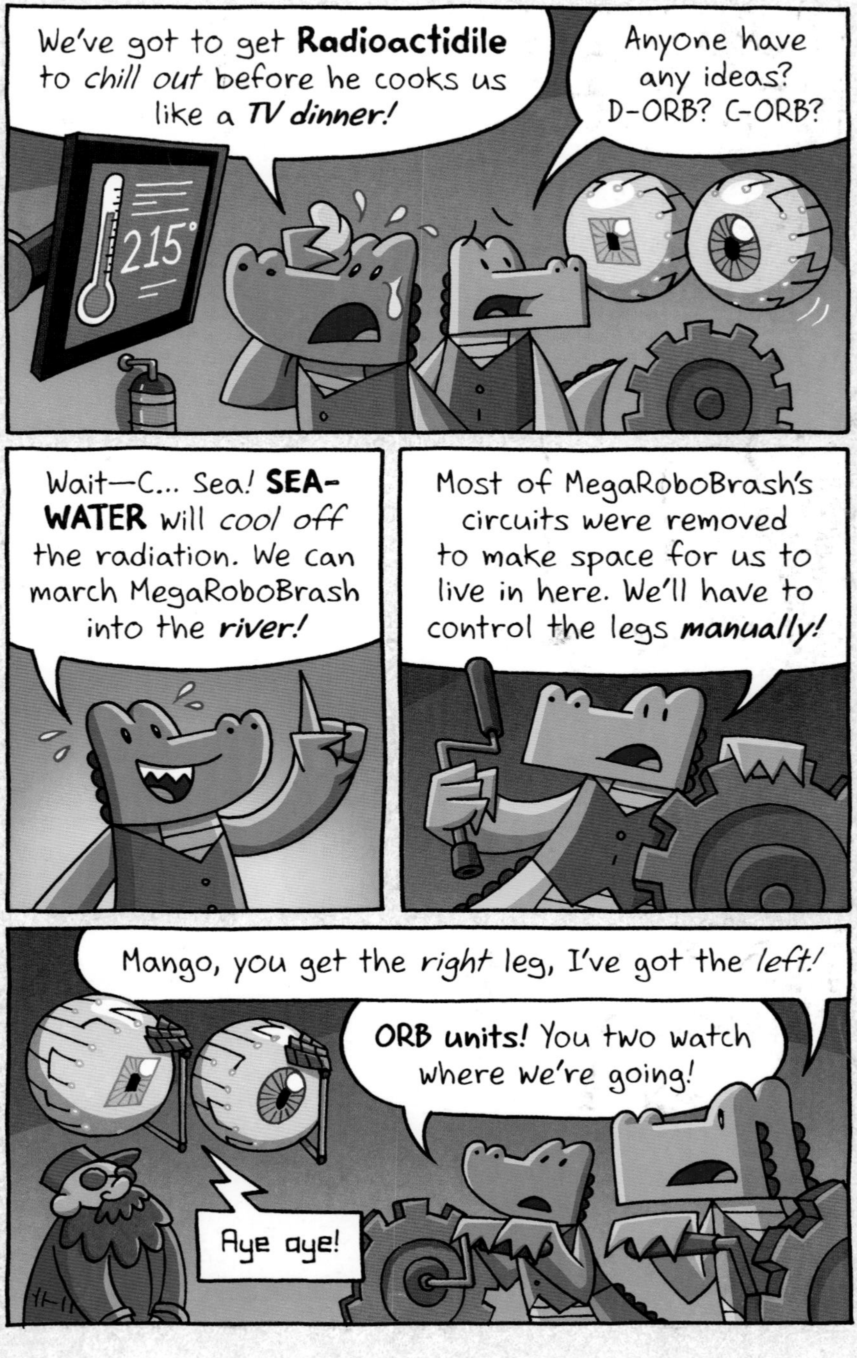
We've got to get **Radioactidile** to *chill out* before he cooks us like a ***TV dinner!***
Anyone have any ideas? D-ORB? C-ORB?
215°
Wait—C... Sea! **SEA-WATER** will *cool off* the radiation. We can march MegaRoboBrash into the ***river!***
Most of MegaRoboBrash's circuits were removed to make space for us to live in here. We'll have to control the legs ***manually!***
Mango, you get the *right* leg, I've got the *left!*
ORB units! You two watch where we're going!
Aye aye!

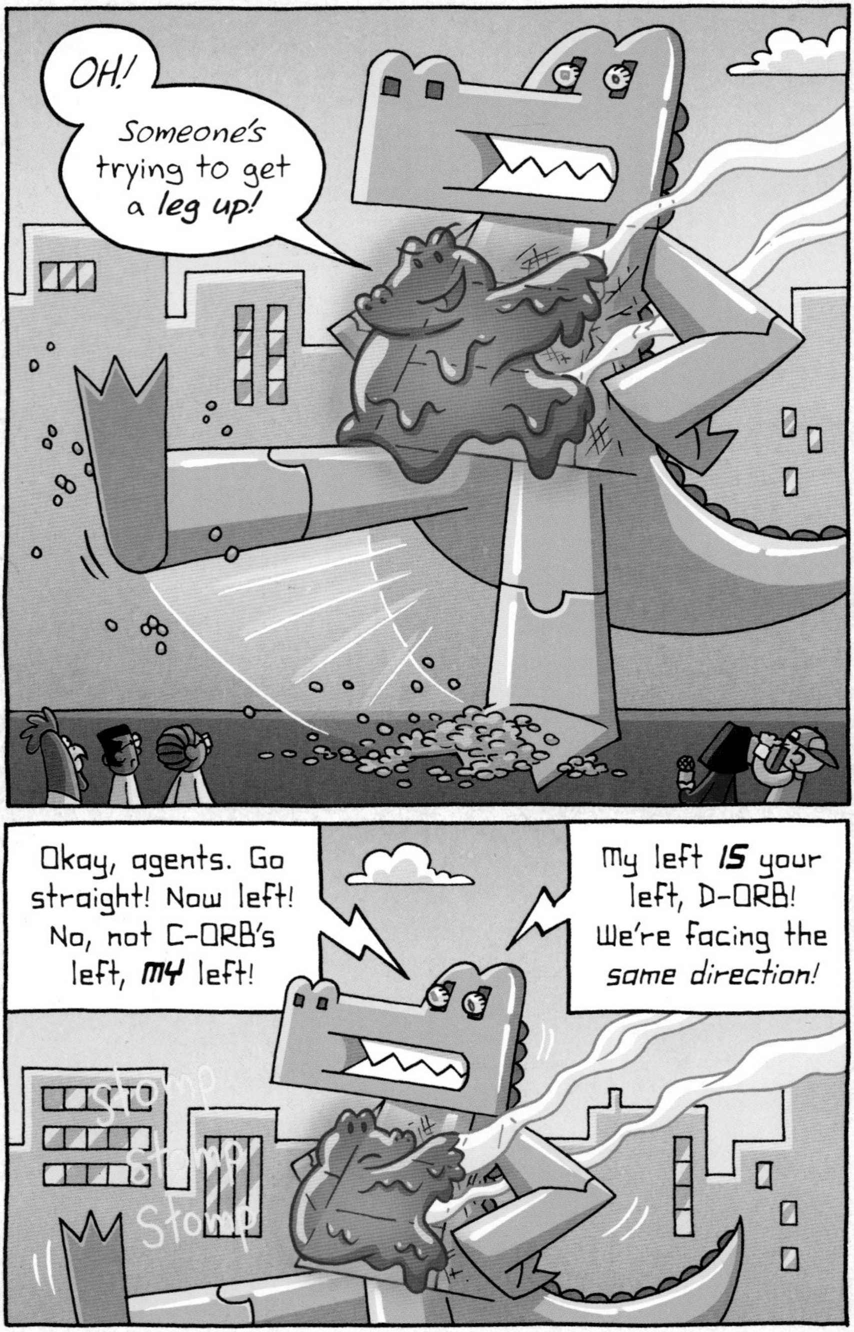
OH! Someone's trying to get a leg up!
Okay, agents. Go straight! Now left! No, not C-ORB's left, MY left!
My left IS your left, D-ORB! We're facing the same direction!
Stomp stomp Stomp

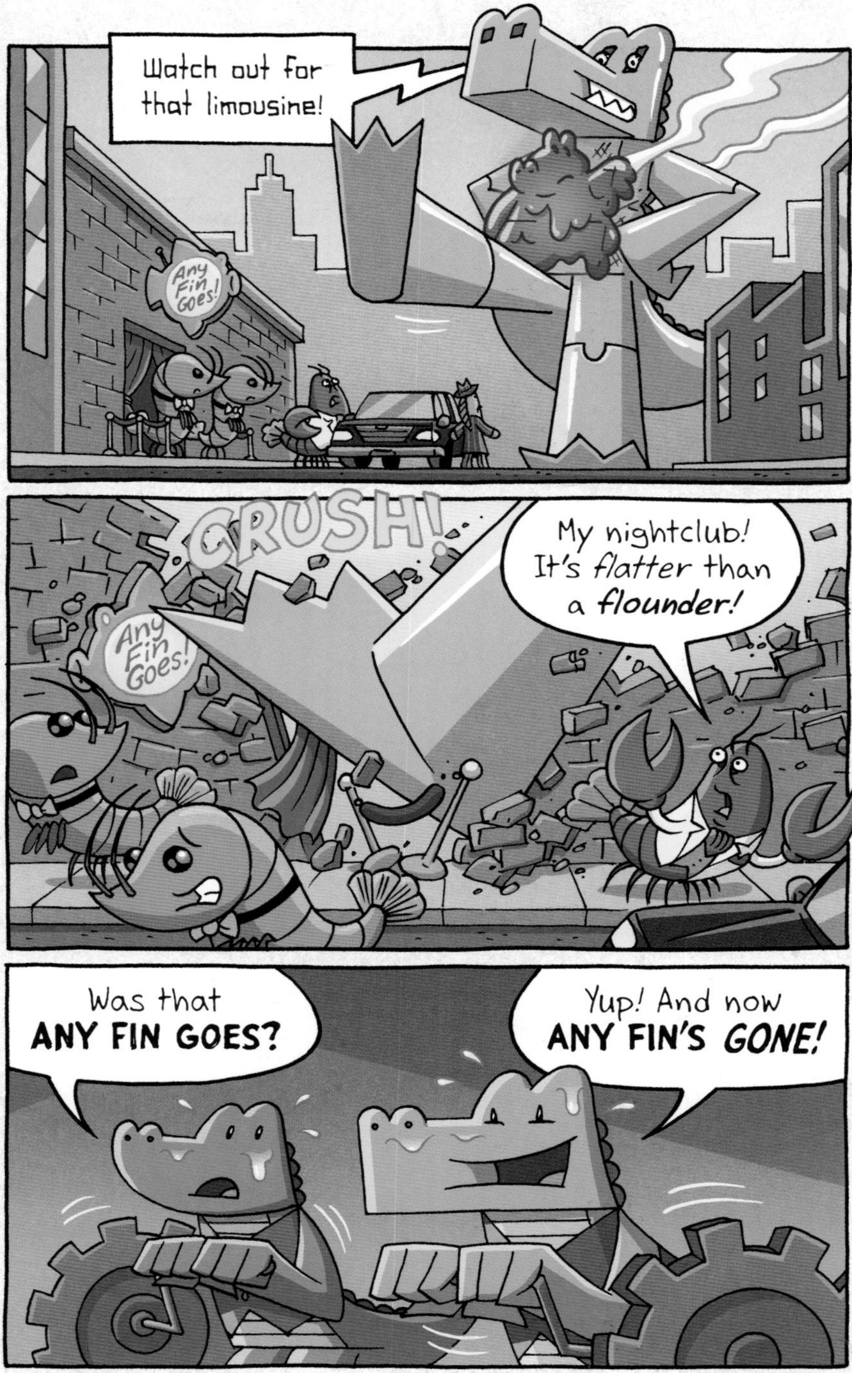
Watch out for that limousine!
Any Fin Goes!
CRUSH!
Any Fin Goes!
My nightclub! It's *flatter* than a ***flounder!***
Was that **ANY FIN GOES?**
Yup! And now **ANY FIN'S *GONE!***

Chapter 19

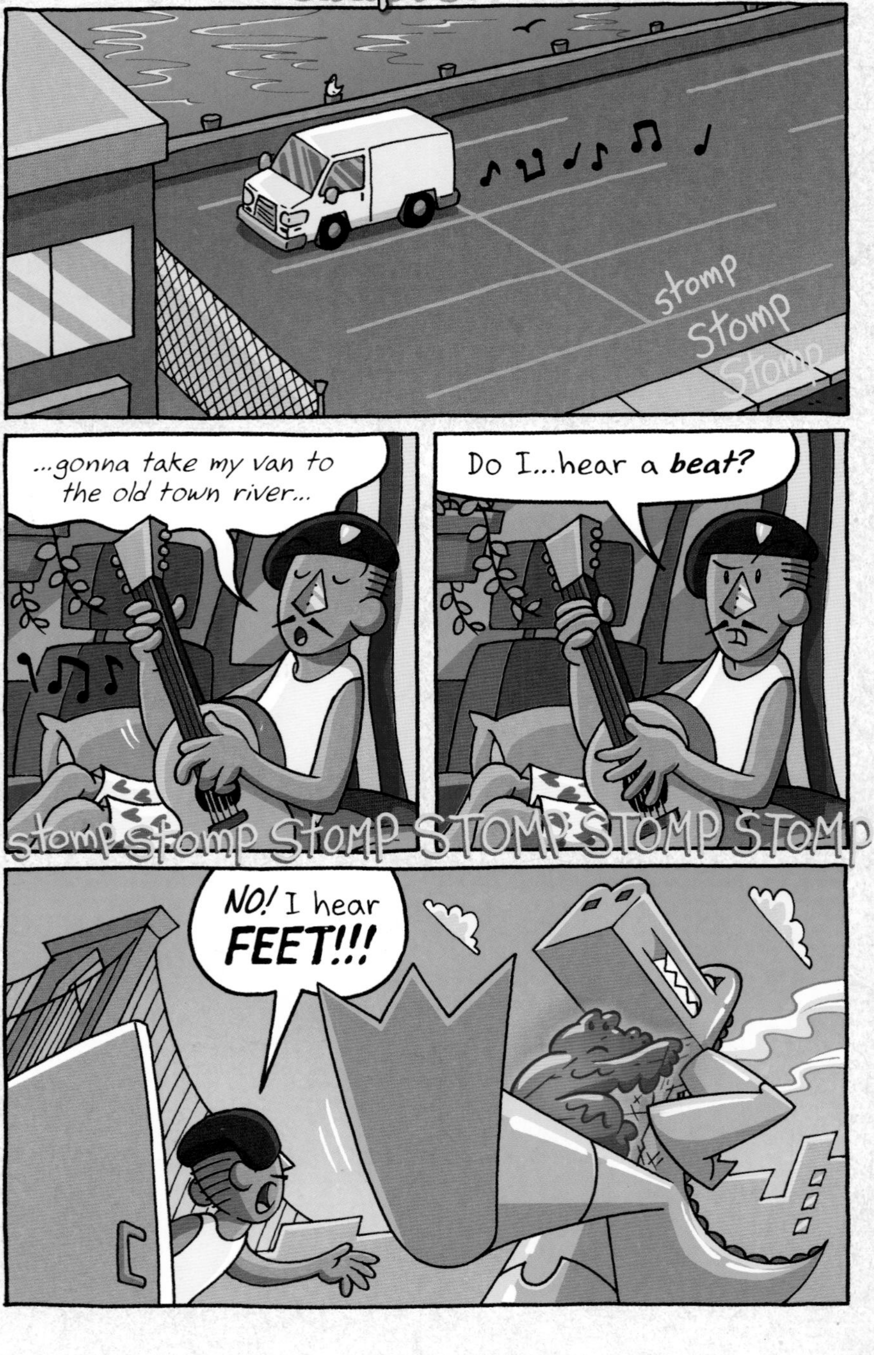
stomp
Stomp
Stomp
...gonna take my van to the old town river...
Do I...hear a **beat?**
stomp stomp STOMP STOMP STOMP STOMP
NO! I hear **FEET!!!**

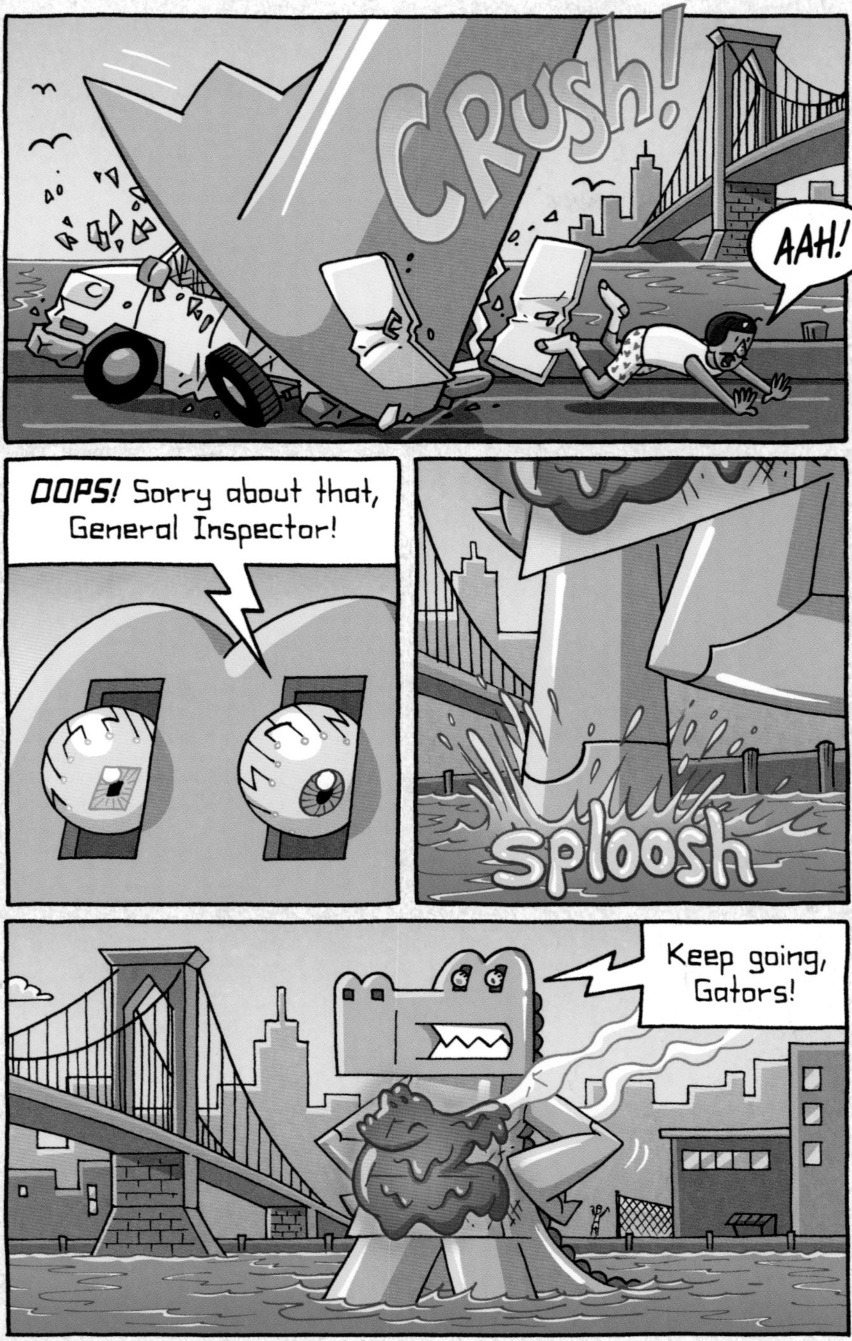
CRUSH!
AAH!
OOPS! Sorry about that, General Inspector!
sploosh
Keep going, Gators!

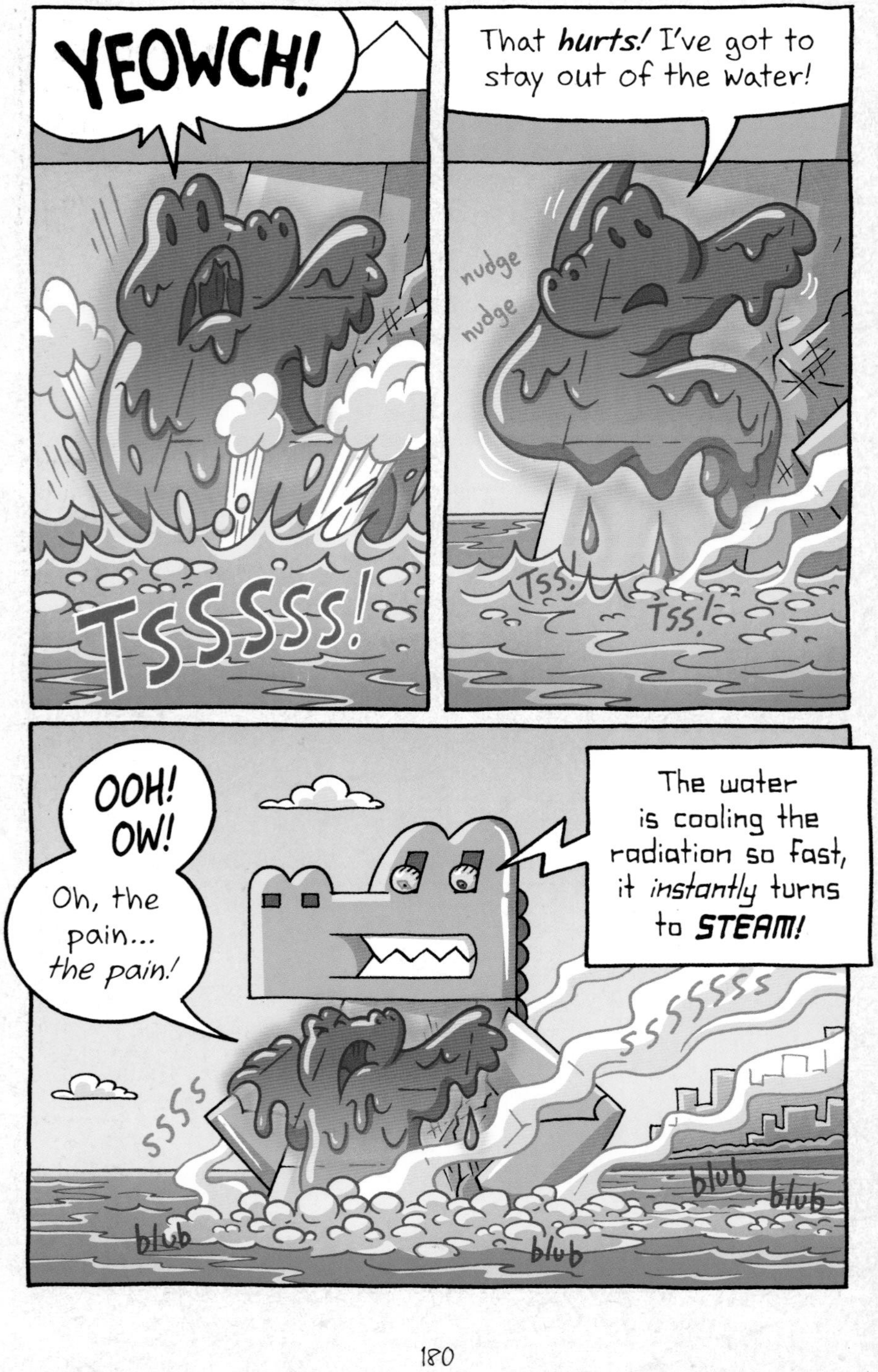
YEOWCH!
TSSSSS!
That *hurts!* I've got to stay out of the water!
nudge
nudge
TSS!
TSS!
OOH! OW!
Oh, the pain... *the pain!*
The water is cooling the radiation so fast, it *instantly* turns to **STEAM!**
SSSSSSS
SSSS
blub
blub
blub
blub

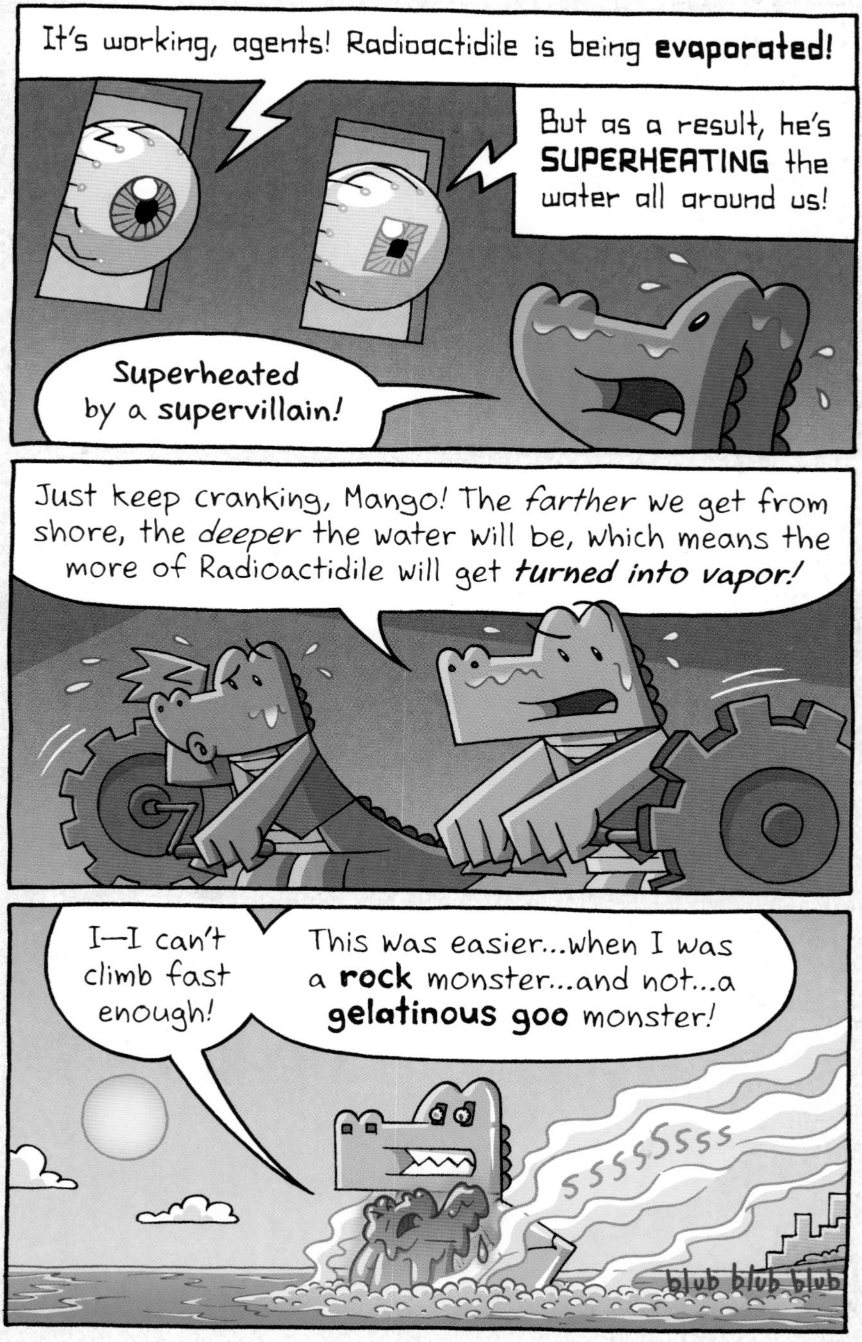
It's working, agents! Radioactidile is being **evaporated**!
But as a result, he's **SUPERHEATING** the water all around us!
Superheated by a **supervillain**!
Just keep cranking, Mango! The *farther* we get from shore, the *deeper* the water will be, which means the more of Radioactidile will get ***turned into vapor!***
I—I can't climb fast enough!
This was easier...when I was a **rock** monster...and not...a **gelatinous goo** monster!
sssssssss
blub blub blub

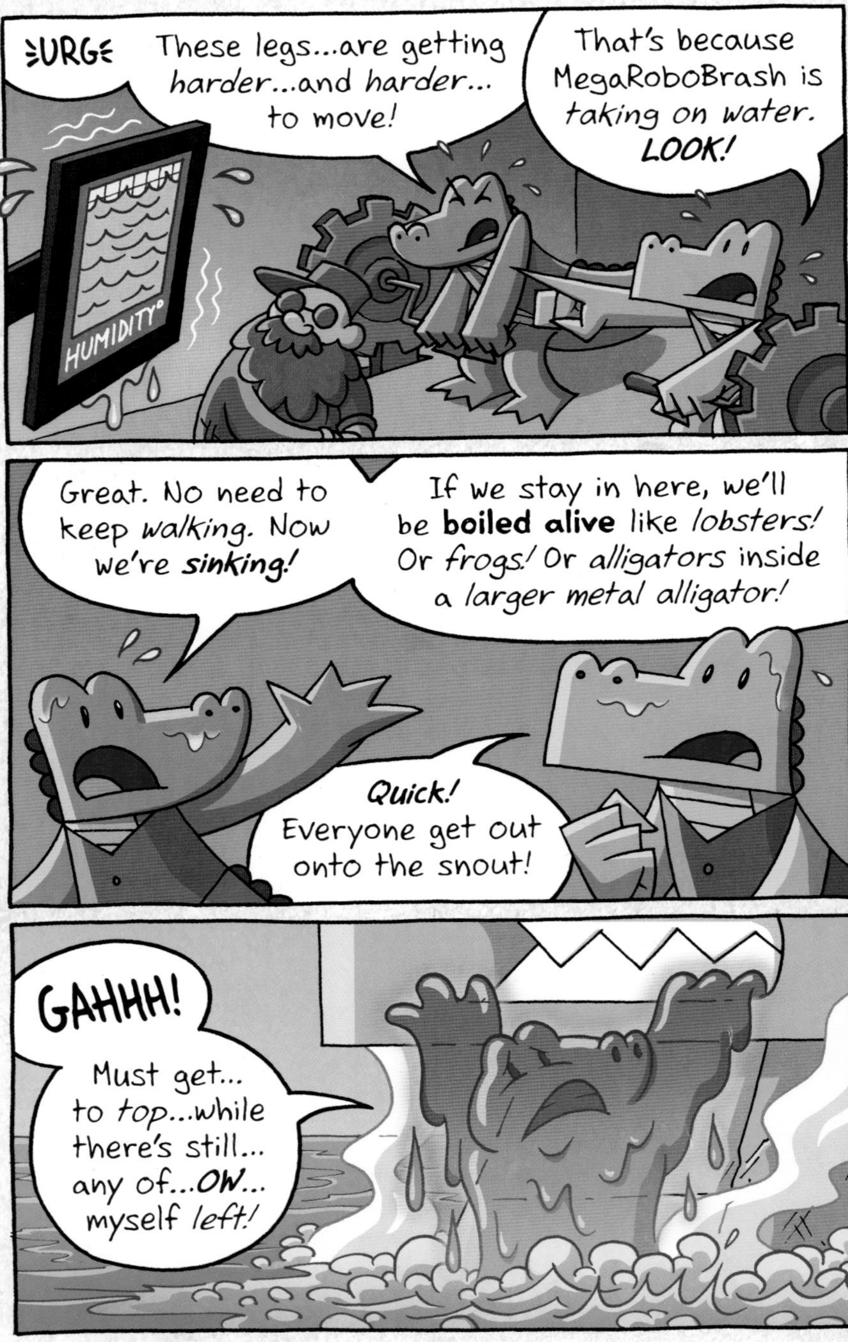
URG
These legs...are getting *harder*...and *harder*... to move!
That's because MegaRoboBrash is *taking on water.* ***LOOK!***
HUMIDITY
Great. No need to keep *walking.* Now we're ***sinking!***
If we stay in here, we'll be **boiled alive** like *lobsters!* Or *frogs!* Or *alligators* inside a *larger metal alligator!*
Quick! Everyone get out onto the snout!
GAHHH!
Must get... to *top*...while there's still... any of...***OW***... myself *left!*

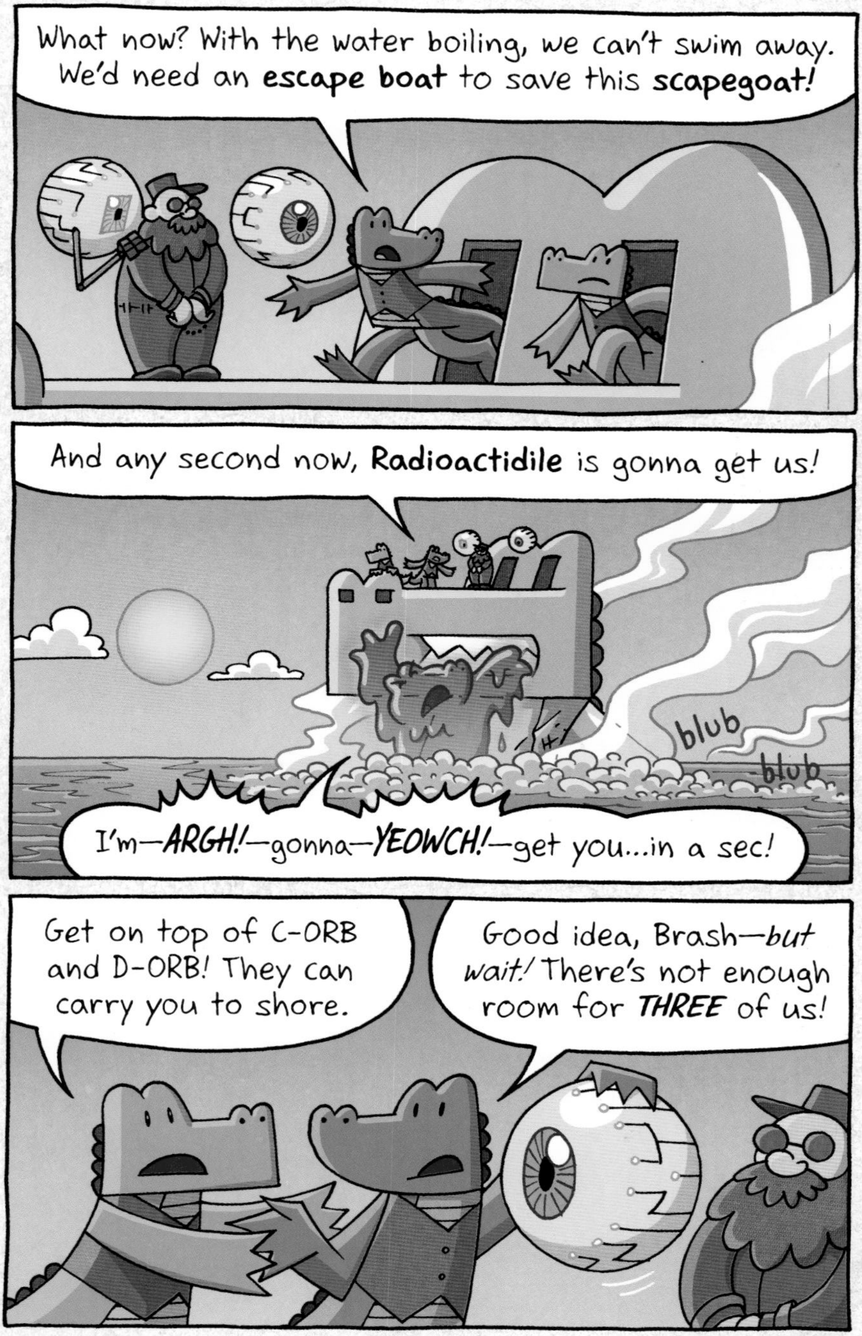
What now? With the water boiling, we can't swim away. We'd need an **escape boat** to save this **scapegoat!**
And any second now, **Radioactidile** is gonna get us!
blub
blub
I'm—***ARGH!***—gonna—***YEOWCH!***—get you...in a sec!
Get on top of C-ORB and D-ORB! They can carry you to shore.
Good idea, Brash—*but wait!* There's not enough room for ***THREE*** of us!

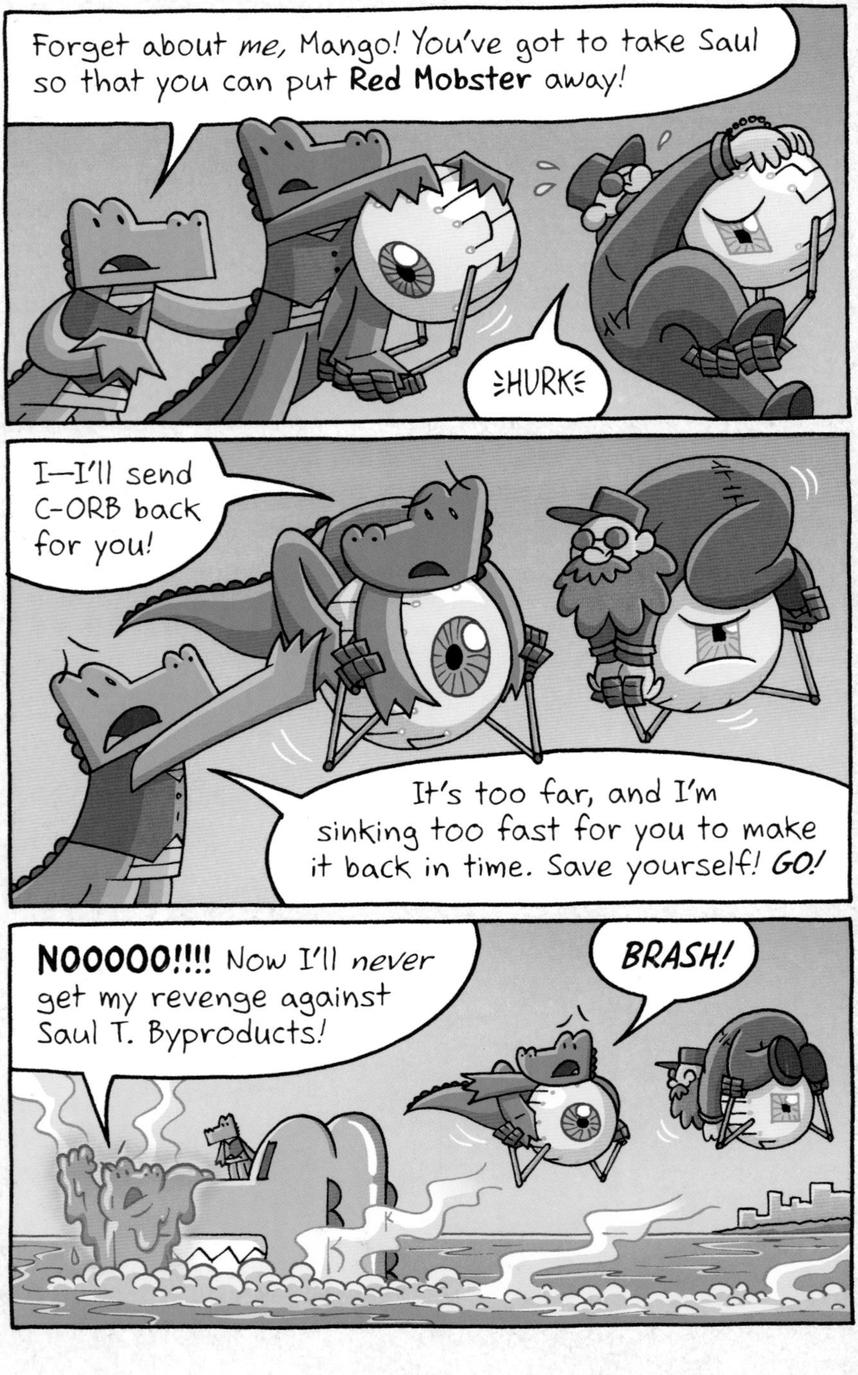
Forget about *me*, Mango! You've got to take Saul so that you can put **Red Mobster** away!
HURK
I—I'll send C-ORB back for you!
It's too far, and I'm sinking too fast for you to make it back in time. Save yourself! ***GO!***
NOOOOO!!!! Now I'll *never* get my revenge against Saul T. Byproducts!
BRASH!

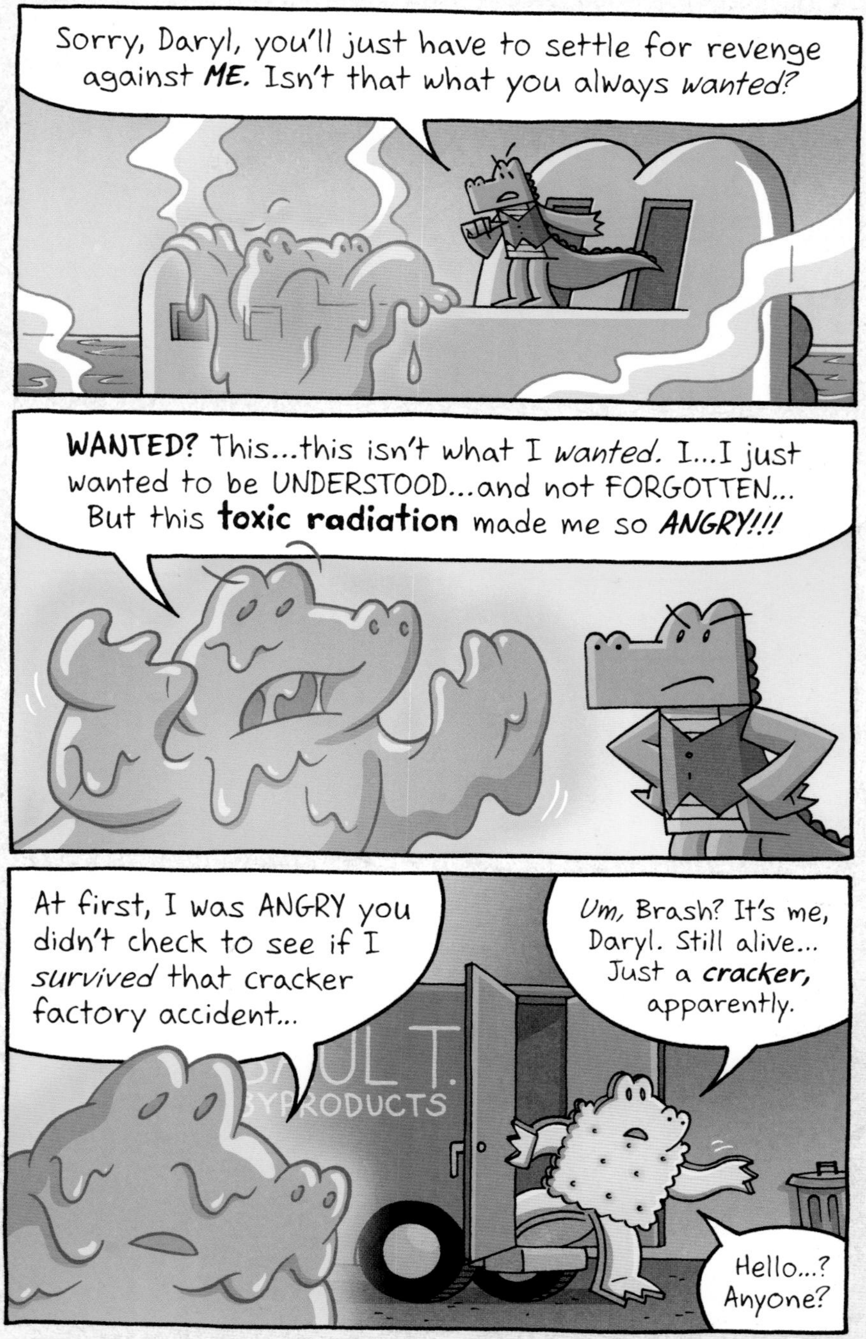
Sorry, Daryl, you'll just have to settle for revenge against ***ME.*** Isn't that what you always *wanted?*
WANTED? This...this isn't what I *wanted.* I...I just wanted to be UNDERSTOOD...and not FORGOTTEN... But this **toxic radiation** made me so ***ANGRY!!!***
At first, I was ANGRY you didn't check to see if I *survived* that cracker factory accident...
Um, Brash? It's me, Daryl. Still alive... Just a ***cracker,*** apparently.
BYPRODUCTS
Hello...? Anyone?

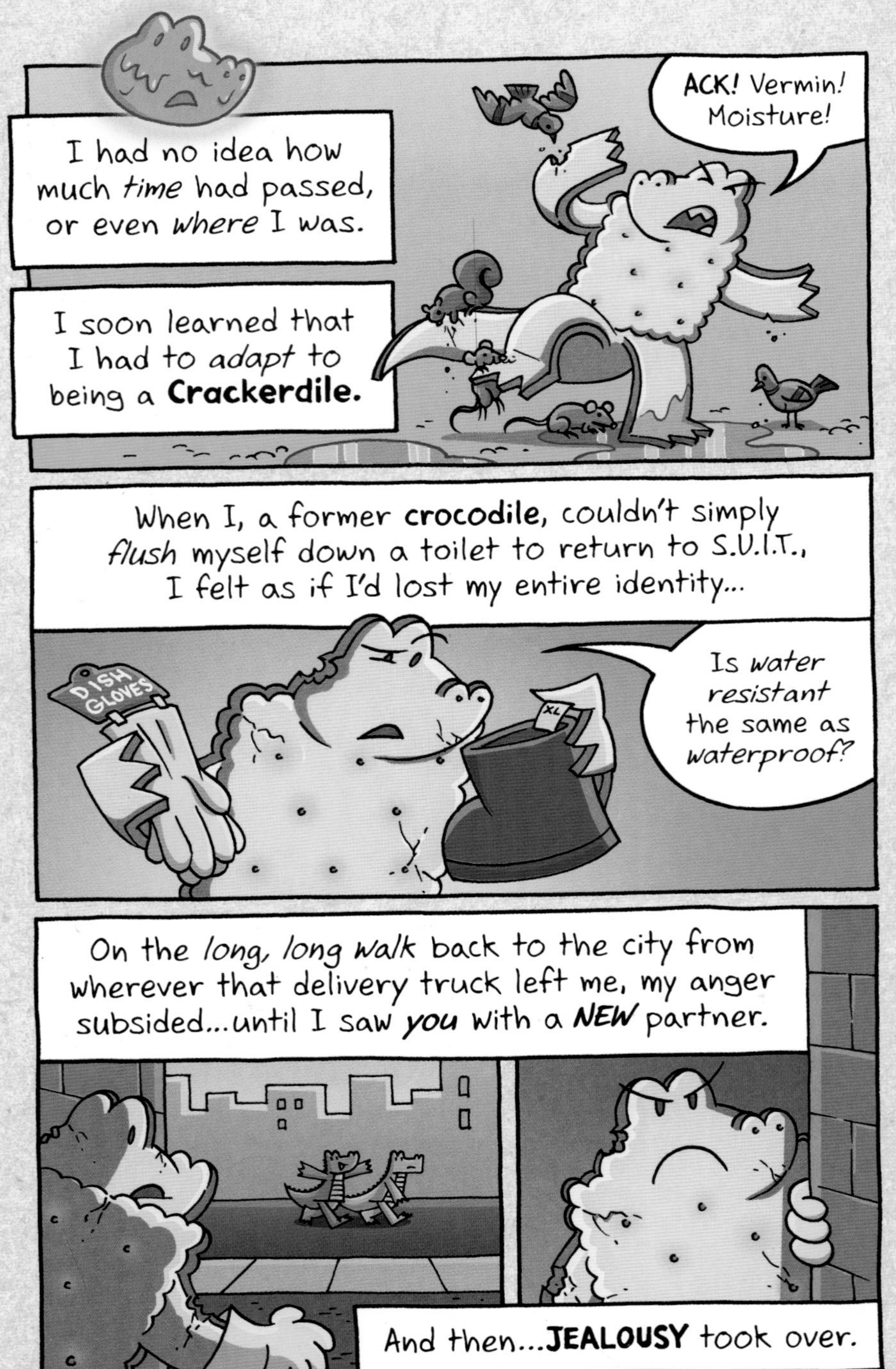
I had no idea how much *time* had passed, or even *where* I was.
ACK! Vermin! Moisture!
I soon learned that I had to *adapt* to being a **Crackerdile.**
When I, a former **crocodile,** couldn't simply *flush* myself down a toilet to return to S.U.I.T., I felt as if I'd lost my entire identity...
DISH GLOVES
XL
Is *water resistant* the same as *waterproof?*
On the *long, long walk* back to the city from wherever that delivery truck left me, my anger subsided...until I saw ***you*** with a ***NEW*** partner.
And then...**JEALOUSY** took over.

I...I didn't *mean* to become a **supervillain**. But my life—and my crumby body—were *crumbling all around me!* And I became filled with **RAGE**. So I blamed *YOU* for what happened to me when I saw how quickly you got over it.

How **QUICKLY I** got over it?!

I **NEVER** got over it! Have you read *ANY* of these books? I'm a *mess!* And now I'm losing you for the fourth or fifth time... I'VE HONESTLY LOST COUNT!

We can't keep going on like this, Daryl! What could you even *turn into* after **THIS?** IT BOGGLES THE MIND!!!

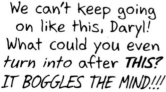

You...You're right, Brash. This **TOXIC WASTE** inside me kept me alive, but also kept me from seeing the *truth...*

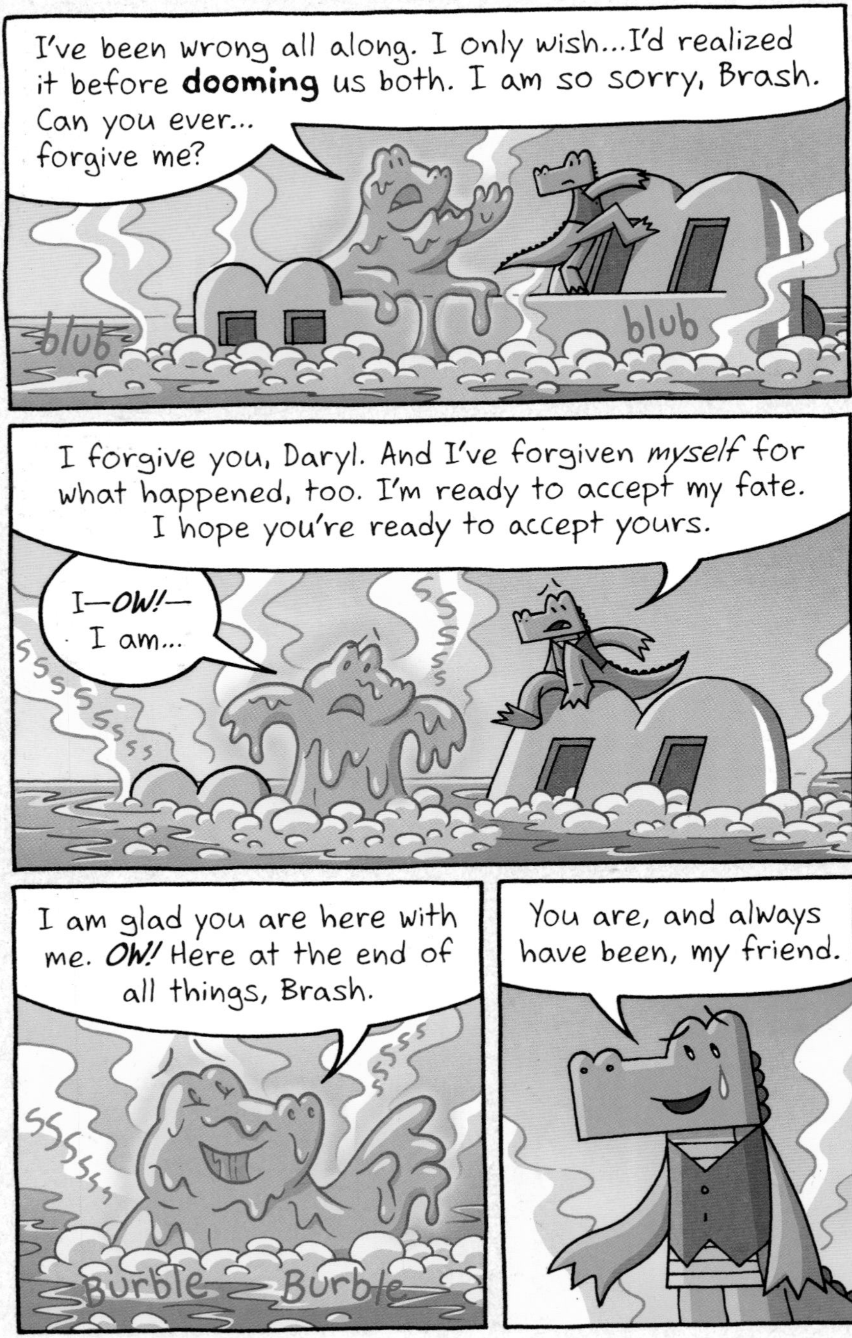
I've been wrong all along. I only wish...I'd realized it before **dooming** us both. I am so sorry, Brash. Can you ever... forgive me?
blub
blub
I forgive you, Daryl. And I've forgiven *myself* for what happened, too. I'm ready to accept my fate. I hope you're ready to accept yours.
I—***OW!***— I am...
I am glad you are here with me. ***OW!*** Here at the end of all things, Brash.
Burble Burble
You are, and always have been, my friend.

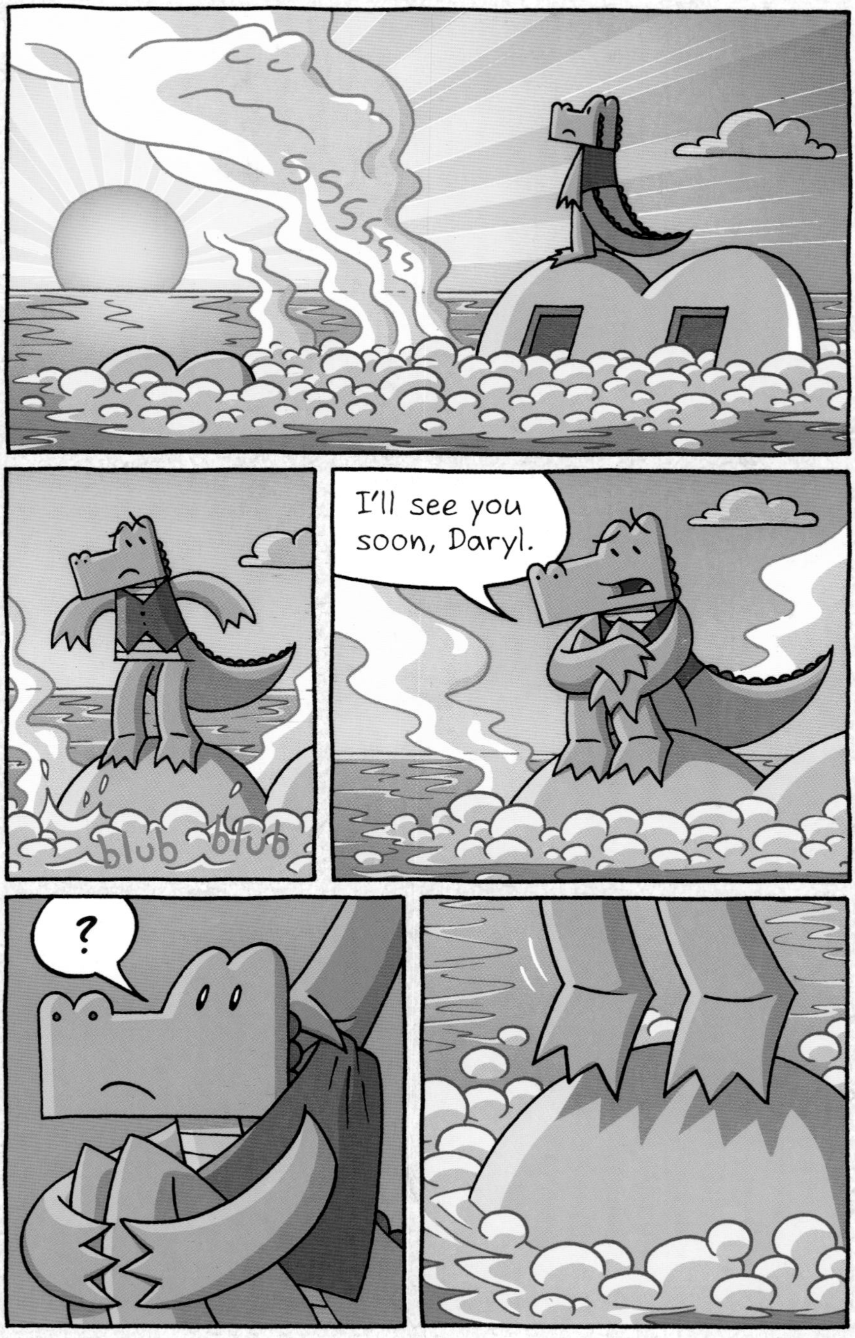
SSSSSSs
blub blub
I'll see you soon, Daryl.
?

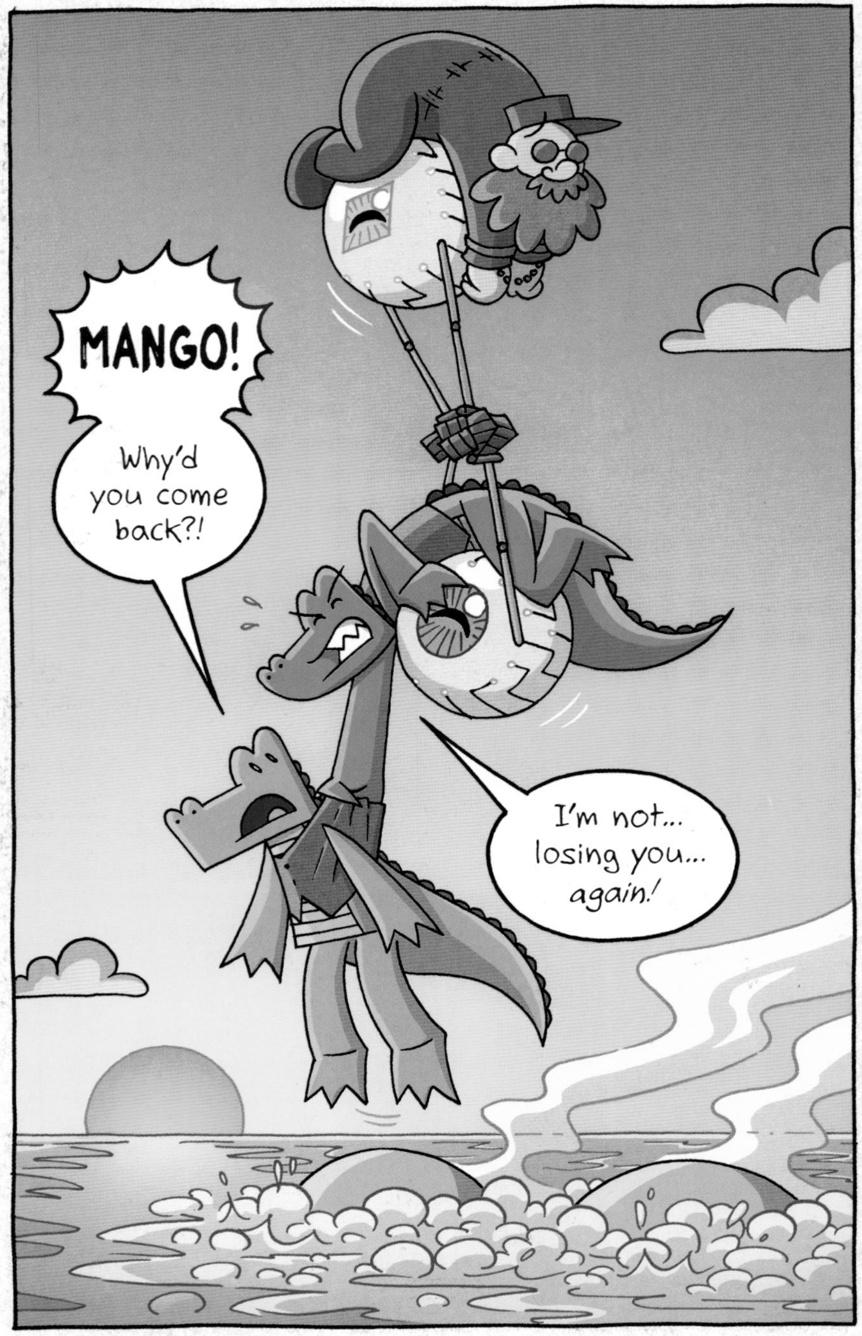
MANGO!
Why'd you come back?!
I'm not... losing you... again!

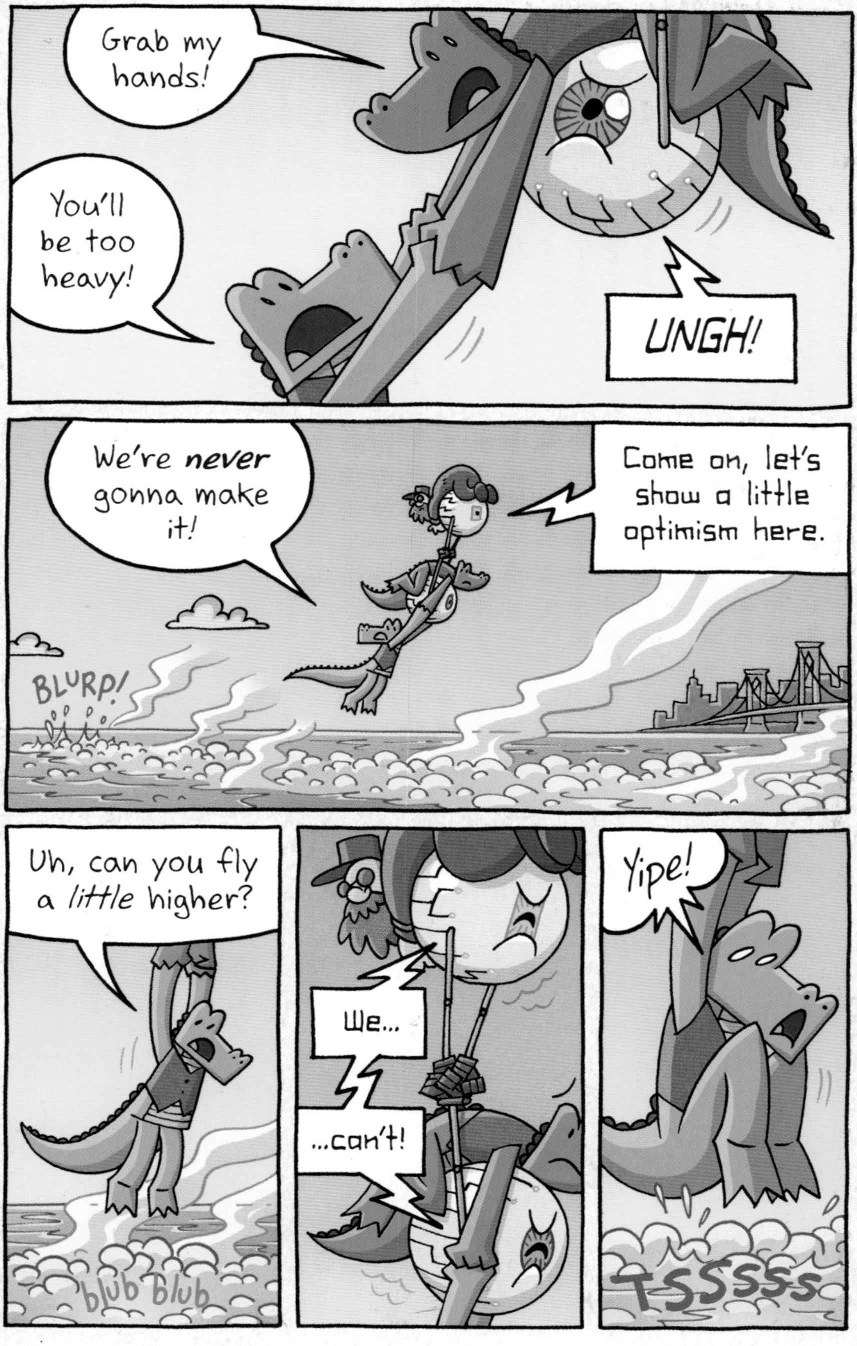
Grab my hands!
You'll be too heavy!
UNGH!
We're **never** gonna make it!
Come on, let's show a little optimism here.
BLURP!
Uh, can you fly a *little* higher?
blub blub
We...
...can't!
Yipe!
TSSSSS

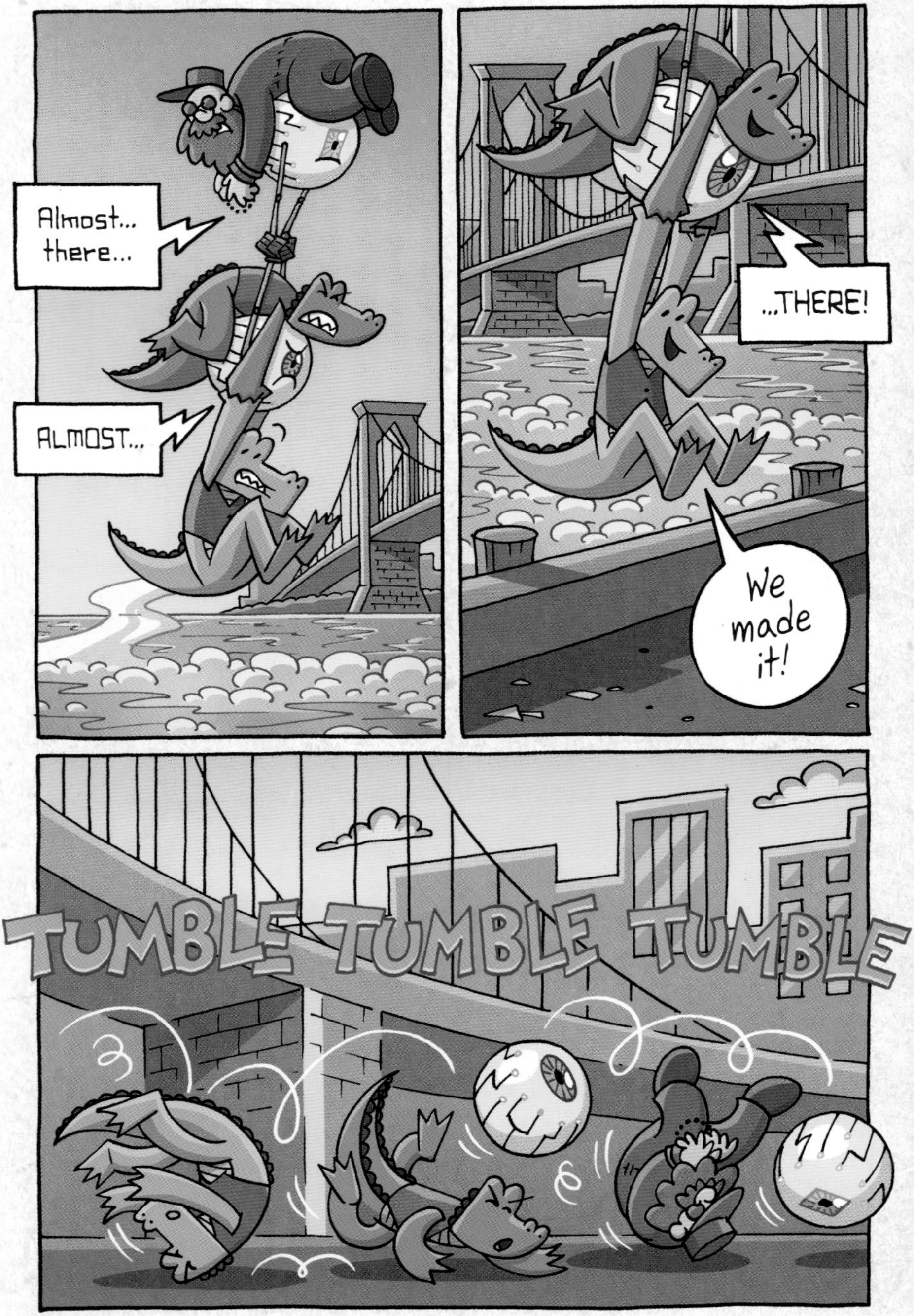

Almost... there...
ALMOST...
...THERE!
We made it!
TUMBLE TUMBLE TUMBLE

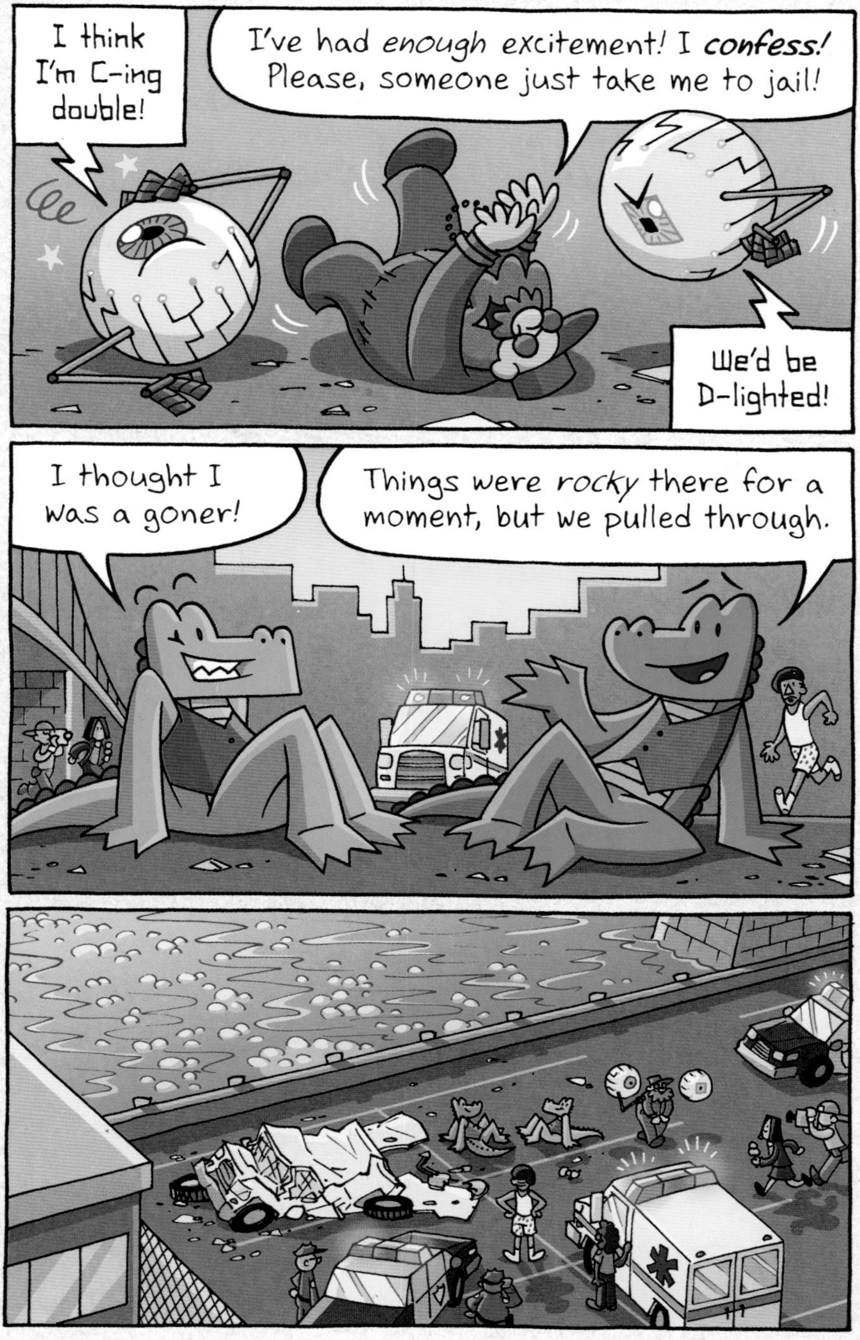
I think I'm C-ing double!
I've had *enough* excitement! I **confess!** Please, someone just take me to jail!
We'd be D-lighted!
I thought I was a goner!
Things were *rocky* there for a moment, but we pulled through.

Epilogue

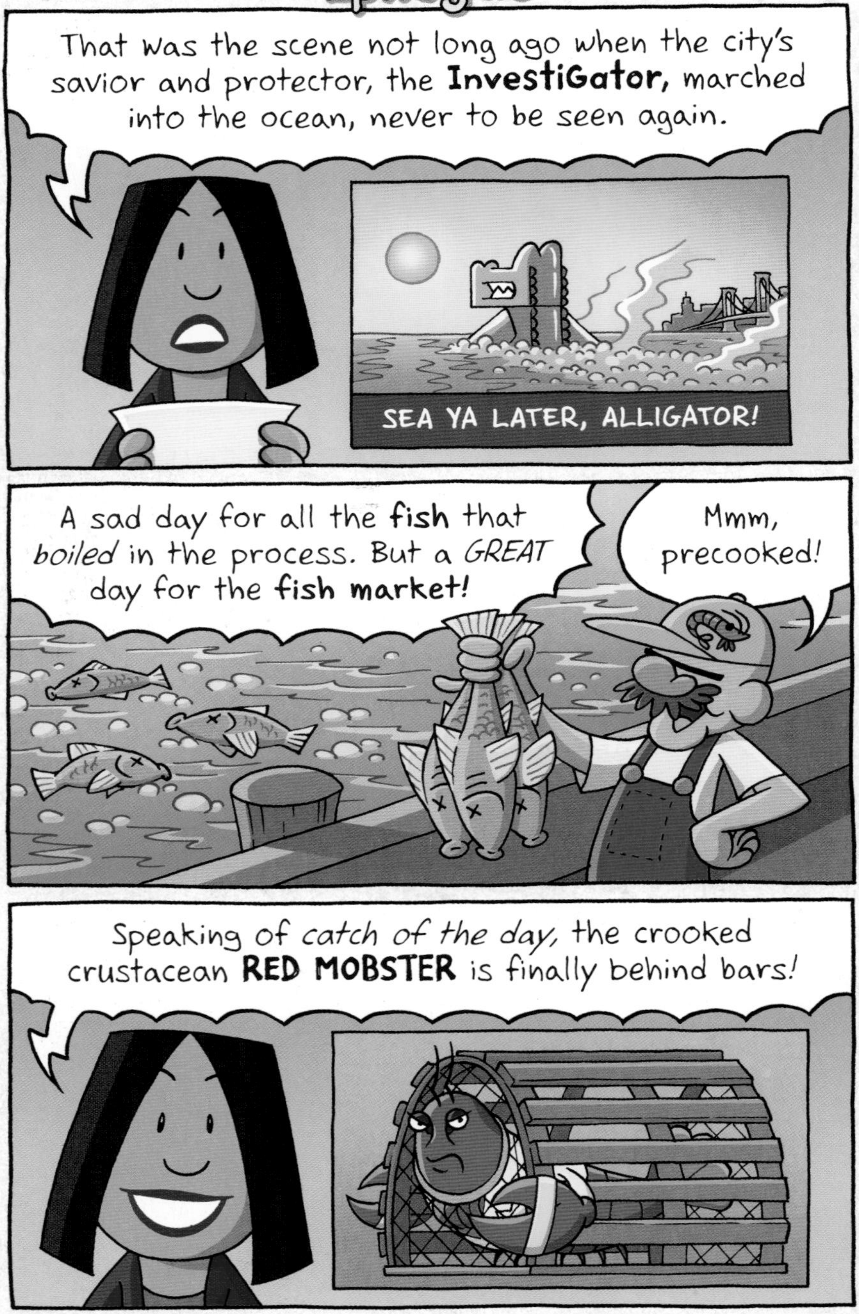

That was the scene not long ago when the city's savior and protector, the **InvestiGator,** marched into the ocean, never to be seen again.
SEA YA LATER, ALLIGATOR!
A sad day for all the **fish** that *boiled* in the process. But a *GREAT* day for the **fish market!**
Mmm, precooked!
Speaking of *catch of the day,* the crooked crustacean **RED MOBSTER** is finally behind bars!

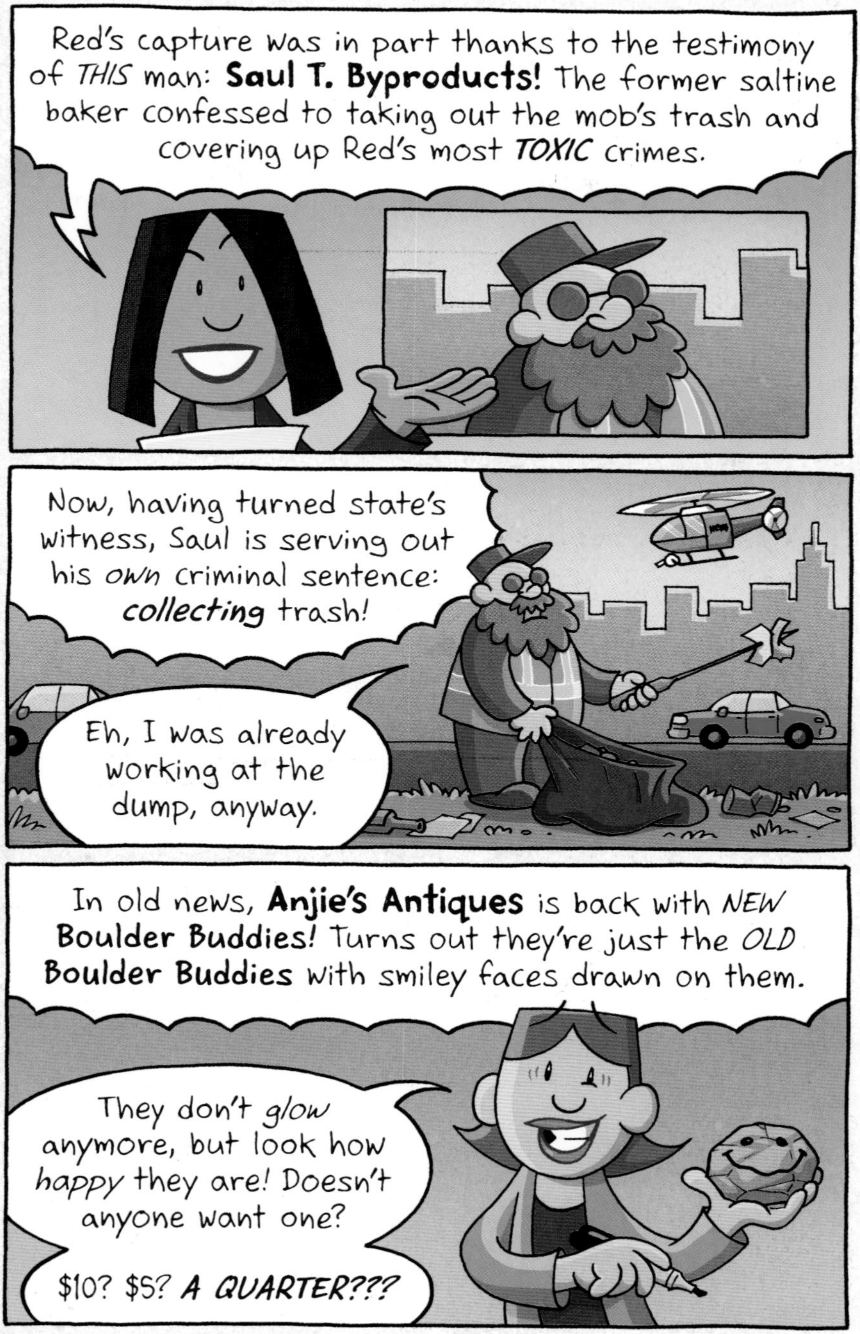
Red's capture was in part thanks to the testimony of *THIS* man: **Saul T. Byproducts!** The former saltine baker confessed to taking out the mob's trash and covering up Red's most *TOXIC* crimes.
Now, having turned state's witness, Saul is serving out his *own* criminal sentence: ***collecting*** trash!
Eh, I was already working at the dump, anyway.
In old news, **Anjie's Antiques** is back with *NEW* **Boulder Buddies!** Turns out they're just the *OLD* **Boulder Buddies** with smiley faces drawn on them.
They don't *glow* anymore, but look how *happy* they are! Doesn't anyone want one?
$10? $5? ***A QUARTER???***

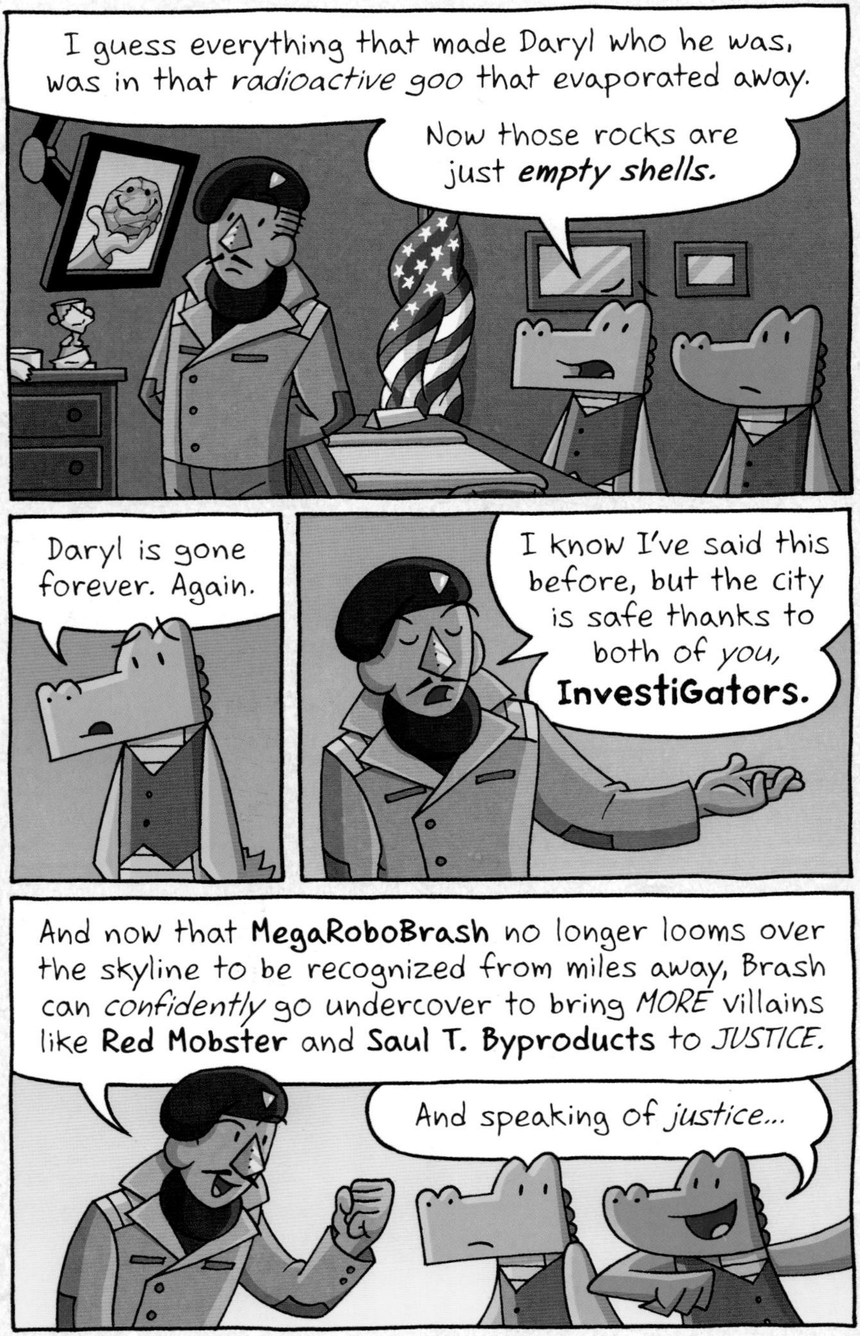
I guess everything that made Daryl who he was, was in that *radioactive goo* that evaporated away.
Now those rocks are just ***empty shells.***
Daryl is gone forever. Again.
I know I've said this before, but the city is safe thanks to both of *you,* **InvestiGators.**
And now that **MegaRoboBrash** no longer looms over the skyline to be recognized from miles away, Brash can *confidently* go undercover to bring *MORE* villains like **Red Mobster** and **Saul T. Byproducts** to *JUSTICE.*
And speaking of *justice*...

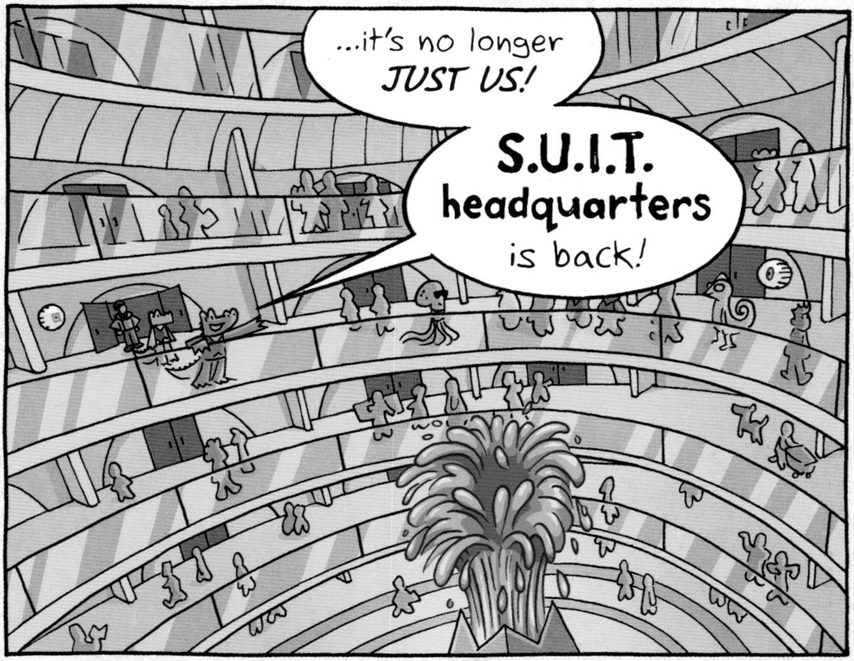
...it's no longer *JUST US!*
S.U.I.T. headquarters is back!

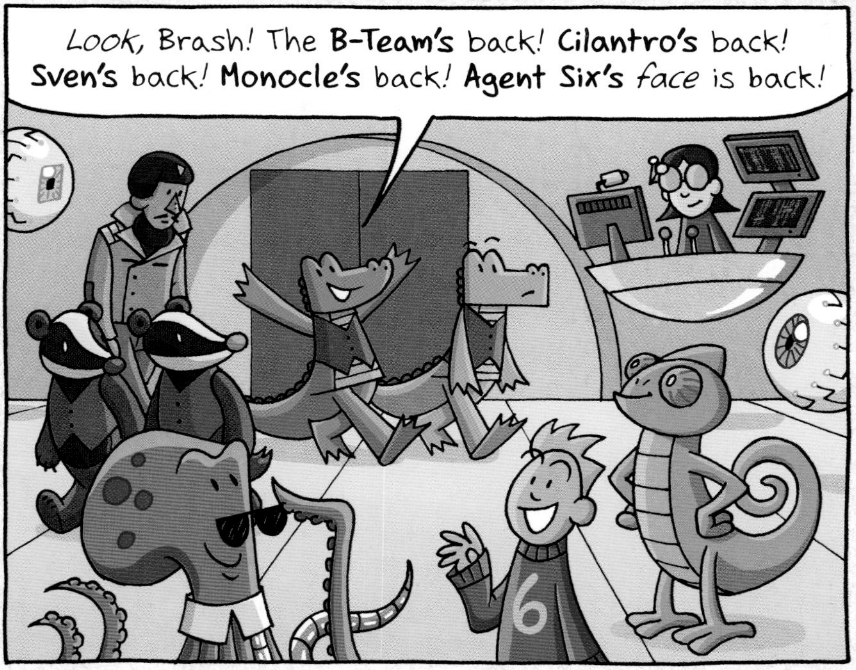
LOOK, Brash! The **B-Team's** back! **Cilantro's** back! **Sven's** back! **Monocle's** back! **Agent Six's** *face* is back!

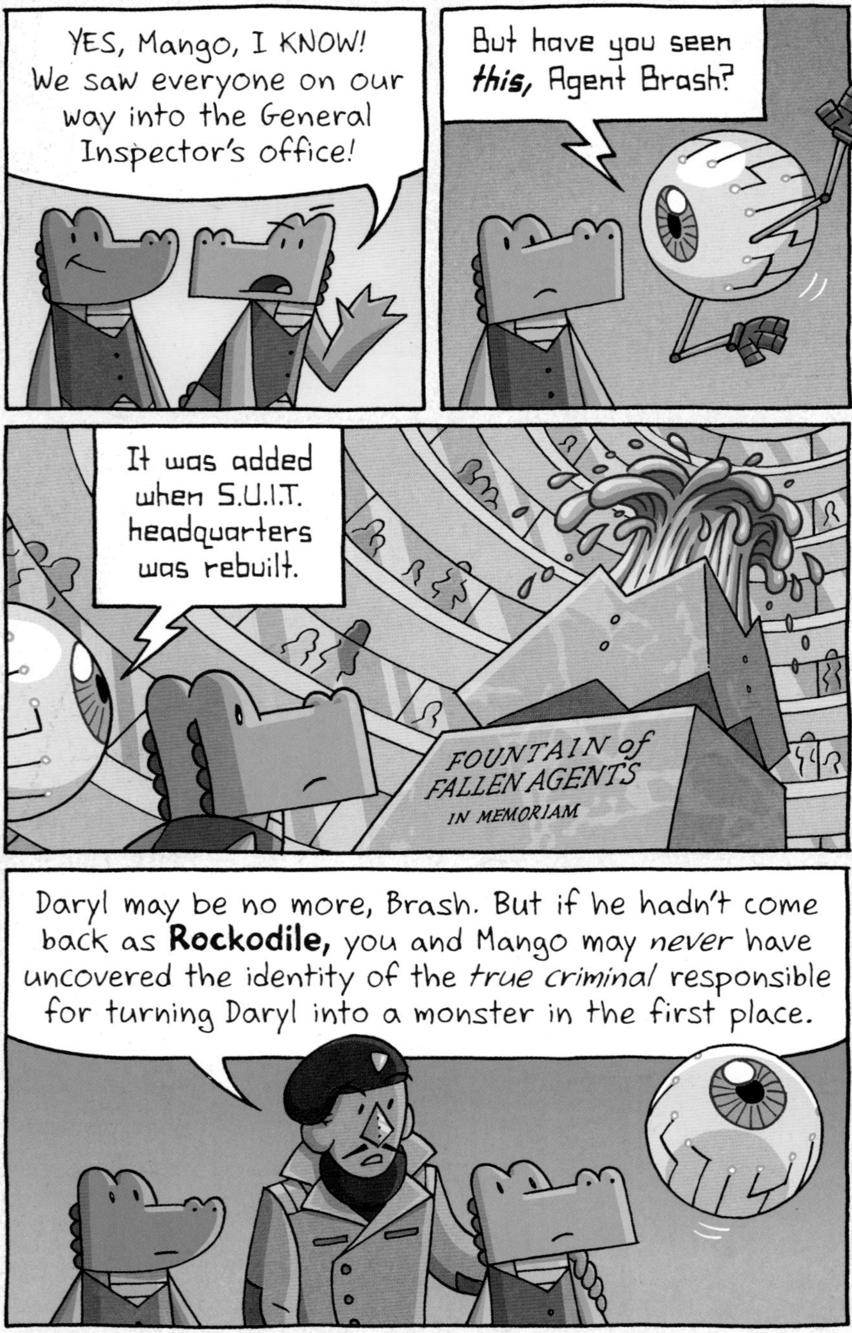
YES, Mango, I KNOW! We saw everyone on our way into the General Inspector's office!
But have you seen **this,** Agent Brash?
It was added when S.U.I.T. headquarters was rebuilt.
FOUNTAIN of FALLEN AGENTS
IN MEMORIAM
Daryl may be no more, Brash. But if he hadn't come back as **Rockodile,** you and Mango may *never* have uncovered the identity of the *true criminal* responsible for turning Daryl into a monster in the first place.

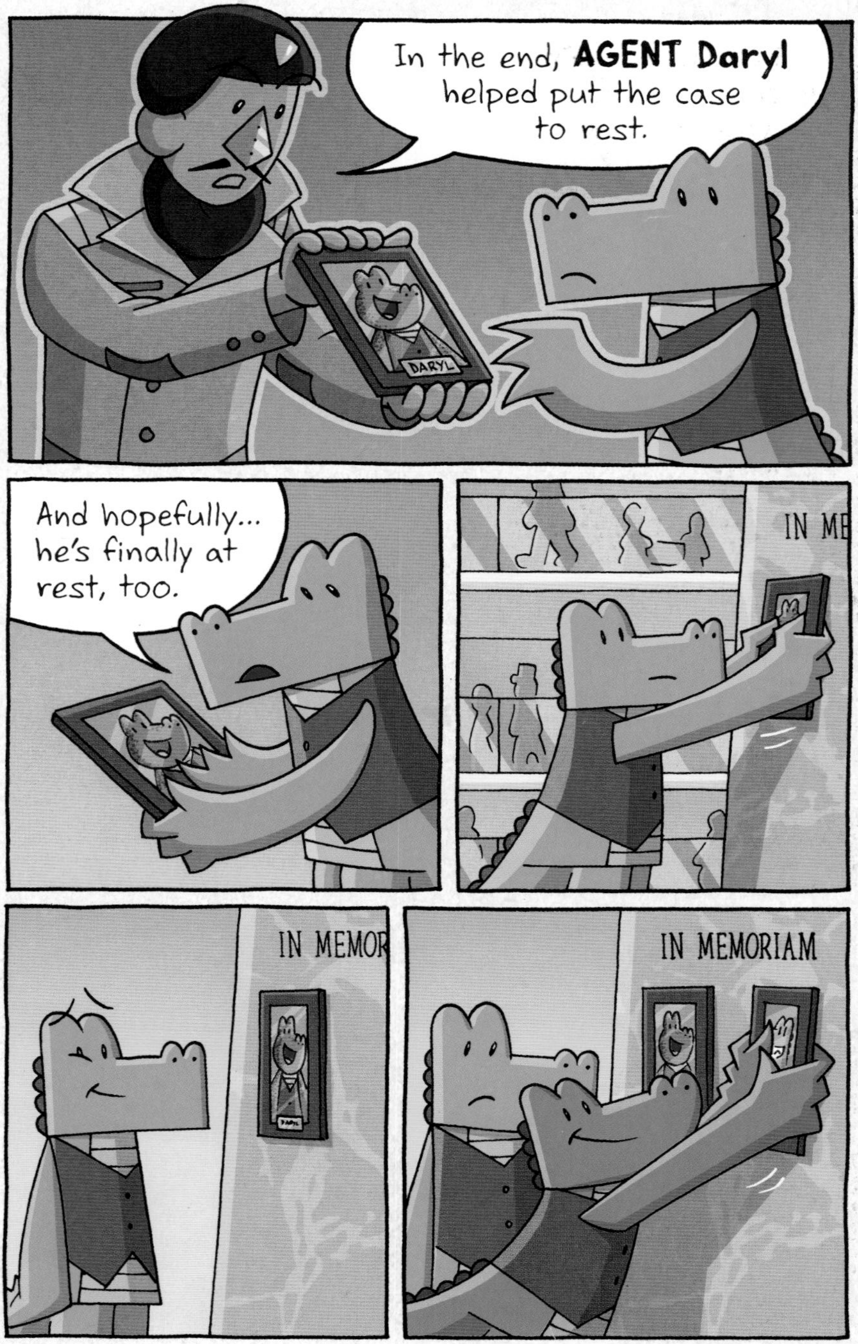

In the end, **AGENT Daryl** helped put the case to rest.
DARYL
And hopefully... he's finally at rest, too.
IN ME
IN MEMOR
IN MEMORIAM

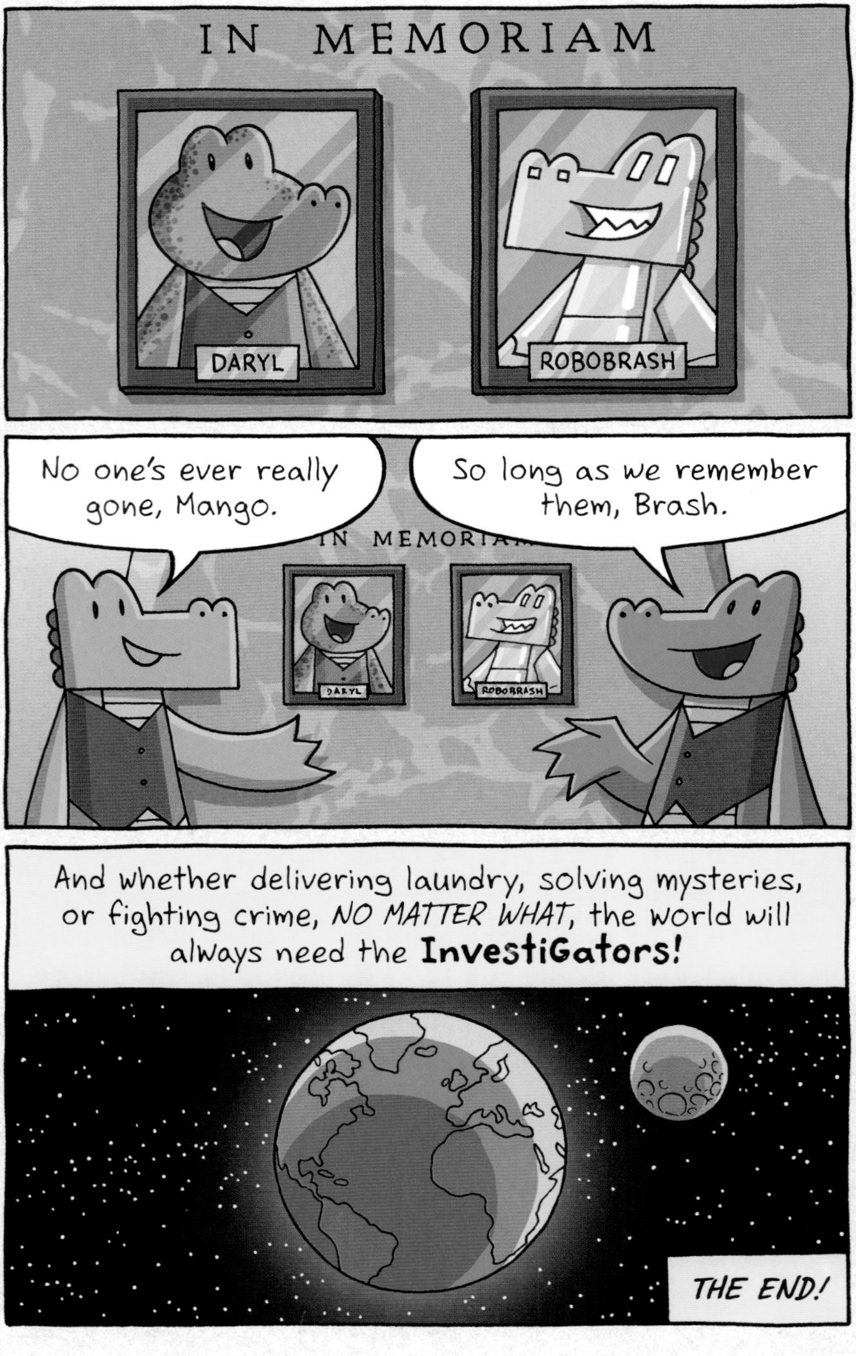
IN MEMORIAM
DARYL
ROBOBRASH
No one's ever really gone, Mango.
So long as we remember them, Brash.
IN MEMORIAM
DARYL
ROBOBRASH
And whether delivering laundry, solving mysteries, or fighting crime, NO MATTER WHAT, the world will always need the InvestiGators!
THE END!

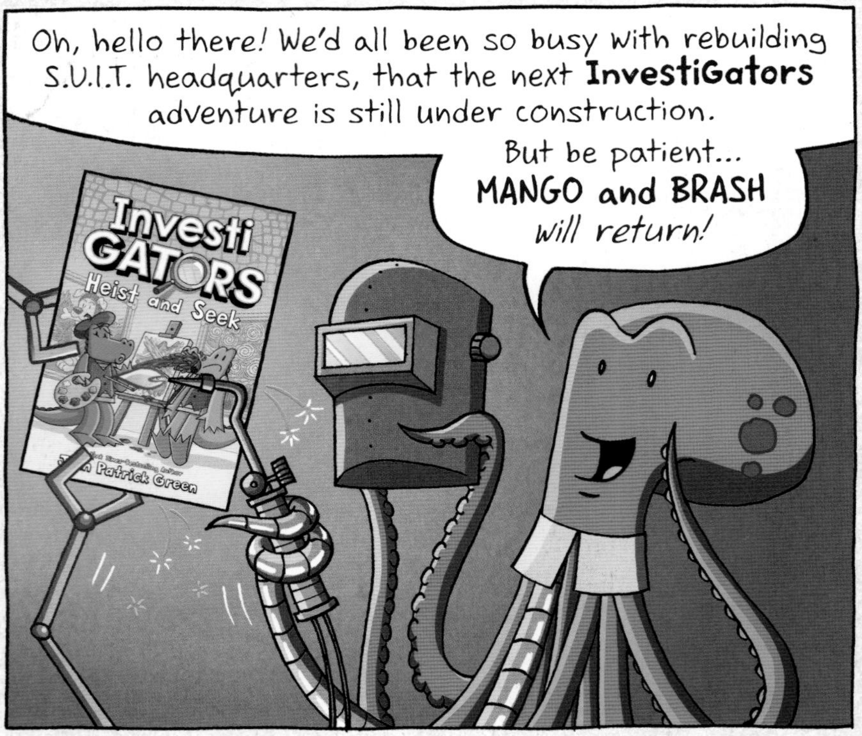
Oh, hello there! We'd all been so busy with rebuilding S.U.I.T. headquarters, that the next **InvestiGators** adventure is still under construction.
Investi GATORS Heist and Seek
Patrick Green
But be patient... **MANGO and BRASH** *will return!*

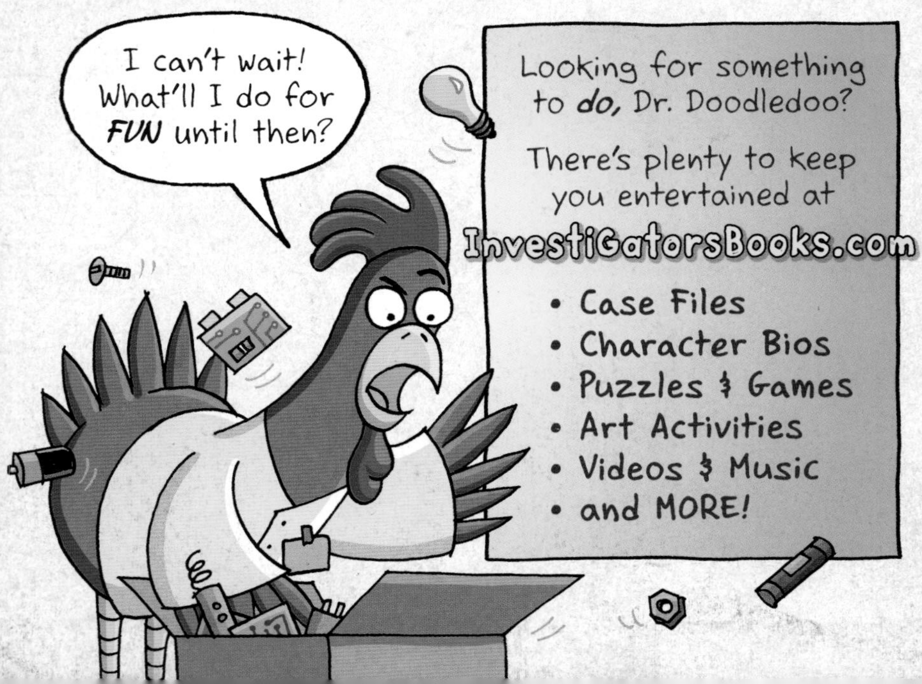
I can't wait! What'll I do for *FUN* until then?
Looking for something to *do,* Dr. Doodledoo?
There's plenty to keep you entertained at
InvestiGatorsBooks.com
• Case Files
• Character Bios
• Puzzles & Games
• Art Activities
• Videos & Music
• and MORE!